THE LAUNDRY FAIRY

J R BUCKLEY

HUSKENDALE
BOOKS

The Laundry Fairy

First published by Huskendale Books in 2019

ISBN-13: 978-1-5272-4372-9

DEDICATION

For my dearest Mum,

For holding me together, when I felt like falling apart.

J x

Do you believe in vampires?
You should; they are closer than you think.

ACKNOWLEDGEMENTS

I wish to express my gratitude, to the many people who inspired me through the writing of this book. For those who have talked things over, read, gave opinionated comments, scribbled over my notes in coloured ink, allowed me to quote their remarks, proof-read and edited – but most importantly kept the cups of tea rolling, because without them I would indeed be a crumbling mess over my never-ending pile of broken keyboards.

CHAPTER I

"No, I don't drink. I find it clouds my clarity and good judgement. I feel it puts me in a state of perpetual bliss, which for my lifestyle, is something I cannot allow!"

Edwin Von Lysander

The village of Baston stands peacefully on the eastern banks of the Cobalt River. Although still classified as a village, Baston has grown immensely in size and population over many centuries, to that of a small town…and *this* is mainly due to the village's primary dealings in washing other people's dirty laundry.

The village is notoriously known for being the last trading place or watering hole before the roads merge into mud-filled paths, which lead into the twisting trails of the Darkened Enchanted Forest of Huskendale.

Many a weary traveller, not familiar with the terrain of the forest, would surely first stop by at Baston for supplies, a pleasant night's rest or just some good old-fashioned company. On occasions, they would leave Baston after having acquired several pairs of freshly pressed underpants…sometimes not even on purpose!

The locals tell stories of travellers that have passed through the village. The *unfortunate ones* that have ventured unprepared into the Darkened Enchanted Forest, only to emerge a few days later with torn clothes, gasping for water and wondering how they got themselves lost on the straightest and most simplest of paths within the forest.

◆◆◆

However, this story does not start in Baston. It begins several miles away with a luxurious stagecoach being hauled over cobblestone roads by two large silky black stallions. They race against time, against a time where the sun starts to rise above the horizon; a time that is getting immensely closer.

The stagecoach wheels rattle and skew in their bearings, repeatedly bouncing over broken stones and rotting tree branches that lay scattered across the road. Ironwork bends and screams in agony as the two stallions pull with all their might, the fully loaded stagecoach, along with its driver and passenger.

The heavens open up and the rain falls. However, this is no *ordinary* rain. This is a heavy rain that descends from every possible angle; the sort of rain that no matter what direction you come from, or wherever you are heading, one thing is very certain…you will be getting extremely wet!

Shadows creep amongst the lifeless woodland trees. The moonlight flickers through their tall, darkened trunks like an old vintage projector; the winds gently murmur across their dull leafless branches and the continued sounds of horseshoes on damp ground, echo throughout the air.

The two stallions let out loud and chilling neighs as the driver pulls the reins hard against their bridles, slowing them *just enough* to navigate over an old rickety wooden bridge, spanning across a deep ravine.

The driver snaps his wrists vigorously against the reins. The stagecoach accelerates hard up the side of a hill and narrowly misses tree branches that overhang the winding road.

'Please…we must hurry, Master!' declares a small mole-like creature, glancing back over his shoulder at the horizon. 'I fear we don't have long at all—'

A deep crimson glow merges with the night sky, as the morning sun begins to rise slowly over the distant mountains of Draeoun.

'You think I do not know that, Corbin?' states his Master, his low-pitched tone resonating through the continuous patter of rain as it hits the solid brim of his black top hat. 'I can only make these two stallions pull so much!'

Corbin directs his attention to the road ahead, repositions himself back into his seat and holds on tightly to his bobble hat. He lowers his head; battling the raindrops that steadily pound at his gaunt face.

'We'll make it!' announces his Master.

'I know we will, Master – I know we'll make it, but the question is…will you still be with us when we do?'

Corbin places his tiny hands together, twiddles his thumbs and awaits a response from his Master.

'Corbin, you amazing and fabulous little—' before an uncomfortable pause. 'Err…what means of creature are you again, exactly?'

Corbin lets out a long sigh.

'I'm technically a mole-sprite, Master. You've asked me that more than a hundred times over the years. Why do I always feel like I'm repeating myself with you?'

'Ah, a mole-sprite. Spr—ite…funny word that!'

Corbin's Master tightens his grip around the horses reins, preventing the wet leather from slipping through his abnormally pointy fingers.

'We are nearly there!' he announces, as the stallions pull the stagecoach speedily past an old wooden sign, nailed very poorly to the rotting trunk of an ancient oak tree. 'Baston – one mile,' he declares.

Corbin turns his head slightly and catches a glimpse of the sign as it passes behind an elderberry bush.

'Interesting that the moon is still out and yet the sun begins to rise, don't you think, Corbin…?' states his Master.

'I've never really given it much thought,' replies Corbin, concerned over his Master's random question.

'You haven't…? Why do you think that is, Corbin?'

'You mean, why do I think the moon is still out? Or, why I don't think about it?'

'Why the moon is still out, Corbin! Now, please pay attention – and you have the audacity to say *you* have to repeat yourself?'

'I don't think that we have the time right now for a lecture in astrophysics…or whatever people call it?'

'Astronomy, Corbin – astronomy!'

Corbin sighs.

'You see…a widespread misconception in general astronomy is that the moon is directly opposite the sun in the sky. In fact, the moon is only in this position for a single instance in the whole lunar month—'

'Please, Master! Right at this moment, I am more worried about the approaching sunlight. I couldn't care less about the position of some celestial object!'

Corbin turns to face his Master; a tall, slender figure, dressed in black, apart from a stiff-collared white shirt and a vibrant red silk waistcoat. He wears a multitude of jewellery; gem faced rings on his fingers and a gold chain around his neck. A large emerald brooch pins his sizeable black cloak together around his neck; a cloak that shields him from the weather. Rainwater pours down the outer skin of his mantle and drips repeatedly onto his highly polished leather boots.

The majority of the time he is seen wearing a pair of round-rimmed amber sunglasses. The darkened amber is just the right shade to blend in with his heredity pale skin tone, and yet dark enough to hide his bright blue eyes. A thick-rimmed top hat, made of soft woven silk, completes his body attire, and despite the pounding rain hammering upon it, the headpiece remains stiff and retains its shape surprisingly well.

'You know, Master…?' says Corbin, pausing briefly to choose his words very carefully. 'It would have been much easier for you to just fly into Baston – I could have just met you there later.'

'And you would have been quite capable of steering these two beasts, would you now?' replies his Master, pointing at the two stallions in front.

Corbin frowns. 'I guess not, Master.'

'Anyway, Corbin…' continues his Master. 'For me to transform into a rather unattractive blood-sucking bat, would certainly not be the best of ideas right now.'

'Why ever not, Master?'

'I might be able to negotiate these roads in the dark and rain, but seriously, Corbin? Despite my experience in bat form, I still haven't managed to master flying in this type of weather – *that's* just asking for trouble. I could cause myself some serious injury – or worst still – I could end up…dead!'

'But you are already dead, Master! You're a vam—'

Corbin holds his words as he stares in panic at the first sign of the sun poking its fiery rim above the horizon. 'You haven't got much time, Master. I suggest you get a move on!'

Corbin's Master lets out a loud hiss. Corbin holds his tongue.

'Please forgive my disrespect, Master. I meant to not instruct or dictate to you,' adds Corbin

Corbin's Master gently nods.

The stagecoach rallies over uneven cobbles; gaining speed and momentum. The two stallions master the mud-filled voids in the road, occasionally tipping the stagecoach onto two wheels as they tear, with lightning speed, around the last few bends. Each wheel clicks with every revolution and builds up a crazed allegro of synchronised rhythm; spinning faster and faster.

Corbin's Master quickly turns and glances over his shoulder, as a sudden urgency to get into Baston a little quicker, starts to settle in.

'Hold on tight, Corbin!' shouts his Master. 'These last few hundred yards or so are going to get a little rough and bumpy. So, hold onto that hat of yours!'

Corbin decides that clinging onto his hat is not the wisest choice and votes to clench his little hands tightly around the rim of his seat. He concentrates on the road that lay ahead; his eyes widening and his jaw fully open.

Being scared around his Master is not an option for

Corbin. He tries desperately to keep his composure as the speeding stagecoach leaves the ground and takes flight for the briefest of moments.

The rain continues to pelt down upon them both; cold droplets running down the backs of their necks. Corbin wipes his brow with the back of his hand and his Master pursues to wipe his sunglasses clean with his cloak. Using one hand, Corbin's Master continues to skilfully maintain complete control of the stallions as they race at full speed into the road's blind corners. The wheels skid across the wet and slippery cobbles.

'How long do you think we have, Corbin?' asks his Master, with a detectable tone of panic in his voice.

Corbin dares not to turn around and embrace what could be his Master's fate. Instead, Corbin chooses to remain in a self-paralysed state, caused purely by the reckless driving his Master is prevailing at.

'Not long, Master!' he screeches, taking a wild guess that his answer is *on par* in being reasonably accurate. 'Not long at all!'

'Oh, *this* is not good at all! This is truly a highly undesirable situation,' replies Corbin's Master, with a look of concern on his face.

Corbin's Master grips the wet reins tightly and raises himself up in his chair to an almost standing position. He pushes his cloak aside, which catches the turbulent air; instantly spreading it wide open. It trails behind him and flaps wildly through the crisp morning air. With the reins, he cracks down hard with sheer force onto the flanks of the horses. The wheels continue rallying forwards.

Terror begins to etch itself into Corbin's eyes, as he catches a glimpse of the first rays of sunlight hitting the upper slopes of the distant mountains behind him.

'You smell of fear, Corbin!' shouts his Master. 'You also seem a little tense!'

'Really? – and you are not, Master?' replies Corbin. 'I can understand you *not* being afraid of the dark and all, but the sunlight is a completely different *kettle of fish* altogether – even for you!'

His Master chuckles.

Corbin sighs.

'If the worse comes to worst, I shall have to put you back in the box again, Master,' announces Corbin.

'I would rather die than go back into that stupid box – mark my words, Corbin! Besides, it is not a box at all…*it's*—it's a coffin!'

Corbin shifts his head very slowly towards his Master and stares blankly at him. He waits patiently for the complex array of microscopic neurotransmitters in his Master's brain to begin to fire, setting off a chain reaction and hopefully leading his Master to conclude, what he just so stupidly said.

'Oh, of course! I'm already dead!' says his Master, with an awkward smile upon his face.

'Look!' screams Corbin. 'We are here…'

The stagecoach rolls gracefully down a gentle slope and decreases in speed as the stallions canter becomes a steady trot. There is a jingle of ironwork as Corbin's Master pulls hard on the reins; bringing the stallions to a sudden and abrupt halt.

Corbin stands on his seat and starts crawling up onto the roof of the stagecoach. He pushes himself onto his feet and stares worryingly at the approaching sunrise. Panic begins to settle in as the rays of sunlight penetrate the darkened shadows of the land…and mile by mile, it comes closer towards Baston.

'Quickly! In here, Master!' instructs Corbin, rushing

towards the village's tavern and stables. He pushes the stable doors open, using every ounce of strength he can muster. The solid oak doors creak on their oil starved iron hinges and without hesitation, Corbin's Master hastily guides the stallions inside the stables, pulling the stagecoach behind them. Corbin closes the two heavy doors, just as a sharp slither of morning sun penetrates through the small gaps in the old woodwork; slicing the dusty air.

There is an eerie silence, broken only by the horses as they exhale slowly. They bury their mouths deep into a water trough and slurp furiously at the icy cold water.

'Well…that was certainly very exciting, don't you think, Corbin?' expresses his Master, as he steps down from the stagecoach and onto the hay lined floor of the stables. 'Oh poop!' he adds.

'You can say that again, Master,' replies Corbin.

'No, look! Poop…and it's all over my brand-new boots. Now I'm going to have to get these cleaned – another chore I don't need—'

Corbin tries to refrain from displaying any facial expressions, but cannot stop himself from letting out a childish giggle, which he cleverly disguises as a sneeze.

His master smirks at Corbin. 'Curse you!' he hails.

'What for, Master…?' says Corbin nervously.

'For sneezing. I can't go around saying *bless you*, every time someone sneezes, can I? I have a reputation to up keep.'

Corbin narrows his eyes.

'Anyway, Master,' says Corbin, as he paces up the side of the stagecoach. 'Next time, I truly believe that you should at least check a map before making such an important journey. That wrong turning you took back there, put a real dent in our schedule and—well, could have caused us some serious issues, if we hadn't made the time up in them last few miles.'

'A map, Corbin!' snarls his Master. 'I have travelled these lands for centuries. I am sure I know these roads better than most folk – and it wasn't a wrong turn at all – I just wanted to take a more scenic route!'

'You missed the correct turn, didn't you?' declares Corbin, directing himself towards his Master.

'No…I just—'

'You got it wrong, didn't you, Master…?'

There is an uncomfortable silence. Corbin's Master hisses and turns his back on his mole-like assistant.

'Well, I may have messed up a little bit,' he states. 'Besides, it's not important. Now…if you would be so kind as to sort out the horses and luggage, Corbin? – I'm rather tired.'

Corbin watches his Master walk towards the end of the stables; sliding and scraping the side of his left boot across the floor.

'Err…Master? I believe it's this way,' says Corbin, pointing across to a large entrance door at the other end of the stables.

It is a sizeable door; a door that would certainly not go unnoticed to most people. The door even has a sign above it saying '*Welcome Ye.*' But then again, this is Corbin's Master.

'Oh right, yes,' replies Corbin's Master, adjusting his top hat, shaking himself off and wiping his sunglasses clean. 'Okay, let's see if there's any life in this here establishment – onwards we go!'

Corbin's Master steps up to the large wooden door.

The front of the door is highly decorated with a mass of decorative ironwork. With minimal effort, Corbin's Master lifts a large brass knocker, before banging it down several times against the stained wood. He waits patiently.

There is a sudden loud thud, a shuffling noise and a distant scream, before a latch drops on the other side of the door. A key turns in its lock.

Then, a moment's pause…

The door flies open and there stands a large bulky man. He casually props himself up against the wooden doorframe and randomly swirls a large tankard of frothy liquid, through the air.

'Good night, morning and a pleasant afternoon to you, dear fellow,' slurs the man.

'You are very drunk, sir,' declares Corbin's Master. 'Your smell is also—well, let's just say…acquired.'

'I am not!' bellows the man, as he struggles to keep himself upright.

'Besides, what…*may I ask*, do they call you?'

'Me? They call me *Dunc*—Duncan Goodbrew. I'm the keeper of this fine establishment…and you are?'

'I'm Corbin's Master.'

'Who is Corbon?'

'No, Corbin…*Cor—bin*. He is my loyal assistant – and he's just over there – sorting out the stallions.'

Duncan narrows his eyes in an attempt to locate and focus in on Corbin, who is now being tossed across the room by a slightly annoyed stallion; a stallion that is more interested in burying his head into the water trough, than being pulled annoyingly by a little mole.

'Anyway…' says Duncan. 'What can I do you for? And surely you have a worthier name than simply, Corbin's Master?'

'My name is Edwin…Edwin Von Lysander.'

'That's a *somewhat* erotic name, err…I mean exotic. Where did you get that one from?'

'It was given to me at birth.'

'Really? It sounds like a bought title!'

'I can assure you…it is not.'

Edwin straightens his waistcoat, places each of his thumbs into its side pockets and allows his pointy fingers to hang down gently. 'I'm looking for a room to rent for a few days if you please, tavern keeper? I prefer one with a window that faces west, if possible. Would that be a problem?'

Duncan stares at Edwin in confusion, as if waiting for some punchline to a joke he didn't comprehend and determining if he should start laughing or not.

'Well, Edwin…' begins Duncan. 'That will cost you three pieces of silver per night – but that does include a hearty breakfast, served from *whenever* the cook decides to get up.'

'I shall not require breakfast, my drunken friend. Also…I'm afraid I do not do silver. It is too much to carry around. It also seems to give me awful cramps when I least want them – but what I do have…is gold.'

Edwin digs deep into his left waistcoat pocket and pulls out a shiny gold coin. Duncan's eyes light up with excitement as he licks his lips in anticipation.

Edwin holds the gold coin out in front of him. He rolls it several times through his bony fingers, before stopping suddenly and placing the coin into the top pocket of Duncan's linen shirt. He gently pats Duncan several times on the shoulder.

Duncan adjusts himself into a more elegant upright position, which causes him to spill a quantity of his ale onto the floor. He removes the coin from his pocket, and with a scrutinous eye, examines it; rolling it continuously between his thumb and forefinger, before placing the coin in his mouth; biting down on it hard.

'That'll do nicely, Ed! Very nicely indeed!' declares Duncan, wrapping his fist tightly around the coin.

'Edwin if you please? My name is Edwin!'

Duncan shifts his body and staggers back into the tavern, mumbling and muttering to himself; a huge grin occupying his face. Before long, his concentration gets the better of him and he walks straight into some wooden barrels, lining the hallway.

'Darn stupid place to put beer barrels,' he mutters. 'Err…Ed—I mean Edwin…why are you still standing in the doorway?' he adds.

Edwin raises a hand up to his sunglasses. He pulls them down gently to the end of his nose to reveal his brilliant blue eyes. They stare piercingly at Duncan.

'Oh, Duncan…' announces Edwin. 'I'm a very respectful soul – I do have a certain level of social etiquette and manners. I was *simply* waiting for you to invite me in. I didn't want to seem rude.'

Edwin continues to stare at Duncan, who is now either feeling the impact of too much honey mead, or the effects of some hypnotic gazing stare.'

'I see,' replies Duncan. 'Well, in that case, come on in – let's grab a drink together!'

Edwin pushes his sunglasses back up the bridge of his nose and whistles across the stables to Corbin, indicating with a wave to follow him into the tavern.

'Thank you, Duncan,' replies Edwin. 'Thank you *very…very* much.'

Edwin takes a nervous step forward. While crossing the threshold, a rogue gust of wind howls through the back passageway and tickles the flames of the candles that light the way. Corbin drags a wooden chest firmly behind and occasionally stops to adjust its direction, before reaching up and closing the door behind him.

Duncan leads Edwin and Corbin through a series of narrow passages, before climbing up a couple of small wooden steps and into a large open area.

A few random characters lay scattered across the floor, while still holding their drinking receptacles in their hands. Empty bottles of brandy occasionally roll past them; bottles that only a few hours earlier had been fuelling a pretty lively night.

'Don't mind them, Edwin. They'll be passed out for most of the day,' says Duncan. 'Oh look! There's the cook over there – on the floor. I guess it's lucky you *didn't* want any breakfast.'

Edwin frowns.

Duncan leans up against a wall; creeping alongside it until he approaches the edge of the bar area. He ushers himself along to a small keg of honey mead, which is wedged into position with his personal crate of cherry brandy and a jar of pickled eggs. He tries to remain balanced and retain some composure as he removes the tightly packed bung from the side of the keg. Thick mead flows into his tankard, and just as it is about to overflow and spill onto the floor, Duncan forces the bung back into place.

'May I interest you in a sample of this fine brew, Ed?—I mean Edwin,' asks Duncan, raising the tankard up close to Edwin's face. Edwin immediately raises his arm and forces the tankard away with the back of his hand.

'No, I don't drink. I find it clouds my clarity and good judgement. I find it puts me in a state of perpetual bliss, which for my lifestyle, is something I cannot allow.'

'Ah, fair play, Edwin – Fair play indeed,' replies Duncan. 'That's more for me, then!'

Duncan raises his tankard and swiftly gulps down its contents. He drops the empty tankard to the floor, before wiping his bushy moustache with the back of his hand and attempts to position himself upright.

There is a loud thud as Corbin parks his Master's wooden chest next to the bar. He takes a small step back, before momentarily collapsing on the floor.

'What on Earth is that?' screeches Duncan, reaching desperately for a large butcher's knife, hanging off an iron hook, on the wall behind.

The sound of the sharpened steel blade as it cuts through the air, launches Corbin from his previously horizontal position, to standing defensively behind his Master's left leg.

Edwin stares down at Corbin.

'Oh, Duncan, this is just my good assistant Corbin,' announces Edwin.

Duncan positions himself over the edge of the bar and holds the butcher's knife high above his head. He stares menacingly at Corbin.

'Oh…my…goodness, that has got to be the biggest darn rat I have ever seen in my life! Look at it, Edwin!'

'No-no, Duncan! This is not a rat. This is merely Corbin, my faithful associate.'

'Oh, gosh, just imagine the size of the pie I could muster up!'

'No, Duncan! You cannot make a pie from Corbin. Corbin is not a rat – he's a—err…what are you again?'

Corbin sighs.

'I'm a mole-sprite, Master!' says Corbin. 'And this man is very drunk,' he adds, pointing to Duncan, who appears to be dribbling over the bar top.

'Quite so…' says Edwin. 'Anyway, Duncan, if you would be so kind as to *not* harm my assistant. Also, I do not want to come across as being pushy or rude – but can you perhaps get around to passing me the key to our abode for the next few days please?'

Duncan continues staring down at Corbin before regaining his composure. He sets his posture straight and returns his knife onto its hook.

Duncan then pulls open a small wooden drawer, from underneath the counter. He reaches inside and takes out a dainty brass key. It dangles on the end of a chain, alongside a small pink fluffy ball.

'Room four, Edwin. That is—*hic*—up the stairs, around the corner and the second door on the left,' mumbles Duncan, dropping the room key gently into Edwin's open hand.

Edwin nods, tips his hat and crouches down to pick up his chest.

'Come now, Corbin…I feel restless,' says Edwin, as Duncan stumbles and falls to the floor. Edwin raises his eyebrows. 'You are correct, Corbin – very drunk indeed,' he adds, stepping carefully over the stretched arms of Duncan, who has passed out behind the bar.

CHAPTER II

**"This bike is a prime example of complex engineering, precision craftsmanship and modern styling, that can only come from Dwarven eng—
Ooooh look, a drinks holder!"**

Melvin 'Melv' Copernicus

The Darkened Enchanted Forest of Huskendale is full of magical mystery. Nothing is ever quite as it seems as you venture deeper and deeper into its depths.

The densely packed tree trunks project up into the sky; casting eerie shadows on the forest floor. Tales have been told of travellers reportedly seeing shadows move amongst the trees; shadows that leave a faint trail of a blue aura behind them.

The forest holds many mysteries, but unknown to many, it also hides a secret pathway; which twists and turns through the vast landscape. It is only during the inky black darkness, highlighted by the light of the moon that the path reveals itself; however, only to those known and trusted by the eccentric Spellbinder Wizard, Melvin Copernicus.

This guardian pathway is one of the very few direct routes that lead to the majestic Huskendale Castle; the home of Melvin Copernicus.

The castle is invisible to the outside world, through a clever spell involving magnets, a large mirror and a small scale model of the castle, which took Melvin several weeks to complete.

◆◆◆

The small, pebbled courtyard inside the castle lay silent, with only the faintest whistle of the wind as it blows lazily through the outer passageways and tunnels, which line its exterior walls.

Melvin, the Spellbinder Wizard, stands motionless. His vibrant royal blue robe spreads out behind him and sparkles in the morning sun. He places his hands on the side of his face and pulls down hard on his rosy red cheeks, to a point where his jaw is fully open. His eyes shift slowly from side to side; scrolling over every inch of his new purchase, which stands before him.

Melvin, lost for words, starts to jump up and down on the spot in excitement. He holds on tight to the rim of his spellbinder's hat, which is on the point of being dislodged from his small head.

'Would you just look at that, Dex?' states Melvin, while clapping his hands together repeatedly like some crazed walrus. 'Would you just look at this fine beast of a machine?'

Dexter, Melvin's pet dragon, turns his head slowly towards Melvin, his purple skinned body remaining perfectly still, and with only the slightest adjustment of his pointed and flared wings altering his posture. His tail twitches on the pebbled ground.

'Err…what is it exactly?' queries Dexter, shuffling himself forward to get a better look at the item, which has Melvin *so filled* with joyful excitement.

'What do you mean, what is it? You don't know?' asks Melvin.

'I've not seen anything like it before in my life,' replies Dexter, scratching his head in confusion and trying to conjure up enough brain power to conclude what the *thing* in front of him, could possibly be.

'This fine piece of machinery is the latest creation from my good friends, down at the Earth Foundry. I've had this marvel on back order for months now – and ta-dah!…Here it is,' announces Melvin.

'That's absolutely wonderful, Melv. It really is. But seriously – what *is* it…?'

'It's a steam-powered bicycle,' says Melvin, as he carefully runs the palms of his hands over the freshly painted bodywork.

'What on Earth do you need one of these for…?' questions Dexter, tilting his head downwards to take a closer look at the vast array of pipes and valves that protrude from its framework.

Melvin pretends not to hear what Dexter had just said; something that he was very good at doing when the moment called for it. Instead, he focuses all his efforts on continuously inspecting every shiny part of his brand-new bicycle; checking for any imperfections and defects.

'Does it come with instructions?' asks Dexter.

'It's a bicycle, Dex. How hard can it be to ride a bicycle?' replies Melvin.

'Have you ever ridden a bicycle?'

'No.'

'You haven't?'

'No – but as I said…how hard can it be…?'

Dexter lets out a long drawn out sigh.

'Holy-moly! Check this out, Dex!' screams Melvin, pointing to a substantial pot-bellied shaped chamber, located deep in the middle of the bicycle. A large grilled door protrudes out from the top of the casing, held tightly closed by a huge cast iron wheel.

'This must be the boiler…or part of it – yes look! Here is where you must fill it with water, which will eventually create the steam,' continues Melvin.

'Yes, Melvin, it's all very marvellous stuff! I'm truly lost for words,' replies Dexter. 'Forgive me, but I don't understand what all the major fuss is about? It's just a bicycle…'

Melvin lets out a sigh. 'This bike is a prime example of complex engineering, precision craftsmanship and modern styling, that can only come from Dwarven eng—Ooooh look, a drinks holder!'

Melvin continues to prod and poke at the various components of his bicycle. He pulls off caps that probably shouldn't have been pulled off, before carefully examining them and pushing them back in place. He fiddles with levers; moving them up and down; giving them a shake, without a clue what they actually do.

Dexter strolls around to the far side of the bicycle. He carefully analyses every part in detail and tries to deduce a basic understanding of how the contraption *actually* functions.

He taps gently on a length of pipe with a sharpened claw. The pipe makes a hollow echoing sound.

'Careful now, Dex! 'You'll scratch the paintwork,' screeches Melvin, as he quickly rushes over to check the pipe. He removes a clean white handkerchief from his robe pocket and spits into it, before frantically and crazily rubbing the surface of the pipe, occasionally checking that the shine matches the surrounding pipes.

'That's just a copper pipe. It has no paint,' states Dexter, calmly.

'Yes, it does!' bellows Melvin. 'It's got copper paint at my request.'

'Err…copper painted on bare copper. Well, there's something new…huh?'

Melvin narrows his eyes at Dexter, who continues to educate himself with the anatomy of the bicycle.

Melvin quickly realises it would be a good idea to try and follow suit and pulls some pretty intense facial expressions as he tries to work out in his mind, how his new bicycle works. He cautiously hides the fact from Dexter, that he has absolutely no clue on how it works and continues to point his finger at random parts, occasionally muttering to himself in an attempt to look intelligent.

Melvin steps back and folds his arms tightly, before raising one arm and resting his chin in his hand.

He watches Dexter as he annoyingly becomes very familiar with the operation of the bicycle. Melvin is even more surprised that Dexter could even be onto something.

There is a pause before Dexter turns to face Melvin. At the same time, their eyes meet.

'Are you thinking what I'm thinking, Melv…?' asks Dexter, in a slightly excited tone. Both their eyes widen.

'Water…we need water! – and something to light this furnace with.'

'What fuel does it run off, Dex?' queries Melvin.

'I guess anything that burns hot; hot enough to heat the water consistently. I would guess coal. Do we have any…?'

'Not coal, we would have to purchase that from the village. What else could we use that we've a plentiful supply of?' Melvin pauses his actions and thinks hard.

'Wood!' he yells. 'We have a lot of wood. We are surrounded by it here in the forest. Do you think that could work, Dex?'

'Well, it could I guess. It will not be as good as coal.'

'Okay, great! Now, let's go and grab some wood.'

'Or, we could just use that over there?' says Dexter, pointing to a wooden bench, lining the courtyard walls.

'That'll do nicely,' replies Melvin, joyfully. 'You sort out the wood – I'll go and fetch some water.'

Dexter watches Melvin leap with excitement and then skip merrily across the courtyard, while pulling the bottom of his robe up high around his knees to prevent him from tumbling over. He disappears into a dark passageway.

Pacing across the courtyard, Dexter heads towards the bench, staring continuously at it and thinking to himself how he is ever going to attempt to move it.

The bench seemed so much smaller from a distance, now that Dexter was standing right next to it. He realises it is going to be an impossible task to even get it to budge.

He stumbles up onto the bench top and begins frantically jumping up and down on it; hoping that it will break in half. However, it doesn't and after several minutes of clawing furiously at the bench leg with his sharp claws, Dexter finally gives up and collapses to the floor next to a huge pile of sawdust.

Dexter's momentary rest is promptly interrupted by the chaotic sounds of Melvin returning across the courtyard, carrying a large bucket of water. Melvin concentrates; being cautious not to spill any of the bucket's contents as he rushes back to his bicycle.

'Oh, Dexter, I thought you would have had all the wood broken into pieces by now,' exclaims Melvin, placing the bucket of water down carefully. He wipes his hands dry on the side of his robe.

Dexter returns to his feet, lets out another long sigh and lowers his head to the ground. He doesn't even attempt to answer Melvin, or give him any kind of response, because Dexter knows perfectly well, that in the end, Melvin really doesn't care.

There is a massive explosion and a flash of brilliant blue light, as the bench that had previously stood next to Dexter, explodes into hundreds of tiny fragments.

'You could have waited until I had moved out of the way, Melv!' shouts Dexter, brushing off splinters of wood and dust from his scaly body. He extends his wings and gives them a couple of shakes, before closing them tightly behind him.

Dexter picks up a few large pieces of wood that lay scattered on the ground around him and shuffles carefully back towards Melvin. He drops the wood at Melvin's feet.

'Okay, my little purple friend, let's get this thing fired up!' exclaims Melvin, picking up the bucket of water and holding it steadily above the water tank.

Dexter tightens his claw around a small cap atop the tank and slowly unscrews it. It pops off and gently rolls effortlessy into Dexter's clawed paw.

Melvin carelessly pours the water out of the bucket and into the tank; spilling a few random drops, which trickle down the side of the tank and onto the ground below. Melvin hastily throws the empty bucket over his shoulder, which then crashes to the ground and disintegrates into pieces.

'Well, you could have used that as wood, Melv?' sniggers Dexter.

'Oh yes,' replies Melvin, letting out a small chuckle. 'Okay…what's next, Dex?'

'Hmmm, well…the fuel, I guess,' mutters Dexter, as he stares intensively at the multitude of components in front of him. 'Well, I'm no expert engineer, Melv, but I would assume that the fuel goes straight into this small furnace here. We'll then light the fuel and close this door. The intense heat should then boil the water in this tank; producing steam, which under pressure will travel through those pipes, into these pistons, which should then turn the wheels.'

Dexter takes a deep breath, relaxes and stares back at Melvin, trying not to look smug.

'Okay…let's light it, then!' says Melvin excitedly.

Dexter picks up a few pieces of wood from off the floor; strategically placing them for maximum burning efficiency inside the furnace.

'Would you kindly do the honours please, Dex?' asks Melvin.

'Err…you seem to forget, Melv,' retorts Dexter. 'I can't breathe fire anymore, remember? I occasionally sneeze out a copper coin or two, but other than that nothing…and would you please stop experimenting on me, trying to get me to sneeze out gold coins? I'm still a little sore from what happened last time. Those little bananas are an absolute pain to try and sneeze out. It's their highly irregular shape more than anything. They get stuck easily!'

Melvin lets out a loud laugh, which he muffles by quickly covering his mouth with his hand.

Dexter, although being a dragon, can't breathe huge balls of fire and flame, like all *other* dragons. Instead, he has developed a severe sneezing disorder, triggered by years of being constantly surrounded by Melvin's love of plants and flowers. The musty air has caused Dexter's fire vents in his snout to clog up, tickling his nostrils; producing uncontrollable sneezing outbursts.

Melvin had previously attempted to fix this for Dexter, but the spell was unsuccessful. It did however, cause Dexter to shoot out colourful rainbows every time he sneezed, much to the disgust of Melvin, who was *merely* disappointed in himself.

Not to be defeated, Melvin saw this as a prime opportunity to make lots of money and enchanted the rainbows to drop a shiny gold coin every time Dexter sneezed. Unfortunately, Dexter is only able to sneeze out copper coins...and now, no rainbows.

AAAAAACHOO!

A copper coin flies out of Dexter's left nostril and ricochets off the back of the bicycle frame, narrowly missing Melvin's foot.

'You see...? That's one right there!' snarls Dexter, wiping the end of his snout with the back of his claw and pointing to a shiny copper coin, resting on the pebbled courtyard.

AAAAAACHOO!

'And another!' adds Dexter.

Melvin carefully crouches down, picks up the coins and places them into his robe pocket.

'Okay...I'll light it, then...no problem at all,' says

Melvin. 'Right, let's see – we light the wood – then shut the door and turn this wheel until tight.'

Dexter gently nods.

'So, do you have a match, Dex?' questions Melvin.

'Why would you ever think that I would be in possession of a match, Melv? I mean…yes, sure, I carry matches with me all the time, being a rare non-fire breathing dragon and all!' states Dexter, sarcastically. 'Anyway, Melv, you are a spellbinder – and a superb one as far as I can see. Surely you can conjure up the slightest of sparks to ignite the wood? You've just made that old bench disintegrate into hundreds of wooden shards with a slight flick of your wrist!'

Melvin leans down and peers into the open furnace at the neatly stacked piles of wood. He pauses and then whispers a couple of words; as if he's *actually* talking to the wood.

The splintered wood instantly ignites and burns with an intense flame. Melvin stands up, closes the door and twists the wheel hard until it locks. He gently pats the boiler casing. The fire roars as Melvin opens a small valve to the side, allowing air into the furnace; feeding the flames.

◆◆◆

Back in Baston, the rising sun shines its warmth across the centre of the village. The sunlight radiates off a large stone water fountain; a fountain that spits out water from the mouth of a creature; a creature that can only be described as a cross between a large fish and—well…a giraffe!

One by one, the residents of the village start to wake. Doors and window shutters fly open in unison, faint distant conversations begin taking place and the *all familiar* sound of hammer on anvil from the village blacksmith, echoes in the distance.

Birds gently sing in chorus; hiding amongst the surrounding trees. Occasionally they are interrupted by a loud squawk from a corpulent black crow, which has recently taken up residence in the village hall.

Timothy Oakes, the Mayor of the village, steps out of his office and onto a large wooden veranda, which overlooks the stone fountain.

Timothy, a colossal giant of a man, stands with an overwhelming presence. He places his hands firmly on his hips as his enormous round belly protrudes out in front of him. A brass buckle holds a wide leather belt tightly around his waist, which squeezes his freshly pressed white linen shirt, firmly against his skin.

Timothy yawns as he stretches his arms high above his head, pulling his shirt out from his trousers and exposing his belly, which flops out and wobbles under its own weight.

He promptly grabs the bottom of his shirt and his fat mass; stuffing it all back into his oversized trousers. He breathes in deeply as he tries to get the buckle to engage into the next notch of his belt.

The ambient sounds of the village are suddenly heightened by a bell ringing from the nearby church. It catches Timothy's attention. He glances over and watches the bell swing back and forth atop the church's wooden framed tower.

He steps down from his veranda onto the dew-covered grass and strolls towards the fountain.

Pausing at the rim, he stares down into the water at his reflection, which shimmers as small ripples pass over it.

With a huge swing of his arm, he scoops up a handful of water and splashes it onto his face. Icy cold droplets run down his double chin and back into the fountain. He shakes his head violently from side to side, before running both of his large hands over his slick black hair and forcing it hard against his scalp.

Timothy takes in a breath of crisp morning air, just as a loud wolf-whistle from across the village, pierces his left eardrum.

He shifts his attention towards the church, where the village Reverend is waving crazily at him.

'Timothy!' shouts the Reverend. 'Good morning, Timothy!' he adds, continuing to wave frantically with one hand, while attempting to unlatch a small white gate in front of the church, with the other.

'Oh, dear Lord,' mutters Timothy.

Timothy's words were not meant in disrespect, but rather a desperate plea to the Lord, in why *he* had, in his divine wisdom, chosen a man such as the Reverend Clementine to represent him.

Nobody knows what the Reverend Clementine's first name is, but many have ideas that it could be something like Shirley or Davina, or maybe some other feminine name. Not that they are terrible names, in fact, they would suit the Reverend reasonably well.

'Ah, good morning to you also, Reverend,' says Timothy, as he strolls towards him.

'Well, the Lord has presented us all with another splendid day, has he not?'

'He certainly has! So…what gets you up so early?'

'Well, Timothy…I wanted to talk with you in a little more detail, about an upcoming competition.'

Timothy frowns. 'What competition?'

'We have been selected this year to take part in the

Village of the Year Award. Exciting isn't it?'

'We have? I was not aware such an award existed.'

'Well, you do now, Timothy. What do you think?'

Timothy is an extremely busy man, who doesn't have much time for pointless ventures. He is more interested in making money…and lots of it.

'I think it's a complete waste of time, Reverend,' retorts Timothy. 'But please…do not let me stop you from entering us. How does it all work?'

The Reverend smiles.

'The village will be scored on a variety of different criteria…such as our community spirit, cleanliness, contribution to society and other things like—'

'That's very well, Reverend. But it seems rather pointless, just for a title for a year. What's in it for us?'

'If the Lord blesses us with success, we can have our village mentioned in the local newsprint next month – and—'

'*Pfft!* Is that it? That's hardly worth the effort.'

'If I may continue please, Timothy? – and the first prize winner of the best village, receives one thousand gold pieces.'

Timothy's eyes widen.

'One thousand gold pieces, you say…?' mumbles Timothy, rubbing both his hands gently together. 'Interesting…*very*…interesting.'

Timothy places his chubby hand on the Reverend's shoulder and ushers him towards his office.

'Well, I think you and I should sit and discuss this competition a little more,' declares Timothy. 'Why don't you come on in and we can chat over the details with a nice cup of elderflower tea?'

'Well, Timothy, I do have morning service to conduct shortly – I really must be—'

'I'm sure *that* can wait for a little while, Reverend,' interrupts Timothy. 'This is God's will – and you must carry out his will…yes?'

The Reverend gives Timothy a confused look.

'Well, yes…I guess you are right. It is the will of God.' The Reverend pauses, thinking momentarily to himself. 'Yes-yes! I will join you for a cup of tea,' replies the Reverend, excitedly.

Timothy places his bulky arm firmly around the Reverend and directs him up the wooden step, leading onto his veranda.

'So tell me, Reverend…' begins Timothy. 'When is this competition again?'

◆◆◆

Dexter and Melvin stare at a gauge on the bicycle's handlebars.

'Well, Melv…it looks like, when the needle here reaches this green segment, there is sufficient steam pressure,' announces Dexter.

Dexter taps his claw gently on the face of the dial, where a thin pointed needle is slowly turning.

'I see,' replies Melvin. 'Then it's all ready to go?'

Dexter follows the extraordinary array of pipework with his claw, pointing at the random valves and levers.

The bicycle starts to hum and hiss gently. The smell of burnt wood begins to fill the air.

'It seems that when this lever gets pulled – and this here large wheel turns – steam gets transferred to the pistons and the bicycle will move,' states Dexter.

Melvin smiles in glee and spins around a few times on the spot, before jumping up and punching the air with his fist.

'I'm a little concerned though, Melv,' adds Dexter.

'Why is that?' replies Melvin.

'I'm having concerns about the wood. I really don't think it is going to be able to burn hot enough, or more precisely, burn long enough to generate the amount of steam required to make this bicycle of any use. We need coal or something similar.'

'As I said before, we can get coal in Baston.'

'So, you are planning to get to Baston using wood to power this bicycle? I mean, you'll have to keep feeding wood into the furnace. How would you store it? Or worse still, how would you drive the bicycle if you had to constantly keep reaching for pieces of wood?'

'It has a sidecar. We can store it there.'

'We…?' questions Dexter.

'Yes, you are coming as well. Besides, I have just formulated a marvellous plan!'

Melvin reaches deep into his robe; his whole arm disappearing into his pocket. He rummages around as Dexter gazes in amazement, at how Melvin's whole arm can fit into such a small space.

'Err…and what's your plan, Melv?' queries Dexter.

'One moment, it's in here somewhere! I've nearly got it,' replies Melvin, reaching further into the depths of his pocket.

'Aha! There we go,' exclaims Melvin, pulling out a tiny glass bottle. 'This is the plan…' he adds.

'I don't like it when you have a plan, Melv. Nothing ever seems to go right when you have a plan. I find it is much better to make it up as you go along…just like I do…well, most of the time!'

Melvin lets out a comical chuckle, before reaching back into his robe and pulling out his eye monocle, which is tethered to his robe by a short piece of string. He raises it up close to his right eye, holds it steady and carefully reads the small label.

Dexter waits patiently as he hears Melvin mutter to himself.

'This is the stuff!' hails Melvin. 'A few droplets of this into the furnace, should stir things up a little.'

'What is it?'

'This, Dexter…is a highly potent liquid. It's the venom of a dragon I raised many years ago, back in my youth.'

'Is that the same one you lost here in the castle?'

Melvin narrows his eyes at Dexter.

'I didn't lose him. I simply can't find him. There is a difference you know? And no – this is from a totally different dragon…one that—well, let's just say has severe issues with a certain fire like element.'

'Isn't that the same sort of venom they use in the mines? You know – for explosives?'

Melvin pauses. 'Err…well yes, but a few droplets of this into the furnace, will more than surely get us up to speed. We do not require a lot of it.'

Convincing Melvin not to use the venom would be entirely out the question, because deep down inside Dexter knows that, although a crazy plan, Melvin has already made up his mind.

Melvin carefully removes the tiny cork from the head of the bottle and hands it carefully to Dexter. It rests on his scaly paw.

'Okay, stand back, Dexter!' bellows Melvin. 'I don't know how this stuff is going to react!'

Dexter shifts back several steps and then a couple more for good measure. He closes his eyes. Melvin reaches out and flicks open a small vent; exposing the burning wood. He stretches his arm out as far as it will go and leans back slightly. He carefully tilts the bottle; tapping its sides a few times with his forefinger. A single droplet of thick syrup-like liquid falls into the chamber.

Dexter opens one eye.

'Err…what happened, Melv?' asks Dexter.

'I'm not sure,' replies Melvin, with a confused look on his face. 'I'll try another little drop,' he adds, before repeating his previous actions.

Melvin takes a step back and waits, before taking another look at the label on the bottle.

'I'm really not sure what is going on…' begins Melvin. That should have at least brought the fire to life – even if just a little bit.'

Dexter hands back the tiny cork to Melvin, who then pounds it into the glass bottle with the palm of his hand. Moving forward, Dexter closes the vent and looks over to the dial. The needle has not moved.

The bicycle continues to hiss and whistle gently.

A small puff of greenish smoke ejects itself from the little ventilation holes that are drilled through the vent cover. Melvin and Dexter continue to wait patiently in anticipation, for either something remarkable, or something anticlimactic to happen…

BOOM!

A loud explosion pushes the vent aside, shooting out a fiery tower of bright orange flames into the air. The sudden force knocks both Melvin and Dexter off their feet.

The furnace roars intensively, and as quickly as they started, the flames ease off. Dexter moves in closer and flicks the vent cover back into position with the tip of his claw. He lifts a wing and uses it as a shield from the intense heat.

'Ha-ha! Now that's what I'm talking about, Dex!' exclaims Melvin, his eyes now wide open with delight. 'Look at the dial now – we are at full pressure!'

Dexter picks himself up from the pebbled ground, which he is now getting very familiar with and brushes himself off for the second time.

Melvin starts to load the sidecar with the fragments of wood that still lay beside the bicycle; chucking them randomly over his shoulder. They each miraculously land neatly stacked on the passenger seat.

'Who needs coal, huh?' says Melvin, chuckling to himself. 'So, Dexter…do you fancy a little trip?'

Dexter briefly turns his attention to the bicycle, before turning back to Melvin.

'On that thing? No way!' roars Dexter. 'Besides, where would I sit?'

'Just sit behind me and hold onto my robe, but don't dig into too hard with those claws of yours!'

Dexter shakes his head. 'No-no-no. I can't believe that you would even think that I would get onto this machine; this machine which has just exploded a massive fiery vent into the air. I mean, look at it, Melv!'

The bicycle growls, roars and hisses. It shakes violently and occasionally lets out a very high-pitched whistle.

Melvin pulls tightly at the edge of his spellbinder's hat, stretching it over his ears and forehead. He gently tugs at the rim, ensuring it's secure.

'There's not one single thing that would come even close to making me get onto that bicycle, Melv,' says Dexter, in a worried tone. 'It would simply have to be out of pure desperation, of such great importance, or a matter of life and death to even—'

'The store in Baston has that new cheese that you like,' interrupts Melvin.

'Oh, they do? Where do I sit...?'

◆◆◆

Timothy steadily raises a ceramic teapot; grasping its large curved handle firmly with his hand. Holding the lid on tightly, he tilts the teapot, allowing the steaming hot and freshly made elderberry tea, to flow effortlessly into the Reverend Clementine's empty mug.

The Reverend sits down elegantly on the end of a rickety wooden chair. He cups his hands together and rests them neatly on his finely ironed clerical attire; a blackened robe that hangs full length from his neck to his feet. It clinches tightly to the Reverend's skinny and lanky body.

'So...Reverend, we only have three more days? Is that what you are telling me...?' asks Timothy, as he hands over a small bowl of sugar to the Reverend, who lifts a hand to refuse politely. 'That doesn't give us long at all to prepare and do all that is necessary. Why did you leave it so late?'

The Reverend Clementine pauses, lifts his tea from the table and takes a small careful sip. He ponders why Timothy, who only a few moments earlier was not interested in the idea, is now suddenly being rather enthusiastic about the whole scheme.

'Well, yes...I do realise that we don't have long,' replies the Reverend, as he carefully places his cup and saucer back onto the table. 'But in all fairness, I don't believe that we have too much to prepare. The village is in a pleasing shape. It's tidy, has character and its residents are hard-working folk. There may be a small list of requests, with your permission of course, that I would like to see addressed – just so I'm confident that the village has ticked all the boxes – and most likely something the judges may pick us up on, if not.'

'These requests being?' asks Timothy.

'Maybe we can replant a few flowers around? We can move some from the edge of the forest. Also, a lick of paint or two on some of the—well, let's say…*duller* areas of the village.'

'Make it so, Reverend. Do what you need to do. Use any resources you require. Let's put Baston back on the map for an entirely different reason!'

The Reverend smiles at Timothy's overwhelming, but surprising enthusiasm.

'Oh…and another thing…' adds the Reverend. 'Maybe it would be a wonderful idea to give our village fountain a little makeover? Well, it is one of the first things the judges will see on entering the village. We want to make a good impression, don't you think…?'

'I completely agree, Reverend.'

Timothy slumps back in his chair, puts his hands behind his head and cups over his notorious bald patch. The wood of the chair creaks and twists as he places one of his legs over the other. He stares through the window, at the village outside.

'Well, I suppose it's a great benefit to us that we have the good deeds of our little friend,' says Timothy, as he turns his head towards the Reverend.

The Reverend pauses. 'Our little friend?'

Timothy winks at the Reverend.

'Oh, yes…our *little* friend,' replies the Reverend, picking up his tea and winking back knowingly at Timothy.

'I assume that she will not let us down?' enquires Timothy, rising from his chair and strolling across to the window.

'Who? Oh, yes…I really can't answer that question. I don't control what she does and when she does it, Timothy…and besides, I'm not even sure if *she* is a she, or—well, you catch my drift!'

Timothy gives a gentle nod of his head.

'Well, our little friend will be a great aid to this operation – she is a key part in helping us win this competition. I pray that she continues to do what she does. In fact, I may wish to speak to her—'

'What do you mean – speak with her? No one has ever seen her, yet had the privilege of talking to her.'

The Reverend takes another sip of his tea, as Timothy stands deep in thought. 'Well…' adds the Reverend. 'Old Jude, at the far side of the village says that she's seen her. However, I wouldn't put my faith in what she says. Last week, I saw her cradling a leg of ham in her arms and singing softly to it. I don't know what was more disturbing.'

Timothy grins and shudders at the pure thought of that image.

'I trust that she will not cause us any problem in the judging process?' asks Timothy, as he cups his hands behind his back and paces slowly around the Reverend.

'What do you mean?'

'I mean, will she be seen as giving the village an unfair advantage…?'

The Reverend stands up from his chair and walks across to Timothy. He places a hand gently on his shoulder.

'What no eye has seen and no ear has heard,' he whispers. Timothy acknowledges him with a slow and steady nod, then releases himself from the Reverend's firm grasp.

'I want us completely ready, Reverend. I mean, I want the village at its absolute best,' states Timothy, with the blackened tone of a man on a mission.

'I understand, Timothy,' replies the Reverend. 'I'm so thrilled and excited that you have taken a serious interest in the village and the community.'

Timothy continues to stare through the window.

'You know your morning service?' asks Timothy. 'What time is that meant to start?'

The Reverend walks across to the window and glances at the clock on the bell tower of the church.

'Oh, fifteen minutes ago.'

'Yes, just as I thought. I've been staring across at the church for a while now – and I must say, I haven't seen a single soul waiting at the church door.'

'Oh…well, that's completely normal,' responds the Reverend, turning back and picking up his tea. 'I rarely get anyone coming for morning service these days.'

Timothy gives a sudden bewildered look.

'So, why do you bother with it?' asks Timothy.

'Because that's what Reverend's do, Timothy. They do morning service!'

◆◆◆

Melvin sits centre of his bicycle, with his hands tightly gripping its formed iron handlebars. They are warm to the touch; caused by the intense heat generated from the raging fire that is burning in the furnace beneath.

Dexter perches himself behind Melvin and digs his claws into the dense fabric of Melvin's robe. He tucks his wings in tightly; shielding himself.

Melvin moves his hand towards a large lever and hovers above it. He hesitates briefly before grasping it in a tightened fist. The needle flickers back and forth violently; struggling to find some logical sense in what pressure it truly wants to read.

'Dex!' shouts Melvin. 'Are you okay back there?'

'What…?' replies Dexter, as he shifts his ear into Melvin's direction.

'Are…you…okay…back…there?' repeats Melvin.

Dexter digs his claws deeper into Melvin's robe; an action that indicates to Melvin, that Dexter is ready to go. There is a slight pause…

Melvin pulls down hard on the lever. It slots into place; making metal-to-metal contact and producing a defining click. Melvin wiggles the lever in his hands and checks it is correctly positioned. He glances up at the passageway ahead and starts to slowly turn the large wheel anti-clockwise.

The bicycle growls and starts to shudder violently. Melvin turns and looks down at the pistons that are rattling loudly inside their housings.

Melvin continues to open the wheel a little further. The bicycle roars in agony as the multitude of pipe-work starts to clang and rattle underneath them.

'It's the brake, Melv! Release the brake!' screams Dexter, who is now holding on for dear life.

'Oh, yes…the brake. This is it, isn't it?' replies Melvin, as he points to a spring-loaded lever to his side.

'I can't see from here, can I?' screeches Dexter. 'Just pull it…push it…do anything with it!'

Melvin releases the lever, and only just has enough time to place his hand back on the handlebars, before the bicycle howls like a rabid wildebeest, and races at tremendous speed across the courtyard.

The wheels spin at unforgiving speeds, as hot steam shoots out from the exhausts and leaves a long trail behind the bicycle. Pebbles ricochet off the walls as the large rubber tyres catch them underneath and flick them violently into the air.

Melvin pulls hard on the handlebars and tries his absolute best to keep the bicycle straight and inline.

They pass with excessive speed through a narrow passageway, across the long wooden drawbridge of the castle and enter the Darkened Enchanted Forest.

'It's too fast, Melv! You're going *too* darn fast!' howls Dexter, with an overwhelming tone of panic in his voice. 'Turn the wheel back – the wheel, Melv!'

'It will not budge!' screams Melvin. 'It's locked in place. What shall I do?'

'Pull the brake…do something to slow us down!'

'I can't reach it, I'm trying to steer and if I let go—well, it's going to get very messy! Can you reach it from there, Dex?'

The bicycle rallies through the densely packed trees of the forest; narrowly missing branches and bushes. Melvin shifts his weight from side to side, which aids the bicycle around a large trunked oak tree. Leaves and twigs fly aside as the bicycle ploughs across the forest floor. The fresh morning dew that lay untouched on the surrounding vegetation, is quickly showered in a blanket of hot steam, as the bicycle continues to race deep into the thick woodland…

'I can't move, Melv!' roars Dexter. 'I'll fall off!'

'Use your claws – climb up onto my back!'

AAAAAACHOO! AAAAAACHOO!

Two copper coins fly out across the forest, one hitting a nearby boulder and the other disappearing amongst a small patch of dewdrops.

Dexter slowly claws his way up Melvin's back, not paying too much attention to the small tears and rips he is making in Melvin's robe. He digs his claws deeper into the fabric; cautiously avoiding Melvin's skin as he tries desperately to clench onto Melvin's shoulder.

'Now, try and climb down here, Dex!' says Melvin, loudly, shifting and nodding his head and indicating where he wants Dexter to move to.

There is a huge bang. The bicycle moans as the front wheel hits a small rock, causing Dexter to suddenly jump and grab onto Melvin's hat. The brisk passing air catches Dexter off guard and triggers his wings to unfold; flapping fully open.

AAAAAACHOO!

Another copper coin flies out of Dexter's snout.

At this precise moment, the sight of a high-powered steam bicycle travelling at tremendous speed, trailing a considerable vent of hot steam behind it, would seem pretty normal to any onlooker. The fact that a crazed wizard is trying to steer it; blinded by a dragon that is perching on his head, wings out full and sneezing copper coins, begs to differ the normality of this extremely bizarre situation.

'I can't see, Dex! Pull up my hat!' bellows Melvin.

There is a look of panic on Dexter's face, as he focuses all his strength on closing his wings, which are preventing him from moving forward. He promptly resets Melvin's hat and continues to climb down the front of Melvin's robe.

'Can you see the brake down there?' hails Melvin.

'Yes!'

'Pull it!'

'What do you think I'm trying to do?' snarls Dexter, who now wishes he hadn't got onto the back of the bicycle and was instead curled up and resting in some shady corner of the castle.

There is a sudden ping and a loud snap.

'Melv? Err…we have a big problem,' says Dexter, painfully.

'Have you pulled the brake? It doesn't seem like we're slowing down at all!'

'You mean this?' says Dexter, as he presents Melvin with the brake lever.

'Oh…my—you broke it?'

'Well, it broke off…yes!'

The bicycle continues to rip through the forest trails; slicing through patches of plants and flowers, which seconds earlier, swayed gently in the morning breeze. The wheels bounce over rocks and small stones. Melvin tries to avoid them at all costs. A trail of hot steam showers the forest floor.

Melvin focuses on the pathway ahead. The forest begins to open up, and to Melvin's delight he catches a glimpse of the village of Baston, in the near distance. But his delight is premature, as it turns into a panic.

'We need to slow down, Dex…we're coming in way too fast!' shouts Melvin.

'You don't say?' shrieks Dexter, wearing a terrified look, at the sight of the approaching village. 'We need to kill the air to the furnace; stop it burning – simple physics, Melv!'

'Huh?'

'The vent…close off the air to the vent – starve the fire of air. Didn't they teach you anything at school?'

'I'm struggling to reach it from here…I'm trying to—*WHOOOOAH!*—steer the bicycle!' shouts Melvin, as he narrowly misses two rabbits, which scuttle across the front of the bicycle.

'Okay, I'll try and reach it!' roars Dexter, stretching himself across to the vent cover, while wrapping his spiky tail around Melvin's waist and holding on tightly to the edge of Melvin's robe. 'Nearly got it!'

With the very tip of his sharpened claw, Dexter scratches at the vent cover, causing it to rotate slowly, before fully locking it shut. The bicycle moans and groans.

'Has it worked, Dex?' asks Melvin.

'I think so, but we now have another problem.'

Dexter pulls himself back and sits on Melvin's lap, facing him.

'What it is?' asks Melvin.

'We are now on fire!'

◆◆◆

'Look out for the step!' booms Timothy, addressing the Reverend, who nearly loses his balance walking down from Timothy's veranda.

With huge pounding strides, Timothy makes his way towards the village church. He listens patiently to the Reverend Clementine ramble on, in the finest of detail, how he is going to give the village back some of its missing beauty.

Timothy nods his head repeatedly. He mumbles a few words to himself as he pretends to listen and process the amount of information the Reverend is offloading onto him. There is a look of pure joy in Timothy's eyes as he thinks about the bigger picture; getting his slimy hands on all that prize money; and what he…and he alone could do with it all.

'I say…it certainly does look like it's going to be another pleasant and beautiful morning here in God's country,' states the Reverend, looking up at the clear blue sky.

Timothy adjusts his belt and pulls up hard on his trousers; just enough to allow him to bend over and tie his bootlace, which is dragging itself through the dew-covered grass. After several moments persevering to get down to that level, he gives up, hiding the fact from the Reverend, by pretending he is doing some morning stretching exercises.

The Reverend gracefully pushes down on the latch of the church gate. It makes a distinctive clicking sound and the gate swings open. He steps through and pulls the gate closed in front of Timothy, who is still trying to decide what to do with his bootlace.

'Well, I guess I must be getting on, Timothy. I have so many things to plan and arrange,' calmly states the Reverend, who is genuinely itching to get started on preparing the village for the competition.

'That you do!' declares Timothy, repeatedly patting the Reverend firmly on the back.

The Reverend straightens his robe and adjusts his collar; ensuring he looks somewhat presentable, on the slim chance, that today is the day, that a villager finally decides they will attend a morning service.

'I must say though, Reverend. I am rather proud of our little village,' states Timothy, trying not to sound overly deep and meaningful. 'Well, it's not so little anymore, but it's a charming and wonderful place.'

The Reverend calmly entertains Timothy's every word, knowing perfectly well that this is not Timothy's normal behaviour.

'I like the people here…' continues Timothy. 'The atmosphere here is great. I think we have such a vibe in this village…don't you think?'

The Reverend nods gently, aided by a sudden state of confusion about what Timothy has just said.

'Sometimes the locals can get a little rowdy and feisty – especially around our tavern late at night. But I have to say – I'm proud to live here,' adds Timothy.

An overwhelming silence lay between them both, interrupted with perfect timing by the sounds of a few villagers taking their first steps into the morning sun. Both the Reverend and Timothy quickly turn and wave at them.

'Good morning to you, Timothy! Good morning to you, Reverend!' screeches a voice from nearby.

'Oh, my Lord…look out! It's Mrs Stamps on the warpath again,' whispers Timothy, nervously. 'Quick, let's hide.'

'Hide? She has already seen us.'

'Is she coming over?'

'She is – and with her multitude of chickens!'

Mrs Stamps, the local Postmaster's wife, is known by many as being—well, an annoying old bag, but even more annoyingly, one with a heart of gold. There is never any pleasing Mrs Stamps. If you gave her your absolute best, she would still want more. Her husband, Mr Stamps, sometimes wishes he could wrap her up, stick a stamp on her and post her far away.

Timothy alters his stance to face Mrs Stamps, who quickly storms across the village green with her army of chickens, while carrying a bowl of corn in her hands.

'She doesn't look too happy, Timothy,' mutters the Reverend.

'Timothy!' bellows Mrs Stamps. 'I *simply* will not tolerate this any longer! I've tried to reason with them – I've even tried to explain the situation several times to you. This will stop now!'

Although being a rather larger gentleman, Timothy suddenly feels as if he's been reduced to the size of an ant, in the presence of Mrs Stamps.

'Err…well, what seems to *b—b*—be the problem, Mrs *S—S*—Stamps?' asks Timothy, with a nervous stutter in his voice.

'Look! Look at it!' shouts Mrs Stamps, dropping the bowl of corn and spilling its contents over the grass.

Timothy tilts his head down at Mrs Stamps' feet, where a dozen very skinny chickens are gormlessly and randomly pecking at the air. Not a single one of them is taking the blindest bit of notice of the copious amount of corn in front of them.

'That's corn, Mrs Stamps,' states Timothy, clearly.

'Don't you dare, Timothy!' bellows Mrs Stamps. 'Don't you dare use that patronising tone with me! You are not too old for a good spanking over my knee!'

The Reverend sniggers and quickly turns his head to hide it from Mrs Stamps.

'Whatever would your poor mother say if she could see you right now?' adds Mrs Stamps. 'God bless her substantial cotton socks.'

'Blessed,' interrupts the Reverend, grinning smugly.

'Thank you, Reverend,' replies Mrs Stamps, tugging at a wooden crucifix, hanging around her neck.

Timothy lowers his head as a darkened mist of shame and embarrassment falls upon him.

'I know it's corn, Timothy!' continues Mrs Stamps. 'You don't have to tell me that. But this is *bad* corn – my babies won't eat it, look!' snarls Mrs Stamps, pointing to her chickens as they pace in crazed circles around her feet.

'Err…*h—h*—have you thought that maybe your *c—c—c*—chickens don't like eating corn?' says Timothy carefully, his voice reaching an impressive squeaky tone towards the end of his sentence.

'What chicken doesn't like corn? Don't be so stupid, Timothy!' rants Mrs Stamps. 'They ate it last week and the week before that. There is something wrong with this corn – I want to know what you're going to—'

'What on Heaven and Earth is that...?' howls the Reverend, stretching out his arm and pointing into the distance.

Mrs Stamps and Timothy hold eye contact for a few moments. They both squint menacingly at each other, before turning and re-directing their attention to where the Reverend is pointing.

'What the—' begins Timothy.

◆◆◆

'Melv, we are coming in *way* too fast!' shouts Dexter, while forcing himself into a sneezing frenzy, using them to try and extinguish the raging fire that is roaring out of control underneath them. Copper coins rapidly fly out from Dexter's snout, pinging off the bicycle's ironwork in all directions, and scattering the landscape around them.

'Cast a spell, Melv!' screams Dexter. 'We need water a water spell would be extremely helpful right now!'

'I can't, Dex!' replies a panicked Melvin. 'I'm trying to keep control of the bicycle – I need both of my hands to casts spells. Oh what a pickle we are in – what a pickle!'

'You're telling me, Melv!' screeches Dexter 'But it's getting extremely hot down there – you've got to do something!'

Dexter knows, that although he can fly, jumping off

the bicycle and spreading his wings at this speed, will most likely cause him great injury. He subconsciously votes to take his chances with Melvin.

'I'm thinking, Dex! It hurts, but I'm thinking,' says Melvin, in a sheer state of panic. 'I'm truly running out of options here – and you shouting at me, isn't helping the situation!'

The bicycle now aflame and pouring out a long, dense trail of hot steam, speeds across the lower foothills that lead into Baston. The bicycle hisses, groans and sings out a chorus of sounds that would certainly not go amiss at a singing lesson for beginners.

In a hurried attempt to slow them down, in sheer desperation and the thought of not coming out of this alive, Dexter digs his claws deep into Melvin's robe. He perches himself up high and extends his wings out as far as they will stretch. The turbulent air catches the thin membrane of his wings as Melvin lets out a girly scream. Dexter persists in trying to create some drag to decrease their speed; only to end up with very sore and cold wings.

The bicycle rattles violently across the cobbled road that leads into the village. Pieces of metal that are extremely important in holding the bicycle together, start to unscrew and dislodge themselves; dropping to the road underneath and rolling out of sight.

'Well, Dex,' announces Melvin. 'You're not going to like this, but I've come up with a plan.'

'A plan is good – any plan is good, Melv!' replies Dexter. 'And the plan is…?'

Dexter closes his eyes.

'In simple terms, Dex, we are going to crash!' says Melvin, nervously.

'The plan is to crash?' screeches Dexter.

'That is correct, my little purple friend!'

'What are you planning to crash into, Melv…? Something soft, I'm hoping?'

Melvin narrows both his eyes, scouts the rapidly approaching village and looks for an ideal place to crash the burning steam-powered bicycle. His eyes widen as he spots the perfect place.

'You know you said we needed lots of water, Dex?' questions, Melvin.'

'Huh?'

'Well, I think I've found some!'

◆◆◆

'Well…whatever it is, it's coming in rather fast – and I believe – yes! It's definitely on fire,' says the Reverend Clementine, as he forces his way past Mrs Stamps and Timothy.

'It also seems to be discharging some sort of huge smoke screen,' adds Timothy. 'But that seems a lot of smoke for such a small fire – no?'

Mrs Stamps shifts herself forward and places each of her chubby hands firmly on her hips, before moving one up to her face to shield herself from the bright sun.

'That looks like my dear friend Melvin,' states Mrs Stamps.

'Melvin?' queries Timothy.

'You know? Melvin? The spellbinder who lives in the castle in the forest?' adds Mrs Stamps.

'Never heard of him,' says the Reverend, scratching at his forehead. 'I say, he is not showing any signs of slowing down, is he? Actually, he does look like he's in a spot of bother.'

Timothy edges forward. 'You know what? I think

you're right, Reverend. I believe he's going to crash – and by the looks of it, right into our village fountain!'

The Reverend gasps.

'And also us if we don't all—MOVE!' yells Timothy, grabbing Mrs Stamps by the arm and pulling her off to the side. Her estranged chickens follow in a straight line behind her; clucking aimlessly.

'Get your grubby hands off me!' demands Mrs Stamps, while trying to break free of Timothy's clutch.

Suddenly, there is a huge explosion, the sound of metal hitting stone and a small splash; followed very quickly by a more considerable splash.

THE AIR HISSES.

'Oh…my…goodness gracious me,' announces Mrs Stamps, tugging herself away from Timothy's grip and making a dire attempt to shield herself from the blanket of hot steam heading their way.

'Oh, darn it-darn it!' announces Melvin. 'Dex, are you okay?'

'Oh, yes, I'm perfectly fine, Melv!' begins Dexter, trying to remain calm and composed. 'I'm extremely thrilled that I've managed to land safely and unscathed in this abyss of cold water. The fact that my claw is stuck underneath this smouldering tyre, is absolutely no problem at all.'

Dexter pauses…

'Of course I'm not alright, Melv!' roars Dexter. 'I mean, you have done some pretty dumb things in your time, Melvin, but this one—well, this one has got to be the stupidest thing you have ever done!'

Melvin sits in the centre of the fountain, his knobbly knees barely breaking the surface of the water. He reaches up and tugs his spellbinder's hat, which slides effortlessly down the side of his wet face. He uses both hands to ring and squeeze the water out of his sodden hat, before placing it atop his head and pulling it down tightly over his forehead.

'Hello…? Is all okay in there?' queries the Reverend, fighting his way through the hot dense steam, which is still discharging from the bicycle's boiler.

Timothy and Mrs Stamps follow behind.

'I'm not!' yells Dexter. 'Will someone please get me out of this mess…?' Dexter tugs at his foot claw with both of his hands. It remains stuck.

'Oh, yes, hello…who's that?' questions Melvin, raising himself out of the cold water; the water rushing down his silky robe.

The Reverend pauses. 'It's me – the good Reverend Clementine,' he replies. 'Are you hurt?'

'Not at all. However, I must attend to my whining little dragon over there.'

Melvin peers through the steam and makes eye contact with Dexter. The look Dexter gives Melvin, more than *sums up* his mood.

The Reverend rushes over to the edge of the fountain, steps into the cold water and wades across to assist Melvin in rescuing Dexter from underneath the bicycle wheel, which has now stopped spinning on its axle.

Both Melvin and the Reverend simultaneously roll up the sleeves of their robes. They lift the bicycle off Dexter, who shifts to free himself, just as Timothy arrives with Mrs Stamps.

'Melvin! A wonderful surprise,' titters Mrs Stamps.

Melvin turns towards a familiar voice. He just didn't want to believe it was that of Mrs Stamps.

'Oh, Mrs Stamps – long-time no see. It's good to see you again. How are the chickens?'

'They are perfectly fine…just over there,' pointing back towards the church. 'It's nice to see you with your clothes on for a change.'

Melvin blushes as Timothy and the Reverend look at each other in shock.

'Yes…well, that's enough of that—*cough-cough*—now-now,' stutters Melvin. 'Anyway, my large man – what's your name?'

'My name is Timothy – Timothy Oakes. I'm the Mayor of this village, although most folks tend to call me Timbers – I really cannot think why…?'

Melvin frowns and waits for Timothy to let out a joking chuckle. It never comes.

Melvin continues to ring out his attire; crunching and twisting the fabric in his hands and releasing jets of water back into the fountain. He picks up the front of his robe, the back still trailing in the water below and steps out of the fountain, onto the grass.

'Well, Timbers,' enquires Melvin. 'I don't suppose there is anyone in your village that can put complex Dwarven engineered bicycles back together, is there?'

'There's Eric, the Blacksmith,' replies Timothy 'He has a small workshop just behind our tavern,' he adds, pointing through the steam. 'I must say you are in luck – he's a Dwarve! But a word of warning – try to refrain from any comments regarding his—well, his height!'

'Ah, jolly good. Oh…and—err…sorry about your fountain. At least it's holding together and hasn't fractured.' Melvin lets out an embarrassed giggle.

'Yes, the fountain. Oh, well…don't worry yourself about it. Nothing a little stone and mortar can't fix. Besides, the Reverend here is going to give it little makeover in preparation for the—err…what's that sound?

Pop! Pop! Pop! – Pop!

Everyone stops and listens carefully.

Pop!

'There's another one,' says Timothy.

Pop!

'And, another one!'

'It's coming from back there,' states Mrs Stamps, pointing towards the church.

Timothy leads the way back through the hot steam, followed carefully by the others. 'It's getting rather hot in here', he states, wiping a few beads of sweat from his brow.

Pop! Pop! – Pop!

'Well, the sound is not consistent, but it's certainly getting more frequent,' says the Reverend.

'And…much louder,' adds Timothy.

'Quiet!' bellows Timothy, halting in his tracks. The others huddle up behind him.

'What do you see, Timbers?' asks Melvin.

'Err…well, it looks like the corn that Mrs Stamps dropped here a moment ago has started to explode in the heated air. It's—well, it's popping open!'

Pop! Pop!

'Huh? The corn is popping open?' queries Dexter.

'Yes, here look!' says Timothy, reaching down, picking up a piece of irregularly shaped corn from the ground and handing it over to Dexter.

'Well, I never—' says Dexter. 'It seems the intense heat surrounding us has forced the water molecules deep within the corn kernel to heat up under extreme pressure; causing them to explode.'

Dexter throws the popped corn into the air, sticks out his long tongue and catches the corn on its way down; flicking it into the back of his mouth. 'Rather tasty also…perhaps a little salt wouldn't go amiss…?' he adds.

Timothy shuffles forward into the mass of corn that lays scattered across the grass. He watches as each one explodes; creating a chorus of loud popping sounds.

CLUCKAAAAWWWK! cluck! cluck!

'Oh look, Mrs Stamps,' announces Timothy, with a small grin upon his face. 'It seems like your chickens are enjoying this so-called…*popped* corn.'

Mrs Stamps gives Timothy a piercing stare.

'Do me a little favour, Timothy!' blasts Mrs Stamps. 'Shut up! Oh…and another thing…would you please tie your blasted bootlace? You're making the place look untidy!'

CHAPTER III

"I remember I was once pulled over on my horse, by an Officer of the Law. He said 'Papers,' so I replied 'Scissors, I win!' and galloped off."

ERIC BRONZEFOOT

On the outer edge of the village, behind the tavern and where the Cobalt River spans out into smaller rushing streams, stands a blacksmith's workshop; a building constructed from large wooden beams, beautiful stone walls and a mass of supporting ironwork. Even from afar, the building is a pure marvel to see.

A mighty wooden waterwheel turns gracefully and majestically, as the rushing waters underneath, drive it around. The large paddles slice through the crystal-clear water; water that finally cascades back into the river amongst a whitewash of spray and foam.

A considerable diameter drive shaft enters the stone wall of the building. Coated heavily in grease and oil, it shimmers as the sunlight reflects off it. The shaft purrs effortlessly with precision through a set of large cast-iron bearings.

Dark grey slated tiles line the roof of the workshop, each placed in an integral woven pattern, which allows the rainwater to flow directly into a maze of cleverly designed piping, filling up anything that can be filled; from the large water storage tank standing on the far side of the workshop, to an array of pots and pans; even the kettle inside the building.

A tall circular chimney protrudes from the centre of the roof and into the sky. Its darkened stained funnel is a common sight on the village skyline, as smoke pours out of it on a daily, or even nightly basis.

Two large wooden doors mark the entrance to the workshop. They are supported either side by colossal hand-made iron hinges, which are firmly secured to the building with over-sized domed iron rivets. A complex system of cogs and pulleys span out from the other side of the door and link ingeniously to the smallest of keyholes on the front. By twisting the key within, it sets loose a chain reaction of moving sprockets, chains and pulleys; all moving in unison. They clank and clink in perfect timing, before finally releasing the doors from the clutches of huge iron retaining bars.

However, at this time of the morning, the doors are fully open, revealing a hum of activity inside. For deep within the stone walls, dwells a highly talented and skilled individual; a master of the hammer, an overlord of molten earth and a manipulator of fire and flame. *This* is home to the village's blacksmith…or Eric…as most people in the village call him.

You could be forgiven for thinking that this stocky Dwarve wouldn't be strong, or even bold enough to lift a heavy hammer and pound it hard down on red-hot iron. But in this case, it is the opposite, as this blacksmith is from the family Bronzefoot; a highly respectable name within the blacksmithing world.

Eric sits comfortably on a small wooden stool and positions himself over his anvil. His long grey bushy beard twisted neatly together with leather straps, as it hangs down in front of him. He occasionally strokes it softly; caressing the long hairs with his rough hands. Reaching into his pocket, he pulls out a small flask and removes the cork, before taking several small swigs of its contents.

He pauses…

Wiping the sweat from his brow, he returns to his feet and paces briskly towards his stone-built forge. The continuous echoing of air being sucked into large bellows, is a haunting sound for anyone not used to hearing it. The forge runs hot and ablaze. It roars as air releases from the bellows and into the heart of the fire, which casues a large piece of red-hot iron inside to crackle and spit.

He carefully steps up to the front of the forge and skilfully removes the hot glowing metal with a pair of large pincers. He manoeuvres the metal onto his anvil.

Using a variety of tools, he turns the liquid looking metal over and over, occasionally pounding down on it with his hammer; releasing hundreds of tiny sparks, which dance across the room, before fading.

Sweat continues to pour off his forehead, and his shirt is stained with the smell of labour and drudgery.

Finally he takes the crafted item, still glowing red-hot and lowers it into a water bath. The water boils and steam hisses and leaves a lucid smell; relished by the creator.

There is a distant knock on the wooden door.

'Well then…what do we have here?' queries Eric, removing his charred and soot coated gloves. 'Visitors to my fine establishment? I'm truly honoured.' Eric places his gloves down carefully on top of his heated anvil. 'Come in-come in…pull up a pew, or a crate…or *even* a barrel.'

Melvin and Dexter enter the workshop and glance around at the mass of tools and devices that hang from the walls and rafters.

Eric follows them both with his eyes as they each find a barrel from the corner of the room, and roll them across to Eric. Melvin swipes his robe to the side and gently lowers himself down onto the cold iron barrel rim. Dexter jumps up onto his barrel and perches patiently. He turns his head continually in all directions, and *eyes up* all the amazing and marvellous wonders of Eric's workshop.

'I must say…you are both looking a little wet. It's not raining outside. Ah, let me guess…you went for a swim in the river?' questions Eric.

Melvin runs both his hands down the front of his damp robe. 'No, not at all. We just had a little trouble earlier with your village water fountain.'

'Oh, how funny!' responds Eric, whilst chuckling loudly. 'You fell into the fountain!' Did you both have a bit too much to drink at our tavern?'

'No, we were not drunk at all,' says Melvin. 'We—well, simply had a little bit of trouble—'

'I've been drunk several times,' interrupts Eric. 'I have managed very successfully to find the cold waters of that fountain on many a night – while leaving the tavern. Mostly with a belly full of honey mead. That Duncan sure knows how to blow my taste buds and my mind at the same time. Have you had the pleasure of meeting him yet?'

'No, but I dare to say that we shall meet him at some point,' replies Melvin.

There is a pause as Melvin stares at Eric and Eric stares at Melvin.

'Oh, I do apologise…how very rude of me. Let me introduce myself,' says Eric, offering out his small, yet chubby hand towards Melvin. 'The name's Bronzefoot – Eric Bronzefoot.'

'Melvin Copernicus of Huskendale,' replies Melvin, reaching out to meet Eric's hand, and embracing in a firm and manly handshake.

'Hmmm…Copernicus? Not the same Copernicus from the castle in the forest?' asks Eric.

'Yep, that's me! Guilty as charged,' answers Melvin excitedly.

'I thought you died…?'

'No, I'm most definitely still alive,' replies Melvin in a shocked tone.

'No…no you surely died. I read all about it in the local newsprint – a couple of years back. You sort of died on purpose to gain entrance to the underworld – or something silly like that!'

Melvin takes off his hat and adjusts it, before placing it firmly back onto his head.

'Ah, no…you must be thinking of my parents, in particular, my father…and yes that would be true. He did die on purpose, along with my mother. They both studied death and were aiming to do some research in the underworld, but they forgot two crucial things.'

'What were they?' asks Eric.

'Well, one…how on Earth they were going to get back to the world of the living – and two…just how much fun they were having while dead.'

Eric smiles out of courtesy.

'On a happier note, it's good to meet you, Melvin,' says Eric. 'And…who is this little dragon?'

'Everyone calls me Dex,' answers Dexter. 'I'm not little actually. I'm quite large for my age!' Dexter grins. 'Unlike some,' he adds, under his breath.

'Okay…steady on, little fellow. I only asked you your name,' adds Eric, taking a casual step back. 'So, I guess the *big* question is – what can I do for you both on this fine crisp sun-filled morning?' Eric rubs his hands together.

'Well, I was hoping that you would be able to spare some time to fix my bicycle. It's well…in a little bit of a pickle,' announces Melvin.

'It's in little bits alright,' sniggers Dexter, turning his head away from Melvin, who catches precisely what Dexter had said. He gives Dexter a piercing stare.

'Sure thing! Let's take a look at it. What exactly is wrong with the bicycle?' enquires Eric.

'Err…let me think. Well, I believe that the word I would use to describe it best would be – everything,' answers Melvin, slightly embarrassed.

'What do you mean…everything?' questions Eric. 'Is it outside somewhere? Come; let us see what the problems are.'

'No, it's not *exactly* outside here, it's—err…'

'Spit it out now, lad!' growls Eric, growing a little impatient.

Dexter raises his head and turns to look up at Melvin, who starts to play nervously with his fingers.

'What Melvin is trying to say…' begins Dexter. 'Is that – his bicycle – his brand-new stream-powered bicycle – is currently in multiple pieces and scattered across the village green. Oh…and I believe some parts are submerged in the fountain.'

Eric places his hands on his legs, takes a huge breath and exhales slowly. He brings himself upright and reaches back into his pocket to take a few more swigs from his flask.

'Please tell me you are not talking about a Dwarven steam-powered bicycle?' says Eric, in a worried tone.

Melvin slowly lowers his head and nods gently.

'How did this happen?' asks Eric. 'Do you realise the amount of time and effort that goes into building just a single bicycle?'

'Simple really…' begins Dexter, raising his claw and pointing to Melvin. 'This clever-clogs here, with his infinite wisdom, thought that it would be a brilliant idea to fuel the bicycle's furnace with wood. Of course, I told him that is was a bad—'

'With wood, you say?' snorts Eric. 'A complex piece of engineering genius such as that, needs to be fuelled by coal – to make the furnace burn hot enough to power the bicycle.'

Dexter's head bobs up and down in excitement.

'Yeah…' continues Dexter. 'He then adds some super-duper venom of *some* dragon, which then causes the boiler to overheat and catch fire. It didn't help that *I* then broke off the brake lever…and then—well, the rest is pretty self-explanatory.'

'You crashed the bicycle into the village fountain?' exclaims Eric. 'I do not know if I want to laugh or cry right now. I mean…where have you two just come from? The Realm of the Numpties, or something?'

Dexter and Melvin turn to one another and shrug their shoulders in confusion.

'You're so lucky that our village lawman didn't see what you did,' explains Eric. 'Good job he's out of town for a day or two.'

'Oh my!' replies Melvin.

'Yes…he surely would have locked you up for a long time in that jail of his.'

A look of concern appears on Melvin's face and an uncomfortable silence falls across the workshop.

'Nah, I'm only messing with you,' replies Eric. 'He wouldn't do something like that. I remember I was once pulled over on my horse by an Officer of the Law. He said "*Papers,*" so I replied, "*Scissors, I win*" and galloped off.'

Eric chuckles loudly, followed by a few spluttering coughs. Dexter and Melvin quickly adopt fake smiles.

'Well then, we'd better go and take a little look at this broken bicycle of yours – or what's left of it anyways,' announces Eric, picking up his leather gloves and sliding them back onto his hands. 'Can you smell that?' he adds.

'Smell what…?' replies Dexter, lifting his snout and flaring his nostrils.

'The air, Dexter,' states Eric. 'The smell of fire, flame, smoke and molten iron. That will certainly put a few hairs on your chest, no? Give the old testosterone levels a little stirring, Melvin…huh?'

'I definitely think that Melvin needs his testosterone levels increasing,' answers Dexter. 'To be perfectly honest though, I think they're going the *other* way and decreasing. I mean, if his testosterone levels drop any lower, he'll turn into a butterfly.'

Eric chuckles as Melvin goes into deep thought.

'Hmmm, that would be quite interesting to become a butterfly…' begins Melvin. 'No wait. I would rather be a big bee. Just imagine that!'

Dexter laughs. 'The day you turn yourself into a giant bee, will be the day I wear a pink flower on my head for an entire month.'

Dexter jumps off from his barrel; obviously bored with the conversation. He moves across the workshop and starts fiddling with a large contraption sitting on one of the many workbenches.

'Don't touch that!' screams Eric. 'That's one of my newest creations.'

'What is it?' asks Dexter.

'Quite simple, really,' says Eric, turning a few small dials and adjusting a couple of levers. 'You put a single slice of bread in here – watch it as it goes through there – over this bit and along these rails, until it finally pops out here…like so—'

'That's all very fancy, Eric…but what does it do…?' repeats Dexter.

'It makes the bread crispy – look!' answers Eric, holding a piece of charred bread up in front of Dexter.

'Looks burnt,' says Dexter. 'Anyway, why would you need crispy bread, Eric?'

'I would have thought that is pretty obvious?' says Eric. 'It helps in keeping my sandwiches from getting soggy in the rain.'

Dexter watches another piece of bread work its way through the machine; sifting through the array of small wire belts and trays, before entering a small glowing red box at the centre.

'Anyway, I haven't got all day…and *certainly* no time to waste,' announces Eric. 'Let's go and see this bicycle of yours. Come on…chop-chop!'

Eric ushers Melvin and Dexter out of the building.

'Thank you, Eric…very much appreciated,' says Melvin, as he stumbles out of the workshop.

'Oh, wait. We might need this,' says Eric, pulling out a wheeled object, which is leaning up against the side of the workshop.

'What is that…?' queries Dexter.

'Again, this is one of my latest creations. I've spent weeks developing this. It's quite complex. It requires the pain-staking forging of multiple pieces of ironwork at elevated temperatures; bending them into optimal angles with sweat breaking precision, before quenching them in cold water to give them maximum strength.'

'What do you call it?' questions Dexter.

Eric pauses. 'I call this one…a wheelbarrow!'

◆◆◆

Duncan picks himself up from the cold stone floor of the village tavern. He rests briefly on one knee to catch his breath, before using his long, bulky arms to aid himself up to the counter level. He runs the palms of his stubby hands down his sweaty face; pulling at his sticky and damp skin. In one swift movement, he grabs hold of a wooden cup full of water and throws it hard against his stubbled face.

He violently shakes his head from side to side, as water droplets hit the tavern's floor and *pretty much* everything else within Duncan's vicinity.

Carefully negotiating the gap in the bar countertop, Duncan tugs at his collar and twists his shirt around to allow him to wipe his bushy moustache. He lets out a loud belch, before attempting to increase his vision, by squinting his drowsy eyes.

Duncan has never been a man who takes personal hygiene seriously. In fact, he is notorious for having an odour that is—well, certainly less than desirable. He acknowledges this himself by raising his arm and taking in a sniff of the pungent smell that wafts from his sweat-stained armpit. He cringes and smiles at the same time.

Gazing across the tavern, to the few locals that still reside on the damp floor, Duncan debates if he should start to clear up the chaos created from the drunken activities of the previous night. His thoughts are interrupted by the tavern's door opening, which lets out a long drawn out squeak, as it's pushed aside.

'Good noon to you, Duncan,' announces the Reverend, passing through the door, followed by an extremely large man and a rather skinny man, both dressed in militia attire.

'Hello, Reverend. Oh my, is it that time already? I really must start to think about getting something to eat.' Duncan shifts his attention to his cook, who still lays passed out on the floor. 'Err…maybe not at this moment, then,' he adds.

'Duncan, may I introduce you to some good friends of mine…?' begins the Reverend. 'This is Corporal Ringelstein and Private Babe, from River's Bend. They are both here to assist me in preparing the village for the upcoming competition.'

'Competition…?' questions Duncan, in a state of confusion.

The Reverend sighs. 'Oh, never mind.'

Duncan has always accepted that he is a large man, but compared to the Corporal, who stands with an overwhelming presence; Duncan is half his size.

Corporal Ringelstein's substantial size in both

height and width gets him noticed wherever he goes. He sticks out like a sore thumb.

His bulging pale-skinned body pushes the limits on the seams of his undersized attire. His legs stand firmly on the wooden floor of the tavern; poised like two massive trees trunks.

'The Corporal is the neighbour of my cousin Frank, who is the local *man of the cloth* up in the town of River's Bend,' announces the Reverend. 'Do you remember him from the party we had last Christmas?'

'How could I forget?' replies Duncan. 'It took me a good amount of time to get him to leave here, after spending most of his evening emptying my jar of pickled eggs. Oh, does he still divulge in his favourite of jellied eels in gravy?'

The Corporal laughs loudly. 'That he does!' he says, before forcing a handful of popped corn into his mouth, which the Reverend had picked up earlier.

'Is that corn you are eating, Corporal?' questions Duncan.

'I hear it's called *popped* corn,' splutters the Corporal, spitting out fragments of half-masticated corn kernels onto the tavern's floor. 'It's spread all over the village green!' he adds.

'Yes…and Mrs Stamps is collecting a lot of it in large boxes – to feed her chickens. They seem to enjoy it,' states the Reverend.

Duncan stands still, with a gormless look upon his face. After years of drinking his renowned honey mead, it always takes Duncan's brain cells a little longer to process his thoughts and compute any form of logical response.

'Ah, yes!' responds Duncan. 'I heard there was a little commotion earlier. Someone crashed his or her bicycle right into our fountain. What a muppet!'

'Here, try some,' says the Corporal, handing over some of the popped corn to Duncan, who immediately throws it to the back of his open mouth.

'Not bad at all,' he announces. 'A little flavouring and I believe that I may be on to something.'

'I think Timothy may have already beat you to it,' states the Reverend.

'Damn that man!' sneers Duncan.

'Well, Duncan…' begins the Reverend. 'I would love to stay and have a little chit-chat with you, but my friends and I do have some rather important business that needs addressing. Please do you have a table…? Oh…and perhaps one with matching chairs – and preferably ones that are still intact.'

Everyone laughs.

Duncan leads them across the tavern to a wooden table by the main window. He picks up a couple of up-turned chairs from the floor, on the way.

A glass bottle shatters and crunches under the Corporal's huge leather boots. The sound echoes across the building's walls.

Private Babe takes the chair nearest the window, followed by the Reverend and finally the Corporal, whose physical size and mass outweigh the size of the chair, which creaks under the Corporal's weight.

'Can I interest you gentlemen in a midday drink?' asks Duncan.

'I'll try a tankard of your finest honey mead please, Duncan,' answers the Corporal, in a deep husky tone.

'Me too,' adds the Reverend.

Duncan glances across the table at Private Babe, who has been remarkably mute since entering the building.

Private Babe is a fraction of the size of the Corporal. A slender and thin character, with hardly an ounce of fat or muscle about his skinny body. He dresses with distinction and pride; each and every piece of his clothing immaculately pressed and his boots polished to perfection. An excellent example of how a recruit of the River's Bend Battalion, should be.

'And for you, Babe? I mean—err…sorry – that kind of sounded very wrong.'

'Don't worry about it – I get it all the time from *him*,' says Private Babe, pointing across the table at his friend and superior, Corporal Ringelstein. 'Well, I'm not a big fan of mead, neither am I a huge drinker, but I think I'll treat myself today.'

'Another mead it is, then,' announces Duncan.

'Oh no. I was thinking more along the lines of a very small tumbler of your finest white wine, if you please?'

The Corporal lets out a roaring laugh.

'What?' questions Private Babe.

'A small tumbler of white wine? Really?' snorts the Corporal. 'Get some mead down you man – loosen you up a little. That's an order!'

Private Babe makes eye contact with Duncan and gently nods at him.

'Three meads it is, then!' exclaims Duncan. 'Which is good – because that is pretty much the extent of my beverage list…mead or water.'

Duncan chuckles and heads back to the bar area.

'Okay, huddle up people,' says the Reverend. 'As you both know, I have called for your assistance in making our village beautiful and spectacular for the *Village of the Year Award.* There is lots to do and very little time to get it all implemented.'

The Corporal reaches deep inside his jacket pocket

and pulls out a long cigar. He eyes across at his Private and waits for him to produce a means to light the cigar.

Private Babe immediately reacts and pats at his chest with both hands; checking his multitude of pockets for a small flare of matches.

The Corporal shakes his head in disappointment.

'I could have sworn that I placed them here in my top jacket pocket…' begins Private Babe. 'They were certainly here earlier when—'

'No worries – here,' interrupts the Reverend, who takes out a small band of matches from inside his tunic. He slides them across the table towards the Corporal, who puts the cigar between his lips, strikes a match and lowers his head towards the naked flame.

'I was about to question if a Reverend should be drinking…' states the Corporal, 'But now you smoke as well?

The Reverend smiles. 'Oh, no-no, I use those matches to light the many candles in the church. As for drinking…I can see nothing wrong with consuming a little honey mead, once every so often. Besides, the Lord put these bounties on this planet for us to indulge in. I see nothing wrong with that.'

The Corporal nods, draws in hard on the end of his cigar and blows a couple of perfectly formed smoke circles across the table.

'Right, we only have a few days to sort out things. I assume that you can round up the rest of your squad, Corporal?' asks the Reverend.

'Yes, they are ready to be instructed accordingly.'

'Excellent.'

The Reverend pauses. 'Private Babe, would you mind taking a few notes? Much needs addressing – and I want to make sure that it all done in good time.'

Private Babe pulls a small black notepad and a piece of charcoal from his inner pocket. He nods at the Reverend.

'There we go, lads – three tankards of honey mead. That'll warm your cockles!' states Duncan, slamming down the tankards onto the tabletop. 'I'll leave you all to it, then? I've got a few things to sort out.'

'Much appreciated, Duncan,' asserts the Corporal.

'Okay, I have a bit of a long list here. Are you ready, Private?' questions the Reverend.

'I am…' replies Private Babe.

'Number one…I would like our fountain rebuilt. After that little mishap earlier – the judges will not take kindly to seeing that, the moment they enter the village. Can I leave that in your capable hands, Corporal?'

The Corporal nods his head up and down gently while savouring his cigar.

'I would be delighted if you can make it better than it was before. I mean…it will be the first thing the judges will see,' adds the Reverend.

The Corporal continues nodding.

'Number two…where possible, I would like the village to have a fresh lick of paint and perhaps tidy up those dilapidated buildings down by the river – if you don't mind?'

'Any particular colour, Reverend?' queries Private Babe, looking up from his notepad.

'Hmmm, a nice shade of pale blue would suffice,' answers the Reverend.

Private Babe proceeds to scribble notes on his pad, quickly flicking over the pages to try and keep up with everything the Reverend is saying.

The Corporal takes a huge gulp of honey mead and continues puffing deeply on his cigar. He stares at the clock on the wall and then back at the Reverend, who is now on verbal overdrive.

The Corporal sighs as boredom begins to take over.

'How long is that list of yours, Reverend?' enquires the Corporal.

'I have a total of eighty-three different items that need addressing, Corporal,' replies the Reverend.

The Corporal groans in displeasure and takes his tankard of honey mead in his hand, before tipping its remaining contents down his gullet. He signals across to Duncan for another one; pointing at his empty tankard. Duncan nods, before attempting to wake his cook from the floor, by slapping him across the face with his own apron.

The Corporal stares at the Reverend and watches his mouth move up and down. Words are coming out, but the Corporal chooses not to listen or relate to them. He glances to the side at Private Babe and smiles, knowing that he is carefully writing down everything the Reverend is saying.

The Corporal removes his cigar, flicks it onto the floor and stamps it out underneath his boot.

'Eighty-three you say, Reverend…?' quizzes the Corporal.

'That is correct, Corporal,' replies the Reverend.

'What number are we on now?'

'Still on two.'

'Darn it,' mutters the Corporal.

◆◆◆

Dexter reaches down, picks up a twisted piece of metal from the ground and holds it high above his head. He casually flips it from side to side and tries to deduce precisely what part of Melvin's bicycle it came from. Narrowing his eyes, he inspects the burnt and charred remain, before tossing it over his shoulders into Eric's wheelbarrow.

'What a complete utter mess! Such a shame…such a waste,' concedes Eric, glancing around at the debris scattered around the fountain.

'I know,' replies Melvin, with a slight tear in his eye. 'I've only had it a few hours and look what I've done to it?'

'I'm not talking about the bicycle, Melvin. I can fix that! I'm talking about our beautiful fountain!'

Melvin tilts his head in shame and embarrassment.

AAAAAACHOO!

A tiny copper coin shoots out from Dexter's left nostril and hits Eric on the back of the leg.

'Ouch!' yells Eric, turning around and picking up the coin from the floor. 'What's this, Dexter? It looks very much like copper.'

'Oh, yeah. Melvin, Lord of the Numpties, tried to cure me of a problem I have with my fire vents, but he failed…and ever since I've been sneezing copper coins. Sometimes I can sneeze a rainbow alongside them, but that's been much better of late.'

'How very interesting…' remarks Eric. 'May I ask what you do with all the coins, Dexter?'

'I usually leave them where they lay …' answers Dexter. 'The castle grounds are full of them.'

'Interesting…well we may need them now. This bicycle has much copper. How often can you do that?'

'Err…it just happens randomly,' replies Dexter, as he continues to pick up pieces of bicycle and place them into the wheelbarrow.

Melvin removes his damp sandals, lifts his robe to

his knees and steps back into the cold waters of the fountain. The previously crystal-clear water, now stained black; infused with burnt rubber, soot and oil.

He reaches down and penetrates the oily surface with his hand. Rummaging below, he pulls out pieces of his bicycle from its blackened depths. He places them carefully onto the bricked rim of the fountain, which is still resisting to crack and fall.

'Mind your tootsies on the floor, Melvin!' shouts Eric, from a distance.

Melvin treads carefully around the perimeter of the fountain. Using his fingers, he scraps the bottom of the fountain, making sure that none of his bicycle remains, or maybe making sure, none of the *remains* of his bicycle…remain.

Eric strolls towards Melvin, carrying both large wheel hubs under one arm and an exhaust pipe, under the other.

'I think that's most of it,' declares Eric, dropping the items to the ground. 'A question though, Melvin – Why not use your powers of spellbinding to try and put your bicycle back together?'

'NO!' screeches Dexter. 'I mean no, Melv – don't you even think about it,' he continues, with a softer and lowered audio level.

'Why ever not?' questions Eric.

'I don't feel comfortable with it…' begins Dexter. 'I mean…based on the fact that occasionally Melv gets things very and I mean *very* wrong. I don't want him to spoil this bicycle by doing something drastic to it.'

'I think it's a little late for that,' retorts Eric, pointing his finger at the fully loaded wheelbarrow.

'No, Dexter is right,' says Melvin, clearing his throat to explain. 'Spellbinding is a mysterious art; full of randomness and unknowns. However, we do know two things. Firstly…magic can only be performed on something living, something of essence and not anything that is man-made. Sometimes there are exceptions, but that is a general rule. Secondly…I would have to know exactly what it was that I wanted the magic to do. In this case, I don't know anything about rebuilding a Dwarven bicycle. It would be such a complicated spell to even attempt.'

Eric and Dexter stand in shock on hearing Melvin's responsible and mature response.

'Very wise,' states Eric.

Melvin steps out of the fountain and places the few remaining parts carefully into the wheelbarrow. Eric grips on to its handles tightly and with minimal effort lifts the wheelbarrow. He pauses a second, before he starts to push the wheelbarrow back to his workshop.

'Melvin! Oh, Melvin!' calls a voice.

'Blast it! I was hoping she wouldn't see us,' exclaims Melvin, pretending not to hear the annoying and piercing tone of Mrs Stamps' voice.

'Oh, Mrs Stamps, we meet again,' answers Melvin, giving in to the fact that Mrs Stamps is better off acknowledged, than ignored.

'It looks like you *will* be staying a few days here, Melvin? How wonderful. Maybe you and I could have a little catch up at some point? Just like old times, huh?' says Mrs Stamps excitedly, winking at Melvin and giving him a slight nudge with her arm.

'Oh, err…well, I guess you may be right,' responds Melvin, turning a slight shade of red.

'You know, you can stay at the post office? I'm sure my husband wouldn't mind – and I believe we can also accommodate your dragon,' suggests Mrs Stamps.

'Oh, *that's—that's*—err...that's most kind of you Mrs Stamps,' stutters Melvin. 'However, I'm sure Eric will have the bicycle fixed very shortly – will you not, Eric?'

'Good grief, you must be joking? I'm going to need at least two, maybe three days, to get this back together and in perfect working order,' bellows Eric.

Mrs Stamps smiles.

'Nearly three days?' questions Melvin.

'That's right, lad...' begins Eric. 'It looks like you may be introducing yourself to Duncan at our tavern, after all.' Eric chuckles. 'If you tell him I sent you, he may, if he's in a good mood, give you a discount.'

'Oh...oh very well, then,' says Melvin, turning his attention to Dexter. 'Fancy a few days in Baston, Dex?'

'Do I have a choice?'

'Not really...no.'

'Oh, Eric...?' queries Mrs Stamps. 'Would you mind terribly if I borrowed this contraption of yours in a while? I seemed to have accumulated a few boxes of popped corn over there.'

Everyone turns to where Mrs Stamps is pointing; observing her hungry chickens pecking randomly at the ground. They watch as the chickens search for the last few kernels of popped corn, still scattered around.

'It is my absolute pleasure, Mrs Stamps,' answers Eric, as he proceeds to push the wheelbarrow towards his workshop.

Melvin takes a small bow in front of Mrs Stamps and promptly reaches down to pick up the two wheel hubs at Eric's feet. Dexter picks up what's left of the bicycles elaborate exhaust system.

AAAAAACHOO!

AAAAAACHOO!

Dexter launches two copper coins in front of him, which both land softly on the grass.

'Oh, how very cute,' states Mrs Stamps. 'A sneezing dragon!'

'Don't forget to pick up them coins, Dexter,' hints Eric. 'You never know…those two pieces could form part of the bicycle's refurbished cooling system.'

Dexter frowns.

'Cooling system? A lot of good that did us last time,' he mutters.

◆◆◆

'Number seventy-two…the church bell to be polished so that you can see your face in it—' continues the Reverend.

The Corporal yawns.

'This honey mead is absolutely s*h*mashing s*h*tuff!' blurs Private Babe.

'Err…I hope you have been writing down the last things I've been saying, Private?' says the Reverend.

'Oh, s*h*ure…s*h*ure I have,' responds Private Babe, holding up his notepad and pushing it forcefully into the Reverend's face.

'How many meads have you had, Private?' asks the Reverend.

'S*h*even. No wait…eight!'

'Oh dear, Lord!' wails the Reverend.

'You ss*h*ould loos*h*en up*f* a li*dd*le. Here, try s*h*ome!'

'I'm perfectly fine, Private. I have my own.'

'Are you s*h*ure?' splutters Private Babe, as he pushes the sloshing tankard towards the Reverend; spilling a little mead over the tabletop. 'Is*h* really good s*h*tuff!'

The Reverend sighs and glances over towards the

Corporal, who is struggling to focus and keep his drowsy eyes open.

'I guess we are done here, then?' asks the Reverend, disappointed that he was nearly at the end of his list. 'Well, Corporal…I hope that you will give this all of your full attention – starting promptly on this list in the morning?'

The Corporal adjusts himself in his chair. 'It will get our full attention, Reverend.'

'I would hope so, Corporal. For your troubles, I will be paying you each a gold coin.'

The Corporal's eyes shift and widen.

'A gold coin *each*, you say? Well, that's certainly better than I expected,' states the Corporal, who begins to suddenly take a much more serious approach to the Reverend's plans. 'It will all be completed on time, Reverend. You can count on me and—well…well this broken mess of a man!'

'Pull yourself out of this mess, Private!' booms the Corporal, lifting himself out of his creaking chair. 'And stand to attention and salute your superior officer.'

'Yes*h*, S*h*ir!' responds Private Babe, pushing himself up and attempting a salute, before crashing down onto the tabletop and slowly sliding to the floor.

'Oh, he was right,' states the Reverend. 'He doesn't drink very much.'

The Corporal nods.

'I'm afraid, Corporal, that I will have to leave him in your capable hands though…' begins the Reverend. 'The evening approaches and I must prepare for evening service. I have secured two rooms here at the tavern, for yourself and Private Babe, but I understand the rest of your squad will be staying in tents by the river. Is that correct?'

The Corporal finishes the remains of his honey mead and wipes his large bushy moustache with the back of his hand. 'That is correct, Reverend.'

'Good-good!'

'Do you *actually* have anyone attend your evening service, Reverend?'

'Of course not! But it does give me an excuse to take a little tipple of the holy wine!'

The Corporal laughs.

'Oh…you may need these back?' says the Corporal, throwing the band of matches towards the Reverend.

The Reverend grabs the matches and places them back into his tunic.

'I shall see you bright and early in the morning, Corporal…say nine?' proposes the Reverend.

'Nine it is!'

◆◆◆

Melvin dives deep into his left robe pocket and rustles around a little, before pulling out a small tanned leather pouch, held tightly closed by a length of leather cord.

He bounces the pouch up and down in the palm of his hand. With raised eyebrows, Melvin stares strangely up into the roof of Eric's workshop, determining by pure weight alone, exactly how many coins are inside his pouch.

The coins inside jingle as he uses his other hand to pull on the leather cord; opening the top of the pouch and allowing Melvin to peek inside. With delight and yet a slight reluctance, Melvin reaches inside and retrieves a gold coin; placing it down carefully into Eric's waiting palm. At a steady pace, Melvin continues this action, until four extremely shiny gold coins lay neatly positioned in the centre of Eric's sweaty palm. Eric then quickly clenches his fist, encasing the gold coins deep inside.

'As I mentioned before, Melvin, I aim to rebuild your bicycle within two days…maybe three, depending on the amount of damage,' explains Eric, opening his fist gently and eyeing up the gold coins that are now in his possession. He lets out a large grin. 'Oh…and if you can, Dexter…try to collect up as many of those copper coins that you sneeze out. They will certainly come in most handy if I need to reforge some of the bicycle's key copper components.'

Dexter sighs and agrees by nodding his head.

AAAAAACHOO!

A copper coin exits with tremendous velocity from Dexter's left nostril and richochets with a loud ping off the top surface of Eric's anvil, before rolling across the floor and out of sight.

'Well, that's a good start!' declares Eric.

Melvin turns his attention to the wheelbarrow, full beyond belief with parts of his bicycle, which are currently defying the laws of physics and somehow remaining perfectly positioned in a balanced state.

'Are you sure that you'll be able to put my bicycle back together, Eric?' asks Melvin, as he moves across to the side of the wheelbarrow and attempts to pick up a random piece of the bicycle, only to realise that it probably wasn't such a good idea.

'Oh, yes! No problem at all, Melvin,' replies Eric.

'Like—err…precisely the way it was before?'

'Yes, Melvin…please trust me on this one. I might even decide to add a few minor upgrades of my own design.'

'Oh…and the wheels will be the same?'

Eric grins.

'Melvin…please…don't worry. It shall all be done.'

Melvin remains still and strokes his beard slowly, trying to convince himself that the bicycle is in more than capable hands and that he should just let Eric get on with rebuilding it. After a few moments, Melvin concludes that the whole situation with his bicycle couldn't possibly get any worse and nods at Eric.

'Okay, good-good. I shall start working on your bicycle straight away,' says Eric, taking the gold coins and dropping them into his open trouser pocket. 'But first…will you join me in a quick tipple of brandy?'

'Oh—err, no thank you, Eric,' replies Melvin.

Eric turns and offers the small flask to Dexter, who stares back at him blankly.

'Well, then…I must crack on,' begins Eric. 'There is much to do – and I must start by getting this forge up to—'

'What, on good Earth, is that horrible ringing?' yells Melvin, cupping his hands and placing them tightly over his ears.

'Oh, blast it!' bellows Eric. 'Is it that time already? I must get my soils sorted.'

'Time for what…? Soils?' queries Dexter, glancing up towards Melvin, who stares back and shrugs his shoulders.

Eric rushes across his workshop and slides open a wooden door that leads into a small back room. Dexter and Melvin watch with interest as they try to block out the annoying ringing, which currently resembles a hundred tiny church bells, all going off at different times. Occasionally, the ringing is overpowered by the sounds of Eric shouting and moaning loudly at himself from the back room.

A few moments pass and Eric returns carrying a large wooden crate. Dexter sniggers as he observes Eric's barely visible head sticking out from behind the crate; a head that now has an elaborate pair of cotton underpants positioned embarrassingly over it.

The loud ringing suddenly stops as Eric drops the crate to the floor, followed quickly by his underpants, which fall from his face, back into the crate.

'I nearly forgot about all this!' announces Eric, shifting his attention to the contents of his crate.

Melvin releases his hands from around his ears, takes a small step forward and hovers over the crate full of dirty clothes.

'So, tell me…what's all this, Eric…?' asks Melvin, as he repeatedly pokes a finger in and out of his right ear and checking if he can still hear by snapping his fingers together.

'I would say that is completely obvious, Melvin,' states Dexter, while positioning himself over the crate to inspect its contents.

'Hmmm…err—well, as Melvin said, Eric…what is it?' asks Dexter.

'It's my laundry,' replies Eric, with a slightly stunned look on his face, whilst wondering why both Melvin and Dexter struggle to determine the fact. 'I guess during all the excitement of the day, I just simply forgot all about it. I must make sure it goes out the front soon. Hopefully she will get it sorted for me this time.'

Melvin scratches his head in complete confusion and Dexter follows shortly after.

'Who?' questions Melvin.

'Yes, who?' adds Dexter.

Eric takes a step forward and lowers his tone, as if what he is about to say is top secret. He looks around the room; shifting his eyes around the four walls of his workshop. He gracefully ushers Dexter and Melvin towards him.

'Well, friends…' begins Eric. 'That ringing you just heard – it sounds every evening – at six o'clock on the dot. The ringing, as annoying as it is, comes from the wash-house at the end of the village. You must have seen it earlier as you entered the village?'

Melvin and Dexter bob their heads in unison.

'Well…' continues Eric. 'That sounds indicates two things. One of them being very important.'

'It does?' questions Dexter.'

'Yes, it does,' replies Eric, shifting his eyes from side to side and scouting the room again. 'Firstly, it indicates the exact moment that the workers at the wash-house finish their shifts for the day; clocking themselves out. But secondly, and most importantly, it signals to us villagers to take out our dirty clothes and leave them outside our front doors; to be taken.'

'Why do you do that, Eric?' asks Melvin.' I mean, surely a man with your vast engineering knowledge, could devise and build a machine that would do that for you?'

'Well, yes I suppose I could, but I've never thought about it in detail. Besides, I've got used to her doing it for me every day.'

'Who?' queries Melvin.

'Yes, who…?' adds Dexter, pulling a cheeky grin behind Melvin's back.

'Will you stop repeating me, Dexter!' screeches Melvin. 'I'm trying to listen to—'

'Quiet, Melvin! I'm trying to listen to what Eric is saying,' interrupts Dexter.

Melvin sighs.

There is a moments pause, as Melvin and Dexter wait for Eric to say something.

'Yes, friends…the Laundry Fairy,' states Eric.

Melvin steps in closer. '*The*—the Laundry Fairy? I thought she was just a pure myth; some sort of legend?'

'Oh…no, my dear fellow. She is completely real,' responds Eric, reaching down and picking up the wooden crate, before brushing past Melvin and Dexter, who both promptly follow Eric to the front of his workshop.

'How do you know she is real, then…?' enquires Dexter. 'Have you ever seen her?'

'No, I haven't seen her,' replies Eric.

'Has *anyone* actually seen her?' adds Dexter.

'Err…no I guess not, but—err…' mumbles Eric.

'So how do you know that she is real, then? Also, if no one has had the pleasure of seeing her, then how do you know that this *so-called* Laundry Fairy is a she?'

'Err…well—' stutters Eric.

'Load of old cobblers!' announces Melvin.

Eric turns around and continues to carry his dirty clothes out of the building, pretending that he didn't hear what Melvin had just said. Eric lowers the wooden crate and places it down gently atop of an old cut down tree trunk.

'Here, you see this?' says Eric, pointing at the crate. 'In the morning, my dirty and soiled clothes will be washed, pressed and neatly stacked in that crate.'

'That could be anyone that does that, Eric!' argues Melvin, while folding his arms together.

Eric sighs.

'Everyone takes their laundry outside at more or less the same time. It's the same most evenings – look!' says Eric, pointing across the village.

Melvin and Dexter focus their attention at the many locals, who like clockwork, are coming out of their homes and businesses; placing their washing out onto the street, ready to be collected.

'Many villagers have tried to catch a glimpse of the Laundry Fairy…' begins Eric. 'Some have waited patiently all night to see her, as she collects, washes and returns their clothes. Many of them have failed, but yet many have reported seeing a tremendous flash of yellow light – and in the blink of an eye, their dirty clothes have miraculously been washed and pressed.'

'Interesting…interesting stuff,' states Melvin.

'You're not wrong there, lad…' adds Eric. 'And, despite whether you believe in her or not, my dirty clothes will be nicely clean in the morning. Maybe you should allow her to clean your robe and hat, Melvin?'

Melvin runs his hands down the length of his damp robe. 'Well…I would, but I'm only wearing a pair of my favourite underpants underneath and I—'

'Too much, Melv! Too much!' screams Dexter.

Eric paces back into his workshop, grabbing the edge of one of the huge wooden doors on his way and pulling it closed. It snaps into place with a loud crunch, before Eric shifts a lever that sends a large metal rod deep into the workshop floor.

'A few months ago…' begins Eric. 'An elderly chap came into the village and stopped off at our tavern for refreshments. I forget his name…but I also happened to be in there that evening – somehow he and I got into a very deep discussion about the Laundry Fairy. I specifically remember him saying that if you wanted to try and catch a fairy of any sort, then you would have to have lightning reflexes and more importantly be able to slow down time.'

Melvin listens with interest to Eric.

'No wait!' continues Eric. 'Not slow down time, but rather have the ability to let time around you seem slower than it is.'

'Huh? What on Earth does that mean?' questions Dexter. 'That doesn't even make sense!'

'No it doesn't, does it?' replies Eric, trying to think of a better way to explain it.

'If I may?' begins Melvin. 'I think I understand what you mean, Eric. You don't slow down time as such, but may have the ability to slow down your own perception of time. Your timeline stills continues as normal, but you move through that time much slower than other people would experience. So for example, something moving normally at that time, but being observed, would seem to be moving faster to the person who is at the same time, but slower. Does that make sense?'

Eric stares at Dexter and lets out a slight grin.

'Err…nope,' replies Dexter.

'Okay, well let me explain it a different way. If I stand completely still and—'

'No, Melv! It's perfectly fine. We get a general idea,' bellows Dexter.

Melvin lets out an embarrassed smile and starts to twiddle his fingers around each other.

'Anyway…' continues Eric. 'The elderly chap said that there are only a few types of creature within this kingdom that possess such a trait.'

'And they are…?' asks Dexter.

'Well, unicorns for sure – and certain tribal fairies. Oh…what was the third one? Hmmm…oh yes…and vampires!'

'Vampires! I thought they vanished centuries ago?' retorts Melvin.

Eric shrugs his shoulders. 'Beats me…but I have heard that they can all manipulate time and possess the ability to slow it down in some form or another.'

'Yes, I must admit – I am also aware of that fact,' adds Melvin.

Melvin pauses and goes deep into thought. He lets go of his fingers and reaches up to take a long stroke of his beard. 'Interesting this whole time malarkey. There must be some magical essence involved in it all. I'm sure with the right combination of enchants, together with a small bout of logic and a lot of luck, I may be able to conjure up a spell that would display similar effects to that described.'

'Don't even think about it, Melv!' screeches Dexter. 'We are here to get your bicycle fixed and for that task only. Then we are heading home. Oh…and not before I stop off and grab some of my favourite cheese from the store. That's all I came here for, to be honest.'

'It's certainly going to be a while before your bicycle is ready, Melv,' states Eric. 'Why not stay here in Baston for a few days? As I said before – if you go and find Duncan at the tavern and mention that I sent you – I'm sure that he'll be able to accommodate you.'

'NO-NO-NO!' shouts Dexter. 'I'm cold, wet, tired and hungry. I just want to curl up in some corner of our castle and go to sleep. So why don't you be a good spellbinder and open both of us a portal back home?'

Melvin, shocked by Dexter's outburst, steps back.

'Stop being such a cry-baby, Dex!' voices Melvin. 'Besides, it will be fun.'

'Do I really have to…?'

'I'll buy you two blocks of cheese if you do.'

Dexter smiles and quickly accepts defeat.

Eric places his leather apron around his neck and

ties it tightly behind his back. He slides his hands into his matching leather gloves and repeatedly claps his hands together.

'Right, I must crack on for real now. I have a bicycle to rebuild. Oh…and if I were you – I would go and check into our tavern, sooner rather than later – before our Duncan becomes too incoherent to strike up any form of conversation – let alone book you into a room. Oh, and also…don't let Duncan give you room two – there is something wrong with the door lock. It took a good friend of mine nearly three hours to get into her room the other night.'

AAAAAACHOO!

A copper coin hits the floor, rolls a small distance and stops at the tip of Eric's boot.

'Attaboy, Dexter!' yells Eric.

CHAPTER IV

"Please, Master! How many times do I have to tell you? That is not your sock...that is my sleeping bag!"

Corbin

Within room four, located in the far western corner of the village tavern, moonlight penetrates through a pair of thin cotton curtains. They sway gently in a breeze, which creeps through a gap in a slightly open window, causing the moonlight to flicker as it illuminates the room's dusty wooden floor; shadows move and dance across the cobbled faced walls.

The iron hinges on the window shutters squeak as they gently swing back and forth, trying to resist the breeze acting on them. Occasionally, a slight tapping is heard as the shutters close up against their mainframe, followed by a chilling whistle as a gust of air rips through small voids in the woodwork, forcing the shutters ajar again.

The sound of hammer hitting anvil, echoes in the distance. Muffled voices and loud laughter are heard through the floorboards underneath, as the church bell rings out twelve times.

Midnight has arrived in Baston.

Startled by the sound of the church bell, Corbin opens his sleepy eyes and pulls his arms free from the depths of his sleeping bag, which conveniently hangs from a bed knob on the end of an iron framed bed.

He rubs his eyes with the backs of his hands, lets out a yawn and stretches his arms high above his head. He glances around the room, searching for his woolly hat, which he finds on the floor below him, covered in dust. After picking his hat up and brushing it down, he pulls it firmly down onto his tiny head.

Wriggling free from his handmade sleeping bag, Corbin scutters across the floor and fetches a small clay pot from his Master's chest. While clutching the pot tightly to his body, he positions himself in front of an unlit candle, which stands in the middle of an old oak side table.

Corbin carefully grabs hold of a knotted piece of rope infused into a small ceramic bung. With a swift tug, he releases the bung from the pot.

An intense heat radiates out and Corbin instantly offers the pot up to the candlewick, which ignites and burns; instantly lighting up the corner of the room.

'Back in you go,' whispers Corbin, pushing down hard on the ceramic bung, preventing the living flame he had caught several weeks earlier from escaping and possibly having a little bit of heated fun; not just with the room's dry woodwork, but probably the taverns as well.

The candle flickers in the breeze and lights up the room *just enough* for Corbin to observe his Master lying atop the bed. His tall, slender figure rests flat against the mattress, with his arms perfectly positioned by his sides and his toes pointing directly up towards the rafters of the tavern.

Corbin giggles as he notices a hole in his Master's sock; a hole with a rather ugly big toe poking through.

Returning to his sleeping bag, Corbin reaches deep into a side pocket. He pulls out a scanty red waistcoat and with minimal effort slides himself into it. He quickly fastens it with three small brass buttons. With a deep breath, he sucks in his chest and pulls down sharply at the bottom of the waistcoat, before exhaling and allowing the material to fall back and fit firmly over his little, but podgy belly.

'Master? Master, you instructed me to wake you at midnight,' whispers Corbin, trying to project enough volume to wake up his Master, yet quiet enough not to trigger any unnecessary attention from anyone, or anything that may be lurking around. 'Master, time to wake up,' he adds.

Corbin tuts, jumps up onto the end of the bed and moves slowly along the mattress towards his Master's face. He pauses for a moment to listen to his Master sleeping. Corbin smiles, as he knows perfectly well that his Master doesn't make a single sound while sleeping, not even a breath of air, or a snore.

'Master!' yelps Corbin, before covering his mouth and realising that his voice may have been a little too loud that time.

Edwin's eyelids open; widening instantly. His eyes immediately shift to the side, in Corbin's direction.

Their eyes meet and Edwin stares piercingly at Corbin for a few moments. Corbin gives a nervous, but cheeky smile back at his Master.

'I'm guessing it is midnight as you've awakened me, Corbin?' asks Edwin, manoeuvring very quickly from a horizontal to a vertical position.

'Yes, Master,' replies Corbin.

'If you would be as kind as to hand over my cloak please, Corbin…?' asks Edwin, neatly adjusting the orientation of his shirt and tucking it deep inside the waistband of his trousers.

Corbin jumps down from the edge of the bed and makes a slight thud as his tiny feet hit the floor. A small explosion of dust releases up from the floorboards, and dances through the still air, before gracefully settling back down onto the dry wood.

Corbin lets out a high-pitched sneeze and instantly covers his mouth with both hands, in an attempt to silence himself, before another sneeze follows. He decides after a few seconds to release his hands and wipes them both down the front of his waistcoat. He picks up his Master's cloak from atop the chest and hands it over to him.

'Did you sleep well, Master?' questions Corbin, watching his Master unfold the cloak, swing it around his broad shoulders and promptly fasten it around his neckline.

'I did, Corbin – very well indeed,' replies Edwin. 'And you…?'

'Yes, Master…snug as a bug!'

Edwin smiles and runs both his hands over the top of his head, pushing tightly up against his scalp and allowing his glossy black hair to stay in position.

Corbin reacts and rushes back towards his Master's chest. He pulls himself up onto the rim of the chest and tilts himself head first inside. His feet wiggle slightly in the air as he briefly leaves the floor, before emerging from the depths of the chest holding an oval brass mirror. He grips it tightly in his hand and returns to his Master, holding out the mirror towards him.

'Corbin, what is that?' asks Edwin.

'A mirror, Master. You can check your hair with it,' answers Corbin, stepping closer towards his Master.

'Are you not forgetting something?'

'Master…?'

Edwin eases forward, picks up Corbin by the scruff of his neck and elevates him onto his shoulder. Corbin sits still, clutching the fabric of his Master's cloak with one hand and the brass mirror in the other.

'Now then, Corbin! Tell me what you see?' demands Edwin.

Corbin rotates the mirror in the direction of himself and his Master; observing himself floating in mid-air in the mirror's reflection. Corbin instantly realises his foolish mistake.

'Apologies, Master. I completely forgot that you do not have a reflection. I was only trying to assist you,' whimpers Corbin, as he is lowered back down to the floor by his Master, who gasps on noticing the hole in his sock.

'Well…that is not good, is it?' announces Edwin, holding his leg up with one arm. He gently hops on the spot and carefully examines his minor footwear failure in more depth. 'Bother it!' he adds, returning his foot to the dusty floor.

Again, Corbin rushes back to his Master's chest, this

time searching deep down for a needle and a reel of black cotton thread.

'Oh, there's a sock right there! Pass me that would you, Corbin?' instructs Edwin.

Corbin's muffled voice echoes from the depths of his Master's chest.

'What was that, Corbin…? That is not my what?' questions Edwin, still trying to determine and decipher the random muffles of Corbin, who pulls from the chest, a small reel of black cotton.

'I said…that is my sleeping bag…and if you remove your sock, I shall repair it for you, Master,' replies Corbin, feeding the black cotton through the eye of a needle, crafted from a tiny fish bone.

'No, Corbin, this here sock will be perfectly fine,' responds his Master, reaching out and unhooking Corbin's sleeping bag from the bed knob.

'Please, Master! How many times do I have to tell you? That is not your sock…that is my sleeping bag!'

Edwin hisses and curiously eyes Corbin's sleeping bag up and down, before realising that it was in fact, Corbin's sleeping bag.

'Then, I apologise to you, Corbin. A simple fault on my behalf,' says Edwin, projecting a slight tone of embarrassment.

Edwin sits back down on the edge of the mattress, allowing Corbin to freely repair his sock, which he does hastily and energetically.

Edwin lifts his foot to inspect the repair, before standing up and walking across to a wooden dresser, beside the bed. A scattering of Edwin's necklaces, rings and brooches cover the top surface. One by one, he places the necklaces around his neck, the rings onto his pointy fingers and pins the brooches onto the front of his waistcoat and cloak; checking they are secure.

Corbin always tries to keep up with his Master in all aspects. He pursues to be, to the best he can, just like his Master, which for someone like Edwin, is pretty tricky to achieve.

Racing back to his sleeping bag, Corbin removes a large round pin badge attached to its inner lining. While his Master's back is turned, he leans over and secretly attaches the badge to his tiny waistcoat.

'May I ask you a question please, Master?' enquires Corbin, watching his Master slide both of his feet effortlessly into his shiny black boots.

'You may,' replies Edwin. 'And, may I say…you've done an amazing job of polishing my boots. A very nice job indeed.'

Corbin smiles at his Master's compliment.

'Does it hurt when you transform into a bat?'

'No, not at all, Corbin. Sometimes it tingles a little, but I've got used to that now.'

'May I ask another question please, Master?'

'Yes you may, Corbin.'

'Forgive me, but why don't your clothes fall to the floor when you transform yourself? When you are in bat form, you seem—well…naked. Where do all your clothes go?'

Edwin pauses and lets out a slight smile, trying hard to prevent himself from breaking into a laugh and revealing his bright white sharpened fangs.

'That, Corbin, is an excellent question and I'm very impressed that you've noticed that. But I'm afraid that information is a closely guarded vampire secret – and I cannot disclose that to you,' states Edwin.

Corbin acknowledges his Master by gently nodding his head.

'Anyway, Corbin! What is that ghastly thing you are wearing?' hisses Edwin.

Corbin lowers his head. 'This is my new waistcoat, Master,' he replies.

'No, not your waistcoat! That thing attached to it.'

'Err…it's my new badge, Master.'

'Is that a unicorn on the front of it?'

'Yes, Master,' says Corbin nervously.

Edwin takes several steps forwards and leans down towards his spritely assistant. 'I—love—unicorns,' he reads out carefully. 'Is that true, Corbin…? That's somewhat inappropriate don't you think, considering the company you are in right now? Remove it at once!'

Corbin lowers his head in disappointment, un-pins the badge from his attire and throws it casually into a darkened corner of the room, before picking up his Master's hat and handing it to him.

Edwin snatches his hat from Corbin and holds it tightly by the rim with both hands. He tosses it gently into the air and after several spins, the hat lands perfectly atop Edwin's head.

Corbin stares at his Master, who reaches down once more to the top of the wooden dresser and picks up his sunglasses. The irony is the fact that Edwin has never ventured out into the sunlight…and this is for obvious reasons.

Edwin flicks the arms of his sunglasses open with a snap of his wrist and offers them over his ears. He adjusts them slightly to sit midway on the bridge of his long narrow nose.

'So, Master…what's the plan?' asks Corbin.

'The plan, Corbin, is simple,' replies Edwin. 'I… and I alone shall go out into the night and track down the Laundry Fairy. I will creep in the shadows until she tires from her nightly washing duties – I shall then strike and capture her. I will then interrogate her until she gives in to my demands.'

'What if she spots you, Master?'

'I shall be in bat form, Corbin. I will simply be an innocent bat hanging around in the gloomy corners of the village. She will not suspect a single thing.'

'Okay. Sorry for all the questions, Master. But how will you catch her?'

'I'm glad you asked, Corbin,' says Edwin, strolling towards his chest, opening a latch on the side and sliding out a secret drawer. A shimmering glow radiates from inside. Edwin reaches in and lifts out a small cage. The cage itself is cast from a blackened zynite; a metal well known for its abilities to dampen and hinder the magical skills of wizards, mystical creatures and fairies, whenever it comes into close contact with them.

'At a convenient moment…' begins Edwin. 'I shall sneak up on the Laundry Fairy – and when she is least expecting it, capture her in this cage. Her powers will begin to drain and weaken. She can try all she likes, but she will not be able to escape. I will keep her in the cage until accepts my demands. I *will* walk in the sunlight, Corbin – I will! I shall force the Laundry Fairy to wash my clothes in her magical suds, which together with a certain enchant that has to be spoken by her, should allow me to then walk freely in the sunlight, without the risk of getting turned into a pile of dust.'

'I really hope that you get what you desire, Master.'

'Oh, Corbin – I'm very certain I will…very certain indeed. I just hope the ancient manuscripts written by my ancestors are accurate and that this cursed body of mine can day walk. I will not be a prisoner to the darkness of the night any longer.'

'How can I be of assistance to you, Master?'

'Corbin, I have one vital job for you, so please don't let me down. It is of vital importance…and I trust no one but you to fulfil this task.'

'Oh…please instruct me at your will, Master. I am your humble and obedient servant.'

'Well, Corbin. I want you to stay right here and—and…guard the room.'

Corbin sighs.

'Then…how will you carry the cage while in bat form, Master?' questions Corbin. 'It does look rather cumbersome. I think I would barely be able to lift it myself. You would certainly struggle in bat form.'

'Hmmm…I never thought about that. Oh, bother it! Well, it looks like you will be assisting me after all, Corbin.'

Corbin smiles. His eyes widen with pure excitement and his face shines with impish glee.

'Here, take the cage and meet me at the side of the village hall in…say ten minutes? While there, we can check to see if she has got as far as doing the mayor's laundry. If not, we can start to plot against her from that point.'

'Yes, Master,' replies Corbin, picking up the cage with all his might. He bear hugs his short arms around the cold metal; clutching it tightly.

'Oh…and one more thing, Corbin. Try not to be noticed by anyone, especially that drunken tavern keeper, or he'll end up putting you in a pie!'

Corbin gulps. 'Yes, Master…'

Edwin lowers his head and pauses. He grips onto his cloak and wraps it tightly around him. With a brilliant flash of red light and a small turbulence in the air, he transforms into a bat. Edwin hovers, his wings flap gently; stirring the dusty air. His blue eyes stare down at Corbin for a few moments, before he turning and darting towards the window.

There's a thump, followed by a loud thud, as Edwin flies straight into the window shutter, before crashing to the floor.

'Maybe you should have opened the shutter first, Master?' says Corbin, with a cute, but cheeky grin.

◆◆◆

On a small porch, just off to the side of the tavern's entrance, Melvin rocks gently back and forth on the hind legs of a small wooden stool. He rests his hands on his lap as he stares across at the moonlit covered village.

Dexter lays front down on the decked wooden floor with his tail stretching and curling around the back of Melvin's stool. Occasionally the tip of his tail clips the stool as Melvin leans back a little further.

They both relax, tranquil in their own minds as they embrace the rising moon. The stars shine brightly, piercing the darkened blue velvet sky. The air is crisp, but not chilly and a slight gust of wind causes Melvin's white beard to flutter across his face.

'Do you know what, Dex? Considering the long day that we've had – I thought I would be much more exhausted than I'm feeling right now,' announces Melvin, brushing his beard away from his face with a swift flick of his hand.

'Hmmm…?' replies Dexter, opening his tired eyes and adjusting his focus to look up to Melvin, who continues to rock gracefully back and forth on his stool.

'Well, maybe you are tired, Dex,' continues Melvin. 'However, I feel thoroughly awake. I've been deep in thought about what Eric was talking about earlier – you know? About his so-called Laundry Fairy – and more interestingly about slowing down time.'

Melvin pauses, awaiting a response from Dexter. It doesn't come.

'This whole *time thing* does interest me greatly. I wonder…' begins Melvin, drifting off into another one of his little thinking sessions.

Dexter stretches out his arms and claws. They scrape across the dry wooden planks of the porch. He lets out a long unwinding yawn, before repositioning himself upright, next to Melvin.

'What interests you the most though, Melv?' asks Dexter. 'The Laundry Fairy…? Or this time mumbo-jumbo?'

Melvin remains silent.

Dexter stares blankly at Melvin and wonders if any time soon, Melvin would be returning to the realms of normality.

'Melv?' adds Dexter.

'Hmmm…? Oh, err—well, I'm guessing a little bit of both, to be honest, Dex.'

AAAAAACHOO!

A shiny copper coin launches across the green from Dexter's nostrils and disappears into the grass.

'I think I'll leave that little coin for Eric to find,' announces Dexter, folding back his wings and taking a more comfortable sitting position. 'Melv?' he adds.

'Huh…? Oh right, yes,' responds Melvin, followed by a small chuckle.'

'You really seem to be in a little world of your own there, Melv!'

Melvin shifts his weight, allowing the front two legs of the stool to meet the wooden floor with a slight thud. He crosses one leg over the other and leans forward to rest his chin on a clenched fisted arm; his elbow balances perfectly on his kneecap. He continues to think deeply while staring at the floor.

'I wonder when the Laundry Fairy *actually* washes all this dirty laundry?' says Melvin. 'I've been glancing out across the village, and I still see an array of washing baskets full of dirty laundry. If what Eric says is true, then I thinking that maybe we could catch a glimpse of her tonight!'

'Well…I don't think she's got to the tavern yet,' states Dexter. 'That awfully smelly tavern keeper who checked us in earlier – well, his washing basket is still sitting over there. Judging by its pure smelliness factor, the slight yellowish haze above it and the fact that flies look like they are having a party in there, I'm guessing she either leaves this place until last, or there's some washing that is just *too* dirty, for even a Laundry Fairy to cope with!'

Melvin lets out a roaring laugh, breaking himself from his thoughts. He turns towards Dexter.

'Yes, when the wind blows just right, I get a slight taste of that pungent aroma on the tip of my tongue!' announces Melvin.

Another gust of wind whistles through the porch, causing Melvin to react quickly to prevent his hat from being blown off his head.

Melvin gazes up at the moon and the numerous constellations of stars that lay scattered across the night sky, hoping for a divine moment of inspiration, which will lead him to find a way to see and hopefully meet the Laundry Fairy.

His mind is completely focused on creating a spell that will allow him to slow down time, or alter it in some way; enabling him to interact with the Laundry Fairy, who with every moment, seems to become more and more real in Melvin's eyes.

Jumping to his feet, Melvin pulls his robe tightly around himself. The wind is heard in the distance as it rustles through tree branches and whistles over the rooftops of the village buildings. However, no sooner than it started, the wind suddenly dies down.

Melvin focuses on putting some of his grey matter to use. He needs a spell, but not any old spell; this spell has to be completely flawless. He begins to ramble to himself, processing all the crazy ways in which he could achieve manipulating time.

'I must find a spell, Dex…I must,' mumbles Melvin, turning and altering his stance towards Dexter.

'Err, okay…what do you have in mind, Melv?' asks Dexter, extending his wings and shielding himself from the crisp cold air.

Melvin raises his hand to his beard and begins stroking it slowly; caressing its long white hairs. He pulls some intense facial expressions and squints his eyes tightly as he goes into thinking overdrive.

Reaching into his robe pocket, Melvin pulls out a tattered journal; thick parchment pages bound to a spine of solidified amber and wrapped in a darkened hind of a wildebeest. The journal remains closed. Only by Melvin waving his hand over the front cover and chanting some magic incantations, do the pages finally release.

'What's that, Melv?' asks Dexter.

'This, my little purple-scaled friend, is my book of thoughts, spells, enchants and incantations,' answers

Melvin. 'I believe there may also be a couple of recipes in here for delightful green tomato chutney!'

'I love tomato chutney!' adds Dexter.

Melvin begins to casually sift through the pages. He smiles and chuckles to himself as his reads his notes; reminiscing the many pretty stupid, yet damn right amazing times he has had with the spells he's created. He suddenly stops on a single page and his eyes rest on a particular spell.

'No-no, that won't do,' states Melvin, tapping the page briefly with the tip of his finger, before continuing to thumb his way further into his journal; flicking the pages over and over.

'Hmmm…possibly…possibly,' continues Melvin, pointing at another page.

After a few moments, he carefully places the journal face down on top of his stool. Without a thought, he reaches into his inner robe pocket and pulls out a gold pocket watch; casually checking the time.

'Darn it! It's stopped again,' yelps Melvin, bringing the watch to his ear and listening for its faint ticking rhythm that he is so familiar with. 'Dead as a dodo,' he adds, lowering the watch and winding up a small dial on the side, until it clicks.

'Twelve fifteen, before you ask, Melv,' announces Dexter, shifting his head towards the clock on the side of the village church.

Melvin opens the glass face of his watch, adjusts the hands and then snaps it shut. He holds the watch briefly, before placing it back into his robe pocket.

'So, Melv, what unusual and remarkable piece of magical engineering have you got in mind…?' queries Dexter, picking up Melvin's journal and taking a snout at the pages.

'Don't touch that!' screams Melvin, snatching the journal out of Dexter's claws. 'This journal contains some of my *most* powerful magical spells. The power in this journal is not to be meddled with. I beg you not touch it again!'

'Alright, keep your hat on,' replies Dexter.

Melvin reopens his journal and continues scouting through the pages of detailed notes and diagrams.

'What we need, Dex, is something that can allow me to mess about with the structure of time,' states Melvin, as he focuses in on a particular spell and carefully tries to follow his handwritten instructions.

'I don't like how you say that, Melv…mess about with the structure of time. I suppose the definitive word there being *mess*, huh?' replies Dexter.

Melvin gives Dexter a hard stare; a stare that Dexter contemplates whether it means that Melvin is slightly annoyed with him, or the fact that Melvin has had a moment of clarity and is now formulating a masterful and cunning plan to create a new spell.

'This is it, Dex! This is the spell right here,' says Melvin, holding the book page out in front of Dexter, who struggles to focus in on the words on the page.

'Time bending…?' questions Dexter.

'That's exactly right, Dex. That's *exactly* what I'm going to do.'

'Hang on a minute, Melv. Wasn't that the spell you did a few years back, when you ended up bending the fabric of time within the castle walls? – Remember? To save time getting from your bedroom to the pantry?'

Melvin smiles and then lets out a little chuckle.

'That's precisely the one!' states Melvin. 'That ten-minute journey from upstairs to the pantry, took only seconds with this spell.'

'Yes, Melv, but our grandfather clock was never the same after that spell – it *literally* shook itself to bits!'

'Ah, fun times though, Dex…fun times.'

'So…you are going to try to bend the fabric of time again?'

'That is the plan, my scaly companion. It says here that I need a device to control it and a force of nature to bind it. Oh…and I have to read out this enchant.'

'Enchant…?'

'Yes, these words right here, Dex,' pointing to a few rows of mystical words and symbols.

'I see…' responds Dexter.

Melvin reads through his notes and carefully recites the magical enchant under his breath; making sure he pronounces each word and sound correctly.

'Okay, Dex. I think I've got this sorted. I simply need something to control how much I bend time… something with a dial or a lever maybe…hmmm?'

'What about what's in your pocket?' queries Dexter.

'I have lots of things in my pocket, Dex. Can you be more specific?'

'Seriously, Melv? What were you holding not only moments ago?'

'Oh yes! My watch. Good thinking, Dex!'

Dexter lets out a sigh and slaps his claw against his forehead as Melvin reaches back into his pocket for his watch.

'Perfect!' says Melvin.

Melvin clutches his gold pocket watch firmly and carefully follows the written text in his journal with the tip of his finger.

'Darn it! We need a force of nature. I remember now…last time I cast this type of spell, it was raining in the courtyard. We are not having much luck here.'

'Err…Melv? You're a spellbinder, aren't you? So why don't you just make it rain?'

'Rain? Please Dex…I've already got wet through today and I'm still trying to dry off.'

'Wind then? Make it windy. It will also help you dry off a bit.'

'Now *that* is something I can do. Brilliant idea, Dex!'

Melvin moves his stool to the front of the porch and places his journal on top, before carefully sitting his pocket watch atop the pages; holding them open.

Adjusting his stance and raising his arms up into the air, Melvin takes in a deep breath and slowly starts to mutter some magical words under his breath. Dexter listens carefully and tries to capture any words or phrases coming from Melvin's mouth.

Melvin starts to sway from side to side and enters a trance-like state. Dexter stares on in amazement as Melvin begins to move his hands around in the air, while still muttering his ancient words.

Melvin reaches down and picks up his journal and gold pocket watch. He clamps them tightly against each other and begins to read out the magical instructions scribbled over its parchment-like pages.

Occasionally, Melvin stops reading from his journal and switches his attention to the night sky, raising his arm up to the heavens and voicing an entirely different set of magical words.

The air grows colder. Melvin starts emitting a blue-ish aura about his body, which radiates across the porch and lights up the side of the tavern.

A gentle breeze begins to blow across the porch and the rustling sound of trees in the distance starts over again.

Melvin turns his attention back to his journal and

begins to repeat the words he had only a short while ago spoken. His voice grows louder and louder as an intense orb of green light starts to form around his pocket watch. Again, Melvin turns to face the heavens; attempting to invoke the mighty fury of nature and cause the winds to bind with his pocket watch.

Entering a dreamlike state, Melvin chants the words over and over. He drifts from side to side as the gentle breeze turns into howling gusts.

Dexter shifts himself backwards, raises his wings and extends them, before bringing them down in front of him, using them to shield himself from the intense cold wind, slicing past his scaly skin. He peeks over the top of his ribbed wing structure and observes Melvin waving an arm around in the air.

The winds grow faster and start to take a more circular path as they rush around Melvin.

'Melv!' shouts Dexter. 'This is getting a bit intense for my liking. Are you certain you know what you are doing?'

'I can't hear a darn word you are saying, Dex!' yells Melvin, as his pocket watch begins to levitate from his journal and enter the now spinning orb of green light. Melvin's journal drops to the floor as he uses his other hand to try and prevent the orb from spiralling out of control.

Melvin morphs his hands around the orb; crafting and shaping it; just like a potter would with clay. The wind continues to hurl around Melvin and unleash their fury onto his robe, which flaps around him.

Suddenly, without any warning or hesitation, the orb of light radiates a bright glow, before exploding in Melvin's hands and knocking him down to the floor. The winds vanish.

'Well that went better than I expected,' says Melvin, raising himself back to his feet.

'Did it work, Melv…?' questions Dexter, shuffling forward towards Melvin.

'I'm not sure, Dex,' replies Melvin, adjusting his attire and removing the chain of his pocket watch, which has miraculously wrapped itself several times around the sleeve of his robe. 'Well, the watch is still here, but I don't feel any different at all.'

'How should you feel?'

'Well, I thought something would be different. All of that didn't just happen for nothing. Or did it…?'

'I couldn't say, Melv. But I *can* tell you that it looks like your watch has stopped again?'

'Oh, darn it!'

Melvin takes his pocket watch by the chain and lets it hang in front of his face. He focuses in on the hands of the watch as it sways gently back and forth, before cupping the casing in his right hand and letting go of the chain. Melvin lowers himself and picks up his journal, which lay battered on the floor and returns to his stool; a stool that has amazingly remained relatively upright during the last few moments.

'I guessing you'll have to rethink that spell, Melv?' asks Dexter, sitting his hind back down on the wooden decking.

'I guess so, Dex – and mind your wings there, my young buddy. You nearly knocked my hat off!'

'Oh, sorry…'

'No problem.'

Melvin stares at the face of his watch and raises it up to his ear. He gives it a slight shake.

'Yes, it's certainly stopped again,' states Melvin.

'It has,' replies Dexter. 'Even I can't hear it ticking

– and that's saying something with my super hearing.'

Melvin pulls out the dial on the side of the watch and pursues in turning it slowly; winding up the watch for the second time. A slight hum echoes in the air.

Opening the face of the watch, Melvin repositions its tiny hands back to the correct time, only this time something is different…*very*…*very* different.

'Everything okay, Melv?' enquires Dexter.

There's a moment's pause…

'Are you there, Melv?' adds Dexter.

'I am,' replies Melvin. 'And do you know—*I*—I think the spell has actually worked!'

'What do you mean?'

'I'm running very slowly.'

'No you're not. You're sitting down on your stool. You seem pretty normal to me.'

'Not me physically…I mean *time* is running slower for me. I see things in—well, in slow motion.'

Dexter looks on at Melvin; scrutinising his precise movements.

'Well, you are surely acting the same, Melv,' states Dexter. 'How do you hear my voice right now?'

'It's very long and drawn out,' answers Melvin.

'That must be so weird. Can I try?'

'I'm afraid not, Dex. The spell has bound itself to my watch and me. It looks like – whenever I wind my watch – it slows down time around me.'

'Ooooooh, I see. So maybe you can now get to actually see this Laundry Fairy?'

Melvin's face becomes an array of childish delight and happiness, at the thought.

'Oh, yes!' exclaims Melvin.

Melvin straightens his hat and smiles at his new time altering watch.

'I'm guessing that you don't bend time with your watch as you intended, but rather it just simply slows it down for you – and you alone?' queries Dexter.

'I think that's pretty much it. I would try to explain the whole technicalities of the spell and how the wind played a vital part in the binding of it, but firstly…I don't think you'd be that interested – and secondly…I really can't be bothered!' replies Melvin.

Melvin twists the dial on the watch in reverse and waits patiently for time to catch back up to him.

'Ah, there we go,' states Melvin, standing up and placing the watch on the top of the stool.

'Err…Melv? What are you doing?'

'What do you mean?'

'I mean, why are you emptying all your pockets and removing your hat and robe?'

'Duh! I thought if I leave my robe and hat out here, the Laundry Fairy would stop and wash them for me? She can't do that if I'm wearing them, can she?

'So, you are just going to sit here nearly naked?'

'That's right!'

'Naked in the cold air of the night?'

'Correct!'

'Well, don't you think it would be a good idea to sit there and activate your watch again? Or you'll just end up missing her.'

'Oh shoot! I'm guessing you're right, Dex,' says Melvin, clutching hold of the watch in his hand. 'But it's just a long wait if I slow down time. I will feel like I'm waiting a very long time – maybe even forever.'

'You're the one who wants to see the Laundry Fairy, Melv – I really couldn't care less. Well…I'll get a little sleep – if you're staying up.'

Melvin nods his head.

'No worries at all, Dex. Sleep well, my friend.'

'Oh…and one more thing, Melv?

'Hmmm…?'

'How on Earth do you fit all of this stuff into your robe pockets?'

'That is a well-kept spellbinding secret, Dex. I can't disclose that information with you.'

'I see—'

'But here…have a banana!'

◆◆◆

In the darkest shadows towards the rear of the village hall, Edwin suspends himself upside down from the underside of a wooden beam, protruding out from the roof. He waits patiently and silently in the crisp air. His blackened wings wrap tightly around his thin and agile body; his sharp and pointy ears stand completely upright, absorbing all the eerie sounds of the night. He listens carefully and continues to wait for his assistant Corbin to honour him with his presence.

The bell on the church tower tolls once.

The air shudders and a flash of brilliant red light momentarily radiates the side of the village hall.

Edwin somersaults backwards and lands back onto his nimble feet in human form. He promptly shuffles back into the shadows, just as Corbin appears from around the corner of the building.

'Master…are you there?' whispers Corbin, letting out a few heavy pants and stumbling over the damp grass, whilst trying his hardest to keep a firm hold on his Master's mystical cage.

Corbin creeps slowly up the side of the tavern and into the shadows, where he halts and carefully lowers the cage to the ground. He removes his woolly hat and uses it to wipe the small beads of sweat dripping off his brow.

'You are a little late, Corbin,' whispers Edwin, from the shadows.

Startled by his own Master's voice, Corbin jumps and turns to stare into the blackness, trying to pick up the familiar outline of his Master, but not sure whether to expect him in human or bat form. He realises that in all the years he has known Edwin, he has never seen him speak in bat form and thus continues to scout for the tall, slender body of his Master.

'Where are you, Master?' whispers Corbin.

'I'm right here,' replies Edwin, his pale face creeping out from the shadows and giving Corbin a brief stare. His eyes shift from left to right. 'Don't just stand there, Corbin – come closer to me – someone might see you.'

Corbin grabs his Master's cage tightly and drags it across the grass towards him. It digs into the grass, making Corbin huff and puff as he pulls with all his might, before finally releasing the cage at his Master's feet. Corbin falls backwards and rolls over.

Edwin sniggers.

There's a brief pause as Edwin watches Corbin return to his feet and brush himself off.

'My apologies to you, Master…' begins Corbin. 'But it was challenging not to be seen by anyone. Even at these early hours of the morning – there are still some peculiar characters hanging around. Besides, this cage is much heavier than it looks.'

Edwin leans down and carefully picks his cage up from the grass. He lifts it high above his head; rotating it around in his hands and inspecting its integrity.

'Tonight is the night that we capture the Laundry

Fairy,' snarls Edwin, as he glances across the village at the mass of dirty laundry baskets, boxes and other receptacles of various shapes and sizes, which have yet to be touched by the magical abilities of the mystical Laundry Fairy.

'How do you plan to do that, Master?' asks Corbin.

Edwin slowly tilts his head down towards Corbin, picking out the recognisable and familiar outline of his assistant, within the darkness.

Edwin's unique ability to see exceptionally well in the dark, is certainly a trait that he has truly developed, after years of coping with the darkness. Tonight, that ability would become more than handy.

'Very simple, Corbin. I will be in bat form,' explains Edwin. 'I will capture her and place her in this magical cage.'

Corbin folds his arms behind his back. He stares at the ground and drags his left foot back and forth through the grass; making a small slippery trench of mud. He directs his eyes upwards to his Master.

'Master?' questions Corbin.

'Yes, Corbin?'

'Well, how exactly will you be able to capture the Laundry Fairy if you are in bat form…? I mean, are you planning to grab her between your fangs or something? Also…surely you will not be able to use those small claws of yours? They are way too tiny to lift her up.'

Edwin hisses loudly, showing his bright white fangs to Corbin, who takes a sudden step backwards in an attempt to reduce the intensity of his Master's wrath.

'Corbin, sometimes I feel that you just don't respect my judgement and trust my instincts…' begins Edwin. 'Don't you think I've already thought about that? I have spent the last few months preparing every detail for this exact moment. I've analysed all possible angles and I'm extremely confident in saying that my plan is flawless. There is not a single scenario that I haven't considered. Now…as you were saying, Corbin?'

'I asked how you would capture her, Master?'

'Ah yes! Well, when I see the Laundry Fairy – I will sneak up on her and capture her with my bare hands. I will then call for you to open this cage.'

'Um…Master? How will you be able to—'

'Please do not interrupt me!' blasts Edwin, placing the cage gently down next to Corbin, who slowly turns to give it his full attention. 'As I was saying…when I call – you then open the door on this cage, okay…?'

'I guess so, Master.'

'No, Corbin! I don't need you to guess. I need you to do,' hisses Edwin. 'You must open the cage using this little lever,' he adds, demonstrating the function of the lever by flicking it gently up and down with his pointy finger. The zynite cage's latch opens and closes repeatedly.

Convinced that Corbin now knows how the lever operates, Edwin leaves the lever forward allowing the door of the cage to swing open.

Corbin slowly paces around the outside of the cage. With a scrutinous eye he checks out its fine intrinsic metalwork and unearthly craftsmanship

'Will she be able to stick her hands through these bars and release the lever from the inside, Master…?' questions Corbin.

'No, Corbin, she will not! Again, did you not listen to a single word that I said earlier?'

'Master…?'

'This, Corbin, is zynite – and once inside this cage, the Laundry Fairy will be paralysed by its dark power.

She will find it difficult to even stretch a muscle.'

'I see,' replies Corbin.

'Now, where was I…?' asks Edwin. 'I seem to have forgotten my own plan.'

Corbin waits patiently for his Master to conclude his perfect plan.

'I really do not wish to disrespect or question you again, Master,' begins Corbin. 'It's just that I'm a little confused about how exactly you will be able to call me while you are in bat form?'

'Err—I will simply make a sound,' replies Edwin.

'What sort of sound?'

'I don't know, Corbin! A bat-like sound.'

Corbin pauses to think…

'Right, okay – I got it, Master,' responds Corbin. 'But still…how will you capture her while in bat form?'

'I'll have to transform back into human form,' says Edwin. 'I can use my hands to grab hold of her tightly – preventing her from wriggling free and escaping.'

'How will you then be able to see her if you are not in bat form? She will be too quick for you if you have to turn back into human form.'

'Well…that's when I will—err…that's when I—oh drat! I didn't think – okay, a rethink is needed.'

Corbin tries his absolute hardest to prevent himself from letting out a very satisfying and smug smile, but contains himself by sucking down hard onto his lower lip, somehow managing to express a very convincing, sincere and understanding smile, towards Edwin.

'Can I make a suggestion, Master?' asks Corbin.

'You certainly may, Corbin,' replies Edwin, deep in his thoughts, panicking slightly and knowing that at any time, the Laundry Fairy could make an appearance.

'I believe that the best approach would be to simply

capture her in bat form. You can use your claws to grab her – and then all you have to do is wrap your wings around her and drag her to the floor.'

'Go on…' instructs Edwin.

'At that moment, you can then transform back into human form and call me to get the cage ready, or better still…why don't you just leave the cage open? You know I'm right, Master.'

Edwin hisses at Corbin.

'I'm afraid you may *actually* be correct this time, Corbin,' mutters Edwin.

'You…afraid, Master?'

'Huh? No-no, not at all – just a figure of speech. However, I must admit, that is a good plan. I'm a little surprised that I didn't come up with that one myself!'

Corbin sighs.

'And are you absolutely sure that she will not be able to escape the cage, Master?' questions Corbin.

Edwin taps gently on the top of the cage with his fingertips. 'Oh, I'm perfectly sure, Corbin…perfectly sure indeed.'

'Anyway, time is of the essence here. We must get prepared,' howls Edwin.

'Yes, Master—' replies Corbin.

'Corbin, I need you to wait in the shadows until you hear my call. Oh…and please remain still and quiet. We don't want to alarm her.'

'Yes, Master—'

'I will now transform and hang near the mayor's laundry basket. The Laundry Fairy will not see me up in the roof braces – until it is too late for her.'

Edwin lets out an evil sounding chuckle.

'Um…Master? What will your call be?' asks Corbin.

'Oh, Corbin – use your head!'

'Err…okay, Master. What shall we do now?'

'We wait, Corbin…we must wait patiently,' answers Edwin, instantly transforming himself into bat form and flying up onto the roof of the village hall.

'Use my head…?' mutters Corbin. 'What does he mean by that?'

Corbin reaches into his waistcoat pocket and pulls out a small boiled sugar sweet, which he unwraps and places into his mouth. He crunches down hard on it.

CHAPTER V

"I'm terribly sorry, but what's your name again? I was completely distracted by the fact that you are sitting in the cold, wearing only a pair of underpants."

THE LAUNDRY FAIRY

Marginally outside the village and past an old dead tree trunk that many locals say resembles an upside down man, a group of highly trained individuals continue to set up camp along the banks of the Cobalt River.

Trained to work together in perfect harmony and unison, they have each persisted through a scrutinous selection process, after spending months of intensive training; developing their mental stamina and cognitive reasoning, before perfecting their skills in advanced weaponry and hand to hand combat.

These men are at their prime; men of honour and statue. They include some of the most noted and respectful soldiers from the town of River's Bend.

At the lower banks of the Cobalt River, these men are hard at work, preparing to show everyone in the village, why they are the top fighting force within the Kingdom of Auchendale.

'Settle down, lads! Settle down please!' instructs Corporal Ringelstein, who suddenly shifts to the left and ducks; narrowly missing a wooden mallet hurling through the air. 'Oi! I saw that. What's your name, Private?'

The Corporal raises his hand and points his finger at a scrawny little man wearing a pair of glasses, who looks up and stares blankly at the Corporal, before continuing to hammer in a long pole, with a now very empty hand.

'I don't think they are taking the blindest bit of notice of you, Sir,' states Private Babe, looking across at the rest of the squad, many of which had only just recently been recruited into the ranks.

'Do they even know what they are doing?' asks the Corporal.

'Well, it doesn't look very promising if you would like my opinion, Sir,' says Private Babe, staring in shock at his *brothers in arms*, as they use the best of their skills and abilities to attempt to erect two large tents.

'NO-NO-NO! That doesn't go there, does it? You imbeciles!' bellows the Corporal, at a couple of recruits trying their hardest to put a large metal rod into a place where a large metal rod doesn't want to go. 'Oh, my goodness,' he adds.

Private Babe lets out a sigh as he glances across at some familiar and some *not so* familiar faces. He tries to deduce in his mind, the reasons why a bag of potatoes is on fire, a tent is upside down and why an extremely tall man is talking to a seagull.

'I give up, Babe—err, I mean Private Babe,' begins the Corporal. 'It's extremely late, I'm tired, hungry and I really do need to get my head down for a few hours before we meet up later with the Reverend.'

The Corporal and Private Babe stare in shock at several of the squad's recruits causing chaos around them, and making a right *pig's ear* of assembling their accommodation for the duration of their stay.

'This is a complete shambles!' retorts the Corporal. 'And did I just hear one of them chaps over there say, "The Corporal is a ninny"…?'

'I don't think so, Sir,' replies Private Babe. 'I think he said, "Cor-blimey isn't it nippy," or something along those lines.'

'Right, I've really had quite enough of this now. ATTENTION!' bellows the Corporal, bringing all of the squad to a sudden, yet confused halt.

'*I*—I said attention!' repeats the Corporal, pacing towards his recruits like an out of control bull. 'Stop what you are doing and listen up!'

There's a chorus of sounds as various items, some of them very questionable, drop from the hands of the recruits. One recruit in particular, for reasons the Corporal can't comprehend or fathom, is holding a loaf of bread, and using it insanely to hammer a wooden peg into the ground.

'Hey, you – you with the loaf! What's your name?' questions the Corporal.

The man quickly turns towards his superior, while trying with both of his hands, to hold together a disintegrating loaf of fine granary bread.

'The name's Trout,' replies the recruit.

'Trout? As in the fish?' queries the Corporal.

'Yes…as in the fish.'

'I see. Well, Trout, how do I put this politely…?' begins the Corporal. 'Ah yes…how about you shut up, address me as *Sir,* put your loaf on the floor and stand to attention like everyone else is doing?'

Private Trout instantly drops the loaf to the floor and stumbles forward to join the rest of his squad lined up in formation.

The Corporal glances one by one at his band of men, while strolling in front of them with his hands locked behind his back. He reaches the end of the line and makes a quick turn on the spot.

Walking back across the front of his men, the Corporal pauses and turns about-face to a rather short and fat individual, before leaning down towards him.

'What's your name?' asks the Corporal.

'Myles, Sir!' replies the recruit.

'Well, Myles. Can you tell me why you think it is a good idea to put the entrance to that tent facing the water line? I mean, you now have to wade through the river to get inside the tent!'

'Err…I—err…I was—'

'Silence, Myles!' yells the Corporal. 'This nonsense stops now…right now! I'm exhausted, hungry and we all have a busy few days ahead of us. In fact, why am I even still here…? I've a nice warm bed back at the tavern. Babe, will you finish what I've started here?'

A few of the recruits begin to snigger and chuckle.

'Please don't call me that, Sir…especially in front of the squad. In fact, please do not ever call me that at all. My name is *Private* Babe,' says Private Babe. 'And yes, I will finalise addressing the men, Corporal.'

The Corporal digs deep into his jacket pocket and pulls out a fresh cigar. He turns to Private Babe, before letting out a long sigh on remembering that his trusty number one Private has no means of lighting his cigar.

'Here you go, Sir,' says Private Trout, taking a match out of his pocket and striking it hard against his stubble filled face. The match lights instantly. Private Trout cradles the lit match in his cupped hands and carefully offers it up to the Corporal's cigar.

'Good man, Trout!' praises the Corporal. 'You'll go far, son. Mark my words!'

The Corporal gives Private Trout a firm pat on the shoulder, before taking a puff on his cigar and exhaling a huge trail of smoke across the night sky.

Private Babe and the squad watch as the Corporal turns away and starts to stroll back up the hill, towards the village.

'Right then, team…' begins Private Babe. 'Let's get all this mess sorted out. We wouldn't want to displease the Corporal any further, huh?'

'Err…what *exactly* are we all doing here?' asks a tall and lanky recruit.

'Yeah! What's this all about? Dragging us all the way down here…' asks Private Trout.

The squad starts to break out into random ramblings and begins to fire questions at each other. After a brief moment they realise they are getting nowhere with each other and direct their attention to firing off an assortment of questions at Private Babe.

The Corporal, still in listening range, glances back to observe Private Babe in a heated debate with the rest of his men. The Corporal slyly smiles and continues walking up the hill, towards the village.

'I bet it's a top-secret covert operation deep within

the village – to penetrate a mad man's lair and rescue a very important person from certain death,' announces Private Trout.

'No-no-no,' replies another recruit. 'I've heard that we're here to test out a newly developed secret weapon on the—'

'A secret weapon…?' interrupts Private Myles. 'It's obvious what we are here for.'

'It is?' queries Private Babe.

'Yeah…It's obvious that the village has been taken over by zombies and the Corporal is in on it. Didn't you see his eyes? They were all bloodshot! First sign of infestation that, you know?'

Private Babe chuckles. 'I think you'll find that the Corporal's red eyes are simply from lack of sleep. I can also assure you that the village has not been taken over by zombies.'

'Then, what *are* we here for?' asks Private Trout.

'We are here to rebuild a water fountain, plant lots of beautiful flowers and do a bit of painting,' answers Private Babe, reluctantly.

'Awww, really?' moans Private Trout.

'Come on, guys. I know it sounds boring, but the Corporal has promised me that we will be handsomely rewarded for our troubles.'

'Oh? Well, that doesn't sound too bad I suppose,' says Private Myles.

'It doesn't, does it?' replies Private Babe. 'Each of us will be receiving a single gold coin for completing our duties.'

Private Myles lets out a huge smile.

'When do we start?' yells Private Trout, clapping his hands together excitedly, quickly followed by loud cheers and shouts from the rest of the squad.

Private Babe quickly adjusts his attention to looking at what's happening behind the recruits.

'Err…well, the Corporal wants us all down by the village fountain at nine sharpish, but first, may I suggest you think about rescuing your tents? They are starting to float down the river!'

◆◆◆

Melvin sits calmly in a time-altered reality and stares in utter amazement at everything running at a completely different pace to which he is usually accustomed. He lets out a long sigh; a sigh of boredom, which ends up sounding like a huge foghorn going off.

Melvin repositions himself on his stool, adjusts his body parts and changes his posture, in an attempt to keep himself warm from the cold sting of the wind that continuously lashes at his naked flesh.

The night is quiet, although, in the near distance, a hammer can still be heard as it bashes red-hot metal onto the face of a blacksmith's anvil. Melvin smiles, knowing that Eric is hard at work repairing his steam-powered bicycle.

Glancing down at his robe that lay on the ground in front of him, Melvin chuckles, asking himself why he took it off earlier, becoming aware that he should have stayed fully dressed until he actually *has* the pleasure of meeting the Laundry Fairy. He ponders about getting up and putting on his robe and hat. He then sighs; knowing how much time that would take to achieve. He dismisses the idea to alter his watch back to its regular time, accepting that he doesn't want to risk missing the Laundry Fairy, for the sake of the warmth of his robe.

He continues to battle the cold winds that rip past the front of the tavern, wrapping his long arms tightly around his skinny framed body and rubbing his hands across his skin; warming himself briefly.

Spellbinders are taught never to use magic just for the sake of it. From an early age, Melvin has always endeavoured to find a simpler solution to his problems. In this case, Melvin contemplates whether to break that rule and cast a spell to produce fire, just to stay warm.

His thoughts are distracted by a moth flying directly past his face. Melvin turns and watches the beauty of the movement of its wings as they slice slowly through the air in a harmonised state.

Melvin lets out a huge smile, trying to refrain from sinking into boredom and falling asleep.

'It would be more fun if the Laundry Fairy washes the laundry during the day, instead of under the cover of darkness,' thought Melvin, knowing perfectly well, that there would undoubtedly be much more interesting things to look upon during the day.

Melvin chuckles loudly as he pictures the likes of Mrs Stamps in slow motion and even better still, how Dexter would look as he sneezes out a copper coin. His chuckle resonates through the air, sounding very much like a rickety wooden cart, rolling down a hill.

Time ticks away, second by second; minute by minute. Melvin continues to wait.

◆◆◆

Corbin sits with his back against the side wall of the tavern, and under the shroud of darkness waits patiently for a call from his Master, who hangs silently overhead from the rafters.

The wet grass causes Corbin to fidget from side to side as he feels the dampness start to penetrate his thin cotton trousers.

Bored of twiddling his thumbs, Corbin reaches into his waistcoat pocket and pulls out a small yo-yo, which he has hand carved himself from a piece of oak.

Pushing himself back to his feet with his other hand, Corbin winds the worn string around the yo-yo and as quietly as he can, starts to play with it.

Voices from around the corner momentarily halt his attempt at suppressing his boredom. He catches the yo-yo firmly in his hand, backs up tightly against the wall and hides himself from view.

'I'm so ready for sleep, Private,' says the Corporal, puffing away gently on his cigar. 'Oh…and by the way – it looks like you have sobered up a little?'

'I don't think I was drunk, Sir,' replies Private Babe, in a defensive tone.

'*Bah*! Well, you were not exactly sober either.'

Private Babe blushes.

'So, tell me, Private. I assume the men will be ready in the morning?' questions the Corporal.

'Well, if you want my opinion, Sir? Then that would be debatable,' answers Private Babe. .They did seem to get a grip on matters when I mentioned their payment. I told them to meet us by the fountain, at nine.'

'Excellent. Right, I think I'll grab a little bite to eat, before bedtime…assuming Duncan is sober enough to accept my request and that his cook is drunk enough to care.'

Corbin listens to the Corporal and Private Babe's laughter fade as they walk away towards the tavern entrance. He remains still for a moment, before leaning slightly forward; removing his back from the cold wall.

He tilts his head, looks at the roof above him and tries to locate his Master. He squints slightly as his vision tries to penetrate the dark shadows. With no luck, Corbin sits back on the ground and clutches his arms around his Master's cage.

Time moves on and the church bell rings again.

Corbin yawns.

Growing restless, Corbin creeps slowly towards the wicker basket containing the mayor's laundry.

Sneaking up to the side of the basket, he places his tiny hands onto its rim, pulls himself up and takes a quick peek at its contents. He is instantly knocked back by a pungent cheesy aroma that hits him right between the eyes, which causes his nostril hairs to tingle. He returns to the cage, dumps himself onto the ground next to it and wishes that he'd never agreed in assisting his Master in his grand scheme.

THUD!

'Ouch! Darn it!' yelps Edwin, picking himself up from the damp ground and brushing off flakes of mud and blades of grass from his attire. 'Darn it! – Darn it! – Darn it!' he adds.

Corbin rushes to his feet, picks up the cage and hastily manoeuvres it across to his Master. He flicks the cage's lever and the door swings open. He waits for some response from his Master.

'Is that the call, Master?' asks Corbin, nervously.

'No, *it's*—it's not the call, Corbin!' hisses Edwin, removing a handkerchief from his waistcoat pocket and dabbing it onto patches of wet mud that have presented themselves on Edwin's crisp white shirt.

'Did you mess up, Master?' queries Corbin.

Edwin pauses as he tries to conjure an answer that

will save him from not only looking foolish, but also one that would satisfy Corbin and prevent his little assistant from asking more questions.

'No, Corbin. I didn't mess up,' answers Edwin. 'I was however, a little hesitant there, and decided it was best to try to capture her somewhere else.'

'Oh, you got to see her, Master…? I didn't notice anything at all. She must have been extremely fast?'

'Yes, Corbin. She was here, look!'

Corbin follows his Master's long finger as it points directly at the mayor's dirty laundry, which to Corbin's surprise, has been washed and neatly folded.

'I don't believe it, Master,' murmurs Corbin.

'Well, you'd better start believing it,' replies Edwin, taking in a deep breath and smelling the freshness of the washing left behind by the Laundry Fairy.

'Can I ask you a question, Master?'

'Do I have a choice…?'

'What do you mean, Master?'

'Oh, never mind. Yes, go ahead, Corbin.'

'Why don't you just steal other people's clothes that the Laundry Fairy has washed and then wear them to walk out in the sunlight?'

Edwin sighs.

'Do you listen to anything that I tell you, Corbin?' retorts Edwin. 'I have to get her to read out some ancient words, while washing *my* clothes.'

'Ah, I see, Master. What are those words exactly?'

'I have them written down, Corbin…don't worry.'

Corbin nods his head.

'So, err—what happened just then, Master?'

'I simply hesitated too much, Corbin. I left it a little too late; by the time I decided to pounce on her, she had vanished. Of course, I had already transformed myself by the time I had made that decision – hence why I was a little unprepared as I hit the floor.'

'Did she see you, Master?'

'I don't think she did, Corbin. However, we must promptly relocate elsewhere if we are going to have another chance at capturing her.'

'I'm truly yours to command, Master,' says Corbin, leaning forward, slamming the cage door shut and picking the cage up from the ground. 'Where did she go?' he adds.

Edwin stares towards the blacksmith's workshop at the far end of the village. Corbin directs his eyes to join his Master staring.

'She went that way…' begins Edwin. 'But we shall head across to the church. I can still see unwashed laundry outside.'

'Master, you can't step on holy ground, remember?'

'Oh, yes…silly me. I'm surprised I'm still alive after all these years. I mean, err—dead, no wait—well, you know what I mean.'

Corbin grins.

'Okay, let's go to the building next to it. What is that place?' questions Edwin.

'It looks like a post office, Master,' replies Corbin.

'To that post office we go – and swiftly!'

'Yes, Master—'

'And, Corbin…please try and not be seen.'

'Yes, Master—'

With a flash, Edwin transforms into his bat form and quickly disappears into the night sky.

Corbin scutters across the grass, while holding firmly onto his Master's cage. He pauses briefly to catch his breath and to check that the coast is clear, before continuing across the village green.

◆◆◆

Melvin gazes upon his spellbinder's hat, which sits perfectly atop his folded robe on the wooden decking. He tries to remember the exact day that he acquired his hat, and smiles as he recalls that it certainly wasn't as bent and misshapen back then. He reminisces over all the events in his life that could have caused the hat to become so lopsided and out of shape. He chuckles to himself at some of the crazier, stupid and damn right dangerous ones.

It isn't long before Melvin's attention is redirected as he hears voices approaching across the green He shifts his eyes to the left and barely manages to pick out the faint outline of an extremely large gentleman, followed closely by a much smaller individual.

Hoping not to attract any attention, Melvin remains entirely still, steadies his breathing and prays that his pale pinkish skin blends into the tan stain wood of the tavern; camouflaging him from view. He leans down slowly and pulls his legs tightly together. He tries to make himself as small as possible, in an attempt to cover his saggy white underpants, which glow very mysteriously in the moonlight.

A moment of panic comes over Melvin as he realises that he has left his hat and robe directly in the path of the two men. However, it is now too late for Melvin to even think about moving them out of sight and he opts to remain still. He hopes the two men will not notice his attire on the floor, or better still, him.

'Would you look at this, Corporal?' voices Private Babe, as he points down at Melvin's robe and hat. 'Someone has left all their clothes lying on the floor. It looks like some sort of wizard.'

The Corporal takes a quick puff on his cigar, before flicking the stump out into the darkness. A trail of burnt tobacco leaves and embers fly across the night sky in front of Melvin. The cigar stump lets out a slight hiss as it hits the damp grass.

'I believe everyone is leaving washing out, Private,' replies the Corporal. 'It's all to do with this Laundry Fairy character that the village is extremely notorious for…remember?'

'Ah, yes! I certainly remember reading all about her somewhere, Sir. You are right…and you do hear many stories of her – and her well-doing to the villagers here.'

Private Babe stares at Melvin's hat.

'What's so fascinating about it, then? It's just a hat,' asks the Corporal.

'Well, I was just thinking that I've never actually met a wizard before…well, not a real one, anyways,' states Private Babe. 'It very much looks as if this hat is—oh my goodness, yes! It's a spellbinder's hat!'

'Explain, Private?'

'Well, Sir…spellbinder wizards are a unique form of spellcaster as they don't just cast spells – they also create unique ones – and—'

'Yes-yes, I know what a spellbinder is, Private,' interrupts the Corporal. 'But…what's your point?'

Private Babe leans down and takes a closer look at the hat and robe, followed closely by the Corporal, who carefully crouches down behind and looks over the Private's shoulders.

'There are only a few spellbinders that I know of – and one of them lives not too far away from here, in Huskendale Castle. But it's shrouded in some magical spell – rendering it invisible unless you know how to get to it.'

'And…what's this spellbinder's name?'

'The spellbinder is the great Melvin Copernicus,' announces Private Babe.

Melvin lets out a pleasant smile and continues to eavesdrop interestingly on the Corporal and Private Babe's conversation.

'Melvin who?' questions the Corporal.

'Copernicus, Sir. I hear he is one of the most caring, charming, elegant, wise, intelligent and sophisticated individuals that you will ever have the fine pleasure of meeting. A true gentleman. A master of magic and enchants – and a wonderful lover of nature.'

'I see,' replies the Corporal.

'Oh…and I believe he collects and raises dragons,' adds Private Babe.

'Sounds like a *fascinating* individual,' responds the Corporal, letting out a long yawn.

'Oh yes, very much indeed. I hope that one day I will get to meet him. The vast amount of knowledge I could gain from him – and also the many delightful conversations we could have. He must be a wonderful man – full of life.'

Melvin now has the biggest grin spread across his face; caused deeply by the knowledge that people did actually know of the great name of Copernicus.

The Corporal pushes himself upright as Private Babe leans further forward. Fascinated by the intricate detail and fine stitching on the hat, Private Babe begins to remove it from atop the neatly folded robe.

'Excuse me! What do you think you are playing at?' yells Melvin. 'Get your hands off that!'

'Oh, my!' gasps Private Babe, staring shockingly and yet excitedly at a near-naked Melvin, crouched up on a stool. 'Err…hello?' he adds.

Melvin coughs. 'Hello to you also.'

Private Babe rises to his feet. 'I'm terribly sorry; we didn't see you there. Are these yours by any chance…?' asks Private Babe, pointing down to the hat and robe at his feet.

Melvin ponders and tries to decide the best possible answer for this moment; tossing up between telling the truth and most likely ending up divulging information, or to simply lie, hoping that both the Private and the Corporal would ignore him and continue on their way.

'Um…them? No-no, never seen them before in my life,' answers Melvin, letting out another cough.

'Oh, *it's*—it's just that you're pretty much naked…' begins Private Babe. 'I thought maybe—'

'Well, you thought wrong, then!' interrupts Melvin hastily, trying his hardest to end the conversation as promptly as he can, by taking the very practical *rude* approach, which has worked out very well for Melvin, on many previous occasions.

The Corporal moves in closer towards Melvin and eyes him up and down. 'May I ask you your name, old timer?'

'My name is *M*—my name is, err…Dave,' replies Melvin hesitantly. 'And yours…? *Chubby Chops*?'

'Dave, huh…?' retorts the Corporal. 'Well, Dave, I don't believe I like your tone of voice – and the name's Corporal Ringelstein, if you must know!'

Melvin remains silent to the Corporal's remark. He smiles back, in a sad attempt to neutralise the hostile conversation and not make it worse by saying, "You started it," to the Corporal.

'Err…so, Dave?' begins Private Babe. 'May I ask what you are doing? – and why you are sitting out here in the cold, doing it naked?'

Again, Melvin puts his brain cells hard at work, trying to construct the perfect answer that would suit his situation.

'I'm just getting a little air, you know? Tones the skin and keeps me fresh,' answers Melvin.

'So what brings you to Baston, Dave?' questions the Corporal.

'Well, Err, *I'm a*—I'm a builder…yes that's what I am! I'm here to aid in the reconstruction of the village's fountain,' stutters Melvin.

The Corporal frowns; unconvinced of Melvin's story. 'Yes, I hear that early yesterday morning some moron decided to crash a steam-powered bicycle into that fountain!' states the Corporal.

'Oh, is that so…?' responds Melvin, with a tone of embarrassment in his voice. '*W—wha*—what a wally, huh?'

The Corporal nods.

'Do you know whose hat and robe this is, Dave?' ask Private Babe.

'Nope, not…a…darn…clue,' replies Melvin. 'I would imagine a guest at this tavern.'

'Oh, goody,' glees Private Babe.

'Come, Private…enough of this nonsense. I smell food – and I'm really starving,' declares the Corporal, stepping up onto the wooden decking of the tavern with a mammoth thud, followed immediately by Private Babe, who then rushes ahead to open the door for his superior.

'Maybe we'll see you tomorrow, Dave?' questions Private Babe, before following the Corporal inside.

The door slowly swings shut and Melvin lets out an immense sigh of relief. 'I believe that's a certainty – a certainty indeed,' he mutters.

The church bell tolls twice.

Melvin lets out a long yawn and continues to wait patiently. His yawn, however, is suddenly broken by a disturbance in the air, which instantly grabs Melvin's attention. He remains still and silent, while shifting his eyes back and forth from side to side. There is a faint ringing sound in Melvin's ears.

'Is this her?' he mumbles to himself, before turning his glance towards his hat and robe; staring at them with great anticipation…and just like that, the one he's been waiting for, suddenly materialises about his hat.

Melvin's jaw hangs low and ajar. He gazes in amazement at the most beautiful sight he's ever seen.

The Laundry Fairy hovers gracefully in the air, her wings sound out an angelic hum, while flapping back and forth in perfect timing. Melvin watches in excitement as the Laundry Fairy reaches into a small pouch tied around her waist and pulls out a handful of orange dust, which sparkles and radiates in her hand.

'Hello…' announces Melvin, quietly.

The Laundry Fairy pauses out of confusion and slowly lifts her head towards Melvin. She is shocked in the fact that she never expects anyone to say "hello" to her, let alone a near-naked spellbinder.

'Oh, err…hello to you,' replies the Laundry Fairy, nervously.

'I'm sorry – I didn't mean to startle you…' begins Melvin. 'Please…please don't be afraid. My name is Melvin Copernicus, but most people call me Melv.'

The Laundry Fairy stares briefly at the sight in front of her, before letting out a cheeky giggle, which she immediately silences by placing a hand over her mouth. She quickly adjusts her wings, glides slowly towards Melvin's face and hovers in front of his eyes.

'I'm not afraid,' states the Laundry Fairy. 'It's just that I was—'

'Shocked?' interrupts Melvin. 'Startled?'

'No, none of them. It's just—I'm terribly sorry, but what's your name again? I was completely distracted by the fact that you are sitting in the cold, wearing only a pair of underpants.'

Melvin looks down and smiles, before turning a bright shade of crimson, in embarrassment.

The Laundry Fairy begins to fly gracefully around Melvin's head; carefully analysing him in every detail, in particular, his glossy white hair.

Melvin attempts to follow her around by twisting his neck, only to then realise it only stretches so far and quickly rotates it in the opposite direction to observe the Laundry Fairy from the other side.

'I was half expecting you to try and capture me,' says the Laundry Fairy. 'Everyone else I notice while doing my rounds seems to try. I think someone tried to do that earlier…hmmm, I not sure. Something happened over near the village hall. I didn't see anyone, but I had the strangest feeling I was being watched.'

'Oh, how peculiar,' replies Melvin. 'And, no-no…I'm not trying to capture you at all.'

The Laundry Fairy smiles.

'I'm actually astonished that you are able to see me,' adds the Laundry Fairy, arriving back in front of Melvin's face. 'Just how are you able to do that?'

'I'm a spellbinder. I can do most things if I put my mind to it. Most of the time the spells I create and cast, end up coming out exactly the way I want them to.'

'Oh, right – I see…'

'And to tell you the truth. I wanted to see if I could get the chance to meet you – and so I conjured up a spell to slow down the world around me.'

The Laundry Fairy blushes.

'Do you have a name?' asks Melvin.

'My name is Amelia,' replies the Laundry Fairy.

'I'm truly honoured to meet you, Amelia.'

Amelia returns to Melvin's hat and robe, before removing a small wand tucked deep inside her tunic. 'I'm guessing that these are yours, Melvin?' poking at the tip of his hat with her wand.

'Yes, they are. I'm rather thrilled that you have—*WHOOOOAH!*—look at that!' shrieks Melvin.

Amelia releases the sparkling dust in her hand all over Melvin's hat and robe. The dust chimes and rings out as if a thousand miniature bells are all going off at the same time…and with an immense flash of orange light, Melvin's attire is instantly washed, dried and folded neatly in front of him.

'Oh, wow!' yelps Melvin. 'That is amazing!'

'It's my pleasure, Melvin,' replies Amelia. 'It is no problem at all.'

Melvin promptly returns to his feet and shuffles forward, while attempting not to reveal too much of his nakedness to Amelia, who tries not to giggle. He picks up his freshly washed robe and slides effortlessly into its soft fabric. Melvin inhales profoundly and takes in the fresh scent of his newly cleaned robe.

'I don't know what I can do to return the favour, Amelia,' says Melvin, reaching down, picking up his hat from the floor and placing it firmly on his head.

'You don't have to do anything, Melvin. It's all in a night's work. I wouldn't be me if I didn't wash laundry for everyone, would I?'

'I guess not,' answers Melvin, returning to his stool.

Melvin begins to pick up his items from the floor

and put them back into his robe pockets; items that immediately have Amelia guessing at why Melvin would be carrying them at all.

'I'm surprised they all fit into your robe pocket, Melvin,' says Amelia.

'Oh yes, they all fit in here,' replies Melvin. 'I once cast a unique spell on my robe. I can't quite remember what was involved, but I do recall having to buy a load of cotton thread.'

Amelia smiles.

'Blast it!' screeches Melvin, turning his attention towards the tavern's door, before dashing up to the side of it and placing his back up against a wall. He slowly creeps in front of the door and cautiously peers through a small gap in the woodwork.

'Is everything okay?' asks Amelia.

'Huh…? Oh, yes. I just didn't want to be seen by a couple of individuals, whom I *may* have just told a little white lie to about my identity. In fact, I did tell them a little lie about who I am – and if they see me in this robe…then its game over.'

'Why did you have to lie to them?' replies Amelia.

'Err, well I was trying to get rid of them – because I wanted to try and get to meet you.' Melvin blushes. 'One of them wanted to meet Melvin…err, I mean, me, so I pretended I was someone else.'

'You are truly a very peculiar character, Melvin. Do you realise that they will probably work out who you are in the end, Melvin? All they have to do is ask the tavern keeper. He is always drunk at this time of night – and I would imagine that he would tell anybody *anything* right now.'

'Do you think?' queries Melvin.

'Well, I can see through the window there – that a

large man and his companion are talking to him right now – and he is pointing over this way. I'm guessing they are the two you speak of?'

Amelia turns towards the village and glances across to the clock on the church tower.

'Oh my-my, Melvin,' begins Amelia. 'I would love to stay and talk more, but tonight I'm running very late. I really must get going. I still have the other side of the village to get through.'

'Oh, well, that is such a real shame,' answers Melvin, while attempting to peer into the tavern through the window.

'Yes, I still need to attack the laundry at the wash-house – which takes a lot of time – plus a load from the post office. That Mrs Stamps and her husband do have some very questionable pieces of clothing in their laundry basket.'

Melvin turns instantly back to Amelia. 'Oh? How very interesting. Like what?'

'I'm sorry, Melvin, I *really* have to be going. It was a pleasure meeting you. Try not to mess your robe up again – or you'll be seeing me again tomorrow.'

Amelia smiles and lets out a sly wink.

'I will find the largest mud-filled puddle and dive straight into it later,' calls Melvin, as he watches Amelia disappear into the night.

Melvin lets out a sigh and reaches into his robe for his pocket watch.

'MELVIN!' bellows a voice from inside the tavern.

'Oh geez!' shrieks Melvin, looking at his watch. 'I think I'd better wind this watch a little more.'

◆◆◆

Mr and Mrs Stamps always hang a lantern outside the post office; a single candle housed in a glass and metal frame. The candle burns constantly through the cold and damp nights. It lights the path for anyone who decides to post a letter or parcel in the very early hours of the morning. The lantern hangs from an iron chain, which hooks over a bent piece of metal, nailed onto the front wood cladded wall of the post office.

Despite its rather small size, the candle inside the lantern shines brightly, illuminating a large portion of the village green, but also…and more importantly, the village's post box, which is in dire need of some serious repair.

It is the lantern burning brightly that is now causing Edwin and Corbin a little bit of trouble, as they both struggle to find a suitable location to hide; a place they wouldn't be noticed; a place somewhere very close to perhaps the biggest laundry basket they've ever seen.

Mrs Stamps is a person known to enjoy her fashion. She is notorious for always continually changing her outfits, depending on her mood, or even the time of the day. She is the sort of person who wakes up in the morning and gets dressed, only to then, a few hours later, change her clothes after finishing her breakfast. She rarely wore an item of clothing for more than two hours. She is well-known for swapping her outfits up to ten times a day.

Mrs Stamps is also known to place garments out for washing that she hasn't even worn, merely to keep them fresh and ready for whenever she chooses to wear them. If you ever stumble across Mrs Stamps in the village, it is most likely she'll be wearing an entirely different set of clothes, to if you then bumped into her again, later that day.

At these hours of the morning, Mrs Stamps is very much asleep and slouched in her favourite armchair in the front room of the post office. Covering herself in a large wool knitted blanket, she continuously snores and pauses only to let out a small whistling sound from her left nostril.

'*Pssst!* Over here, Corbin,' whispers Edwin. 'And be quiet – someone is sleeping inside. I believe it must be the postmaster, or maybe his wife?'

Corbin scutters to the front of the post office, while trying to dodge the areas lit by the candlelight, and remain in the shadows. He pauses to take in a few deep breaths and to scout around for his Master.

'Here, Corbin…by the drainpipe,' adds Edwin.

Corbin raises his tiny head and squints his eyes as he stares into the black darkness. He follows the rusty drainpipe until he meets the sinister outline of his Master, seeping through the shadows. Checking the coast is clear, Corbin rushes across to the drainpipe. In his haste he trips and stumbles over in front of his Master's boot, releasing the cage from his clutch and forcing him to stretch out his short arms to prevent a huge face full of mud and grass.

The cage flies through the air and hits the side wall of the post office, before falling onto the soddened grass below with a slight thump sound.

'*Shsssssh*! You'll wake her, Corbin!' whispers Edwin.

'I'm doing my best, Master,' replies Corbin, picking himself up from the ground and giving himself a brisk brushing down. 'It's hard work carrying this cage and running across the village – trying to avoid things.'

'You wanted to help, Corbin. You've only got yourself to blame,' responds Edwin. 'Anyway, we must concentrate, Corbin. This may be the last chance we have in capturing the Laundry Fairy until tomorrow night. I trust you will be concentrating a little harder this time, Corbin…and not be letting me down again?'

'But, Master, I was concentrating last time – it was you that—'

'Quiet, Corbin!' voices Edwin, in a lowered tone. 'I think that post lady has stopped snoring.'

Edwin and Corbin pause and listen carefully for any indication of Mrs Stamps' snoring from inside. Edwin cautiously steps out from behind the rusty drainpipe and peers around the corner of the building.

Looking through a large framed window into the front room of the post office, Edwin observes Mrs Stamps, still fast asleep in her chair. She holds the woollen blanket tight against her wrinkly face; muffling her snoring. Occasionally she lets out a snort, sounding somewhat like a cross between a snore and a hiccup.

'Okay, Corbin, it looks like she is still fast asleep,' announces Edwin, returning to his spot behind the drainpipe, on the side of the building.

'Will you again be in bat form, Master?' asks Corbin.

'I will indeed, Corbin. But, right at this moment, I'm struggling to find a suitable place to hang. This building is very different from all of the others. There are no beams or places I can suspend from.'

Corbin glances around; his eyes rolling in their sockets as he analyses the building, aiming to please his Master by finding him somewhere to hide and wait.

'May I make a suggestion, Master?' asks Corbin.

'You may indeed, Corbin,' replies Edwin, adjusting his cloak at the collar and pulling it around to be more central with the rest of his attire.

'Why don't you just blow out the candle in the lantern?' questions Corbin. 'It will then be dark and we can both stay here behind this drainpipe.'

'Corbin-Corbin, my little bundle of wonder. I'm sure someone will notice there is no light?'

'*But*—but look, Master, there is no one else about. Besides, it is very windy – people will just assume that a gust of wind has blown out the candle.'

'I guess that could be acceptable,' responds Edwin, leaning down to pick up Corbin and raising him to the side of the lantern.

A hinged door is held shut by a small hook on the side of the frame. Corbin halts and looks through the window of the post office, at a still *very fast* asleep Mrs Stamps. He turns swiftly to the door, unlatches the hook and pulls it slowly open. The door lets out a howling creaking noise, which for the size of the door is more than impressive. It increases in volume as Corbin tries to ease the door open, only slower.

'*Shsssssh*! Corbin…be quiet,' says Edwin, under his breath.

'I am, Master. It's the door – not me,' responds Corbin, leaning inside the lantern and extinguishing the candle with a quick exhale of breath.

The front of the post office is immediately plunged in darkness. Edwin returns Corbin to the floor.

'Okay, perfect,' says Edwin. 'This time I shall just lean up against the drainpipe, next to you – and then, when the moment arrives, I shall be ready to pounce.'

'Pounce on that sleeping lady, Master?'

'No-no, Corbin. Do you think I'm that unkind? I meant the Laundry Fairy – when she presents herself.'

'Oh…I get you,' answers Corbin, smirking at his Master; a smirk, which then makes Edwin aware that Corbin was only messing with him.

'Err…Master?'

'Yes, Corbin?'

'It's getting very late—I mean, very early. 'Do you believe that the Laundry Fairy will still come at this hour, Master?'

'I am surely counting on it, Corbin,' replies Edwin. 'Besides, there is still a lot of washing scattered about the village – and even right here...look!'

'Okay...and we now wait again, Master?'

'Yes, Corbin, we wait...again.'

Corbin, after spending hours in the dark and cold, is now becoming very restless and bored. He is even more frustrated in the fact that he now has to remain still and quiet, in fear of waking up Mrs Stamps. She is the last person that Edwin and Corbin would want invading their plans; they just didn't know it yet.

The wind continues to blow; whistling through the alleyways between the buildings. The eerie squeaks of the lantern swinging back and forth, cuts through the otherwise, silent night. The faint sound of hammer on anvil is still heard in the distance.

Edwin and Corbin wait patiently.

'NOW, CORBIN!' yells Edwin, wriggling around in the damp grass, while clutching his hands tightly together. 'Quick, come to me. I don't know how much longer I can hold her...Ouch! She just bit me!'

Corbin leaps into action and drags the cage across to his Master. He quickly releases the lever to the door, which flies open with minimal effort; assisted with a little helping hand from a small gust of wind.

'Come over here, Master!' shouts Corbin, holding the cage steady in both hands and watching his Master attempt to crawl using both his elbows, through the sodden mud and grass.

Edwin frantically digs the tips of his boots deep into

the soft and damp soil; desperately trying to find a footing that would allow him to push himself forward. His once highly polished boots pile through the mud as he painfully refrains from cursing and shouting at the Laundry Fairy, who is now using every trick in her arsenal to try and release herself from Edwin's tightened grip.

'Ouch! She bit me again!' yelps Edwin. 'Bring the cage closer, Corbin. I can't reach you.'

Corbin pulls the metal cage a few feet closer to his Master, struggling *himself* to move across the slippery ground, which with every counting second, turns into a soddened mud pit.

'Hurry! I'm struggling to hold my grip,' yells Edwin.

After a few moments of rolling around in the mud, Edwin stretches his arm out fully and reaches for his cage. His boots slip and slide across the wet blades of grass; digging a small trench into the sodden earth as he desperately tries to find the last few inches, that would get *his* hands…and yet more importantly, the Laundry Fairy inside the cage.

'You're nearly there, Master,' announces Corbin, poised and holding steadily onto the cage.

'Be ready with the door, Corbin…I'm about to let go!' screeches Edwin, desperately trying to blank out the pain caused by numerous little bites to his hand.

'I'm ready, Master.'

In one swift movement, Edwin releases his cupped hands and rolls backwards. Corbin slams the cage door shut and traps the Laundry Fairy inside.

The cage begins to hum and a slight red aura glows around its metal frame. The Laundry Fairy, weakened by the mystical powers of the cage, lays sprawled out and shaking on its cold metal floor.

Edwin unwinds from his cloak, which has wrapped itself several times around him. He rises to his feet in the most elegant way possible, trying his best to avoid slipping over and landing straight back into the mud.

With concentration and composure, Edwin takes a few steps towards the cage. He lowers himself down and picks it up with two hands. 'I've got her!' he hails.

'She doesn't say too much, does she, Master?' states Corbin, staring up at the cage.

'No, not right now she doesn't – but she will.'

Edwin pokes a finger through the thin bars of the cage and gently prods at the legs of the Laundry Fairy.

'Isn't that right?' he adds, trying to spark a reaction from her.

Suddenly, Corbin turns his head, startled by the sound of a door opening behind him, which then alerts Edwin, who instantly vanishes into the darkness, along with the cage.

'What in the good Lord's name is going on out here…?' bellows Mrs Stamps, rushing through the doorway, while holding a large pitchfork tightly in her hands and waving it around her head like some crazed axe murderer.

Many people would find it rather peculiar in seeing a middle-aged woman running out of a post office wielding a pitchfork, but this is Mrs Stamps…and she is—well, Mrs Stamps.

A faint light from a small flickering candle in the front room of the post office, shines through the doorway. It illuminates the front porch *just enough* to allow Mrs Stamps to observe Corbin, who stands mortified at the sight of her.

It's a pretty normal reaction for anyone to be mortified at the sight of a crazed woman waving a pitchfork in the air, but what's even more disturbing is the fact that *this* crazed woman is doing it all while wearing a full-blown evening gown.

'Err…Master?' murmurs Corbin, turning his head slightly to the side, while keeping full eye contact with Mrs Stamps. 'A little help, Master?' he adds.

'Darn rat!' shouts Mrs Stamps, stepping forward and lowering her pitchfork; poking the air in front of Corbin's face with its sharp tines.

'Oh my, would you look at that? A rat wearing a waistcoat,' states Mrs Stamps.

'Err…hello, lady,' whimpers Corbin.

'Oh my—a talking rat, wearing a waistcoat? I must stop drinking that blumeberry wine…I'm starting to see things now,' says Mrs Stamps.

'Please… I'm not a rat. I'm a—oh, never mind!'

'Begone, you pest!' instructs Mrs Stamps.

Taking the option not to be repeatedly skewered by a pitchfork, Corbin plucks up enough courage to dart into the safety of the shadows. He turns his head and stares back at Mrs Stamps.

'*WHOOOOAH!* Watch it, lady!' yelps Corbin, as the cast iron tines of the pitchfork fly past his left ear and penetrate the soft damp grass behind him.

'Curse it!' booms Mrs Stamps.

Corbin sighs at his lucky escape and continues into the darkness, in search of his Master.

CHAPTER VI

"My husband, the Postmaster, asked me to send him something sexy for his birthday. But he just ended up screaming at me, telling me to get out of our mailbox."

Mrs Stamps

Corporal Ringelstein flicks the tobacco ash from the end of his burning cigar into the murky waters of the village fountain. It sizzles briefly atop a thin film of oil that has risen to the water's surface; oil, which only yesterday evening had been a vital part of a steam-powered bicycle.

He strolls around the perimeter of the fountain wall and occasionally glances down at the small piles of fragmented brick and mortar that lay scattered at its foundations.

The debris crunches and cracks as the Corporal's large boots step over it. The unevenness causes him to struggle to hold his balance as the soles of his boots slip across ragged rocks and shards of metal.

He casually kicks at the debris with the tip of his boot; unearthing a multitude of metallic and shiny objects, undoubtedly from Melvin's steam-powered bicycle, along with splinters of wood, and what looks like strips of burnt charred rubber.

Flicking the last few slithers of ash from the end of his cigar and inhaling in one last drag, the Corporal drops the cigar stump onto the dew-covered grass and promptly extinguishes it with the bottom of his boot.

He glances down at the ground and is startled by the appearance of an object he has disturbed. The object catches and reflects the sunlight, causing it to shimmer and wink at the Corporal. He leans forward, crouches down and attempts to pick up the object in a dignified and elegant manner.

But of course, this is not the case. The Corporal's leather trousers squeak and twist as he adjusts his position, allowing his short bulky arms to stretch just enough to pick the object from the ground.

'Found anything of interest, Sir?' asks Private Babe, approaching from the direction of the tavern.

'Ah, good morning, Private,' replies the Corporal, painfully returning to his feet. 'No, it's just a simple copper coin…but, a pretty new one it looks like…and it feels kind of—well, warm to the touch.'

'How very interesting,' responds Private Babe.

The Corporal places the coin in the palm of his hand and brushes off the dirt with his chunky fingers, before raising it close to his face and scrutinising it in fine detail.

'It's not the first I've seen scattered about here. This is the third coin I've found this morning—' states the Corporal.

'Have you thought that maybe they could be coins that the good villagers have tossed into the fountain, to make a wish with, Sir?' questions Private Babe.

The Corporal stares briefly at the coin and then back at Private Babe.

'Well, they must have been extremely intoxicated or something, as they've managed to miss the fountain every time. It's is a pretty big enough target, don't you think, Private?' queries the Corporal.

Private Babe nods and smiles at his superior.

'So, Private…let's have a look at this list of the things that Der—I mean the Reverend would like us to complete in preparation for this upcoming *Village of the Year Award*,' demands the Corporal.

Private Babe reaches deep into the top pocket of his jacket and pulls out his small notepad. He flicks it open and hands over the first page of scribbled notes to the Corporal.

Reaching into *his* top pocket, the Corporal removes a small pair of brass-framed reading spectacles. He opens them up and carefully places the thin legs over each of his earlobes. The spectacles sit gently on the tip of his nose.

'Seems like we have much to do, Private,' states the Corporal, turning the pages of the notepad over. He squints his eyes and attempts to read Private Babe's handwriting, which seems to get worse as he continues towards the last few pages. The Corporal smirks as he realises this is due to Private Babe's clear intolerance to the copious amounts of alcohol he'd consumed the night before.

'Yes, Sir…' begins Private Babe. 'I'm very much looking forward to giving the village a little spruce up and releasing my creative side.'

The Corporal frowns and hands the notepad back to Private Babe, who then promptly returns it to his jacket pocket.

'I'm just simply looking forward to getting paid,' exclaims the Corporal. 'Today is going to be some very easy money – very easy money indeed. The Reverend is always good to his word.'

'Well, Sir, talking of the Reverend…here he comes now,' replies Private Babe, turning about himself to watch the Reverend approach from across the green.

The church bell tolls nine times.

'Right on time I see, Reverend,' announces the Corporal, stepping forward to greet him.

'Good morning, gentlemen,' says the Reverend. 'Another fine and crisp morning here in the Land of our Lord, don't you think?'

'Yes…very much so,' replies Private Babe.

'Ready to crack on with all your duties for the day Corporal?' asks the Reverend.

'I certainly am; however, I'm not too sure where the rest of the squad are – they are a little late!' replies the Corporal, with a raged tone. 'You did say nine o'clock sharp, Private?'

'Yes, Sir, I did – plain as day,' says Private Babe.

'Well blast me down with a rubber duck…where are they?' retorts the Corporal, growing impatient and glancing across the village, towards the river. He raises a hand to his brow and shields his eyes from the bright morning sun; squinting a little as he looks over the top of his reading spectacles, trying to focus on a distant path that leads towards the riverfront.

'Useless imbeciles,' mutters the Corporal.

'I'm sure they will be here soon, my good friend,' says the Reverend, calmly.

'Hmmm, I sure hope so,' replies the Corporal. 'So, Reverend, tell me more about this wizard fellow that crashed into your fountain yesterday? What's his name again…Melvin? He seems to have made quite a mess!'

The Reverend straightens his attire and adjusts his crisp white collar. 'Oh yes, Melvin. He seems a nice chap…I caught him briefly for the first time yesterday morning. I believe he is staying at our tavern – with his pet dragon. I can't quite remember the dragon's name – Chester or something like that.'

'At your tavern you say?' queries the Corporal. 'He doesn't by any chance have a brother by the name of Dave, does he…?'

'No,' answers the Reverend, slightly confused.

'Hmmm…yes, just as I thought—' mumbles the Corporal, his eyes narrowing with a slight rage.

'Why the interest, Corporal?' asks the Reverend.

'Well, I think I may have already met this Melvin,' begins the Corporal. 'I'm pretty sure we met very early this morning—'

'You think that was him?' interrupts Private Babe, with a sound of joy and excitement in his voice.

'I don't think, Private I *know* that was him,' replies the Corporal. 'But, two things puzzle me. Firstly…why did he lie to us about who he was? – and secondly. …why was he sitting outside in the cold, near naked?'

A look of confusion falls across the Reverend's angelic face.

'Beats me, Sir,' answers Private Babe.

'Crazy old fool,' mutters the Corporal. 'If I ever get to see him again…I'll wrap his—'

'Ah, here come the rest of the squad now, Sir…' announces Private Babe, cutting off the Corporal in mid-sentence.

Private Babe points his finger towards the rest of the squad, who approach in tight formation from the hill. They chant and sing as they march in perfect synchronised timing towards the village.

Both the Corporal and Private Babe look shocked at the fact that the squad are starting to look like real soldiers.

'Come on, lads! We're nearly there!' yells Private Trout, leading the squad into another delightful and colourful marching cadence about a woman named Cynthia…and her one-eyed ferret. 'Follow my lead, lads!' he adds, bursting into chorus again.

Private Trout and the remainder of the gang rally forwards towards their superior, coming to a sudden and abrupt halt in front of him. They attempt to salute in unison at the Corporal, only to fail miserably as one Private, for some bizarre reason salutes backwards, and another manages to poke himself in the eye.

'You are all late!' bellows the Corporal.

'Ah…well, yes – apologies for that, guv! We had a slight issue with getting out of our tents this morning,' explains Private Trout, straightening his jacket.

The Corporal pauses and then sighs, choosing not to attempt to engage in a debate with Private Trout about his timekeeping and excuses.

'Well, at least you are here,' mutters the Corporal, as he looks over at the rest of his squad.

'Who is this?' asks Private Trout, nodding his head in the direction of the Reverend, who stands patiently with his hands cupped together as if in silent prayer.

The Corporal turns his attention to the Reverend

and then slowly back towards Private Trout, who is trying to remove a lengthy hair from deep inside his left nostril.

'I would have thought that a man of even your intellectual level would have worked that one out by now, Trout,' queries the Corporal.

Private Trout stares blankly at the Corporal and then re-directs his eyes towards the Reverend; slowly eyeing him up and down.

The Corporal runs a hand over his face and bites his lower lip.

'This, Trout…is the Reverend Clementine, who also happens to be a good friend of mine. He is the local *man of the cloth* here,' states the Corporal.

'Ah, gotcha now!' declares Private Trout. 'Morning Rev, a pleasure to meet you,' he adds, taking a bow.

'Like-wise,' responds the Reverend, in a tone that suggests he is unsatisfied with Private Trout's informal and disdainful introduction.

'Right then, lads…' begins the Corporal. 'I hope you are all ready for a full days grafting? The Reverend here has given us a full list of all jobs that need completing today. Private Babe will talk you through them all and allocate chores.'

Private Babe reaches into his pocket and pulls out his notepad.

'Oh…and Corporal?' interrupts the Reverend. 'Any materials or supplies you need – please grab them from the local store. I have already spoken to the shopkeeper there. I'll settle up with him later this evening. So, take all you need.'

'You heard him now, lads! Chop-chop!' yells the Corporal, rubbing his hands together; warming them a little in the crisp morning air.

Private Trout takes a sneaky peek at the notepad over Private Babe's shoulder and focuses in on some random scribbles written on the pages.

'Excuse me, Sir?' says Private Trout.

'What is it, Trout?' replies the Corporal, softly.

'Forgive me, Sir…but can I ask you what this means here?' questions Private Trout, stretching his arm over Private Babe's shoulder and pointing to a page in the notepad.

'What does it say, Trout? Come-on, spit it out!' yelps the Corporal.

'Err…well, guv. It looks like a drawing of a small dog, doing a—well…doing its business on a flower,' states Private Trout, sniggering gently.

'Huh?' reacts the Corporal, snatching the notepad from Private Babe, who instantly lowers his head in embarrassment.

The Corporal looks down and tries his hardest not to laugh at the poor attempt of drawing a dog.

'Do you have anything to say, Private…?' asks the Corporal.

Private Babe ushers forward to stare at the creation he has drawn in his notepad. He smiles and looks up towards his superior.

'You did say that I was rather drunk, Sir!' responds Private Babe.

The Corporal snaps the notepad closed and pushes it hard against the chest of Private Babe, before patting him gently on the shoulder.

'That you were, Private…' begins the Corporal, walking straight through his squad, who immediately shift to their side. 'That…you…were—'

◆◆◆

Dexter lets out a long-drawn-out yawn, stretches his short arms and slowly opens his eyes.

He tilts his head to the side, expecting to see Melvin fast asleep on a small metal framed bed, only to notice a ruffled sheet and a pillow on the floor.

Shifting onto his rear legs, Dexter paces towards a large window and pushes hard against its wooden shutters, allowing rays of sunlight to fill their rented tavern room. He embraces the sun's warmth on his scaly skin and draws in a breath of crisp morning air.

His moment of tranquillity is interrupted on hearing sounds of splashing water coming from behind a small door at the far end of the room.

'Melv…is that you?' questions Dexter, turning and facing the door.

Dexter's sharp claws tap out a rhythm as he moves across the wooden floorboards. He leans his ear gently up against the ajar door, pauses and carefully pushes it open. The door lets out a chilling creak, just as a voice bursts into a beautiful array of hums and whistles.

Dexter peers around the edge of the door and observes Melvin sitting in a tiny metal bathtub, with his knobbly knees poking through the water's surface. He stares momentarily at Melvin, who is gracefully running a mermaid's comb through his long, wet beard.

Dexter places a claw immediately over his mouth and tries his hardest not to burst into fits of hysterical laughter, only to grab Melvin's attention by stumbling into the door; pushing it wide open.

'Yikes, Dex! Do you mind? I'm trying to bathe here!' bellows Melvin, quickly covering his nakedness with a mass of foam and bubbles.

Dexter chuckles, slides back behind the door and pulls it half closed.

'But…Melv, you hardly bathe. Why now all of a sudden?' questions Dexter, sliding his body down the front of the door and sitting onto the floor.

'Err…well—I guess I'm—oh be quiet, Dex!' blasts Melvin. 'Can't an old man enjoy a nice hot morning bath, once in a while?'

'I guess,' replies Dexter. 'Anyway, did you manage to have any luck in meeting the Laundry Fairy, earlier on?'

There's a slight pause and a splash of water.

'Actually, I did, if you must know, Dex!'

'You did?' gasps Dexter, leaning back against the door so hard it flies open again, causing him to roly-poly back into the room.

'Her name is Amelia – and she is the most beautiful woman I have ever seen in my life,' says Melvin, in a soft and loving tone.

'Probably the most beautiful woman you've ever *met* in your life,' mutters Dexter, under his breath.

'What did you say…?' queries Melvin, shifting his glance towards Dexter.

'Err…nothing,' responds Dexter, picking himself up from the slightly damp floor.

'She is absolutely and truly amazing and—no wait! She is elegant…gorgeous…wonderful – a complete pleasure to be with.'

Dexter pauses and goes into deep thought about Melvin's unusual and sudden strange behaviour.

'So…Melv, did she say much to you?' asks Dexter.

'Not much, my little purple friend…' begins Melvin, twisting his beard with his hands and ringing out the water. 'She was running behind schedule and in a hurry. However, I'm *hoping* to meet her again tonight.'

Dexter grins, smiles and then bursts into laughter.

'What's so funny?' demands Melvin, picking up a linen cloth wrapped tightly around the end of a broom handle and using it to give his back a good scrubbing.

'Oh, nothing, Melv. Nothing at all—'

'No, go on! Please enlighten me with your words of wisdom for the day…'

Dexter jumps up onto a small wooden box, crouches down and lets his tail swing gently behind.

'Well, Melv…I think maybe a certain someone, has a little crush, on perhaps…a little fairy, huh?'

'Don't be so absurd, Dex!' snaps Melvin. 'That is the most darn-right preposterous and stupidest thing I've ever heard come out of your mouth. I'm simply shocked that you have even suggested it!'

Dexter stares blankly at Melvin, who begins to turn a bright shade of crimson around his cheeks.

'Oh, come on, Melv. It's obvious! You have that look of love and lust about you. Besides, that would explain why you're sprucing yourself up. You've got a date, haven't you…huh?'

'No, I haven't! I'm simply—'

'Err…Melv, I think you have. You don't have to lie to your good pal Dexter. Anyway, if you ask me nicely, I may be able to aid you – give you some pointers.'

Melvin instantly drops the broom handle to the floor, pinches his nostrils closed with two fingers and submerges himself under the water. A few bubbles of air rise to the surface. After a few moments, Melvin breaks through the foam at the other end of the tub.

Dexter shields himself from the mass of water droplets flying across the room as Melvin crazily shakes his head from side to side; attempting to dry his hair. Melvin wipes his eyes with the backs of his fingers and glances across at Dexter.

'You…give *me* some advice?' chuckles Melvin.

'That's correct,' answers Dexter.

'Hmmm…oh…and yes, I may be a little fond of her, Dex! But, come on…dating advice from a dragon? Now that's something new…huh?'

'Well, the offer still stands if you need it, Melv.'

'Truly honoured, Dex…but no! I'm sure I'll be fine. Anyway…pass me my robe would you, good chum?'

Dexter jumps down to the floor, picks up Melvin's robe and hands it over to him.

'Oh look! She has even fixed those small rips that I tore in your robe, while on the bicycle yesterday.'

Melvin smiles. His eyes widen.

'Oh, she is wonderful!' he says, in a dreamlike state.

Dexter grins.

'Turn around, Dex, naked wizard coming through!' announces Melvin, pushing himself up and out of the bath. He quickly wriggles into his robe, before reaching for his white underpants, which are folded neatly over the back of a wooden chair.

Dexter turns and saunters back towards the window in the main room. He stares out across the village, where a group of men are now hard at work repairing the village fountain…well, attempting to repair it!

◆◆◆

Timothy pours hot elderflower tea into his cup from a ceramic teapot and carefully places the teapot back onto the tabletop. He picks up the cup and takes a relaxing sip, before slouching back into his favourite armchair.

He gazes out of the window and smiles as he observes the Corporal's men hard at work with various tasks around the village, whilst knowing that in a few days, Baston could win the *Village of the Year Award* and he could be in possession of a nice chest of gold.

With the sun's warmth on his face, Timothy shuts his eyes and dreams about all the exotic items he could buy with the gold. He is relaxed and content as he wriggles his rear into the soft sponge-like material of his chair.

There are several loud taps on the windowpane, which startle Timothy; drawing him from his dreamy state.

'TIMOTHY!' screeches Mrs Stamps, pressing her wrinkly old face hard up against the glass window and peering through into his office. 'I know you're in there, Timothy.'

'Darn it…what now?' mumbles Timothy, quietly rising to his feet.

'Timothy? I can see you're in there…don't you dare ignore me!' bellows Mrs Stamps, as she continues to frantically tap on the glass with her knuckles.

'I'm coming, Mrs Stamps!' yells Timothy, in a nervous tone, while making his way to the front door. 'I'm coming, *you*—you miserable old bat,' he adds under his breath.

He twists the key in its lock, rotates a handle and takes a deep breath, before slowly opening the door.

Mrs Stamps stands with her hands on her hips and stares at Timothy, with a menacing rage in her eyes.

'Good morning, Mrs Stamps,' announces Timothy, with a soft smile on his face.

'Good? What's so *good* about it, Timothy?' snarls Mrs Stamps, awaiting an immediate response.

'Err…Well – I suppose it's because—'

'And, are you just going to stand there? Or are you

going to let me in?' interrupts Mrs Stamps.

Timothy pulls the door wide open, steps to the side and swings his arm in the direction of his office, allowing Mrs Stamps to walk briskly past him. He briefly looks outside, before slowly closing the door behind him.

'*C—c*—can I interest you in a cup of freshly made elderflower tea, Mrs Stamps?' asks Timothy, removing a clean cup from a lopsided shelf, fixed to the wall.

'I haven't got time for tea, Timothy! I want to know what you are going to do about our situation?' replies Mrs Stamps.

'Our situation?' replies Timothy, with a confused and void look on his face.

Mrs Stamps lets out a sigh, pushes her way past Timothy and re-opens his front door. 'That situation!' she yells, pointing towards Timothy's laundry basket, sitting on the veranda.

Timothy shuffles past Mrs Stamps, being cautious not to make any bodily contact with her. This is more for his own self-respect as a human being and not because he wants to save his eardrums from taking another pounding from the high-pitched screeches and squeals of Mrs Stamps.

'What the—' begins Timothy, dropping the cup to the floor, which smashes into several fragments. 'What on Earth is going on?' he adds, rushing to his wicker basket and picking up a soiled pair of trousers and a dirty handkerchief.

'I was hoping that you would be able to tell me, Timothy?' snaps Mrs Stamps. 'I left my laundry out last night and I have exactly the same problem. There is no doubt that we are not the only ones whose laundry has not been washed – just take a look!'

Timothy immediately turns and glances across the village. He picks up the sight of other laundry baskets that appear not to have been washed. A sense of concern and worry settles into his mind.

'Oh…and that's not the only problem we have, Timothy!' begins Mrs Stamps. 'This village has a rat problem!'

Timothy adjusts his gaze towards Mrs Stamps, who has a rather satisfied grin on her face; satisfied that she has made Timothy feel rather uncomfortable.

'A rat problem? What do you mean…?' questions Timothy, with a horrified look upon his face.

Mrs Stamps grabs Timothy's arm and ushers him back inside; pulling him back through the front door like a naughty child that has done something extremely wrong. She closes the door behind her.

'I saw a rat very early this morning…' begins Mrs Stamps, letting go of Timothy's arm. 'It was a very *large* rat as I remember.'

'We have not had any rats in the village for a long time,' states Timothy.

'Are you calling me a liar, Timothy?' retorts Mrs Stamps, waving her finger in front of Timothy's face.

'No…not at all. I'm just saying that it—'

'Well, Timothy…' interrupts Mrs Stamps 'I know what I saw. I was having a lovely little sleep and then I was rudely disturbed by a noise outside. When I went to investigate, I saw a huge rat standing on its hind legs – right outside my door – wearing a waistcoat.'

Timothy stares in complete concern at Mrs Stamps. He contemplates whether he has just misheard what she has just said, or whether Mrs Stamps' old age is finally catching up with her.

'I'm sorry, Mrs Stamps…' begins Timothy. 'Did you

just say, a giant rat wearing a waistcoat was standing outside your front door in the very early hours of the morning?'

'That's correct, Timothy. I want to know what you are going to do about it?' replies Mrs Stamps.

Timothy pauses and takes a few seconds to conjure up a suitable answer that will please Mrs Stamps.

'And it even spoke to me,' adds Mrs Stamps.

Timothy tries to prevent himself from bursting into laughter, by biting on his lower lip. A huge grin begins to occupy his face and his cheeks start to glow a rosy red. He clenches a fist and places it discreetly into his mouth, before biting down hard onto his knuckles.

'What are you grinning at, Timothy?' questions Mrs Stamps, taking a step towards him.

'Oh…err, nothing'—*cough-cough*—'I seem to have something stuck in my throat—' answers Timothy, patting his chest gently. 'So…Mrs Stamps – what you are telling me – is that a giant rat stood outside your door last night and it spoke to you?'

'Yes, Timothy! I've already told you that. Will you stop making me repeat myself?'

'Forgive me, Mrs Stamps…but what, may I ask, did it say to you?'

'Never-mind what it said, Timothy. I didn't come down here just to talk about a rat. I believe we've got much more important things on our list of worries right now; don't you think?'

Timothy nods gently and proceeds to lower himself back into his comfortable chair.

'What in the Lord's name do you think you are doing, Timothy?' queries Mrs Stamps.

'Finishing my cup of tea,' answers Timothy.

'Finishing your cup of tea? *Finishing* your cup of tea?

We've a potentially severe problem here in the village and all you can think about is finishing your cup of tea?'

Timothy takes a few more gentle sips of his hot beverage, before returning his cup carefully onto the tabletop.

'It helps me think, Mrs Stamps…' begins Timothy. 'Besides you are right. I *do* believe we have a problem.'

'Glad to hear it, Timothy,' responds Mrs Stamps.

'But to be perfectly honest, Mrs Stamps…I really have no idea what you want me to do about it. I don't control the Laundry Fairy. It's completely her choice what she does – not ours.'

'Well…err—' begins Mrs Stamps. 'You may have a point. All I can suggest is that you go look for her.'

Most of the time, Mrs Stamps' suggestions are very cleverly thought out and she usually presents the most logical solutions to a problem. However, her latest idea has caught Timothy by complete surprise; a surprise that forces Timothy to chuckle aloud.

'Mrs Stamps…forgive me – but you want me to look for her?' begins Timothy. 'Nobody has ever seen her I have no idea where she comes from or lives. I would have absolutely no idea where to even begin.'

Mrs Stamps sighs. She positions herself next to Timothy and leans her plump rear up against the arm of his chair.

'I cannot recall one single instance – not one *single* moment in my life where I have had to wash my own laundry. I'm certainly not about to start today!' states Mrs Stamps before pausing. 'This is *your* problem and I suggest you sort it out!'

'What on Earth do you mean…my problem? Surely you mean *our* problem?'

Mrs Stamps tuts and raises herself to her feet.

'And talking about problems…here comes another one,' she adds.

There's a light knock at the door. Timothy rises to his feet and shuffles across to the window. He glances through the glass windowpane to observe a very tall and well-dressed man, waiting patiently on the veranda. Timothy turns to Mrs Stamps, who stares back at him with an annoying smirk on her face.

Pausing to take a deep breath, Timothy paces to the door, turns the handle and pulls it wide open.

'Good morning, Samuel,' says Timothy, with a fake, but yet convincing smile.

'Ah, Timothy. I'm so glad I managed to catch you this early,' begins Samuel. 'We need to have a little chat. I have a bit of a problem.'

'I believe we *all* have, Samuel. Please come in,' replies Timothy.

Samuel Arthurs has run the village wash-house for as long as anyone can remember. His father ran it before him and *his* father before him.

Commonly seen wearing very crisp and well-ironed clothes, Samuel has an obscure intellect about him and often knows a lot of topics that most people would not even take the time to learn about.

He is an extremely busy individual, although his cool and relaxed posture would suggest to most, that he has all the time in the world. This is an observation that most people make, whenever they see him.

'Samuel…it's nice to see you out and about this early,' says Mrs Stamps.

'Oh, Mrs Stamps, I wasn't expecting to see you here, but thank you,' responds Samuel.

'Well, neither did I,' mutters Mrs Stamps. 'But it seems we have a joint problem, don't we?'

'Yes, we do. A pretty big one if I do say so myself,' states Samuel.

'Cup of tea, Samuel?' asks Timothy.

'Oh, no thank you. I will not be staying long. I will make this quick, Timothy,' answers Samuel.

'I'm guessing you are here because of our non-washed laundry?' asks Timothy.

Samuel removes his flat cap, folds it in half and places it neatly into his jacket pocket. He runs the palm of his hand firmly over his hair, flattens it to the side and makes himself look a little more presentable.

'I am, Timothy. Has something happened to our little fairy?' enquires Samuel.

'I wish I could answer that, Samuel…' begins Timothy. 'But the truth of the matter is—'

'The truth is…we don't know!' interrupts Mrs Stamps. 'And *our* Timothy is just too darn lazy to do anything about it!'

'I did not say that at all, Mrs Stamps,' says Timothy, with a sigh. 'I just said…I don't know what you want me to do about it!'

'*Wh* what's the difference, Timothy?' snarls Mrs Stamps. 'What's the ruddy diff—'

'Excuse me!' interrupts Samuel. 'This arguing is getting us nowhere. Can we just concentrate on the problem at hand and try to at least come to some sort of solution?'

Timothy and Mrs Stamps stare briefly at one another, before both turning slowly towards Samuel and giving him a gentle nod of their heads.

'Now…' begins Samuel. 'We must establish the facts. Do we actually know if she has gone missing, or has she just given up on us? She may have gone missing on purpose.'

'We don't know, Samuel,' replies Timothy. 'How would we even begin to find that out?'

'Yes…how would we?' adds Mrs Stamps.

'Well, we'd better quickly get our thinking caps on, as before long, we are going to have much bigger problems…' announces Samuel.

'Bigger problems?' queries Timothy.

'Well, put it this way, Timothy…' begins Samuel. 'Yesterday I had a huge delivery of dirty washing from the surrounding towns and villages. Later today, I'm expecting another delivery. I just can't keep up with the demand – I'm short staffed as it is. I feel if our little fairy doesn't appear later tonight, then the washing will simply not be done and I'll lose the business.'

'Hmmm…yes, that is alarming,' says Timothy, in a concerned tone.

'And on top of that…most of the washing delivered earlier is from the town of River's Bend. I can tell you now – there are marks on those clothes and sheets that are of a very questionable and disturbing nature.'

'Like what?' asks Mrs Stamps.

'I'd rather not discuss it to be honest, Mrs Stamps – client confidentiality…you see?' responds Samuel.

Mrs Stamps stares at Timothy, who shrugs his shoulders. She then turns her attention back to Samuel.

'Client confidentiality?' begins Mrs Stamps. 'What a load of puppy—'

'And I hear on the grape vine…' interrupts Samuel, with a raised voice. 'That our village has been entered into the *Village of the Year Award*?'

'Yes, it has!' announces Timothy.

'Well, I can tell you this now…' begins Samuel. 'My aunt took part in a similar event when she used to live in the town of Dyll, on the east coast of Auchendale. I remember her saying that the judges didn't take too kindly to the local's dirty laundry being left out – and that's nothing compared to our mass of it.'

'Oh, really?' questions Timothy.

'Yes,' answers Samuel. 'And judging by – *no pun intended* – this morning's sun, it's going to be a fairly hot day. I've already noticed many people's laundry still outside, gathering flies and various other insects. With the heat – it will only get worse.'

Timothy places a hand over his mouth in shock.

'I'm just saying,' adds Samuel.

'It's really that bad, then?' asks Mrs Stamps, taking considerable interest in what Samuel is saying.

'It certainly is not going to help if the day produces sweltering heat, especially with all the washing from River's Bend. Before you know, the village will be overwhelmed with horrible smells; smells of rancid blood, sweat and tears, which will moulder and fester in the heat. This will then lead to an infestation of flies, bug, maggots…and even rats, which will—'

'Rats you say?' interrupts Timothy.

'Yes, rats! Really – big – rats!' announces Samuel.

'See, Timothy…I told you I saw a rat last night!' bellows Mrs Stamps, storming towards Timothy and waving her pointy finger back and forth in front of his face. Timothy backs away from Mrs Stamps, trying desperately to regain a little personal space.

'Yes, I know, Mrs Stamps…but I think Samuel is talking about *real rats* and not the kind that speak to you – or wear mini waistcoats.'

A look of shock and confusion falls across Samuel's long-drawn face as Mrs Stamps lowers her head in total embarrassment. Samuel stares at Mrs Stamps, turns to Timothy for any verbal response, and then slowly shifts his attention back towards Mrs Stamps.

'I'm certainly going to be busy for most of the day – and I would imagine well into the night to get this washing all sorted. I don't want to assume the Laundry Fairy will be back tonight…and to make it all worse – it's my birthday today. I was really looking forward to spending the evening with my wife and child.'

'I didn't know it was your birthday, Samuel. You kept that quiet! Happy Birthday!' roars Timothy.

'Yes…many happy returns,' adds Mrs Stamps. 'Hoping for any nice presents?'

'Thank you. No, just to spend some quality time with the family – that would be more than enough,' answers Samuel.

'My husband, the Postmaster, asked me to send him something sexy for his birthday…' begins Mrs Stamps. 'But he just ended up screaming at me…telling me to get out of our mailbox!'

There's an uncomfortable silence…

'So, what's the plan, Timothy?' asks Samuel.

'I'll need some time to think about it all,' replies Timothy.

'Well, time is ticking…' begins Samuel. 'And I don't think you'll be getting too much spare time today.'

'What do you mean?' asks Timothy.

'Well, take a look outside,' instructs Mrs Stamps.

Timothy pushes Mrs Stamps aside, slides briskly past Samuel and opens his front door to an array of villagers, queuing outside his office. He pauses briefly, takes in the sights of the many angry looking faces, before being bombarded with a loud chorus of questions and comments concerning their unwashed laundry.

'What on Earth?' mumbles Timothy.

'Looks like you've got a pretty busy morning yourself, Timothy,' comments Samuel, from behind.

'I think you may be right there,' adds Mrs Stamps, who continues to wear a large smirk across her face.

'CALM DOWN! Calm down, will you? I'll get to see you all shortly,' yells Timothy, before slamming the door shut behind him and taking a long deep breath; exhaling it slowly.

'Err…Timothy? What's that sound I hear…?' asks Mrs Stamps.

Timothy pauses and listens carefully.

'Oh, that's just the villagers – outside – having a good rant about their laundry. I'll talk to them in a while,' replies Timothy.

'No, not that – listen,' continues Mrs Stamps.

'I don't hear anything at all,' states Timothy.

'Me neither, Mrs Stamps,' adds Samuel.

Pop!

'There it is again!' says Mrs Stamps, slowly creeping towards the back of the room.

Pop! Pop! – Pop!

'Oh, darn it!' shrieks Timothy, rushing past Mrs Stamps, into the next room.

CHAPTER VII

"Err...he *ca—ca*—calls it a *re—re*—refrig—a refr—a cooling down thing."

Mr Dylan Kalar

Melvin carefully places his spellbinder's hat atop his head; pulling it down gently until it meets the tops of his ears. He grabs the rim and slowly tilts it from side to side; adjusting it several times, until satisfied with its position.

He runs a hand slowly down the fabric of his robe, using it to iron-out any minor creases or imperfections. The royal blue coloured material shines as it reflects a shard of morning sunlight, which bursts into the room through an open window.

He begins to comb his beard, running the comb gracefully through his long white hairs, before grabbing the hairs and twisting them around several times. Holding them tightly with one hand, he reaches into his robe pocket with the other and pulls out a small cord of leather. He wraps the leather around the end of his beard and ties it off in a fancy knot.

This whole *twisted beard* thing, according to Melvin, is the latest fashion in the spellbinding world, and finishing it off with a fancy leather cord, is Melvin's attempt to look cool, hip and trendy. In Dexter's eyes, it's a darn good attempt indeed.

'How do I look, Dex?' asks Melvin, twirling himself around on the spot and fanning out his robe.

'To be perfectly honest, you look like an absolute gem, Melv. I'm truly stunned at how exquisite and distinguished you look,' states Dexter.

Melvin blushes at Dexter's compliment.

'So, apart from perhaps meeting a certain little fairy later on – what are your plans for the day, Melv?' asks Dexter.

'Not a clue...' replies Melvin. 'I thought perhaps I would see how Eric is getting on with rebuilding my bicycle. I keep hearing the blows of his hammer in the distance. I imagine he must be advancing well with it.'

'Yes, that hammering went on through the night. I eventually managed to doze off,' states Dexter.

Melvin smiles.

'Oh...well, if you are heading over, could you please give him these?' adds Dexter, handing over to Melvin, a sack full of shiny copper coins he had collected.

Melvin clutches the top of the sack and gives it a violent shake.

'Holy-moly, Dex...' begins Melvin. 'Had a little bit

of a sneezing marathon of late, have you?'

'I wouldn't be having sneezing marathons at all if you hadn't gotten your stupid spell wrong in the first place, Melv!' retorts Dexter, raising his eyebrows up at Melvin.

'Why do you have to keep bringing that up…?'

'I'll tell you why, shall I? It's because the last time you tried to fix it; you made a right—'

'It looks like it's going to be another beautiful day, here in Baston,' interrupts Melvin, in a raised voice.

Dexter sighs and accepts that he is not going to get any further response from Melvin, on the matter.

'Oh, darn it!' exclaims Melvin, looking out of the window at the mass of people working on the village fountain.

Melvin instantly shifts himself to the side of the window; shielding himself from view. He cautiously pokes his head around the window frame, before a sense of panic and worry slowly starts to settle in.

'What now?' questions Dexter.

'The Corporal…' whines Melvin.

'Who?'

Dexter paces across the floor towards Melvin, positions himself behind him and carefully looks out of the window.

'The Corporal,' repeats Melvin.

'Which one is he, Melv?'

'He's the rather large—bulky—err…the big one, Dex! The *really* big one!'

'Err…okay? So, what exactly is the problem here, then, Melv? Also…why is there a small tree moving about next to him?'

'What do you mean – a small tree?' queries Melvin, squinting a little through the glass pane. 'Oh…no that's not a tree, Dex. That's one of his men. Private Babe is his name, if I remember correctly.'

'Oh, I see,' says Dexter, chuckling to himself.

'Well, Dex…I kind of told a little fib very early this morning – to that giant of a man – and I think I may have fallen short in my deception, as he—well, I wasn't a very good liar – put it that way. I may have insulted him and tried to hide the fact of who I am. I now feel that I may have to face him in the near future.'

'Why did you lie though, Melv?' asks Dexter.

'I was trying to wait patiently for Amelia…' begins Melvin. 'The Corporal and his associate happened to come my way. I thought I could remain still and they wouldn't see me. But they did – and started to question why I was sitting out in the cold…naked!'

'Okay…and?'

'They then noticed my robe folded neatly on the floor – and *that* Private Babe has some silly, obsessive fascination with me…so I lied and told them both that I wasn't Melvin – just so they'd leave me alone.'

'Oh, I see…'

'Then, to make it worse…and *just* as I thought I had got away with my deceit, that drunken tavern keeper puts me right in it, by telling them both that I was me – if that makes sense? They must have asked Duncan whom the robes belong to when they entered the tavern.'

'Oh…how embarrassing.'

'You're right there, Dex. No doubt I will bump into him at some point.'

'Can't you just hide or maybe dress up in some other clothes? You know – so they don't recognise you?'

'I only have this one robe, Dex. I wasn't planning on staying in Baston this long.'

'But you're a spellbinder, Melv…remember? Just transform yourself.'

There's a moment's pause as Melvin tries to conjure up all the marvellous ways in which he could prevent himself from interacting with the Corporal. He giggles at the more elaborate ones.

'Actually, no. I think I will just *man up* and face the music,' declares Melvin.

'Yeah…it's not over until the fat man punches you in the face…huh, Melv?' jokes Dexter, bursting into a roaring laugh.

Melvin steps back into the room, circles around the dusty floor and goes into thought about the best way to eventually approach the Corporal and Private Babe.

Dexter watches as Melvin mutters loudly to himself, generates multiple ideas and then sighs as he realises all of their flaws. Melvin continues to repeat this loop for several minutes.

'Well, I wouldn't worry too much, Melv,' announces Dexter. 'What's the worst that can happen?'

'That's what worries me, Dex,' answers Melvin.

'Just simply apologise for your mistake…and if that doesn't work – then just cast some spell on him,' jokes Dexter.

'Yes! That's exactly what I am going to do…' states Melvin, breaking the momentary silence. 'I'm going to cast just a little, teeny-weeny spell on him. Nobody will ever know.'

'Oh, I do really not like the sound of that, Melv,' announces Dexter, repositioning himself.

Melvin reaches into his left robe pocket. His hand disappears deep inside the fabric, along with half his arm. He rummages around. Dexter watches with interest as Melvin stretches further into his pocket, pulling some extremely funny facial expressions; many of which involve Melvin sticking his tongue out.

A melody of rattles and clinks are heard as Melvin pushes aside various objects that are buried in the depths of his pockets.

'A-ha! That'll do the trick, Dex!' announces Melvin, pulling from his pocket the tiniest glass bottle that Dexter has ever seen. Melvin holds it steady, pinching it gently between his thumb and forefinger, before giving it a slight shake from side to side. A thick yellow liquid oozes down the inner surface of the bottle.

'Err…okay, Melv – what is that?' asks Dexter.

Melvin holds the bottle high above his head and lets the sunlight from the window shine through the bottle; illuminating the liquid.

'This, Dex…' begins Melvin. 'This is a very potent vial of, what people call…Angel's Fern; the nectar of a rare orange flower that grows on the northern slopes of the Cewin Foothills. It has some—'

'The same place my favourite cheese comes from?'

'Yes, that's right, Dex. But please don't interrupt me mid-sentence.'

'Sorry, Melv.'

'Now, as I was saying…it has some unique mind and emotion altering effects – for those who breathe in its magical aroma.'

'So, it's basically a love potion, then?'

'NO! It's not a love potion. It's nothing like that at all!' blasts Melvin, placing the bottle carefully into an inner pocket of his robe. 'It's a potion that—it can make…err, it's a—oh, okay it's a love potion of sorts.'

Dexter chuckles.

'A simple whiff of this liquid and the Corporal shall be under my complete control…' begins Melvin. 'As soon as the vapours hit the back of his nose, he will feel no more hatred towards me and all my worries of late, will disappear. I may have to mutter a few magic words to enable the liquid to work in my favour.'

'Are you sure it's safe, Melv?'

'Of course, I am. I have used it several times in the past – in various different situations, that—well, have needed a little gentle persuasion.'

'What happens if you use too much?'

'I'm not sure, Dex. I don't think I've ever given anyone *too* much. One way to find out though – right?'

'So, how are you going to get the Corporal to sniff the vapour in?'

Melvin smiles at Dexter.

'That's the hard part,' explains Melvin. 'I'm sure I'll think of something—'

'Are you sure it will work on the Corporal? I mean he is a pretty—well, he's a larger sized gentleman.'

'Yes, I'm fairly certain it will. Besides, what's the worst that can happen…?'

'I asked *you* exactly the same thing a while ago.'

◆◆◆

As the morning sun slowly rises over the Darkened Enchanted Forest of Huskendale, the Corporal and his men disperse themselves across the village of Baston. Working together in small teams, the men push on with completing numerous tasks and small jobs, as instructed by Private Babe, who with the assistance of a new recruit, attempts to plant a variety of flowers and small trees, in the less colourful areas of the village.

'I can think of better ways to assist than planting flowers,' moans Private Simmons, clawing a small hole into the ground with his bare hands.

'Actually, Simmons…I believe that this is by far the easiest and the most pleasant of all the jobs I have assigned,' replies Private Babe, kneeling down onto the damp grass and caressing the leaves of a small tree.

'I really would prefer to do something a little more masculine to be honest.'

'Masculine?'

'Yes, you know? Maybe something with swinging swords around, or even using one of those new devices that fires iron balls at people. I hear the balls can cause great pain…you know?'

'Balls that hurt people…?' questions Private Babe, with a concerned look upon his face.

'That's right. Can't think what it's called.'

Private Babe straightens the roots of the tree that had previously been growing on the edge of the forest, before lowering it carefully into the small hole dug by Private Simmons.

'Oh…I believe you mean a pistol, Simmons,' states Private Babe.

'That's it! Yes, a pistol. Why can't we do something using a pistol?' questions Private Simmons, filling in the hole around the tree with soil and patting it down gently.

'Because, Simmons…I really can't think of anything that requires the use of a pistol – one that would aid us in making the village ready for the competition.'

'Hmmm…well, I guess you are right. Maybe if we don't win, we could use one on the judges?'

Private Simmons chuckles loudly, followed briefly by Private Babe, who begins to check the stability and levelness of the tree they've just planted.

'Okay, Simmons. This one looks good. Let's move

down a bit further and plant another one,' says Private Babe, pushing himself to his feet.

'How many more of these darn flowers and trees do we have to plant?' asks Private Simmons.

'Plenty more to go,' responds Private Babe. 'We've got to make the village look at least a little cared for and ready for judging.'

Private Simmons sighs with boredom.

'I would have preferred to help them two…' begins Private Simmons, pointing at a couple of other men who are repairing some fencing around the church. 'Or even assist that pair over there in trimming those tree branches down a little. But no…I have to plant boring flowers with you.'

'Well, Simmons…we are all getting paid the same amount, so does it matter?'

'No, not really. But I'm not worried about that.'

'What are you worried about, then?'

'The rumours that'll start.'

'Rumours…?'

'Yes, rumours. I'll get called all sort of names for planting flowers. What makes it worse is…I'm planting flowers alongside you.'

Private Babe pauses with an appalled look on his face; troubled at the reasons why Private Simmons would feel uncomfortable in his presence.

'What do you mean, exactly?' queries Private Babe.

'Well…you know?' mumbles Private Simmons.

'Err…nope?'

'You and the Corporal.'

'What about me and the Corporal?'

Private Simmons begins to sweat a little from his brow, growing a little nervous at the aggressive tone of Private Babe's voice. Titling his head back, his eyes meet Private Babes, which stare piercingly back at him.

Private Simmons lowers himself to his knees and defensively tries to avoid answering Private Babe's question, by clawing furiously into the soil.

'Another one here, then?' he asks.

'Yes…fine,' replies Private Babe.

There is a slight pause as Private Babe waits for a response.

'And…?' begins Private Babe. 'What about the Corporal and I?'

'Well…you know? Your relationship with him. He must be feeling rather jealous, no?' answers Private Simmons.

'Relationship? Jealous?' retorts Private Babe. 'I can assure you that there is absolutely nothing like that going on between the Corporal and I. Who would even say such a cruel thing?'

'The rest of the lads.'

'Well, they are just petty and ridiculous rumours, Simmons! Please ignore them.'

'What about you and the Reverend…? Are they also rumours?'

Private Babe chooses to remain silent and not relish Private Simmons with an answer. He leans down to a pile of pulled trees, picks one up and begins tenderly separating its roots, ready for replanting.

'Just out of curiosity…' begins Private Simmons. 'What's next after we have finished with planting all this flora around the village?'

'Cra—err I mean poop,' answers Private Babe.

'Poop?' questions Private Simmons, alarmed at the word.

'Yes, poop! Lots of it.'

'Oh?'

'Well, Simmons…we'll be removing all the animal manure that's scattered across the village.'

'Oh, come on…really?'

'Yes. Horse, cow, deer and—well, let's just say… manure of a *questionable* origin.'

'Darn it!' bellows Private Simmons. 'Why do I always get the crap jobs?'

◆◆◆

The Reverend Clementine carefully sits down on the edge of a raised wooden platform that leads to the church alter. He bends his knees, brings them up to his chest and wraps his arms tightly around them.

He proceeds to gently sway back and forth while humming very loudly; a ritual that he completes most mornings. He says it helps him to cleanse the mind and soul of worries, but it also gives him extremely painful backache.

There's a loud knock on the wooden door at the rear of the church, followed by numerous smaller knocks that echo through the nave of the church. The repeated knocking startles the Reverend, who then looks up at the door. He watches as the door handle turns, which releases an iron latch. The door creaks in pain as it's slowly and carefully pushed ajar.

'Hello, Reverend!' shouts Mrs Stamps, her voice booming through the church atrium. 'It's me…are you there, Reverend?'

The Reverend sighs. He does not even have to ask who "it's me" is, as he's already very used to the loud and screeching bellows of Mrs Stamps, who seems to spend more time in the church, than with her husband at the post office.

'Good morning to you, Mrs Stamps…' begins the Reverend. 'Another splendid and beautiful day in the Land of our Almighty Lord, don't you think?'

'It is satisfactory,' replies Mrs Stamps, pushing the door wide open and revealing the bulk of Timothy, standing in the doorway.

'Oh, Timothy. Good morning to you also,' says the Reverend, raising himself to his feet as Timothy closes the door quietly behind him.

'Morning, Reverend,' says Timothy.

'What do I owe the pleasure?' queries the Reverend, slightly confused at why Mrs Stamps and Timothy have turned up together.

Mrs Stamps walks gracefully and calmly towards the Reverend with her hands locked behind her back. She glances around at the church interior, before bringing her attention to the Reverend.

'Well, I'm guessing you've heard the bad news?' asks Timothy.

'The bad news?' answers the Reverend, adjusting his robe and straightening his collar.

'Yes…we have a *little* bit of a problem – you are not going to like it one bit!' adds Mrs Stamps.

'Oh, deary-me…' begins the Reverend. 'Has one of the Corporal's men managed to destroy something already? Oh-no, it's the fountain isn't it? the fountain has finally collapsed on us…that's all we need!'

'I hope not,' chuckles Timothy. 'It was still pretty much intact as I walked past it just now.'

'Oh, has Shirley, the baker's wife, given birth to their child?' continues the Reverend.

'No…not quite, Reverend,' answers Mrs Stamps, running her finger slowly across the back of a pew; checking it for dust.

'Oh, such a shame,' answers the Reverend. 'I do enjoy a good baptism. So, what is this bad news?'

'Well…have you checked the status of your laundry this morning, Reverend?' asks Timothy.

'My laundry…?' begins the Reverend. 'Why would I check my laundry? It will be exactly where I left it last night, only sparkling clean.'

'I wouldn't be too sure of that, Reverend,' remarks Timothy.

'What do you mean?' questions the Reverend.

Timothy halts himself from answering. He gazes across to Mrs Stamps for any support on relaying the news about their *missing* fairy to the Reverend, who continues to be baffled at why Timothy and Mrs Stamps are in the same room together; let alone why they arrived at the same time.

'Oh stop beating about the bush, Timothy? Just spit it out to the Reverend, would you?' retorts Mrs Stamps, who is now casually running the tip of her finger across the pulpit.

'Well, Reverend…' begins Timothy. 'She has gone missing.'

'Who?' replies the Reverend.

'Our friend,' adds Timothy. 'Our Laundry Fairy.'

'What do you mean…missing? That's not possible is it? What would make you even suggest such a thing?' questions the Reverend.

'Come…I'll show you,' says Timothy, placing his hand gently on the Reverend's shoulder and ushering him towards another door at the rear of the church.

Mrs Stamps stares at the tip of her finger, before letting out a short sigh and wiping it down the side of her dress. She proceeds to follow Timothy and the Reverend, out of the church.

'Oh, my dear—' begins the Reverend, staring down at his unwashed laundry, which is laying at the bottom of a poorly made wicker basket.

'Reverend!' shrieks Mrs Stamps. 'I hope you were not about to use the Lord's name in vain?'

'No, not at all, Mrs Stamps,' replies the Reverend.

'It's the same for most people's laundry in the village,' says Timothy, moving himself closer to the Reverend. 'This is going to cause us some issues with the upcoming competition,' he adds, whispering into the Reverend's left ear.

The Reverend gently nods.

'So, we have absolutely no idea where the Laundry Fairy has gone? Or even why she is missing?' asks the Reverend.

'No,' replies Timothy. 'Not a clue at all. She has just simply failed to do our laundry.'

'That is disturbing,' states the Reverend, staring into his laundry basket at small piles of black tunics, white collars and some vibrant and colourful silk underpants. 'We must report this immediately to Officer Locks at the village jail.'

'That's exactly what I said, Reverend!' interrupts Mrs Stamps. 'I suggest we go and see Officer Locks straight away.'

Timothy raises his eyebrows. 'Mrs Stamps, we have discussed this…' begins Timothy. 'Let's just see what happens tonight. We don't want to be jumping ahead. If she doesn't appear tonight, then you have my word that we'll go and see Officer Locks in the morning.'

'Very well,' responds Mrs Stamps.

'Are you sure that's wise?' asks the Reverend.

Timothy pauses and leans himself closer towards the Reverend; shielding his face from Mrs Stamps. 'I just don't want there to be any unnecessary panic, if you catch my drift, Reverend?'

The Reverend gives Timothy a gentle nod of his head, in acceptance that, at least one of them has a grip on the situation.

'Well, I pray for our Lord to find her well and return her back to us safely,' announces the Reverend. 'If you could please keep me fully updated with all that—'

'What on Earth is all that commotion going on over there?' interrupts Mrs Stamps, marching across the church graveyard, stomping over the graves and giving no regard for the dead.

'Yes, what the—' adds Timothy, following her.

The Reverend dallies behind.

◆◆◆

'Get off me…you, crazy old fool!' shouts the Corporal, trying frantically to shake Melvin off his back.

'Not a chance, *Corporal Chubby Cheeks*!' replies Melvin, wrapping both his arms tightly around the Corporal's giant head; clutching on desperately. The Corporal spins around on the spot, occasionally swapping direction in an attempt to shake Melvin off, only to become more frustrated as Melvin jabs a finger into his right eye.

'When I finally get hold of you, I'll—OUCH!' yells the Corporal, as Melvin pokes his finger into his other eye. 'I can't see. Darn you, wizard!'

Melvin reaches into his inside robe pocket and pulls out the vial of Angel's Fern. He grasps it tightly in one hand as he holds on to the Corporal with his other. He manages to promptly flick the cork off the bottle with his thumb. It falls gently onto the grass below.

◆◆◆

'What the devil is going on over here, Private Babe?' questions Timothy, gathering his breath. Private Babe cringes as he watches his superior take a *royal* beating from a skinny old man wearing a robe and hat. 'Private Babe?' repeats Timothy.

'The Corporal and that wizard fella are having a bit of a quarrel,' interrupts Private Trout.

'I can see that. But are you not going to help him?' asks Timothy.

'Err…nope. This is way too much fun to watch,' responds Private Trout, before chuckling to himself.

The Corporal roars as Melvin clamps down harder around the Corporal's head. Melvin raises his legs and positions them atop the Corporal's shoulders as he begins running around the village fountain, shouting and cursing at Melvin, who relishes the situation by pretending he is in a rodeo contest.

'YEEHAAAARGH!' yells Melvin.

Timothy, Mrs Stamps, the Reverend and half of the Corporal's men stand staring in complete amazement, followed by Dexter, who arrives just in time to see Melvin's skinny legs being hurled through the air.'

Dexter lets out a roaring laugh. 'Oh my—that has got to be one of the funniest things I have ever seen!'

'Are you not going to help him?' asks Mrs Stamps.

'Who me? Nah! He'll be okay. He is a big enough fellow,' answers Dexter.

'I wasn't referring to the Corporal, little dragon,' states Mrs Stamps.

Arms and legs flail about the main square as Melvin tries desperately to remain on the Corporal's shoulders.

'Take a little whiff of this – *you*—you…big oath!'

yells Melvin, placing the vial underneath the Corporal's flared nostrils. 'That's it, my dear Corporal, breathe – breathe it all in.'

'Why you—I'm going to break every bone in—*oh*—oh my…' begins the Corporal.

The vapour of the Angel's Fern flows effortlessly up the Corporal's chubby nose and fill his lungs with its magical properties.

Immediately, the Corporal comes to an abrupt halt. His arms drop to his side as the vapour starts to take its magical and mysterious effect on him. The Corporal develops a large grin across his face and his body begins to relax.

Melvin mutters a few magical words, jumps down onto the ground and moves to face the Corporal.

'Umm…err…Corporal?' questions Melvin, poking repeatedly at the Corporal's arm with his finger.

'Melvin! Come over here you little scally-wag…' begins the Corporal, his eyes widening in sheer delight. 'Don't you be afraid, you sweet bag of goodness – come give me a squeezing!'

'Err…okay—*WHOOOOAH!*—Steady on there, big man!' answers Melvin, as the Corporal pulls him closer.

'Aww…you are *so* soft – and look at your cute little face,' adds the Corporal, pinching at the cheeks of Melvin, who is now slightly concerned about how much vapour the Corporal has breathed in.

'Have I told you how much I love you today, Melvin?' asks the Corporal, while attempting to give Melvin a huge sloppy kiss.

'Err…what?' begins Melvin. 'Love me? I think—'

'Well I do…very much!' interrupts the Corporal, squeezing Melvin tighter as if he is the Corporal's long-lost childhood teddy bear.

Private Trout and Private Myles remain staring at their superior and Melvin. They both take bets on who will come out the victor of the brawl.

'He's got him in a bear hug now, Myles…look!' announces Private Trout. 'Go, Sir! The spellbinder will never get out of that hold!'

'Yeah and it also looks like the Corporal is using some ancient biting techniques and trying to bury his mouth into the wizard's neck,' adds Private Myles. 'I'm not too sure why he is stroking the wizard's hair like that…and face…and he is very near to his—'

'Too much information, Myles!' interrupts Private Trout, while carefully rolling a cigarette.

Mrs Stamps gazes across the village green at the gathering of the Corporal's young recruits; her eyes ablaze at the sight of several finely tuned bodies and angelic faces.

'Oh, I do like a young man in a uniform,' states Mrs Stamps, turning towards Timothy, who is completely engaged in watching the antics of Melvin and the Corporal, taking part in, what can only be described as the weirdest brawl he has ever seen.

'Hmmm?' responds Timothy.

'That one right there is certainly a handsome chap!' expresses Mrs Stamps, pointing across at Private Trout, who is busily trying to locate a flare of matches from his jacket pocket.

'Well go and say hello if he is *that* handsome, then,' instructs Timothy, ushering Mrs Stamps towards Private Trout and Private Myles.

'That I will!' states Mrs Stamps, rolling her eyes at Timothy and huffing.

Mrs Stamps pulls gently at her dress, raises it from the damp grass and paces across the green. She glances quickly back at Timothy with a smirk on her face. She sticks her tongue out at Timothy, who ignores it the best he can.

◆◆◆

'Well…hello, young man,' says Mrs Stamps, tapping Private Trout on his shoulder. 'I must say…you do look rather delightful in your uniform, with your toned and muscular body,' she adds, placing her hand on Private Trout's large bicep and slowly stroking his arm.

'Oh, hello there, madam,' replies Private Trout,' turning a slight shade of crimson. 'And you are…?'

'Most people just simply call me Mrs Stamps…but you can call me anything you like…' responds Mrs Stamps, slowly walking behind Private Trout and trailing her hand across his back. 'What's your name?'

'I'm Trout…and this is Myles,' announces Private Trout. 'Well, Mrs Stamps…what can I do for you?'

'Oh, I can think of plenty of things you can do for me,' replies Mrs Stamps, winking.

Private Trout looks at Private Myles for some sort of comic relief or comment. It doesn't come.

'I'm pretty sure you could,' responds Private Trout, giving Mrs Stamps a soft and faint smile. 'But seriously, Mrs…err—Stamps, was it? What can I do for you?'

'Oh, nothing. Can't a woman come out to play once in a while?' questions Mrs Stamps.

'I guess,' answers Private Trout. 'Don't suppose you have any matches do you, Myles?' he adds, still patting down his jacket, in search of a flame.

'Nope,' answers Private Myles.

'Oh, I would imagine the Reverend over there will have some,' begins Mrs Stamps. 'Perhaps Myles can go and ask him for you, Trout?'

'A very good idea! Well off you go, Myles,' instructs Private Trout.

Private Myles sniggers as he leaves Mrs Stamps and Private Trout alone.

◆◆◆

'Oh, Reverend...I forgot to tell you this earlier. I had to chuckle as she was telling me...' begins Timothy. 'Mrs Stamps believes that we have a problem with rats, here in the village.'

'Rats? That doesn't sound too good at all, Timothy,' replies the Reverend, slightly shocked.

'Ah...I wouldn't worry too much. I think the old dear has finally lost her marbles!'

'Really? I thought she already had.'

The Reverend and Timothy let out a quiet chuckle.

'So, what has she been saying about rats?' asks the Reverend.

Timothy pulls the Reverend in close, just as Private Myles arrives behind them. Private Myles pauses as he sees them both in mid conversation and waits patiently for a convenient moment to interrupt.

'Well, Reverend...' begins Timothy. 'She told me earlier that a giant rat had come to her last night and attempted to steal her dirty laundry. What's even more disturbing, is that she said the rat was wearing a red waistcoat – and it actually spoke to her.'

'Well...that's just absurd!' replies the Reverend, trying not to burst out laughing.

'I know – tell me about it! The village – being taken over by giant killer rats; rats that are stealing people's laundry...whatever next?'

The Reverend and Timothy giggle.

Private Myles stands in shock at overhearing brief parts of Timothy and the Reverend's conversation; the parts being exactly what Timothy has just said about giant killer rats taking over the village and stealing people's laundry. With a confused and bewildered look, Private Myles sneaks up behind the Reverend.

'Ah, Myles isn't it?' questions Timothy, turning his attention towards him. 'You sort of crept up on us there. What can we do for you?'

'Oh…err—do any of you have any matches please?' responds Private Myles, presenting a striking motion with his hands.

◆◆◆

'I really think that someone is getting just a little bit too friendly, don't you?' says Melvin, to the Corporal, now wishing he hadn't let the Corporal breathe in quite as much Angel's Fern vapour as he did.

'Nonsense!' says the Corporal, trying to take Melvin by the hand. 'I'm just showing how much I adore you and what a splendour you are to be around. Although, I must apologise for my earlier rants. You know I was only messing with you – yes?'

Melvin nods gently and pulls himself away from the Corporal's bulky arms.

'Now-now, Corporal. I must be—I've got to go—I have to go and do something,' announces Melvin.

'Oh, how bothersome,' mutters the Corporal. 'Well, how about you join me and the lads later on – for a few drinks at the tavern?'

'Well…I could, I suppose,' responds Melvin, giving himself some distance from the Corporal, who is continuing to attempt to hug and squeeze Melvin, as if his whole life depended on it.

'Melv! Having fun, are you?' chuckles Dexter.

'Oh, don't you start, Dex!' replies Melvin. 'It was nice to see you aiding me in my moment of need.'

'Well, it looks like you now have everything under control, Melv! It could have been a lot worse, no?' Anyway, I'm off to get some cheese – I'm getting a little peckish. Don't worry about buying it, Melv – I've got my own means. Besides you look a tad busy.'

Dexter turns and heads towards the village store, chuckling as he hears the Corporal again express his feelings towards Melvin.

◆◆◆

Mrs Stamps stands aside Private Trout, flirting to the best of her ability, although Private Trout, being the type of gentleman that he is, relishes in her games and flirts a little back.

'It's very kind of you to say, Mrs Stamps, but I really think that my arms should make the choice of who they wrap themselves around – don't you?' states Private Trout. 'Besides, I really must be going now.'

'Oh, what a party pooper!' replies Mrs Stamps. 'But I suppose I must let you do your duties. I'm sure I can find someone else to—well, entertain in your absence.'

'Oh?' responds Private Trout.

'Oh, yes…like I said earlier to Timothy – I do like a man in uniform; wearing his attire to its full potential.'

Mrs Stamps pulls herself away from Private Trout and shifts her attention. 'MELVIN! Oh, Melvin! Come to me…you sparkly blue hunk of a man!' she yells.

◆◆◆

Mr Dylan Kalar sells a wide range of goods and wares to his customers, from his store in Baston. Although not a vast space, it's the type of store you would go into and walk out carrying precisely what you needed.

The store lacks a woman's touch, since Dylan lost his dear and devoted wife Coral, several years earlier. Wherever you look, a thick layer of dust rests on every surface. It coats every shelf, table and display stand. Even the various glass jars that Mr Kalar sells dust in, are covered in dust.

Everything sold in the store is at extremely low, or discounted prices and the dust comes at no extra cost.

Mr Dylan, as he is more commonly known, is a busy soul at this time of the morning; getting all the weekly orders ready for delivery and boxing up a variety of vegetables, meats, rice and numerous dairy products. He always ensures that his produce is to the highest of standards and this is perhaps why all other items in his store are *so* neglected and gathering dust.

Without warning, a small brass bell jingles and the front door flies wide open. In rushes Dexter like a raging bull. He skids to a sudden halt in the centre of the store.

Mr Dylan lowers a completed order to the floor and looks over the counter to greet his first customer of the day. Struggling to see through the dust cloud Dexter has created, Mr Dylan doesn't notice him mid floor and continues to box up more orders.

Dexter makes his way towards the counter, looking about himself and trying his hardest to avoid knocking over piles of stacked boxes and display cabinets that stand in his path. He raises his clawed hand to the countertop and thumps a small bell. It pings loudly, ejecting a small cloud of dust.

'Err...*sh*—shall be *w*—with thee in—a—jiffy,' stutters Mr Dylan, from the floor behind the counter.

Dexter turns his head, and with a scrutinous eye he glances around the room at the mass of merchandise the store has to offer.

Mr Dylan pops up from behind the counter, opens his cash register drawer and pours some small coins inside. He looks up as he closes the drawer. The sight of Dexter takes him by complete surprise.

Since his wife passed, Mr Dylan has developed a stutter in his speech. The fact that a small purple scaled dragon has just walked up to his counter, is surely making him feel *very* nervous. He now feels his stutter will get the better of him, which it always did when he felt intimidated or not sure about something. In this case, the *something*, is whether a purple dragon is about to burn his store down or not.

'Err...*a*—and *y*—*y*—you are?' questions Mr Dylan.

'The name's Dexter...and you?' replies Dexter.

'Mr Dylan...*a* and what *br*—*br*—brings you here on *th*—*th*—this fine *d*—*d*—day?'

'Cheese!' announces Dexter.

Surprised at Dexter's response, Mr Dylan pauses and attempts to compute what he's just heard; trying to make a little logical sense in why a dragon would be asking for cheese.

'*Ch*—*ch*—cheese?' asks Mr Dylan.

'That's right...' begins Dexter. 'But it has to be the finest Cewin cheddar cheese. None of that cheap stuff!'

'Oh, of *c*—*c*—course. Only the *b*—best here.'

'It's my fix you see, Mr Dylan. The aroma – the texture – the flavour – and most importantly the taste.'

'How *m*—*m*—much would you like?'

'Well, that depends on how much I can afford.'

Mr Dylan stares blankly at Dexter, trying to reason with himself how, or even *why,* a dragon would be carrying money, let alone why he is trying to buy copious amounts of cheese with it.

'Indeed! It is *ra*—*ra*—rather expensive, even *f*—for a *dr*—*dr*—dragon,' states Mr Dylan.

'But, so delicious, is it not?' replies Dexter.

Mr Dylan nods and crouches down to a peculiar looking device, which sits on the floor. He opens the door on the device; pulling up on a large handle. A slight hiss is heard from within. He reaches inside and lifts out a massive block of Cewin cheddar cheese, which rests firmly on a round plate. He places it down on the counter, in front of Dexter.

'What on Earth is that?' questions Dexter.

'It's *ch*—*ch*—*ch*—cheese, like you asked for…no?' replies Mr Dylan, slightly embarrassed that he may have misheard Dexter's request.

'No…not the cheese – that *thing* on the floor?' adds Dexter, pointing at the device behind Mr Dylan, which is radiating a chilling haze across the store.

'Oh…*th*—*th*—that is one of our village *bl*—*bl*—blacksmiths many *in*—inventions,' states Mr Dylan.

'I see. What's it called?'

'Err…he *ca*—*ca*—calls it a *re*—*re*—refrig—a refr—a cooling down thing.'

'How interesting,' mutters Dexter, sniffing at the delightful fragrance of the cheese in front of him.

'Oh no! Here we go, Mr Dylan…I hope that you're ready!' announces Dexter, as small dust particles from the countertop enter Dexter's nasal passages.

'Ready for *wh*—what?' replies Mr Dylan.

'Wait for it…wait for it!'

Dexter pauses and pulls some pretty intense facial expressions. He tilts his head back and stretches out his small arms, digging his claws deep into the woodwork of the counter.

'Oh my—' begins Dexter, holding on tightly.

AAAAAACHOO!

A copper coin shoots out of Dexter's left nostril and ricochets off the countertop, before hitting a small box behind Mr Dylan and rolling across the dusty floor.

Dexter wipes his snout with the back of his paw, before launching into an uncontrollable series of sneezes.

AAAAAACHOO! AAAAAACHOO!

Copper coins shoot across the room in multiple directions; a deafening chorus of twangs and pings, as they deflect and bounce around the store.

Mr Dylan stands in amazement, a glowing smile stretching the thin skin on his tight drawn cheeks. He paces around his store, picking coins up from the floor and *anywhere* else they have managed to come to rest.

'I have *n*—*n*—never seen *th*—this before in *m*—my life!' stutters Mr Dylan.

'Aye…but it's very uncomfortable.' replies Dexter, bringing a little composure to himself.

'If you *k*—*k*—keep this up, *w*—we'll be rich – very…very, rich!'

More sneezes follow. More copper coins.

'Do you *g*—*g*—get that *of*—often?' asks Mr Dylan.

'Only when I feel like sneezing,' says Dexter. 'I think I'm about spent out for now though—'

AAAAAACHOO!

'Nope – one for the road!'

'Well, I think you've *g*—*g*—got more *th*—*th*—than

enough coins to *p*—pay for *th*—*th*—the cheese now,' announces Mr Dylan, still busy collecting the coins from around the store.

Dexter wipes the dribble accumulating on the end of his snout. He watches in anticipation as Mr Dylan slowly begins to cut the cheese with a large knife, only to pause.

'Here, you *ca*—*ca*—can have the whole *l*— lot,' says Mr Dylan, happily.

'Very noble of you, Mr Dylan,' replies Dexter, as Mr Dylan carefully wraps the block of cheese in some brown paper and places it into a small wooden crate.

Dexter picks up the crate. He struggles to hold it steady with his small arms as he moves to exit the store.

'Thank you…*c*—*c*—come again!' yells Mr Dylan.

Dexter flicks his tail up into the air, in recognition of Mr Dylan's comment, before suddenly freezing on the spot.

'Oh…Mr Dylan…How much for your jars of dust?' queries Dexter, with a thoughtful tone in his voice.

'Oh, for you…completely *fr*—*fr*—free,' responds Mr. Dylan.

'Marvellous…I'll take two!'

CHAPTER VIII

"Seriously, Myles? I sometimes question the whole point of your petty existence in our little world."

PRIVATE TROUT

Today, the village church bell doesn't toll twice as it usually does at two o'clock in the afternoon. Instead, it tolls out a very irregular, chaotic total of twenty-two muffled and unbalanced thuds.

These sounds are not due to some catastrophic mechanical failure with its clapper, or because it's gearing mechanism has developed a mind of its own. It is *simply* by the virtue of two of the Corporal's most highly trained men, who at this precise moment, both have their arms wrapped tightly around the perimeter of the brass bell, while holding on for dear life.

'I thought you said you had tied both of us to the rafters, Myles?' yells Private Trout.

'I thought you had!' shouts Private Myles, his boots trying to find their footing on the shiny surface of the bell.

'Obviously not – you complete muppet! And stop moving us around or we're going to fall!' adds Private Trout.

The bell swings gently back and forth from a large wooden beam above. It creaks and strains as it takes the added weight of Private Trout and Private Myles.

'Okay, I think we need to move the bell, Myles,' suggests Private Trout, struggling hard to maintain his grip. 'I'll push up a little and you try to lower yourself. We need to try and shift its centre of gravity.'

'Its what…?'

'Its centre of—oh, never mind. Just do what I just said – and then when the bell is swung towards me – you manoeuvre yourself upwards – and I'll go down. We can then get the bell swinging…okay, Myles?'

'Gotcha, Trout!'

There have been some very strange and peculiar sights in Baston over the years, but none, until this day, have been quite as strange as seeing two fully-grown men hanging from the side of a church bell.

'When I tell you to – jump off onto the side – and I'll follow after you,' instructs Private Trout.

The bell manoeuvres back and forth, aided by the unorthodox movements of Private Myles and Private Trout.

'Okay…NOW, MYLES!' hollers Private Trout.

Private Myles lets go of the bell, pushes himself aside and lands with both feet onto a side rafter. He clutches hard to the wooden framework of the tower and finds his balance. Private Trout follows suit and lands safely on the other side of the church tower. The bell lets out a few tolls, each one less prominent than the last, before finally coming to rest.

'I think it may be a good idea if we both attach ourselves to the rope now, Myles…' begins Private Trout. 'For a few moments there, I certainly thought that was the end of us.'

Private Myles acknowledges with a small nod.

'So, Trout? How many more jobs have we got left? Why on Earth did we get this one?' asks Private Myles.

'Not too many, Myles,' responds Private Trout, wrapping the rope around his waist and tying a huge knot. 'This is one of the last jobs on the list for us – apart from a few things later – we are then just about done. I really don't know why Private Babe asked us to do this. Perhaps he knew it's because we are more than capable of getting the task done with minimal effort and problems?'

Private Myles lets out a joyful smile. 'Yeah, that'll be it, Trout!'

'Right, let's get this sorted. Pass me a cloth would you, Myles? And watch where you place your feet or you'll be back on the bell again.'

Private Myles chuckles, reaches down and takes a cotton cloth out of a tin bucket. He ruffles it up into a ball and throws it over the top of the bell in Private Trout's direction. It bounces off the top of Private Trout's head and falls down the bell tower.

Private Trout and Private Myles laugh.

'Okay…let's be serious now and get this done. Pass me another, will you?' asks Private Trout.

'So, Trout? That post office woman seems to have

taken a bit of a liking to you, huh?' questions Private Myles, throwing another cloth towards Private Trout.

'I don't know what you're going on about,' answers Private Trout.

'What's her name again? Mrs Stamps?'

'Err…maybe, yes.'

'She seemed to be flirting a little with you, no?'

'Absolutely not, Myles!'

'Yes, she was! What's also worrying – is that you were also flirting back. Got a little fancy on have you, Trout?'

'No, Myles, I was just being my typical friendly self…anyway shut up and let's get this bell polished!'

There is a moment's pause…

'Besides, it looks like she's got a thing going for that wizard bloke from earlier. You know? The one that crashed into the fountain yesterday,' reveals Private Trout.

'Ah yes! The Corporal seems to be getting on very well with him. Although, he has certainly changed his tune from when I saw him shouting and cursing at the wizard earlier. It's like they are both the best of friends now.'

'He's a spellbinder, Myles. Probably put him under some trance-like spell or something!'

'Yeah…maybe.' Private Myles chuckles.

'Anyway, Myles…? What was all that commotion about earlier – something about lots of dirty laundry has gone missing?'

'Well, Trout…don't say anything – this is between you and I. But I think I heard that Reverend chap say to that fat mayor guy, that people's washing has been stolen by some giant killer rat – and the whole village is being kept under tight wraps?'

'That's absolutely ridiculous, Myles!' voices Private Trout. 'Why would a rat be stealing people's washing?'

'I'm only saying what I heard,' responds Private Myles.

'Or, saying what you think you heard?'

'What…?'

'Oh, never mind, Myles…*never mind.*'

Private Trout and Private Myles take their cotton cloths and rub away at the surface of the brass bell. They make sure that every trace of grease, grime and the occasional crow's droppings are removed; leaving a glistening and highly polished shine.

'How are you getting on over there, Myles?' asks Private Trout, buffing up a few areas of the bell.

'Nearly done here. Just a little more to go.'

'Can you see your face in it?'

'In what?'

'In the bell, Myles. Can you see your reflection in the bell?'

'My what?'

'Seriously, Myles? I sometimes question the whole point of your petty existence in our little world.'

'Thanks. I guess…?'

Private Trout moves around the outside of the bell tower and checks that the bell itself has been polished to the Reverend's exact specification, of being able to see your face in it.

'Okay. I think we are good to go here,' says Private Trout. 'Right, let's see what those last few jobs are again, shall we? A little painting if I remember? You still have the notes Private Babe gave us, haven't you, Myles?'

'I certainly have,' replies Private Myles, reaching into his trouser pocket and pulling out a scrunched-up piece of paper. He carefully unravels it and scrolls over the last few items scribbled at the bottom of the page. Private Myles lets out a grin, followed by a chuckle.

'What is it, Myles?' questions Private Trout.

'You are right in saying we've got some painting to do…' begins Private Myles. 'It also looks like we have a little repair work to complete at the same time.'

'Ah. Easy stuff, then?'

'Err, I guess—'

'So…where have we got to do this painting?'

Private Myles pauses.

'Well, it says here that the village's post box needs a little attention and some paintwork is required on the front facia of the post office building. You know what that means…don't you, Trout?'

'I do…?'

'Yes…you'll get to see *your* Mrs Stamps again.'

◆◆◆

Melvin repeatedly knocks hard on the large oak doors of Eric's workshop, trying his best to overcome the sound of Eric's hammer as it makes multiple deafening blows onto the surface of soft glowing metal.

'ERIC!' shouts Melvin, cupping his hands around his mouth and making a funnel with them. 'ERIC! ERIC!' he continues.

Melvin sighs at Eric's unresponsiveness and steps into Eric's workshop, while carefully minding pieces of newly beaten metal panels that lean up against the workshop walls. He glances to the floor and recognises parts of his bicycle. He steps cautiously over the shiny crafted components laying neatly on the floor. Each one is tagged and marked up with a systematic numbering system, which only someone like Eric would be able to create and understand. A look of confusion falls over Melvin's face as he tries to make sense of what the numbers mean, before shrugging his shoulders and giving up. He accepts, that as long as Eric knows where the parts go, that is all that matters.

'Melvin, my good fellow! Sorry I didn't see you standing there. Have you been waiting long?' yells Eric, removing his goggles from his soot coated face and leaving two skin coloured rings around his eye sockets.

'No, I've just arrived,' replies Melvin, in a raised voice.

'Well…give me a few moments, Melvin. I'll just finish up with this piece – and then I'll be right with you.' Eric places his goggles back onto his head.

'No rush, Eric. I'll just mingle amongst all of your marvellous creations.'

'Help yourself to a small tipple of brandy, Melvin. My flask is sitting on top of that barrel.'

'Very kind of you, Eric…but no thank you.'

'Fair play, Melvin…*fair play*.'

Eric raises his hammer. He continues to strike at a deformed piece of metal, which he turns through various angles with a set of pincers, before stopping momentarily to wipe beads of sweat from his brow.

Melvin places the sack of Dexter's copper coins on to a tabletop, pushing aside a vast variety of springs, cogs and gears. They accumulate into a small pile. He glances around at all the wondrous and characteristic pieces of mechanical machinery that Eric has built over the years, wondering in his mind what the majority of them did, let alone what they actually were.

'Nearly sorted, Melvin…' begins Eric. 'I'll be with you shortly.'

Melvin is filled with amazement as he watches Eric grab the bashed metal with his pincers and guide it very carefully into the roaring furnace. The metal creaks and crackles; spitting out glowing sparks of metallic dust. The metal glows a rosy red.

Melvin steps in closer; mesmerised by the flickering flames engulfing the metal. He stares in fascination as Eric slowly removes the hot glowing metal from the furnace and promptly places it onto his anvil. He gives the surface a few final blows with his hammer, before dropping the completed component into a large vat of cold water. The water bubbles and hisses as steam ejects upwards into the roof of the workshop.

Eric carefully places his hammer and pincers atop his anvil, before removing his gloves and goggles; resting them neatly next to his tools.

'Sorry about that, Melvin. I was sort of right in the middle of an important process, as you saw,' explains Eric, rushing across the room and offering his hand out to shake Melvin's hand. 'So, what brings you here? I wasn't expecting to see you this way until the bicycle was nearing completion.'

'Well, to be honest, Eric, there is not much else to do. I thought I'd just pop in to see how you're getting on,' replies Melvin.

'Ah, I see,' responds Eric. 'Well, as *you* can see, I'm getting on very splendidly with rebuilding most of your bicycle. I've had to make a few parts completely from scratch – as the original pieces were simply unusable – following your unfortunate episode…but you'll not be able to tell the difference. I promise you that!'

Melvin nods and continues to cast his eyes over all the intricate pieces of the bicycle that Eric has crafted.

'I'm very impressed, Eric. You must stay up late and

not get much sleep?' asks Melvin.

'I don't tend to sleep much at all, Melvin,' replies Eric. 'I feel as if I'm wasting time if I do.'

Melvin smiles.

'No dragon today?' questions Eric, peering around the side of Melvin. 'What's his name again?'

'Dexter,' replies Melvin.

'Ah yes – that's it…'

'And no, he is off buying cheese from the store.'

'Cheese? What do you mean – cheese?' quizzes Eric.

'Yes, cheese. He is a little bit of a cheese fanatic, is our Dexter. Oh, he did ask me to give you that sack on the table.

Eric turns and walks across to the table. He picks up the sack with one hand and with minimal effort, gives it a firm shake.

'Oh wow! Copper coins I'm guessing, huh?' asks Eric, with a happy grin.

'That is correct.'

'A rather hefty load it feels like,' states Eric. 'Dexter sure has been very—well, busy is perhaps not the best word to use. Anyway, send him my thanks, Melvin.'

'I will. I'm not going to stay too long though, Eric. This really is just a flying visit, but as you said…and from what I can see, you are making extremely good progress with the bicycle.'

Eric smiles at Melvin's kind words.

'I must say, Melvin, your robe and hat are looking extremely clean and sparkly today. They were in a right tattered mess the last time I saw you,' states Eric.

'Oh yes. Well, after your talk that evening, I thought I'd take your advice.'

'You left your robe out to be washed?' asks Eric attentively.

'I did. You were right; The Laundry Fairy washed – and even repaired them for me…look!'

'Sorry for all the questions, Melvin. But this was *last* night that you left your robe out?'

'Yes, it was—'

'What time was that?' adds Eric.

'Umm…I can't really recall exactly, but certainly after midnight. Why do you ask?'

Eric moves behind Melvin and instructs him to follow him to the front of his workshop. He raises his arm and points to the spot, where he had only last evening, in the presence of Melvin, placed his laundry out to be washed.

'You see that, Melvin?' asks Eric, pointing at his washing basket. 'That has been there since last time I saw you. It hasn't moved.'

'It hasn't moved?' questions Melvin.

'Nope. That's precisely how I left it yesterday.'

Melvin paces slowly across to Eric's laundry basket and gives it a nudge with his knee. He turns slowly back towards Eric and stares blankly into thin air.

'Are you okay, Melvin?' asks Eric.

'I am. But I saw her last night – she was right there in front of me. She washed my robe… look! Why would she have left all this other laundry?'

Eric strolls towards Melvin and places a firm hand on his shoulder.

'I believe you, lad,' assures Eric.

'She did say that she was a little behind…but I don't understand why—'

'There are rumours going around that our Laundry Fairy has gone missing.'

'Missing! What do you mean – has gone missing?' blasts Melvin. 'Where could she have gone?'

'I wish I could answer all those questions for you Melvin – I really do.'

A shroud of sadness and concern quickly falls upon Melvin's face. He rushes back to Eric's laundry basket and begins to frantically remove Eric's soiled clothes from the basket; throwing items mindlessly over his shoulder in an attempt to find any clue as for why Amelia has disappeared.

'Steady on, Melvin. Tossing my washing about isn't going to solve anything, is it?' questions Eric, reaching down to pick up a pair of his soiled trousers.

'Something has happened to her…I just know it,' whimpers Melvin, as one of Eric's dirty socks hits the workshop door and falls to the ground.

'Are you crying?'

'Not at all! Spellbinders don't cry. They eject watery concoctions of toxins and endorphins, triggered by emotional responses to stressful and sad situations.'

'Err….right,' responds Eric, trying his hardest to understand what Melvin had just said, let alone what he meant.

Melvin lets out a sniffle and then draws the sleeve of his robe across his nose.

'I must attempt to find her,' states Melvin. 'Has this ever happened before?'

'You mean, has she ever gone missing?' replies Eric.

'Yes.'

'Hmmm…I can't recall a single moment in my life time that she has not turned up and done the washing for myself. I'm not sure about the other villagers.'

Melvin hangs his head low and begins to twiddle his fingers, before removing his pocket watch from his robe pocket.

'What's that, Melvin?' asks Eric.

'This is how I got to see the Laundry Fairy, Eric. I found a way to alter our perception of time.'

'How fascinating. How does it work?'

'I'm really sorry, Eric. I really don't have the time to explain that at the present. I must figure out how I'm going to find Amelia.'

'Amelia?'

'Oh – that's the Laundry Fairy's name – and yes before you ask, *she* is a she.'

Eric smiles out of social politeness, before watching Melvin spin around and head out across the village.

'What are you planning to do, Melvin?' shouts Eric.

'I don't know, Eric. I make most things up as I go along! Something I'm getting very good at!'

◆◆◆

Private Trout swings his long-handled wooden mallet violently through the air. It smashes into the side of the village's post box, which then explodes into a mass of wooden fragments and twisted rusted metal.

Private Myles sits on the wet grass and experiments with the many *possible ways* in which a human being of his persona can remove the lid from a tin of paint.

'What on Earth is all the racket out there?' bellows Mrs Stamps, opening the front door and stepping out onto her wooden porch.

Private Trout, hoping not to engage in a lengthy conversation with Mrs Stamps, kneels on the floor, lowers his head and hastily scoops up the remains of the post box into a large bucket.

'Well, hello boys,' announces, Mrs Stamps, placing her hands on her hips and seductively moving them very slowly from left to right.

'Oh, Mrs Stamps, a very pleasant evening to you. I must say you are looking very dashing and radiant,' compliments Private Trout.

Private Myles tilts his head up and nods at Mrs Stamps, as he prepares to pierce the lid of the tin with the tines of Mrs Stamps' pitchfork.

'Well, that's very kind of you to say, Trout,' replies Mrs Stamps, blushing and casually stroking the side of her face. 'Oh my! What have you done to my post box, Trout?'

'Oh, please don't worry about it, Mrs Stamps…' begins Private Trout, raising himself to his feet. 'I was instructed by the Reverend that you need a new one built. I'm simply following orders.'

'Did he now?' queries Mrs Stamps.

'My aim is to build you a new one, fully crafted to perfection, using these bare hands,' adds Private Trout, showing the palms of his hands to Mrs Stamps.

'Oh, how exciting! I do like a man who is good with his hands,' smirks Mrs Stamps.

Private Myles raises his head and cringes at her statement, before holding the pitchfork high above his head and aiming it at the centre of the paint tin.

Private Trout lets out an embarrassed smile as he reaches down and picks up several lengths of sawn timber, which lean up against a large boulder.

Private Trout has always been extremely masterful with his hands. He is the type of person that you could send into a jungle holding just a toothpick and who would emerge the other side after building you an entirely new village. However, in the presence of Mrs Stamps, Private Trout is having a rather difficult time in performing the simplest of tasks, while fabricating a new post box.

'NO, MYLES! Don't use that!' yells Private Trout, racing across and snatching the pitchfork out of Private Myles' hands. You need to get the lid off…not put multiple holes in it, you prune! You'll not be able to get the paintbrush in it, will you?'

'Right, of course,' replies Private Myles, scratching his head in confusion.

'Use something else,' adds Private Trout.

'Fine,' mutters Private Myles.

Mrs Stamps sits herself on the end of her wooden steps and places her hands into her lap. She stares dreamily at Private Trout as he measures numerous pieces of wood, and prepares to cut them using a length of cutting wire.

'Hmmm, Trout. You are so very clever,' states Mrs Stamps, in a soft and pleasant tone.

'Err…thanks,' replies Private Trout.

'I was also thinking that if you are free later, you'd maybe like to join me for a drink or two?'

'Oh, err—um, well—that's very kind of you, Mrs Stamps,' stutters Private Trout. 'But I'm very—'

'Very what…?' interrupts Mrs Stamps.

'I'm *very* tired from all the work I've been doing today,' continues Private Trout. 'I'll have to decline.'

'Oh, such a dreadful shame…such a shame indeed,' declares Mrs. Stamps. 'Maybe some other time, then?' she adds, winking slyly at him.

'NO!' yells Private Trout, jumping to his feet. 'What is wrong with you?'

'No?' questions Mrs Stamps, shocked at Private Trout's blunt response to her question.

'NO, MYLES! What are you playing at?' screeches Private Trout, ripping his long-handled wooden mallet out of Private Myles' hand.

'What now?' mumbles Private Myles.

'Seriously, Myles? You really want me to tell you the outcome of using this mallet on the tin? I mean, what on Earth do you think was going to happen?'

'Err…?' responds Private Myles.

Private Myles has always been a little slow when it comes to simple things. His common-sense levels are on a completely different scale to that of normal people. Unbelievably though, Private Myles does have a rather highly developed mind when it comes to some of the more complex things in life, like boiling an egg.

'Well, you'll have ruddy paint everywhere…won't you? Use your common sense, Myles…please?' retorts Private Trout.

Private Myles stands still and contemplates on his next cause of action. He casually folds his arms and glances around.

'Here…use this,' instructs Private Trout, handing him a crafted pocket blade.'

'Actually, Trout…' begins Mrs Stamps. 'Would you mind terribly if I borrowed your mallet this evening please?'

'Err…I guess not,' answers Private Trout. 'What do you need that for…may I ask?'

Mrs Stamps pushes herself up, walks slowly towards Private Trout and places her soft hand gently on his shoulder.

'Well, it's just in case that killer rat comes back,' explains Mrs Stamps. 'This time I'll be ready for him.'

'Killer rat?' queries Private Trout.

'I told you!' yelps Private Myles, standing to his feet and waving the blade crazily around in front of his face. 'I told you a giant killer rat is loose around the village!'

'Yes-yes, Myles…calm down,' says Private Trout.

'You'll have to be very careful, Mrs Stamps. I heard killer rats eat brains for breakfast,' announces Private Myles.

Mrs Stamps places a hand over her mouth and lets out a joking gasp.

'Don't be so silly, Myles…' begins Private Trout. 'That is a ridiculous thought and—'

'Yes, that is an absolutely stupid thing to say—err…Milo is it?' interrupts Mrs Stamps.

'No, ma'am, it's Myles,' replies Private Myles.

'Well, My—les,' continues Mrs Stamps. 'Zombies eat brains – not giant killer rats. But in your case, I don't think it would matter either way.'

Private Trout and Mrs Stamps laugh uncontrollably.

Private Myles lowers his head and gets on with opening the paint tin using the blade. He sharply inserts it under the lid rim and with a flick of his wrist, the lid pops off; revealing a pale shade of blue paint.

Private Trout watches Private Myles pick up the tin of paint and a paintbrush. He continues to watch Private Myles stroll towards the front wall of the post office and waits in anticipation for him to make another clumsy or foolish mistake.

'Err…pardon me for noticing, Mrs Stamps. You seem to have rather a lot of dirty laundry piling up on your porch,' states Private Trout.

'Oh, tell me about it, Trout?' remarks Mrs Stamps.

'Do you need a hand to wash it?' asks Private Trout.

'Wash it? No-no, I don't need to wash it. The Laundry Fairy does all that. Although in saying that, she does seem to have gone missing.'

'The Laundry Fairy…?' questions Private Myles, sloshing a thick layer of blue paint across the front fascia of the post office.'

'Yes, who is this Laundry Fairy? And what do you mean, missing?' enquires Private Trout.

'Oh shoot! I've said too much,' reveals Mrs Stamps.

◆◆◆

As the sun begins to set over Baston, Timothy and the Reverend stroll casually around the village fountain, captivated by the amazing repair work the Corporal's men have conducted on it.

'I really must say, Timothy…our village is looking absolutely remarkable! Are we nearly ready?' asks the Reverend.

'Oh yes, I completely agree,' begins Timothy. 'It *really* does look different. Your Corporal friend and his men have done an absolute smashing job. I believe he mentioned earlier that there are still a few more tasks to finalise, but they'll be addressed in the morning.'

'Excellent,' replies the Reverend.

The Reverend tightly clutches his tunic and raises it slightly, before gracefully sitting himself down on the edge of the fountain. He dips his right hand into its crystal-clear waters and swirls the surface around with his fingertips. Timothy positions himself beside him and stares at their reflection in the water.

'I'm slightly worried though, Timothy,' says the Reverend, raising his hand from the water and giving it a shake.

'Worried?' replies Timothy.

'Yes…about the village being overwhelmed with masses of dirty laundry.'

Timothy turns towards the Reverend.

Most of the time Timothy is the type of person that only looks out for himself. His concern for others is practically non-existent, but the Reverend's sudden lack of compassion for the Laundry Fairy's well-being and safety, strangely grabs Timothy's attention.

'Surely you are worried about the whereabouts of our little Laundry Fairy?' questions Timothy, in an aggressive tone.

'What do you mean…?' responds the Reverend. 'Naturally I am.'

'You made it sound as if it's more important that our village is clear of dirty washing and not a moment's thought about the safety of our Laundry Fairy.'

'Oh…I didn't mean to sound so arrogant. I pray to our Lord that our Laundry Fairy is in good health. Please accept my apology.'

Timothy nods his head slowly in acceptance to the Reverend's answer.

'If the Laundry Fairy doesn't appear later tonight, Timothy, we'll proceed with what all of us discussed earlier and report this to Officer Locks…' begins the Reverend. 'I'm not too sure what he can do though. Nobody has ever seen the Laundry Fairy and so the Officer would not have much to go on. I mean, where would he even begin to start looking?'

'That is true,' mumbles Timothy. 'I feel it may—'

'But we really need to start thinking about what we are going to do with all this dirty laundry!' interrupts the Reverend. 'After talking earlier with the master at the wash-house, our village is simply going to be overwhelmed, with not just our laundry, but all-sorts of fabrics and linens from all over the area. It's been the Laundry Fairy that has been keeping the wash-house on top of things.'

'You don't believe that the wash-house will be able to cope without her?'

'No, Timothy, I really don't. The wash-house has nowhere near enough people to cope with it all. It will simply pile up. Just imagine the judge's faces on seeing piled up dirty laundry in our village.'

The Reverend stands to his feet, paces forward and glances out towards the tavern at the other side of the village. He cringes as he notices a laundry basket sitting outside; the laundry basket that belongs to Duncan.

'That's exactly what I'm talking about, look!' says the Reverend, in a raised voice and pointing across to Duncan's laundry basket.

Timothy joins the Reverend and stands beside him; his hands on his hips.

'Hmmm…yes. Now *that* is a real problem,' states Timothy. 'And going by what Mrs Stamps said earlier about her giant rat…if that be true, then that pile of Duncan's soils is surely not going to help.'

The Reverend and Timothy continue to stare at Duncan's laundry basket, which has started to attract a mass of flies and bugs. Some of the flies stop and rest atop Duncan's shirts, feeding off the sweat marks, as well as stains of beer and food. The laundry basket lets off a potent odour and a visible haze; a haze that grows larger by the hour.

'What are we going to do about it?' questions the Reverend. 'It's not just Duncan's laundry basket - it's also yours, mine and everyone elses that will eventually get to that state.'

'As you said before, Reverend. Let's wait to see if the Laundry Fairy appears tonight.'

The Reverend picks up his silver crucifix that hangs around his neck on a long chain. He brings it up to his lips and gives it a gentle kiss.

'I pray she does, Timothy,' mutters the Reverend.

The Reverend's spiritual embrace with the Lord is momentarily shortened by cheers and laughter coming from inside the tavern.

'They are having a good time,' states the Reverend.

'Yes, that'll be the Corporal and his men celebrating from a hard day's labour,' replies Timothy, squinting his eyes to gain focus through the tavern's window.

'The Corporal seems to be getting on very well with Melvin,' states Timothy.

'A little *too* well it looks like,' adds the Reverend. 'I swear the Corporal just grabbed Melvin and sat him upon his knee!'

'It certainly seems that way, doesn't it?'

'I'm not too sure what Melvin did or said to the Corporal earlier, but it must have been something amazing to soothe the Corporal's rage towards him.'

Timothy chuckles. 'Yeah, most likely cast a spell on him. Those spellbinders are always trying to make the world a better place.'

Timothy continues chuckling, while he observes Melvin trying to escape from the clutches of the Corporal's large and bulky arms.

'Next you'll be asking Melvin for his help in sorting out this laundry problem of ours,' continues Timothy.

'Interesting, Timothy…' responds the Reverend.

'Umm…what?'

The Reverend moves towards the tavern. A plan formulating in his head.

'Here's a crazy thought…' begins the Reverend. 'Why *don't* we ask for Melvin's assistance in tidying up this messy laundry? I'm sure he can cast a spell to make it all disappear, or even wash it for us. He did wreck our fountain…he can simply re-pay us for his unfortunate accident.'

‘Actually, Reverend, that is not a bad idea at all!’ yells Timothy. ‘If the Laundry Fairy *doesn’t* appear tonight, I’ll approach Melvin first thing in the morning. I’m sure he’ll assist if I keep mentioning our fountain.’

‘Excellent,’ replies the Reverend, rubbing the palms of his hands together.

CHAPTER IX

"I've always wondered about the person who discovered milk. I mean, what exactly was he or she doing with the cow at that precise moment?"

Officer Locks

Midnight arrives in Baston.

Corbin pushes a small wooden stool across the dusty floor towards the window. He leaps on top of the stool and uses all his strength to open two large wooden shutters; flooding the room with moonlight.

There's a slight bluish glow from the corner of the room; a glow that radiates from Edwin's magical cage, which currently holds the weakened Laundry Fairy, against her will.

Corbin steadies himself as he jumps back down to

the floor and watches his Master casually light a candle-wick with the touch of his finger. A slight breeze seeps into the room through small gaps in the roof, which causes the candle flame to flicker gently.

Edwin unclips his cloak, folds it in half and places it down carefully upon the bed mattress. He reaches up, removes his top hat and with the back of his hand attempts to brush off some dried mud that has settled on the top rim. Frustrated that his hat may be ruined, he throws it onto the bed, next to his cloak. Edwin sighs as he looks down at his boots and stamps them repeatedly on the wooden floorboards, in an attempt to remove the thick dried mud that has cocooned them.

'A few days ago, these boots were pristine…' begins Edwin. 'Now look at them!'

'Would you like me to give them a clean and polish, Master?' questions Corbin, rushing to his Master's feet and tugging at his crusty black bootlaces.

'No, Corbin – that can wait!' hisses Edwin.

'Master…?'

'I have more important things to worry about than my boots, Corbin – more important things indeed.'

Edwin takes a few small steps forward towards the corner of the room. He fixes his eyes on Amelia, who lay trembling on the bottom of the zynite cage. The moonlight shines through the cage's thin and narrow bars; illuminating her. Amelia gradually opens her eyes.

'Oh, she is awake, Master,' announces Corbin.

'I'm quite capable of using my own eyes, Corbin!' bellows Edwin.

Corbin scutters up behind his Master's legs, grips onto his Master's trouser fabric and peers gently around; fixing his stare on the captive Laundry Fairy.

'What now, Master?' asks Corbin, tilting his head.

'Well, Corbin. I think this fairy and I should have a little chat,' replies Edwin.

'Is there anything I can aid you with, Master?'

Edwin pauses, before crouching down towards Corbin. He pats him gently on his head and dislodges his little bobble hat slightly. Corbin promptly re-adjusts his hat and smiles at his Master.

'Yes, Corbin…' begins Edwin. 'I have one very important job for you.'

Corbin claps his hands together in anticipation and awaits his Master's instructions.

'I would like you to go to the stables and see to the stallions,' instructs Edwin. 'Please be careful not to be seen – especially after the incident last night with that crazy old lady at the post office – you could have got yourself killed!'

Corbin sighs. 'Yes, Master.'

'Off you go, then. Hurry-hurry!'

Corbin scutters towards the window, opens it and jumps out onto a narrow ledge.

'I didn't see you trying to help me as a pitchfork went past my head,' he mutters, sliding down a rusty drainpipe to the ground.

Edwin lifts himself back to his feet and steps closer to the Laundry Fairy.

'It's just you and me now…Amelia,' announces Edwin.

'*Wh*—what? How do you know my name…?' asks Amelia, struggling to find the strength to sit up straight.

'Let's just say, you are not the only fairy I have had the pleasure of capturing,' answers Edwin.

'Let me out of here!' sobs Amelia. 'Why are you doing this to me?'

'Oh…I will. Just as soon as you do a little something for me. Something of great ease for you.'

'I will never do anything for your kind! Never!' yells Amelia, before letting out a spluttering cough.

'My kind?' asks Edwin.

'Yes, your kind! A vampire! I hear tales of vampires hunting fairies for their magical abilities; tearing off their wings…leaving them for dead!'

Edwin paces forward. 'I can assure you I am not like that at all.'

'I don't believe you. Now let me out of this cage!'

'You see…' begins Edwin. 'I have but one humble request from you. If you honour my request – I will simply let you go and you will hear from me no more.'

Amelia slowly lifts herself to her feet and stumbles towards the front of the cage.

'And what request would that be?' asks Amelia.

Edwin turns, heads back to his cloak and removes a small rolled up parchment from a secret pocket in its inner lining. He carefully unrolls it and scans over the ancient text. He lifts his eyes and stares at Amelia.

'Well, it's like this…' begins Edwin, clearing his throat. 'Generations of my family have spent centuries trying to devise methods for us vampires to be able to walk out in the sunlight, without the risk of being turned into dust. It just so happens that my great grandfather had managed to come across some ancient text, allowing this vampire trait to be removed; lifting the curse. But it would involve the help of a certain style of magic – a magic that can only come from—'

'That can only come from a particular type of fairy,' interrupts Amelia.

'Precisely!' acknowledges Edwin. 'I have spent years researching the likes of many fairies, searching for that particular magic and then—then I read about you. So, let's cut to the chase – and if I can ask you to just read out these words and do your thing please. I assume I need to strip down to my underwear?'

'Your underwear?' queries Amelia.

'For you to wash my clothes,' responds Edwin.

'Why would you want me to wash your clothes?'

Edwin pauses and flicks across the text on the scroll, slightly confused.

'I'm expecting you to wash all my clothes in your magical suds – the magic will infuse into the fabric and my skin – allowing me to safely walk in the sunlight?'

Amelia chuckles. 'You think that's how it all works do you, vampire?'

'Please…the name's Edwin – and yes I thought that is how it works.'

'Well, you are completely wrong! Now please let me out of here!'

Edwin leans down towards the front of the cage and brings his face closer to Amelia. 'What do you mean, I'm wrong?' he asks.

Amelia shakes the cage in rage, but falls back to the floor in defeat. She lets out a long sigh.

'It's not the suds…' begins Amelia. 'That is just simply a bit of jazz on my part. I do not need to wash your clothes, Edwin. But you are right in saying that I do have a certain type of magic – and also your great grandfather is correct in—'

'Was,' interrupts Edwin.

'Sorry?' replies Amelia.

'He *was*…you said, "Is." You see – he had a rather unfortunate and un-timely death, that to date, many of my family still humour themselves with.'

'He probably deserved it!' snaps Amelia, as she

thinks about tales her family have told about what vampires did to *her* past generations.

'Not everyone deserves it!' hisses Edwin. 'Especially not from tripping over a large boulder and impaling themselves on a wooden garden post, after a drunken night out!'

Amelia gasps in horror at the thought.

'Anyway…as I was saying – your great grandfather *was* correct. I can help you,' states Amelia.

'Great news. Okay, well let's get this—'

'But I won't…'

'Why is that?'

'Because, I assume that parchment you are holding contains written enchants from a very old vampire coven; one that divulges in the darkest of magic…The Sycen?'

'Your assumption is correct,' answers Edwin.

'And I'm guessing that I would be required to read out the words, so the magic is drawn out of me to cure this curse of yours?'

'Your guess would *also* be correct.'

'If I mess with such magic, I could be killed,' states Amelia, turning her back to Edwin. 'That is why I won't do it!'

Edwin rolls up the parchment and places it carefully into his trouser pocket. 'Then…you leave me no other choice. You have forced my hand.'

'What do you mean?'

'You wouldn't want anything to happen to…well, let's say to your brothers and sisters, would you now?'

'WHAT HAVE YOU DONE WITH THEM?' screams Amelia. 'How did you ever find them?'

'Oh, they are safe – for now – and will remain safe if you give into my simple request. How I found them is of no relevance to the topic in discussion.'

Amelia grabs hold of the cage bars with both hands and tries to muster a little strength to shake the cage, while cursing under her breath at Edwin.

There is a knock at the window.

Edwin turns and hisses at Corbin's smirk little face staring back at him through the clouded glass. Edwin momentarily gazes at Amelia, before turning to open the window and letting Corbin back into the room.

'Were you seen, Corbin?' asks Edwin.

'No, Master,' replies Corbin, catching his breath.

Edwin gentle nods, carefully closes the window and proceeds back to Amelia, who sobs quietly in the cage.

'You have until tomorrow midnight to make up your mind,' whispers Edwin. 'If not, then…well, let's just hope that *then,* doesn't come.'

Corbin scutters across the floor and smirks at Amelia.

'But for now, I must feed. I have a sudden craving for some fresh—'

'Broccoli, Master?' interrupts Corbin.

'No Corbin. Not broccoli,' hisses Edwin, as he instantly transforms into his bat form and darts off towards the window.

THUD!

Edwin hits the window pane and falls to the dusty floor below; the sudden impact forcing him back into human form.

'Darn it!' exclaims Edwin. 'That's the second time I've done that this week!'

◆◆◆

Melvin lifts the bulky arm of Corporal Ringelstein with all his might and raises it high above his head. He stops momentarily to take a deep breath, before rolling out from underneath the arm and lowering it carefully to the floor. The Corporal twitches and mumbles some random words. Melvin pauses and remains still, hoping not to have awoken the Corporal, who in the last few hours, Melvin has been in very close company with.

The Corporal yawns and shifts his body. Melvin quickly jumps to his feet, straightens his hat and wipes his robe with the back of his hand, attempting to dry off the damp patches of spilt honey mead and wine that have accumulated there throughout the evening.

He carefully steps over the Corporal, who along with all his men, lay passed out on the floor of the tavern; a result of a lengthy celebratory session, fuelled by vast amounts of Duncan's honey mead and some old casks of wine found in the tavern's cellar.

Duncan snores loudly. With his mouth wide open, a long trail of his drool flows slowly over his bottom lip and oozes onto the bar counter.

'Hello, Melv!' yells Dexter, letting out a huge grin and holding a rather large tankard of honey mead with both his claws.

'Shush! Be quiet will you, Dex…? You'll wake everyone up – especially the Corporal,' replies Melvin, trying to keep his audio levels at a minimum.

'Fine-fine. Anyway—*hic*—why all the creeping about?' queries Dexter, struggling to maintain his natural posture and balance.

'Are you drunk, Dex?'

'Define drunk, Melv? I feel perfectly fine—*hic.*'

'Hmmm, I don't believe you. Anyway – can't stop. I must try to find Amelia.'

'Do you think she'll show up?'

'I don't know, Dex. I have to try though.'

Dexter carefully places his tankard of honey mead onto the tavern floor and creeps around the head of Private Myles, narrowly missing him with the end of his tail.

'Then what precisely are you going—*hic*—to do?' slurs Dexter.

'Sit outside and wait, that's all I can do. I'll use my watch and see if she turns up. Other than that, I'm really not sure what else to do.'

Dexter lowers his head and pats Melvin on his arm.

'I'll be right—*hic*—here if needed, Melv,' adds Dexter, watching Melvin exit the tavern.

THERE IS A BRILLIANT FLASH OF LIGHT.
THE AIR HUMS.

Melvin waits and time ticks away…

After several hours of waiting patiently outside the village tavern, Melvin realises that what Eric had said to him earlier was perhaps right; the Laundry Fairy is missing. A small tear begins to roll down Melvin's cheek, which he promptly wipes away with the side of his forefinger.

The moon casts its eerie shine over the village as Melvin glances across at the many laundry baskets and boxes, which still remain untouched from the previous night. A festering stench fills the cold night air.

Melvin lets out a long sigh and begins to ponder on what else he can do; failing to formulate any plan at all. He lowers his head, stares down at the pocket watch he holds tightly in his hand and watches the intricate mechanism slowly tick away. The small cogs rotate and mesh with the gears. Suddenly they all stop and Melvin is released from his time slowed trance.

He reaches down and grips the small dial on the watch, between two fingers. After a moment's pause, he snaps the pocket watch closed and returns it to his robe pocket.

Standing up, Melvin straightens his robe and paces back towards the entrance of the tavern.

Duncan awakens to the sound of the tavern's door opening. He pushes himself up off the bar, stretches his chubby arms up into the air and lets out a long yawn, before stumbling backwards.

Catching the edge of the counter with his hand, Duncan finds his balance and leans up against the back wall. He lets out a huge belch as he watches Melvin stroll across the tavern floor; observing him step over the mass of bodies carelessly sprawled out around him.

'Melvin, you've returned. Had any luck?' questions Dexter, struggling to remain upright.

Melvin turns slowly towards Dexter and lowers his head in disappointment.

'Oh…' adds Dexter, following Melvin slowly up the wooden stairs to the second floor of the tavern.

Melvin pauses at the top of the stairs and turns to face a square framed mirror hanging off the hallway wall. He smiles as he stares at his reflection, before reaching forward and re-orientating the frame to a more level position.

A distant door closing, followed by the sound of footsteps coming down the hallway, startles Melvin and Dexter.

'Oh, pardon me,' says Edwin, taking a small bow towards Melvin. 'A very good—well, early morning to you…oh…and your small dragon there also,' he adds, noticing Dexter.

'Hello. Good morning to you also,' replies Melvin.

'Ah…a spellbinder,' states Edwin, staring Melvin up and down.

'I am. Pardon me…and you are?' asks Melvin.

'Edwin…Edwin Von Lysander.'

Melvin holds out his hand towards Edwin, who refrains from engaging in a manly handshake; deciding to place his hands casually behind his back. Melvin slowly lowers his hand and lightly shrugs his shoulders at Dexter.

'You seem to be having a slight nose bleed there, Edwin,' comments Melvin, pointing his finger at a small trail of blood trickling over Edwin's lips.

'Oh, excuse me. I get them sometimes…' begins Edwin. 'It's all the flying—I mean travelling that I do!'

'I see,' responds Melvin.

'Anyway, a pleasure to meet you both,' says Edwin, hurryingly. 'I must clean up. A good morrow to you.'

Melvin and Dexter move aside as Edwin slides elegantly past them both and walks down the stairs.

Dexter gasps, covers his jaw with both of his claws and adjusts his enlarged eyes towards Melvin. Edwin glances back with penetrating eyes at Dexter, who smiles gently back at Edwin as he disappears from view.

'Rather scruffy looking fellow, if I say so myself,' says Melvin. 'All covered in mud and blood.'

'Did you just see that?' says Dexter, tugging gently at Melvin's robe.

'See what…?'

'Exactly! You didn't see anything, did you?'

'What in blazes are you talking about, Dex?'

Dexter leans forward and checks down the stairs for any sign of Edwin, before prompting Melvin to lower his posture down to Dexter's level.

'That, Edwin. He had no reflection in the mirror.'

Melvin briefly turns towards the mirror and then slowly back towards Dexter.

'Don't be so darn ridiculous…' begins Melvin. 'I'm thinking that perhaps someone has had one too many drinks, don't you?'

'I know what I saw, Melv – and I saw nothing!'

Melvin removes his hat and scratches his head in confusion. 'I'm too tired to argue, Dex. I just want to get some sleep.'

Dexter pauses…

'Ah, you're right, Melv…' begins Dexter, exhaling a large breath. 'I'm probably just seeing things. My mind playing those nasty tricks on me again, huh?'

Most likely, Dex – most likely!' responds Melvin, turning around and heading towards their room.

Dexter stands in front of the mirror and waves his claws slowly in front of it; checking his own reflection.

'What was I thinking?' mutters Dexter, to himself, following Melvin down the hallway. 'Maybe he was one of them vampire type people I've heard about?' says Dexter, chuckling loudly. 'I hear that *they* don't have reflections.'

Melvin's eyes widen.

'A vampire you say…?' queries Melvin, pushing the room door slowly open.

'Yes…' begins Dexter. 'Am I right – they don't have reflections?'

There's a moment's pause as Melvin closes the door slowly and quietly behind Dexter.

'That they don't, Dex,' states Melvin, before taking a deep breath. 'That – they – don't.'

◆◆◆

The morning sun begins to rise and the church bell strikes eight times. The heavens open up and the rain pelts down hard on the roof of the village hall.

Timothy stands at his office window, holding a hot cup of elderflower tea; cupping both his hands gently around his cup. He lets out a small chuckle, while watching the Reverend comically race across the village green towards him; hopping and skipping over patches of soddened grass as he shields his face from the cold pounding rain.

Timothy blows across the top of his cup to cool the surface of his hot tea, before sipping at it gently. He casually walks across to his front door, unlocks it and waits aside for the Reverend to enter.

As the Reverend pushes the door wide open, the heightened sound of the rain hitting the wooden veranda, fills the room momentarily. The sound is instantly muffled as the Reverend firmly closes the door behind him.

'Good weather for ducks this morning,' states the Reverend, shaking the raindrops off his tunic and adjusting his hair. 'I see you've got some hot tea on the go…would you mind?'

'Not at all, Reverend. Please, help yourself,' replies Timothy. 'I also assume that you have checked your laundry this morning, Reverend?'

'I most certainly have – nothing's changed. I even had to bring it inside to stop it from getting soaked and shrinking. I never knew laundry could be so heavy.'

'Then…as discussed, I think a little visit to Officer Locks, is in order. We must also think about what we are going to do about all this laundry that is piling up. The villagers are constantly on my case about it all. I don't know what else to tell them.'

'Absolutely, Timothy – with all the judges arriving tomorrow for the judging of the village – we don't have much time at all.'

Timothy gently nods and stares blankly out of the window.

'I just hope this rain subsides,' adds the Reverend. 'The Corporal's men still have a few minor jobs to do around the village.'

The Reverend paces towards Timothy and stands aside him, as he stares into nothingness. He ponders on how the day would pan out and more importantly, how the village will be judged tomorrow.

'Oh, my dear Lord! What on Earth is she wearing?' howls the Reverend, pointing through the window pane at Mrs Stamps as she trudges across the village green from the post office.

Timothy shifts forward. 'They have got to be the biggest pair of boots I have ever seen. Look…they certainly beat the Corporals!'

'They are bigger than her whole legs, aren't they? That can't be normal, can it?' questions the Reverend.

'Yes – and if she isn't careful, that extremely large umbrella she is desperately clinging onto is going to put her airborne, if the wind catches it right.'

Timothy follows Mrs Stamps with his eyes as she attempts to step up onto Timothy's veranda, in the most elegant way possible.

'What on Earth is she doing?' begins Timothy. 'She can't even step up onto the veranda in them boots.'

The Reverend chuckles. 'What a silly old—'

'TIMOTHY!' shrieks Mrs Stamps. 'Timothy, open that door at once! I believe we have an engagement with Officer Locks? Stop messing about!'

'No rest, huh, Reverend?' sighs Timothy.

'You're right there, Timothy,' states the Reverend. 'Come on, we'd better head across – see what Officer Locks can do for us.'

Timothy grabs his overcoat from a hook on the wall. Alongside the Reverend, he paces out hurriedly to greet Mrs Stamps, who waits very patiently outside. Together they battle the treacherous rain and cross the village towards a stone building known as The Lockup.

Baston does not have a typical jailhouse, like many of the surrounding towns and villages, but it does have a tiny room where the local lawman resides, and all the naughty people get sent.

'Well, it looks like someone is in,' states Mrs Stamps, battling with her umbrella and resting it up against the stone wall of the jail.

She thumps hard on the large framed wooden door and waits for any response.

'GO AWAY!' shouts a muffled voice from inside.

Mrs Stamps steps back slightly in shock and turns to Timothy for any answer to why the local lawman would be telling people to go away.

'Here, let me try,' says Timothy, shifting forward and banging a few more times on the door. 'Open up, Officer. It's me…Timothy. It's rather cold and wet out here.'

'It's really not a good time right now. Please go away,' responds the voice.

Timothy turns to Mrs Stamps and then towards the Reverend. He shrugs his shoulders.

'*LET US IN!*' bellows Mrs Stamps, banging hard on the door repeatedly.

There's a long pause and then the sudden twist of a key in a lock, followed by a latch dropping. The door creaks open.

'Ah…there you are, Officer,' says Mrs Stamps. 'Well, don't willy-nilly about – let us in!'

'Mrs Stamps…' begins Officer Locks. 'What do I owe the pleasure…? Mr Stamps doing naughty things with the mail again, is he?'

'No-no, nothing like that. But we need to talk – so move aside and let us in,' replies Mrs Stamps.

Officer Locks is a very skinny man; with not an ounce of fat upon his body. He sports a bushy beard, complete with an excessive amount of hair on his arms and back. His clothes show rips and tears that have been repeatedly repaired.

'Good morning, Reverend…morning Timothy,' adds Officer Locks, ushering them and Mrs Stamps inside the building, before closing the door slowly behind him.

'Well, I'll cut to the chase, Officer…' begins Mrs Stamps, peering around the dainty little room, which is barely large enough to accommodate all four of them. 'Our Laundry Fairy – she's gone missing.'

Officer Locks chuckles, 'Missing you say? How so?'

'For the last few days our laundry that we've left out has—' begins Timothy.

'Has not been washed at all – and it's now beginning to stink – and I'm desperately running out of fresh clothes to wear!' interrupts Mrs Stamps, while giving Timothy a piercing and satisfying stare.

'This is the same for everyone else in the village?' asks Officer Locks.

'Yes,' responds Mrs Stamps.

Officer Locks leans himself against an upturned wooden crate and ponders the thought; scratching the side of his head gently.

'How very interesting,' he states. 'I really can't think

of a single moment since I've been in the village, where I've had reports of our fairy friend going missing.'

'That's absolutely correct,' remarks Mrs Stamps, crossing her arms together in front of her. 'So, what are you going to do about it, Officer?'

'Pray deeply I would say,' chuckles Officer Locks, turning to the Reverend and winking slyly. 'But in all honesty – I'm really not sure what you would like me to do?' I would really struggle to start investigating and looking for someone that nobody has ever seen. I can try filing a missing person's report, but the information will be rather limited. It seems silly reporting a person as missing, if we have never seen or met them, doesn't it? That would just make us all look ridiculous.'

'Can you not just go out and look for her using your detective-like skills?' enquires Mrs Stamps.

'Oh, yes…sure thing, Mrs Stamps,' replies Officer Locks. 'I'll just nip into the pouring rain right now, with a torch, a whistle and a Laundry Fairy tracking device – we'll find her in no time.'

'Really? Splendid!' glees Mrs Stamps.

'No, Mrs Stamps, I can't. I don't think that such a device even exists, let alone me owning one. However, Eric would certainly be more than interested in that concept, don't you think?'

'So, are you saying that there is nothing at all you can do for us, Officer?' asks the Reverend.

Officer Locks stands to his feet, walks slowly across to a small wooden table and pours himself a mug full of warm cow's milk from a large ceramic jug. He raises the mug to his mouth and takes several gulps of the creamy liquid, before pausing; savouring the taste.

'Do you know…? I've always wondered about the person who discovered milk. I mean, what exactly was he or she doing with the cow at that precise moment?' questions Officer Locks.

'Err...' replies Timothy, shrugging his shoulders and wondering why Officer Locks had asked such a random question.

'Interesting thought that,' adds the Reverend.

'Really, gentlemen? I can tell you exactly what that person was doing...they we're—' begins Mrs Stamps.

'*Ahem,* I don't think we need to know the specific details, Mrs Stamps,' interrupts the Reverend.

Officer Locks nods gently and raises his mug once more to consume the last few mouthfuls of milk. He places the empty mug back onto the table and goes into deep thought.

'So, let's think about this logically...' begins Officer Locks. 'You're telling me that you believe our Laundry Fairy has gone missing and that we have no idea where she could be at all? Which I accept, as we have no idea where she comes from or even resides when not doing the washing. Now...this makes it very difficult for us to even think about where to start looking.'

'I agree completely,' states the Reverend.

'But we must start somewhere, Officer,' bellows Mrs Stamps. 'All this laundry that has piled up is not going to wash itself, is it?'

'I understand that completely, Mrs Stamps, I really do,' responds Officer Locks. 'But shouting and cursing about it is not going to help the situation at all, is it?'

Timothy turns to the Reverend and lets out a gentle smile, which suddenly turns into a smirk.

'I'm afraid that Mrs Stamps is kind of right in a way, Officer...' begins Timothy.

'How so...?' asks Officer Locks, turning towards Timothy and raising an eyebrow at him.'

'Well, you see…tomorrow we are being judged for the *Village of the Year Award* and—'

'Ah, that old malarkey!' interrupts Officer Locks. 'I was wandering what all the fuss with the village was about – all this sudden—well, maintenance.'

'Yes – and as I was saying…' continues Timothy. 'The village is covered in a mass of unwashed laundry and its appearance, as well as its vile smell, is starting to become of a real concern. It certainly is not going to go down too well with the judges tomorrow. If we don't locate the Laundry Fairy soon and find out what the problem is, then the village will have a dilemma of monstrous proportions on its hands as we all run out of fresh and clean laundry.'

'Why don't we just take it all to the wash-house?' queries Officer Locks, with a slight look of confusion.

'I believe that is not possible. Samuel has already stated that he's running at full capacity and struggling enough as it is.'

Officer Locks leans up against the side of the one-man cell and grips his hands onto its thick iron bars. 'Well, it seems like we have two problems here…' he states. 'And you mentioned that the judges for this competition are arriving tomorrow?'

'Yes,' replies Timothy, worriedly.

'Then we really do not have a lot of time to spare,' announces Officer Locks. 'I suggest that firstly, you address our *actual* dirty laundry problem, while I formulate some sort of plan in trying to find out what has happened to our Laundry Fairy.'

'And how do you propose that we do that, Officer?' snaps Mrs Stamps. 'It's not like we've all got some magic wand that we can wave about everywhere and make it all go away, is it?'

Timothy turns to the Reverend and lets out another smirk, knowing that there could potentially be a simple solution to one of their problems. He pauses for a few moments to conclude that his earlier thought of getting Melvin to assist, could actually work. His eyes widen.

'Timothy, are you okay?' asks the Reverend.

'Hmmm…? Oh, yes. I was just having a little think,' replies Timothy.

'Care to share your thoughts?' asks Officer Locks.

Timothy steps forward and slowly glances around at Officer Locks, the Reverend and Mrs Stamps; holding eye contact with them briefly.

'Ah, I assume you are thinking about what we talked about before, Timothy?' questions the Reverend.

'Yes, I am indeed,' answers Timothy.

'Do you actually believe that he will assist in helping us with this problem?' adds the Reverend.

'I'm sure he will. I can't—'

'What are you both blabbering on about?' interrupts Mrs Stamps, placing her hands firmly on her hips.

'I'm thinking – why don't we just ask Melvin to give us a helping hand with our dirty laundry problem?' announces Timothy, letting out a slight smile.

'Melvin?' queries Mrs Stamps. 'Don't be so stupid Timothy. He can't do washing clothes – he wouldn't even know where to begin!'

'Yes-yes, Mrs Stamps, you may be right there, but what he can do – and I hear he is very good at…is spellbinding.'

Officer Locks pulls in closer to the conversation.

'Are you really suggesting, Timothy, that we ask this spellbinder to conjure up some sort of spell to help us clean up the village of our dirty laundry?' asks Officer Locks.

'I certainly am!' gloats Timothy.

'That's actually a splendid idea,' glees Mrs Stamps.

'And you believe that he will aid us, do you?' asks Officer Locks, interestingly.

'Oh, you leave that dear old fool to me,' says Mrs Stamps, rubbing her hands together softly. 'I have my ways in getting what I want,' she adds.

Everyone stares momentarily at Mrs Stamps.

'Err, well…that potentially solves *that* issue, then…' begins Officer Locks. 'I will continue to think about how I can be of further assistance in locating our Laundry Fairy.'

Everyone gently nods.

'Err…Officer?' asks the Reverend. 'Have you had a slight hair cut this morning?'

'Huh?' responds Officer Locks.

'You've got hair all over the floor, look!' states the Reverend. 'Quite an excessive amount of it – and why is there a shackle around your ankle?'

'Oh, Reverend…?' begins Timothy, whispering into the Reverend's ear. 'You remember I once told you that the Officer is rather sensitive to the moonlight?'

Timothy pulls back and winks slyly at the Reverend.'

'You did?' questions the Reverend, with a void look on his face.

'Yes,' mumbles Timothy, trying to refrain from getting Officer Locks' attention. 'Especially when the moon is out and at its fullest,' he adds, while winking uncontrollably.

'Oh…yes, I remember now,' mutters the Reverend, feeling slightly embarrassed.

'Well, I believe time is of the essence,' states Officer Locks, calmly ushering Timothy, Mrs Stamps and the Reverend out of the door and into the pouring rain.

'I'll go and find Melvin at once,' announces Mrs Stamps, wading across the green in her over-sized boots and holding tightly onto her umbrella.

'She looks like one of them weird knights…' begins Timothy. 'You know? The sort that do those jousting tournaments.'

The Reverend chuckles, before he bursts into loud laughter at the thought of Mrs Stamps riding a horse, while wearing those gigantic boots of hers.

◆◆◆

Duncan knocks several times on the door to Melvin's room; the loud bangs resonate through the upper walls of the tavern. He waits patiently for any response, while adjusting his shirt and hair, in an attempt to make himself look a little more presentable.

Duncan has never been truly sober. He rarely gives the alcohol in his body any chance of dispersing, before filling his fat gut again with more honey mead and starting the cycle off once more. However, this fine morning, Duncan is sounding rather coherent.

'Err…hello? *Mr Wizard Man,* are you there?' says Duncan, softly through the door. There is no reply. Duncan ponders a few moments and tries knocking a second time. 'Hello, are you in there, *Mr Pointy Hat Magic Man*? It's Duncan the Tavern Keeper. I have a very anxious person downstairs who wants to see you.'

The sound of rummaging feet and shuffles are heard from inside the room, followed by a moment of silence.

'Who is it?' bellows Melvin. 'I'm really not in the mood to talk to anyone today – thank you very much.'

'Forgive me, *Mr Sparkly Man* – but it seems very

important. It's the woman from the post office. She needs to speak to you urgently.'

'Oh, blast it!' yells Melvin. 'What does she want?'

'I have no idea. Shall I tell her to go away?'

'No. I'm coming, darn it! Oh, is that Corporal fellow still down there by any chance?'

'Yes, he is passed out next to the fireplace.'

'Ah good,' replies Melvin, unlocking the door and opening it slowly. 'Oh…and out of pure interest – I met another of your guests earlier – Edwin is it?'

'Oh, yes…Edwin, staying just down the hall there,' responds Duncan. 'Unusual fellow he is – haven't seen him too much of late.'

Melvin pops his head out of his door and peers down the hallway. 'I see, right…'

'Shall I tell that Stamps woman that you are coming down?' asks Duncan, as he paces towards the stairs.

'No, I'll come down with you right this moment,' answers Melvin, while muttering some sentences, that include the words *bothersome*, *blasted* and *sanity*.

Melvin takes his time as he wanders down the wooden stairs to the ground floor of the tavern.

'Ah, Mrs Stamps, I understand you wanted to see me about an important matter?' enquires Melvin.

'Yes, Melvin – that I do. How are you this pleasant morning?' responds Mrs Stamps, leaning herself up against the bar counter.

Melvin narrows his eyes and tries to deduce exactly what Mrs Stamps wants from him at this time of the morning. He cautiously strolls towards her; cautious of whether she would require something intellectual from him, or something a little more personal and intimate. The thought of the latter makes him edgy and nervous.

'I've had better days, thank you,' responds Melvin.

'Anything I can do to make it better? A hug maybe?' says Mrs Stamps.

Melvin cringes at the unpleasant thought of Mrs Stamps engulfing her arms around him and takes a small step backwards, wrapping his own arms around himself, in a sort of pathetic defensive stance.

'That will not be necessary, Mrs Stamps…' begins Melvin. 'Anyway, what can I do for you?'

'Well, we have a little bit of a problem here in the village – and Timothy, the Reverend and I thought that *maybe* you would be able to help us out with it?'

With a befuddled and confused look, Melvin stares directly at Mrs Stamps. He takes a few moments to process what it could possibly be that would require Mrs Stamps to ask for his assistance, let alone the mayor of the village and its Reverend.

'I think I know what you are about to say, Mrs Stamps,' explains Melvin. 'To be honest, I must politely refuse. I don't have the time to worry about your stupid popping corn business ventures with Timothy and the Reverend. I have much more important matters to worry about at the present. Please apologise to the others for me, but I must concentrate my efforts on other things today.'

'What in blazes are you rambling on about, Melvin? I'm not talking about the stupid corn.'

Mrs Stamps raises herself off the bar counter and takes a few steps towards Melvin, who starts to twiddle his fingers in nervousness.

'I need your skills, Melvin – your magical abilities…' begins Mrs Stamps. 'As you are no doubt aware, we have the judges arriving today for the competition – this afternoon if I recall the Reverend correctly. We need to create a good impression. So we were—'

‘Oh, not a chance, Mrs Stamps! I really would like to aid you with some elaborate fireworks display this evening – and all the jazz to go with it, but—’

‘Fireworks? I’m not talking about ruddy fireworks, Melvin!’ interrupts Mrs Stamps. ‘I’m talking about all the mess outside. The villager’s unwashed laundry.’

Melvin casts his eyes across the tavern. He stares through the glass of the front window at the mass of laundry baskets and containers still sitting outside the buildings in the village. Each and every basket, buzzes with bugs and flies.

Melvin sighs, realising that this wouldn’t be the case if Amelia hadn’t gone missing. He turns back towards Mrs Stamps, who continues to look Melvin in the eyes, awaiting a response.

‘Okay…and what about the villager’s dirty laundry?’ asks Melvin.

‘I’m saying it doesn’t look good as a first impression for the judges – plus it’s also starting to smell extremely bad. The amount of complaints that Timothy has received from the villagers is ridiculous. In fact, my washing pile is getting—well…unbalanced.’

‘What would you like me to do about it all? Get my washboard out and scrub the day away? I can assure you that I will refuse to do anything of the sorts! Surely the village wash-house can help? I saw it as I arrived the other day.’

Melvin pauses, knowing perfectly well the reason why the villagers’ dirty washing has not been cleaned, and concludes that Mrs Stamps is also aware of the fact. He also sums up that Mrs Stamps would surely not have any knowledge of his recent rendezvous with the Laundry Fairy. Melvin decides to play dumb with Mrs Stamps.

'The wash-house is short staffed and struggling to maintain all the other washing that is coming in,' says Mrs Stamps. 'Our Laundry Fairy would have addressed their washing also – she is just being lazy.'

Melvin's skin prickles.

'Don't you talk about her like that!' yells Melvin, as he ushers Mrs Stamps to the other side of the room, to prevent her waking the drunken mass of the Corporal and his men, who still lay spread out across the floor.

'What do you mean…her?' questions Mrs Stamps.

'Amelia…oh darn it! I shouldn't have said that. I really shouldn't have said that.'

'Who is Amelia…?'

'Amelia is…she is the Laundry Fairy.'

Mrs Stamps gasps.

'You *know* her? How do you know her?' continues Mrs Stamps, getting right up in Melvin's face.

'Shush woman, keep it quiet!' retorts Melvin, peering back over his shoulder. 'You'll wake everyone.'

'You must know where she is, then? Tell me now Melvin… or I swear I'll hang you up by your—'

'I don't know where she is,' interrupts Melvin.

'You don't? Hmmm…'

'I don't,' replies Melvin. 'But I may have an idea,' he mutters, staring up at the ceiling.

For the next few moments, Mrs Stamps rallies off question after question to Melvin, trying to establish the *ins and outs* of how Melvin met the Laundry Fairy and what he knows about her disappearance. Melvin replies to Mrs Stamps by simply returning yes and no answers, much to Mrs Stamps' frustration.

'Bah! I give up even trying, Melvin…' begins Mrs Stamps. 'So…are you going to help us or not?'

There is a slight pause as Mrs Stamps gives Melvin

a loving smile, followed by a flashing of her puppy dog eyes; a skill which Mrs Stamps uses frequently in order to get her own way.

'Err…I'm not sure I should be interfering with her work. Besides…I have already caused too much of a mess here in the—'

'Pretty please, Melvy,' adds Mrs Stamps, fluttering her eyelashes and puckering her lips.

Melvin nervously strokes his beard.

'Oh, darn it! Okay-okay. I'll do it,' announces Melvin. 'But I'm not doing this for you, Timothy or the Reverend.'

'You're not?' asks Mrs Stamps.

'No…I'm doing it for Amelia. Give me a while to prepare my mind – and I'll meet you by the fountain.'

Mrs Stamps smiles and skips out of the front door of the tavern. 'Still got it,' she mumbles to herself.

'Melvin, is that you…?' says the Corporal, still half asleep on the floor.

'Err…nope…this is—is err…' responds Melvin, before quickly retreating out of the building and making himself scarce.

CHAPTER X

"I'm just like a copper-coin filled fruit machine. A winner on every sneeze!"

Dexter

'Well that's just a stupid and ridiculous idea, Melvin!' curses Timothy, treading across the village green and glancing around at all the glamour and glory of his newly overhauled village. He pays particular attention to the recently repaired fountain.

Melvin strolls slowly behind, occasionally speeding up to a more skipping like motion, in order to keep up pace with Timothy.

'You do realise, Melvin…' begins Timothy. 'That in several hours – we are expecting the judges to arrive to judge our village for the competition – and you want everyone, including the wash-house itself, to bring all of their dirty laundry and pile it all up – right here – in the centre of the village? Are you insane?'

'Yes, that's absolutely correct!' answers Melvin, coming to a halt next to Timothy.

'To which?' responds Timothy.

'Probably both,' expresses Melvin, letting out a tiny smirk and adjusting his hat back into position.

Timothy grins at Melvin's carefree and relaxed response.

'Well, look at it like this…' begins Melvin, placing his hands firmly into his robe pockets. 'You—well, Mrs Stamps, came to me and asked for my assistance with *your* problem. So here I am – trying to help. I can, just as easily walk away.'

Timothy sighs. 'I must admit, Melvin, that is true,' he replies, as he turns on the spot and *eyes up* masses of dirty laundry baskets, scattered across the village.

Timothy tries to picture how the village would look without them in place and smiles knowing that if they can be cleared, or better still washed, then the village may have a good chance of winning the competition. It would also stop Mrs Stamps from moaning at him constantly, and…the majority of the village.

◆◆◆

Amongst the darkest shadows within room four of the tavern, Edwin lay fast asleep atop the metal bed. He positions himself perfectly straight down the length of the mattress, completely mute and with no signs of movement. He truly looks at peace.

The gentle flicker of a candle flame shines just

enough light into the room to illuminate the outline of Edwin's body; the low light occasionally reflecting off the buffed shiny buttons of his waistcoat.

Slowly, the light in the room begins to fade as the last few strands of candlewick burn. They sizzle gently in the molten wax and leave a charred and burnt smell in the air.

Corbin opens his eyes and peers into the darkness that has overcome the room. He gives himself a few moments for his eyes to adjust, before picking himself up from the floor and creeping slowly and quietly towards his Master's wooden chest.

Corbin reaches out and feels his way across the lid of the chest. He grips it tightly in his right hand and slowly pushes it open, being careful not to cause any unnecessary sound that would wake his Master.

Rummaging around inside the chest, Corbin pulls out a fresh candle and stares at it briefly, before scuttering across to the table and jabbing it down into the warm wax left by the previous candle. He reaches out with his finger and pokes the candle into a more vertical position. He squints his eyes and tilts his head slightly to check the candle's orientation.

Corbin returns to his Master's chest and picks up the ceramic pot containing the living flame; using it cautiously to ignite the new candlewick. The room is immediately flooded with light, which casts shadows that dance across the walls. Corbin carefully returns the living flame back inside the chest and pushes it tightly down into his Master's belongings, to prevent it falling over, or worse still, falling over and opening.

Corbin turns to face his Master and smiles, knowing that he has managed not to stir or wake him. He quietly scutters to the other corner of the room and stares piercingly into the magical zynite cage, to observe a very weakened Amelia, laying asleep on her side. He pauses, before sliding his hand through the thin bars and giving her a gentle poke.

Amelia lets out a slight grunt. Corbin smiles and retracts his hand from the cage.

His playfulness is interrupted by some loud shouts and voices from outside. He immediately shifts his attention to the window shutters, before rushing over to a wooden stool and jumping up upon it. He pauses; intrigued at what all the commotion outside could be.

Shuffling his little feet forward across the top of the stool, he reaches up and places his hands on the two large wooden shutters. The small gap between them lets a very thin shard of sunlight shine into the room; it cuts through the dusty air and leaves a slithery beam across the floor.

Corbin hesitates, knowing that if he attempts to even slightly open the shutters, the room could be flooded with sunlight, which would surely be the end of his Master; leaving him as a huge pile of dust upon the mattress.

'Open it! Do us all a favour,' murmurs Amelia, from the corner of the room.

'Oh, hello. You're awake, then?' replies Corbin, in a softened tone. He turns to face Amelia. 'Now, be quiet, or you'll wake my Master,' he adds.

Amelia turns her back to Corbin and groans in pain as she re-positions her body.

Still concerned at the noises from outside, Corbin plants his gaunt face up against one of the shutters, narrows an eye and tries to focus through the gap.

Outside on the green, the majority of the village inhabitants gather around a monumental pile of smelly and dirty laundry; various attires stacked up high, nearly reaching the height of the cast iron weather vane on top of the church.

Corbin squints an eye and then immediately widens it again at the sight of Melvin and Timothy directing the last few baskets of dirty laundry to the top of the pile. He gasps as he observes Mrs Stamps darting across the village green at full pace. Corbin tilts his head slightly to the side and continues to follow her, until the shutters block his view and she disappears from sight.

He pulls himself away from the shutters and takes a small step backwards on the wooden stool; watching carefully not to fall off the edge. He pauses briefly, before turning towards Amelia, deep in thought.

After a few moments, Corbin slowly turns his head to look at his Master and checks that he is still asleep. He carefully reaches up to a handle on one of the shutters and grips it tightly in one hand. He follows with his other hand, clutches onto an iron latch and lifts the latch very quietly off its catch-plate. It makes a muffling pinging sound as it releases.

'NO, CORBIN! What do you think you are doing?' shrieks Edwin, quickly shifting to an upright position and stretching across the bed towards the shutters; forcing them both closed with his bony hands.

'Oh, Master…I wasn't—I mean, I only wanted to open them a—'

'Silence, Corbin!' yells Edwin. 'I don't care about what you think you wanted. It only takes the smallest gust of wind and those shutters would fly open; letting in the sunlight. Keep them closed at all times!'

Corbin jumps to the floor and hangs his head in shame.

'I really don't like going into my coffin…' begins Edwin. 'The bed is much more comfortable to sleep on. You wouldn't like it at all if I told you to fetch my coffin from the stagecoach, would you?'

'No, Master.'

'I will not tell you again, then – keep them closed!'

Corbin gently nods his head and sits his bottom down on the dusty floor. He watches his Master clutch onto his right hand, which has been severely burnt by the slither of sunlight shining through the shutters. Corbin gazes in amazement as his Master's hand effortlessly starts to heal itself in front of him.

'Anyway, Corbin…what is so important that you felt the need to open the shutters?' questions Edwin.

'The villagers seem to be piling lots of dirty laundry up outside, Master – and not just a little bit, but a huge mountain of dirty laundry – right in the middle of the village,' responds Corbin.

'Piling it up? What do you mean?'

'All the dirty, unwashed clothes from the village, Master. Everyone is piling it up – in one colossal pile.'

'Now, why would they be doing that?' asks Edwin, pondering for an answer to his own question.

Edwin returns to laying down atop the bed and stares at the ceiling.

'They must know that their Laundry Fairy has gone missing, Master!' announces Corbin.

'Of course, they know, Corbin! Of course, they do,' retorts Edwin. 'But why pile all of it up in the centre of —oh, I see now…'

'You do, Master?' asks Corbin.

'I do…I do indeed…' begins Edwin. 'Did you by any chance manage to see a rather skinny man in a blue robe and a pointy hat out there?'

'I believe I did, Master. Why?'

'A spellbinder, Corbin.'

'What?'

'A spellbinder wizard, Corbin. I believe he is going to attempt to wash all the dirty laundry – by using some type of magical spell on it…but that is none of our concern now is it, Corbin?'

'But surely, Master…' begins Corbin. 'If they know she is missing – then someone will eventually come looking for her…no?'

'Hmmm…I agree,' replies Edwin.

There's a brief pause before Edwin takes to his feet and strolls across to Amelia. He narrowly misses the thin ray of sunlight slicing across the dusty floor.

'Well, hopefully we will not have to worry about that, will we?' states Edwin, staring into the cage.

There is no response from Amelia.

'Not much time left to make that choice of yours now?' adds Edwin, grinning.

'Anyway, Corbin…' begins Edwin. 'We shall be long gone before they even manage to find her. I would imagine it is only a matter of time before someone does come looking—'

Edwin halts midsentence.

'But, of course…I did promise Amelia that if she fulfils my request, then no harm would come to her and I would simply let her go,' continues Edwin.

'You did, Master?' replies Corbin.

'I'm a man of my word, Corbin.'

'That you are, Master.'

'However, I'm also a vampire, Corbin – anything goes with me—'

◆◆◆

The village green has never seen such a vast amount of people standing about in the same place at any one time, especially around an extremely large mountain of piled up dirty laundry.

The last time the village green was this busy, was when Mrs Stamps decided to have a luxurious birthday party and she invited the whole village along to help her celebrate; although the invitations sent out were more instructions, than actual requests. Many of the villagers chose to take their chances in attending the party, rather than trying to find suitable excuses not to.

However, today the mass of villagers standing about in the green are not here for a party. They have all stopped their daily routines and assembled on the village green to watch the great Melvin Copernicus attempt to solve their laundry issues, by washing, cleaning and folding all of their dirty clothes; a task that even Melvin himself is not quite sure he'll accomplish.

The villagers remain quiet, with only the faintest of mumbles and whispers as they direct all their attention towards Melvin, who stares blankly at the pages of his journal; flicking them back and forth. He scratches his head, tugs at his beard and then ponders to himself whether a page of his journal is missing, or whether he'd previously forgotten to write down something very important.

'How you diddling, Melvin?' asks Timothy.

'Well, Timbers…I believe that this spell should do the trick,' replies Melvin, pointing his finger at a page in his journal. 'But I must admit…I cannot recall ever casting this spell before.'

'What do you mean?' questions Timothy, running the palms of his hands slowly down his chubby face. 'Never used it before? Or never attempted it?'

'Both,' answers Melvin, before biting his lip.

'That's certainly worrying.'

Melvin ignores Timothy's comment and continues to decipher his own scribbled handwriting; trying to deduce exactly what the spell is instructing him to do.

'I think that this spell could possible work…' begins Melvin. 'Although I am a little concerned about two things. Hmmm, I'm really not—'

'Concerned, Melvin?' interrupts Timothy. 'About what? I don't like it when people say that word.'

Melvin continues to slowly caress the end of his beard and cast his eyes repeatedly over the same text on the open page of his journal, which lays neatly balanced in the palm of his left hand.

'It's all the laundry, you see?' says Melvin. 'Most of the clothes are man-made. I don't think that the spell will bind very well to something that is man-made.'

'And you are telling me this now?' shrieks Timothy. 'Right after I've instructed everyone to pile up all their laundry in one huge pile – right here!'

Melvin turns to Timothy and raises his index finger to his lips in a polite attempt to silence him, before shaking his head violently; trying to remove a fly that buzzes past his ear and lands on the rim of his hat.

Timothy follows suit and slams his hand down hard on his chubby forearm, narrowly missing another fly by a fraction of a second.

'Nuisance flies…they're ruddy everywhere!' bellows Timothy. 'If they're not in the washing, they're in the air – if not in the air, they're everywhere else. Little beggars don't deserve to be alive – they should all—'

'That's it!' yelps Melvin, turning to face the laundry pile. 'I believe it may just work after all.'

A look of complete confusion crosses Timothy's

face, followed by a look of shock and concern.

'Melvin?' says Timothy, prompting for an answer.

'Right…I can make this work!' glees Melvin. 'I'll need water and soap – lots of soap!'

Timothy instantly shifts his attention to the village water fountain filled with crystal-clear water, hoping that Melvin hasn't already noticed it, but it was too late.

Melvin faces the fountain and then turns back to Timothy, before raising his eyebrows and smirking.

'Don't you even think about it, Melvin!' bellows Timothy. 'Really? You can't be serious?'

Melvin continues to smirk at Timothy.

'You want to use the water from our newly built fountain?' adds Timothy, breaking into a slight panic.

'Well, Timbers…it's either that or we get all the villagers to use what they can to pail water from the river. However, time is ticking away…the judges will be arriving in a few hours, won't they?'

Timothy sighs. 'Oh, very well – use the fountain.'

The villagers continue to stare at Melvin and patiently wait for him to perform a monumental spell, which will make all of their laundry worries disappear.

'But we'll still need soap, Timbers. As I said before, we need lots and lots of it,' adds Melvin.

'The shop keeper probably has soap, Melvin. If not, we'll have to get it from the wash-house.'

'Make it so, Timbers. I will need time to gather my thoughts – this spell will take a lot of my energy.'

Timothy turns to face a couple of gormless looking young lads, standing nearby. 'Hey, you two, come with me,' he says, leading them both to the village store.

Melvin closes his eyes, snaps his journal closed and places it back into his robe pocket. He steps up onto the recently repaired stonework of the village fountain, overlooks the crowd and focuses on the colossal pile of laundry in front of him.

The crowd of villagers let out small cheers, which Melvin instantly silences by using his arms to instruct them to move aside; forming a passageway to the base of the laundry pile. Melvin takes a deep breath and stretches his hands. His bones click and crack.

'COMING THROUGH! Coming through, people!' yells Timothy, as he races through the crowd towards Melvin. The two young lads stagger behind, each carrying a huge block of scented soap in either arm. They both come to a sudden halt at Melvin and drop the blocks of soap at his feet.

'Not there!' screeches Melvin, at the two young lads. 'On top of the laundry pile...and please break it up into smaller pieces.'

Timothy assists the young lads and picks up two blocks of soap from the floor. He strolls towards the base of the laundry pile, while ripping off fragments of soap with his bare hands and throwing them high onto the top of the pile. The two young lads follow his lead.

'Happy now?' asks Timothy, directing his daggered tone towards Melvin.

'Perfectly,' replies Melvin. 'I think that we are now ready to have a go at this.'

'Finally,' mutters Timothy.

'Okay everyone. You may wish to step back a little,' announces Melvin. 'This may get a little chaotic.'

The villagers turn towards each other and shrug their shoulders. They mutter and mumble a few words to each other, before letting out a unified cheer.

Melvin sighs, adjusts his hat and straightens his robe. He reaches back inside his robe pocket for his journal; instantly opening it at the required spell. He mutters aloud as he tries to read his own handwriting; reciting the magical enchants over and over.

After several moments, Melvin snaps the journal shut. The crowd gasps in anticipation.

'I'm not sure I like all this silence,' whispers Melvin, leaning down towards Timothy. 'I know I need to concentrate, but this is very unnerving.'

Timothy stares blankly back at Melvin.

'Err…what do you want me to do about it, Melvin? Get them all to cheer and shout?' replies Timothy, glancing around at the faces of the villagers. 'Or maybe I could get Mrs Stamps to shout at you lots…would that help take the tension off?'

Melvin cringes at the thought of being shouted at by Mrs Stamps.

'No-no, that's perfectly fine…' begins Melvin. 'I would rather listen to nothing than to—'

'Too late…' interrupts Timothy. 'Here she comes.'

'Seriously?' asks Melvin. 'Oh, darn it!'

Expecting Mrs Stamps to burst into a chorus of random curses, Timothy and Melvin are pleasantly surprised as she strolls through the crowd, halts next to Timothy and casually folds her arms. She says not a single word.

Melvin stares at Mrs Stamps. He quickly re-adjusts his stare elsewhere as her eyes meet his.

There is an uncomfortable pause…

'There's no use in staring at me, Melvin!' barks Mrs Stamps. 'That's not going to make the spell go any faster! Now get on with it…we haven't got all day!'

◆◆◆

Duncan stumbles out from behind the bar counter and feels his way along its edge with his hands. He staggers across the tavern, while carefully avoiding the Corporal and his men, who lay scattered on the floor.

Greeted by a chorus of snores, wheezes and tuneful breathing, Duncan carefully and skilfully negotiates a pathway towards the front window of the tavern. He pauses briefly, before losing his balance and stumbling backwards into a wooden chair; it creaks and cracks as it takes his colossal weight. He lets out a sigh, takes a quick breather and wipes the sweat from his brow.

Duncan's short break is interrupted as he looks out of the window. The uncommon sight of seeing the village green filled with a mass of villagers, forces him to rubs his eyes with his hands, to check again whether what he sees is not some fragment of his imagination, caused by the copious amounts of honey mead still floating about in his stomach.

He musters up a little strength to push himself out of the chair and stumbles across the floor to the window frame. He pushes out his arms and clutches onto the woodwork to prevent himself from falling flat on his face.

He gasps at the number of villagers standing around in the centre of the village and ponders at what all the commotion is about. He scrolls through the many familiar faces and squints his eyes; focusing in on Melvin, standing atop the fountain wall.

Duncan stares in confusion at Melvin. He tries to conjure up any logical explanation as to why Melvin is not only entertaining the villagers, by crazily waving his arms around in the air, but also why a huge collection of dirty laundry is piled up next to him.

Duncan's gaze is interrupted by a series of loud taps

approaching from the stairs. He turns on the spot to observe Dexter casually stepping into the main hall of the tavern.

Dexter pauses at the bottom of the stairs. He turns his head and rolls his eyes at the sight of the Corporal and his men, who are beginning to awaken.

'Ah…morning to you, Duncan,' says Dexter softly, tiptoeing carefully around the mass of bodies sleeping on the floor. 'I don't know why they bothered renting a room, Duncan. It seems they spend most of their time on this floor.'

'Oh…morning—err, Dexter isn't it…?' whispers Duncan, signalling to Dexter to make his way over to him. Dexter nods gently.

'What on Earth—' mutters Dexter, on seeing the huge pile of dirty laundry and the crowd surrounding it. 'What's going on? Is that Melvin?'

'I believe it is,' replies Duncan. 'I thought *you* might be able to tell *me* what's going on?'

Dexter takes a few more steps forward towards the window. He pushes his snout hard up against the glass to catch a glimpse of Melvin, flinging his arms around in the air. He shifts his eyes to the dirty laundry pile and then quickly back to Melvin.

'Oh…he can't be serious?' exclaims Dexter, with a tone of panic in his voice.

'Huh?' responds Duncan.

'I'm talking about Melvin. I *really* do hope he is not attempting what I think he is!'

'What would that be?' enquires Duncan.

Dexter sighs. 'This is going to go horribly wrong,' he mutters to himself. 'I can feel it in my bones.'

'Oh, is he casting some sort of marvellous spell? How exciting!'

'That's what troubles me, Duncan.'

'Him casting a spell?'

'Yes, a pretty huge one – if he is about to attempt what I think he is.'

'Oh?' responds Duncan. 'What's that, then?'

'I believe he is attempting to solve the villagers' dirty laundry problem by casting some sort of elaborate washing spell.'

Duncan redirects his attention to his now empty laundry basket, sitting outside the tavern.

'Looks as if my washing has all gone. I'm guessing it's somewhere within that huge pile? Well I hope it is. I've run out of clean underpants.'

'Your guess would be very correct,' replies Dexter, cringing at the thought of Duncan's underwear failure.

Dexter continues to stare at Melvin. He is nervous at the fact, that although he is fully aware of Melvin's abilities as a spellbinder, he is also aware that even Melvin can…and very drastically, gets things extremely wrong. Most of the time it would be because Melvin has forgotten one key element to a spell, a simple mistake while reading out the magical enchants, or because he has failed to take into consideration something very important.

At this time of the morning in Baston, Dexter has a feeling that this spell is not going to go the way that Melvin intends it to go.

'Is that front door locked, Duncan?' asks Dexter.

'Why?' replies Duncan.

'Well, it may be a very good idea to do so, if it isn't already locked. Make sure its bolted also!'

'I haven't locked that door for as long as I can even remember. Why would I start to lock it now?'

'It's your call, Duncan. Nevertheless, given my

experiences with Melvin, and the amount of times I've seen him cast some of the more elaborate spells – something is bound to go wrong. It always does—'

Duncan and Dexter are interrupted by a huge yawn and groan from the Corporal, who then stretches his arms out across the floor. He slowly opens his eyes and stares at the ceiling.

◆◆◆

Samuel leans up against the white picket fence of the church yard. He rubs his hands together, then carefully places them into his jacket pockets and waits patiently for any activity from the centre of the village green.

The Reverend shifts from side to side in an attempt to find a comfortable position; or one that doesn't involve the tipped end of a fence picket from poking him in places that he doesn't want to be poked.

'It's so wonderful that this Melvin gentleman has decided to help us in solving our immediate laundry problem,' says Samuel, turning to face the Reverend. 'I must admit – I'm a little shocked at the sheer amount of laundry that we have here in the village.'

'I imagine that the majority of that is from the wash-house, Samuel.'

'Yes, I would believe so.'

Samuel pushes himself up from the fence into a standing position, raises a hand out of his pocket and uses it to shield his eyes from the morning sun. He focuses in on Melvin, who is performing some very radical movements with his arms and legs.

'He is certainly a peculiar character,' states Samuel, tilting his head in Melvin's direction. 'Do you think he's—well, all with it?'

'That has crossed my mind once or twice,' replies the Reverend, followed by a small chuckle.

'I'm very surprised that most of the village has turned out to watch. Very strange that!'

'Well…it's not every day that you get to see a spellbinder turn up in your village, let alone one that is about to cast a spell on a huge pile of dirty washing.'

'I guess so,' responds Samuel, before pausing. 'Do you think he actually knows what he's doing?' he adds, questioning Melvin's unorthodox methods and bizarre movements, which continue to baffle Samuel.

'Ah…well, either his spell will solve our problem or it won't,' states the Reverend.

Samuel nods. 'What do you expect will happen?'

The Reverend leaps up from the fence and stands next to Samuel. 'Well…I'm hoping that all the washing does get cleaned, folded and returned to its correct owners. I think that's the basis of what Melvin is trying to achieve.'

'Really? Spellbinders can do that sort of thing, can they?' enquires Samuel.

'Oh yes, they can do some amazing things when they put their minds to it,' replies the Reverend.

'Have you heard of any amazing things that Melvin has done in the past?'

'To be honest – no I haven't.'

'Interesting…' responds Samuel, relishing at the thought of all the wash-house's laundry completely washed, neatly folded and ready to be delivered to various clients in the surroundings towns and villages.

Samuel's thoughts are interrupted by the sound of the Corporal staggering out of the tavern. He observes as the fresh morning air hits the Corporal's face.

The loud thudding of the Corporal's boots echo

across the village green. One by one, the Corporal's men follow, creating a percussive chorus of thuds and thumps as they all try to find their composure after a rather heavy night of singing and drinking.

The Reverend and Samuel continue to wait…

◆◆◆

Melvin closes his eyes and continues to launch his arms out in all directions. He rotates his wrists and elbows; manoeuvring his hands in some near-like impossible ways. His body sways gently back and forth as he takes a defensive stance atop the wall of the village fountain.

He continues to mutter to himself; random lines of magical words and enchants; entering a slow trance-like state, while rotating his head slowly about his neckline. His whole body seems to momentarily slow down, before speeding up again to its normal motion.

Melvin continues to sway his arms out in front of him. He suddenly comes to a halt; pausing in mid-air as if time had simply stopped.

The crowd of villagers stare on in anticipation and excitement. They wait for the slightest movement from Melvin.

There is an eerie still in the air…

Unexpectedly, a sudden gust of howling wind rips through the village green. It takes most of the villagers by complete surprise as a few of them struggle to clutch onto their hats.

The wind moves around the village green in an unusual circular motion; lashing and ripping at the sides of the dirty washing pile.

The earth beneath the villagers' feet begins to tremble and quake, making each of villagers turn to one another in concern. They look down at the ground beneath them and shuffle their feet in an attempt to remain balanced.

A second gust of wind enters the village from another direction; intertwining with the first gust. They both howl and whistle loudly; producing their own tones as they constantly change direction. A chilling and eerie melody fills the air.

The winds continue to circulate the pile of laundry; gathering speed and merging into one huge gust. It rips violently around the unwashed clothes, which start to flap around as the winds lash at them.

Trousers, pants, socks, shirts, aprons, dresses and frilly underwear begin to rise from the pile as they are caught within the vortex of the swirling winds; spinning faster and faster. The laundry pile reduces in size as clothes are sucked up into the sky; tumbling around in the ever increasingly mass of turbulent air.

Melvin begins to emit a greenish aura about him; an aura that radiates from both his hands and spreads up his arms and into his robe. Melvin continues to mutter to himself; repeating the same words over and over.

The crowd takes a step back. The ground continues to tremble underneath their feet. It grows in volume and intensity, to the point where small fragments of mortar and stone begin to fall off the newly repaired fountain wall.

The crystal-clear water in the fountain begins to ripple; each water molecule seeming to shift and align perfectly in a patterned array, as a small tidal force is created. This causes the water to swirl violently around the perimeter of the fountain.

The water increases in speed. It splashes over the sides of the fountain wall and Melvin's sandals. Melvin himself continues to glow brighter, and with minimal effort, he raises the mass of water out of the fountain and into the air.

The crowd gasps in amazement as the water, drop by drop, is sucked up into the cyclone; the cyclone which continues to gather speed.

The sounds of blocks of soap exploding are muffled by the howls of the wind and the sloshing of water molecules as they race through the air.

The crowd looks up and watches their dirty laundry spinning violently across the sky. The pleasant aroma of soap fills the morning air.

THE AIR CRACKLES AND HUMS.

'I'm getting very wet,' yells Mrs Stamps, her vocals trying to drown out the constant howling of the winds. She lowers her head and attempts to shield herself from the cold watery spray.

THERE IS A BRILIANT FLASH OF LIGHT.

The winds disappear and the water falls to the ground, causing a cascade of dirty laundry to fall from the sky. Melvin drops to his knees in exhaustion and the greenish aura fades from his hands.

The crowd screams and goes into a panic as freshly washed pieces of clothing fall on top of them and onto the surrounding grass at their feet.

There is silence…

'Melvin…are you okay?' asks Timothy, stepping forward and helping Melvin to his feet.

'Err…*I*—*I*—I don't know what happened there,' stutters Melvin. '*I*—I couldn't control it. It was too much. I'm sorry – I tried—'

'What on Earth are you talking about?' interrupts Mrs Stamps, picking up a random sock from the ground and giving it a sniff. 'I think you've done it!'

'I have?' replies Melvin.

'Yes…look!' instructs Mrs Stamps. 'It's a shame you that couldn't get it all neatly folded and sorted, but I'm guessing that's *too* much to ask.'

Melvin's eyes narrow.

'*ARGHHHHH!* It moved—' screams Mrs Stamps.

'What did?' interrupts Timothy.

'The sock…*It's*—It's alive!' shrieks Mrs Stamps, dropping the sock to the floor.

'Oh my – she is right!' yelps Timothy.

Suddenly the villagers erupt into shouts, screams and hollers, before running off in various directions in a state of fear and horror.

'What on Earth—' begins Timothy, glancing across the village green.

'They're all alive!' interrupts Mrs Stamps, staring hard at a pair of leather trousers and a silk shirt rising up from the grass, followed by hundreds of other items of clothing.

'Oh…what have I done?' mumbles Melvin.

'We haven't time for questions, Melvin…RUN!' yelps Timothy, pulling Melvin to his feet.

'I'm too weak – leave me here,' whimpers Melvin.

'You heard him, Timothy…let's run!' squeals Mrs Stamps, stumbling across the damp grass, while trying to avoid the rising army of possessed laundry. Timothy follows, leaving Melvin behind.

Melvin falls to his knees, slowly lifts his head up and is greeted by the sight of a leather apron, racing wildly towards him from across the village green.

He retains his focus just enough to observe the Reverend and Samuel beat the apron with a couple of pickets from the church fence. The apron backs away, just as Melvin collapses to the ground.

'It's okay, Melvin – we've got you,' announces the Reverend, as he and Samuel aid Melvin to his feet and escort him towards the church, battling socks, shirts and an extremely large pair of underpants on route.

◆◆◆

The main door to the tavern slams closed and a key hastily turns in its lock. A multitude of iron latches slide firmly into place with a melody of knocks and clangs.

The Corporal grabs hold of a large wooden table with his chunky hands and drags it across the tavern floor; pushing it hard up against the door. He bangs his fists down onto the tabletop, before pausing and taking in a deep breath. He turns to face his men and a couple of random villagers that have also ended up inside the tavern.

'What in the devil's name was that…?' yelps Private Myles, catching his breath as he slides down the bar counter and onto the floor.

'That, Myles…was a pair of freshly washed woollen pyjamas,' answers Private Trout.

'Why were they trying to strangle me? Seriously—I mean…are they supposed to do that? That's really not normal!'

'No, it's not normal at all,' interrupts the Corporal. 'Keep your heads down. There's lots going on out there. We don't want to draw attention to ourselves.'

'It's a laundry apocalypse!' shrieks Private Myles.

'It's not an apocalypse, Myles,' retorts Private Trout. 'Don't be so childish!'

The Corporal peers through the main front window of the tavern, being cautious not to been seen by anything—well…irregular.

'What has happened, Sir?' asks Private Babe, placing his metal helmet onto his head and pulling the leather strap tightly up against his chin.

'I can tell you *exactly* what's happened!' interrupts Dexter.

'Please do,' replies the Corporal, ducking his head, as a couple of red socks jump and bounce across the front of the window; disappearing from view.

'Well...he's messed up again!' states Dexter.

'Huh?' responds the Corporal.

'Melvin - he's messed up again,' repeats Dexter. 'He's cast a complicated spell – forgot something very important – and it's all gone wrong around him. In addition, it's not the first time either. I told you something didn't feel right.'

'You can't go blaming my little Melvin,' bellows the Corporal. 'He's a wonderful man.'

'Err...I think you'll find I can...' begins Dexter. 'As it was Melvin...and Melvin alone that cast the spell – I didn't see anybody else waving their arms about crazily in a trance-like state and glowing brightly.'

'He's right—*hic*—very right indeed!' says Duncan, holding a large tankard of honey mead in his hand.

'So, what are we going to do, Sir...?' says Private Trout, directly to his superior.

The Corporal lifts his head and uses his highly developed analytical skills and deductive reasoning to assess the severity of the current situation. Or in simple terms...he takes a quick look outside.

His eyes widen as he observes a group of white linen shirts marching past the front of the tavern.

'Damn it,' whispers the Corporal. 'I think they just saw me.'

'Who, Sir?' replies Private Trout.

'The shirts.'

Private Trout stares hard in disbelief at his superior, questioning whether he has just simply misheard the Corporal, or if he did actually hear him say the word "shirts." With the current situation, he decides on the latter.

Suddenly, several loud thumps pound at the front door of the tavern, followed by the rattling of the latches. Just as quickly as the thumps are heard…they disappear.

'Are they still there?' says Private Babe, quietly.

'I'm not sure,' replies the Corporal, remaining still and quiet on the floor.

'Well, we can't stay in here all the time, Sir,' whispers Private Trout. 'We need to take some sort of stand – besides, it's only laundry. It's not as if it's an army of monstrous flesh-eating beasts, is it?'

'Or zombies,' adds Private Myles, before smirking.

'Shut up, Myles!' interrupts Private Trout.

The Corporal slowly shifts across the tavern floor and joins the rest of his men at the back of the room.

AAAAAACHOO!

A single copper coin launches from Dexter's left nostril and hits the glass pane of the window with a ping, causing it to crack.

Dexter lowers his head. 'I'm sorry,' he mutters.

'Where are all our weapons, Private Babe?' enquiries the Corporal.

'Oh, well we haven't—I mean they are all back at camp, Sir,' replies Private Babe.

'What?' snaps the Corporal, trying to keep his vocal volume at a reasonable level?

'Well, that's just great…' begins Private Myles. 'Just great! What are we supposed to do now?'

AAAAAACHOO!

Dexter launches another copper coin, which rolls slowly across the floor and comes to halt in the corner of the room.

'Sorry again,' whispers Dexter. 'It's all the dust – it makes me sneeze.'

'We need to get to our weapons,' announces the Corporal, rising to his feet. 'We must attempt to run back to the camp.'

'Do you think that our swords will be more than enough to defeat them all, Sir?' questions Private Myles. 'I've never before had a fight with a possessed piece of laundry.'

'I really don't know, Myles,' interrupts the Corporal. 'What would you rather do to them? Iron them to death?'

Private Trout narrows his eyes in a response to his superior's comment. He glances around the tavern for anything useful that could be used to face-off the possessed laundry. He sighs at the very limited options.

AAAAAACHOO!

'We need a distraction,' announces Private Babe. 'Something to draw their attention to while we make a run for our weapons; something that would make a noise and attract them to it; something we can stay at range from.'

AAAAAACHOO! AAAAAACHOO!

Everyone slowly turns their heads towards Dexter, who nervously takes a few careful steps backwards. 'Err…what?' asks Dexter. 'What are you all staring at?'

'How often can you do that? Err…Dexter, isn't it?' asks the Corporal.

'It's random, but any dust seems to make me sneeze a lot more. However, it just so happens that I have lots more upstairs – well, let's just say – for other purposes.

'You can sneeze out a copper coin each time?' adds the Corporal.

'Yes, pretty much,' replies Dexter. 'Sometimes two!'

'Well, then…that's settled, Dexter. You will be our distraction.'

'Huh? *Wh—wh*—what? Wait a second, I have—' stutters Dexter.

'No time to waste, Dexter,' interrupts the Corporal. 'Go and fetch your dust and we'll formulate a masterful plan.'

Dexter sighs and carefully tiptoes up the wooden stairs to the first floor, just as a window pane smashes and spreads shards of splintered glass onto the floor.

'Hurry, Dexter!' yells the Corporal.'

'Yes, chief,' mumbles Dexter, imitating a salute with his claw. 'I'm just a copper-coin filled fruit machine. A winner on every sneeze!'

CHAPTER XI

"Can you please let me know the next time you use a teleportation spell? My hat is now probably floating around in some interstellar dimesion."

SAMUEL ARTHURS

Melvin sits on the stone-cold floor of the village church, with his legs fully extended and his head hung low. He steadies his breathing; occasionally taking in a long-drawn breath, before exhaling it slowly. He raises his hands and places them softly onto his face; pulling them slowly down across his wrinkly skin. He lets out a long sigh of disappointment.

The Reverend hurriedly paces across to Melvin and hands him a small wooden cup full of cold water, which Melvin immediately grabs from the Reverend's hand and raises it to his parched lips. In a few swift gulps, Melvin devours the contents of the cup, before handing the empty cup back to the Reverend. Melvin wipes his face with the sleeve of his robe.

'Oh, my-my – what have I done?' whimpers Melvin, trying amongst his panic to deduce exactly what had gone wrong in causing all of the village laundry to now seem very much alive. He cringes at the thought of the havoc and chaos they could create.

Samuel reaches down offers Melvin his hand and pulls backwards to aid Melvin to his feet. He assists Melvin in straightening his robe and hat; giving Melvin a little more composure.

'We are safe in here for the time being,' says Samuel.

'I'm really not sure for how long though,' adds the Reverend, staring in concern at the glass windows that line the church walls. 'Those windows are made from very thin and fragile glass. I pray they do not try to force their way inside.'

Samuel and Melvin cast their eyes over the highly decorative glass windows that stretch down the length of the church. They both sigh simultaneously.

The Reverend paces across to the front door of the church and pushes himself up hard against it; checking that it's firmly closed. He reaches out with his hands and individually checks and *double checks* that each bolted latch is fully engaged.

'At least the front door is fully secure,' states the Reverend, turning back towards Melvin and Samuel. 'Ah, shoot! I'd better check on the other door…be back in a few moments.'

'I was only trying to help,' announces Melvin. 'I seem to have made a right mess of this in my arrogance and bigheadedness. But…what went wrong?'

'Let's not dwell on what went wrong, Melvin – or the *who's, why's and when's,*' says Samuel. 'Together we need to work out what we are going to do about it all – now, is there a spell you can use to sort all this out?'

Melvin pauses and gently scratches his head, before reaching down into his robe pocket in search of his journal.

'It's gone!' yelps Melvin, frantically patting his robe, before methodically searching the church floor.

'What has?' enquires Samuel.

'My journal. It's not here – oh darn it! It must have dropped out of my pocket, earlier.'

'Oh…how inconvenient.'

'Well…even if I had it, I don't think I have near enough magical charge left in me to create another large spell. I can barely stand up.'

The Reverend returns from the rear of the church. 'Okay, well we're locked in, but I really don't think we can stay here too much longer – do we have a plan Melvin? Some sort of marvellous and ingenious spell I'm hoping?'

Melvin turns towards Samuel, hoping that he would readdress the Reverend.

'Do we have a plan, Melvin?' repeats the Reverend.

'Patience, Reverend,' begins Samuel, 'Melvin needs to recharge – and we have a little hindrance in casting a spell right now.'

'We do?' replies the Reverend.

'Yes, we do. Melvin seems to have misplaced his journal,' states Samuel.

'Oh, that does not sound good at all,' responds the Reverend. 'What are you going to do? And what do you do to recharge?'

'That's a pretty in-depth discussion for another day,

Reverend,' replies Melvin. 'But basically, I'm low on magical energy…it's all very boring and technical – and despite me having misplaced my journal – right now, I believe we have much bigger issues.'

'What do you mean?' asks the Reverend.

'Look!' yelps Samuel, pointing at the windows.

Melvin and the Reverend immediately redirect their attention to where Samuel is pointing. They watch as the inside of the church darkens; the light from the windows blocked out by the blurry outlines of trousers, shorts and pullovers that linger on the other side of the glass window panes.

'What do they want?' shrieks the Reverend.

'I don't know, but we can't stay in here any longer,' replies Samuel. 'We need to move – and sooner rather than later.'

'Can you move, Melvin?' asks Samuel.

'I'm not sure. I really think it would have been better if you just—'

Melvin is interrupted by the sound of loud thuds coming from the front door of the church, which startle Samuel and the Reverend.

'No, you're right! We do need to move!' continues Melvin, taking a step back from the door.

'But, where do we go?' asks the Reverend, huddling closer to Melvin and Samuel.

'I suggest our tavern,' answers Samuel. 'It's rather secure – compared to all the other buildings. I also saw the Corporal and his men run back inside there earlier – maybe they have a plan? Or maybe some weapons at least.'

'Good idea!' bellows the Reverend. 'Now all we've got to do is to get out of here without being seen and make our way to the tavern.'

'I suggest we just make a run for it,' begins Samuel. 'Either that – or we use those incredibly large candle holders to bash them with – or even the cloth from the alter to shroud us in, and hope that they don't—'

'Gentlemen – gentlemen please,' interrupts Melvin, bringing Samuel to a silence. 'I *could* just teleport us there?'

'Teleport?' queries the Reverend. 'You can do that?'

Melvin raises his eyebrows at the Reverend. 'Of course, yes – I believe I have just enough energy left to take us that short distance.'

Samuel shifts his head towards the Reverend and waits for any comment from him regarding Melvin's solution. It's not that Samuel doesn't have complete confidence that Melvin can perform a teleport spell. It is just the fact that his last spell had some pretty major flaws. Samuel ponders on all the things that could possibly go wrong using a teleport spell.

'Err…very well, then. If you believe you can,' says the Reverend.

'Okay great! Hold on tight!' instructs Melvin, instantly clutching onto the arms of the Reverend and Samuel.

THE AIR HUMS…A FLASH OF LIGHT.

'*WHOOOOAH!* Hold on, wait a—' shrieks Samuel.

◆◆◆

The newly crafted wooden mailbox outside the village post office creaks and moans, before its supporting post snaps in half, causing the box on top to fall to the ground below. It explodes on impact and covers the grassed area in front of the post office in a blanket of splintered and fragmented wood.

Several socks of all colours and sizes slither over the remains of the mailbox; slowly making their way to the front door of the post office. Each sock bounces up the wooden steps leading onto its porch.

Long socks; short socks; stripy socks and multi-coloured socks made from wool and cotton, leap from the porch's wooden planks and attach themselves to the freshly painted fascia at the front of the building. They scale across the pale blue boards and scout for a way inside. A rather large and lengthy blue woollen sock leads the way to the tiled roof of the building, before pausing and indicating to the other socks to follow.

Mrs Stamps and Timothy stare in horror through the front window as two small cotton socks hurl themselves at the glass pane, causing Mrs Stamps and Timothy to take a sudden step backwards into the room. They continue watching as the two socks pause momentarily, before both slowly sliding back down the front of the glass and onto the grass below.

'We're under attack!' shouts Timothy. 'What are we going to do, Mrs Stamps?'

'Yes, I'm completely aware that we are under attack, Timothy,' replies Mrs Stamps. 'But whimpering and skipping around like a toddler is not going to help the situation, is it?'

'They're everywhere – look!' cries Timothy, tilting his head towards the ceiling. 'They're on the roof!' he adds, upon hearing thuds and thumps above him.

'Timothy…if you don't stop moaning and reduce your vocal volume – you are going to find that the back of my hand is going to meet the side of your chubby face – with an extremely violent force!'

Without any delay, Timothy silences himself by

reaching up to cover his mouth with his hand; preventing him from making any un-manly sounds that would distress Mrs Stamps any further. He watches as Mrs Stamps promptly grabs her pitchfork from the corner of the room and wedges it firmly between the door handle and the floor. She tugs it gently to check its integrity for holding the door closed.

'Close those curtains, will you, Timothy?' instructs Mrs Stamps, frantically waving her arm about in the direction of the window. 'And will you please calm down! I need to think…'

Mrs Stamps looks around her front room and searches for anything useful that can be used against the army of socks, which are currently *en-masse*, scaling the walls of the building.

'Do you think they'll be able to get inside, Mrs Stamps?' questions Timothy, taking a peek from behind Mrs Stamps' fashionable and highly decorative curtains.

'No – I don't think so. I think we are safe here for now – unless they work out how to get down the—oh blast it!' yelps Mrs Stamps, rushing through a doorway and into the next room.

'Mrs Stamps…what are you doing?' asks Timothy.

'Oh, shoot,' begins Mrs Stamps. 'Where did I put—oh, there they are. Pass me those matches just there, would you please?'

'Why? Are we going to set them all on fire?'

'Don't be so stupid, Timothy! People just don't randomly set fire to other people's socks – that's just borderline insanity. Besides, I have just seen a pair of my stripy socks on the porch outside. Do you know how hard they are to come by? I paid good money for them – and I'm not about to set them on fire!'

'So why do you need matches?'

Mrs Stamps stares at Timothy in concern and waits for his brain cells to kick in and fire.'

'Seriously, Timothy? Will you just for once today, use that tiny brain of yours? Think, Timothy! Think!'

Timothy takes a few seconds to ponder over the question of why Mrs Stamps would be lighting a fire in the fireplace of the post office. Thuds and thumps continue overhead. Timothy follows the sounds with his eyes and then suddenly realises why Mrs Stamps is about to create fire. He promptly hands her the box of matches.

'This will at least stop them from coming down the chimney – I hope…' states Mrs Stamps, crunching up some old pieces of parchment paper and throwing them onto the base of the fireplace. She reaches to the side and removes several pieces of coal from a small bucket, before placing them carefully atop the paper and topping it off with a couple of large wood logs. She lights a match and inserts it underneath the paper. The paper instantly catches fire and burns.

'Either that, or your husband will certainly not be too pleased that you've burned his beloved post office to the ground,' responds Timothy.

Mrs Stamps raises her eyebrows at Timothy.

'Come – I feel much safer in the front room,' says Mrs Stamps. 'Let that fire burn fast and close this door behind you – and would you please try to remain quiet? Stomping about the place like that – they'll hear you.'

Mrs Stamps and Timothy remain still and silent in the front room. They both stare up at the ceiling and follow the continued sounds of thuds and thumps as the socks move over the slated tiles, on the roof above.

'Shush, Timothy!' whispers Mrs Stamps. 'I think

they've stopped. The thuds and thumps have ceased.'

'Really?' replies Timothy. 'Do you think they have gone elsewhere?'

'I can't hear them anymore – can you?'

'No. What shall we do?'

Mrs Stamps tiptoes across the floor towards her front window and parts the curtains *just enough* to take a sneaky peak outside.

'Well…I can't see any of the socks out on the porch, Timothy,' states Mrs Stamps. 'Maybe we should think about making a run for our tavern?'

'Do you think Melvin will be there…?' questions Timothy. 'I feel really bad for leaving him behind. He could be—well, less alive than normal.'

'Don't you worry about him!' responds Mrs Stamps, trying her best to keep her voice down. 'He has been in much worse situations than this. I'm fairly sure he can take care of himself.'

'Oh, I see…' replies Timothy, staring over Mrs Stamps' shoulder and through the gap in the curtain. 'Can you see anything else out there, Mrs Stamps?'

'Would it make it any better if I could?'

'Not really.'

'In that case – there isn't.'

Mrs Stamps grabs hold of her pitchfork and pulls it firmly to dislodge it from the floor and the door handle. She hands it over to Timothy.

'I think, while the coast is clear – it would be a good time to try and run across to the tavern – what do you say, Timothy?' asks Mrs Stamps.

'Well, I suppose the others will be there,' replies Timothy. 'Perhaps they have already come up with an ingenious plan? You know, we should have just gone straight to the tavern before…'

'Let us hope – and please don't start Timothy.'

Timothy hears random noises from outside. 'Are you absolutely sure there is nothing out there?' he says.

'Err – yes-yes…the coast is *perfectly* clear, Timothy – nothing out there at all,' answers Mrs Stamps.

Suddenly, the sound of glass smashing in the next room startles Mrs Stamps, who then immediately grabs the door handle.

'I think we'd better make a move, Timothy!' yelps Mrs Stamps, turning towards him. 'We can't stay here – I think they've got into the next room.'

'It certainly sounds like it!' responds Timothy, in a panicked tone, before grinning.

'Shall we move?'

'Oh, very much so.'

'Are you ready…?'

'I was born ready.'

'Oh, shut up Timothy!'

Mrs Stamps opens the front door and takes a quick glance outside. She turns her head from left to right; checking for the ideal moment to make a run for it.

'Okay, Timothy…to the tavern's entrance we go,' whispers Mrs Stamps. 'Damn it, Timothy! – wait a second. Would you please tie your bootlaces – not only are you making the place look untidy…again! But on top of this mess outside, we don't need one of the judges being greeted by a clumsy mayor, who has accidently tripped over and impaled a part of his anatomy on a pitchfork, do we?'

There's a slight pause…

'I hope your precious post office burns to the ground,' mutters Timothy, under his breath.

◆◆◆

Several tables and chairs that had previously been neatly arranged around the main room of the tavern, now lay on their sides; strategically placed in front of the windows on either side of the main entrance door.

Another large table is lifted onto its narrow edge and is wedged firmly up against the door. It slides across the floor, before finding its footing and locking up hard against the cast iron door handle.

Other tables are turned onto their sides; lining the length of the room with a barrier of solid wood. Chairs and stools from the rear of the room are smashed together; their legs and braces used to fill in the small gaps between the tables, preventing even the smallest of creatures from slipping through. Spindles from the backs of the chairs are used to lock everything together; pushed through gaps in the surrounding tables.

The decorative wooden legs of the tables, highly crafted by master carpenters, have now been ripped out of their previously housed sockets, each one of them now being held very tightly in the hands of every one of the Corporal's men, the tavern cook, three random villagers and the Corporal himself.

Duncan, tries his hardest to remain upright, while holding a freshly poured tankard of honey mead in one hand and opting to wield his butcher's knife in the other.

'Okay, steady now, lads – steady now,' instructs the Corporal. 'It looks like we are going to have a slight battle on our hands.'

The Corporal and his band of highly trained men, usher sideways and spread themselves out across the tavern floor; lining up against the wooden barricade.

Duncan, the random villagers and the tavern's cook take position behind the bar counter. The Corporal stares over at them and ponders whether it is the ideal place for them to stand from a strategic point of view, or whether Duncan simply knew it was the best place to be in order to keep his tankard full.

'Where did they come from all of a sudden?' yelps Private Babe, clutching hold of a wooden table leg in both hands. He positions himself, ready to attack the wave of dirty washing currently pounding on the windows and doors at the front of the tavern.

'I don't know!' responds Private Myles. 'But this is going to either be a lot of fun or it's going to get very messy.'

'Hold your ground, lads!' bellows the Corporal. 'Don't let them in. Hold them back the best you can.'

The Corporal begins to swing his wooden table leg around his head, before slamming the tip down hard into the palm of his hand. 'It's clobbering time, lads!' he adds, before grinding his teeth in rage.

Private Myles turns to Private Trout and places his hand next to Private Trout's ear; shielding his voice from the Corporal. 'What does the Corporal expect us to do? Bash them to a pulp with these pieces of wood?'

'Do you have a better idea, Myles…?' questions Private Trout, adjusting his helmet and narrowing his eyes at the oncoming wave of laundry.

'Err…I suppose not,' answers Private Myles. 'But what about that Melvin geezer? Surely if he made all of this mess – then he should be able to cast some spell to sort it all out?'

'Well, that would make sense, wouldn't it?' replies Private Trout. 'However, I don't at this very moment in time see him anywhere. So, I suggest you take hold of your leg and start swinging.'

'My leg?' How will swinging my leg help?'

'This leg here! You complete and utter muppet! The one right in front of you,' retorts Private Trout, shaking Private Myles' wooden table leg that he is holding in his hand.

'Oh right...gotcha,' responds Private Myles. 'Well, even still...it would be an ideal time for that wizard to make a little bit of an appearance, don't you think, Trout?'

The Corporal turns to face Private Myles and Private Trout.

'Will you two over there stop mumbling!' yells the Corporal. 'We must concentrate all our efforts on the problem at hand – and where has that dragon gone? We'll need his assistance shortly.'

Outside, a small army of laundry slowly wanders around the perimeter of the building; scouting for ways to get inside. Items persistently pound and thump on the glass window panes and doors, which continue to creak and strain with every blow.

Suddenly and yet mysteriously, a large leather apron appears in front of the window to the right of the main door. It stops and pauses, before creeping slowly up to the glass and pressing up hard against it. It appears to stare inside the tavern, directly at Private Myles, who stares right back at it in terror.

Without warning the large leather apron pounds aggressively onto the glass pane, causing the crack that Dexter had made earlier to propagate out of control.

In a moment of shear panic, Private Myles picks up a small table and hurls it with all his strength towards the window. The glass smashes into hundreds of tiny fragments and falls to the floor.

'What the—what on Earth did you do that for?' questions Private Trout, as he advances to the window and begins beating the leather apron with the end of his weaponised table leg.

'I don't know, Trout – I panicked!' yelps Private Myles, aiding Private Trout by repeatedly clobbering the apron.

After a few moments, Private Trout and Private Myles pause to catch their breath and stare in horror at the apron that lay groaning on the floor. They hold their table legs high in the air; twisting their sweaty hands around their wooden shafts. They both let out a gasp as the apron pulls itself back through the shattered glass on the floor and out through the aperture where the window pane used to be.

'LOOK OUT, MEN!' bellows the Corporal, as a small wave of trousers and shirts advance through the window frame and knock the last few shards of glass onto the floor. 'HOLD THEM BACK!' he adds.

Thuds, thumps, bangs, knocks, smashes and other sounds that you would expect to hear in battle, echo as wooden table legs contact the surrounding furniture and fabrics of laundry. The Corporal and his men try their hardest to battle on against the continued waves of possessed laundry, which make their way through the window frame and into the tavern.

'Look out, Myles! Duck!' shrieks Private Trout, as he swings his wooden table leg over Private Myles' head and makes contact with a crisp white cotton shirt. The shirt moans in pain before falling to the floor. Private Trout kicks the shirt with the end of his boot, causing it to fly back through the window and land on the grass outside. He watches as the shirt returns upright and continues to advance towards them.

Private Trout turns and faces his superior. 'They don't seem to be staying down, Sir!'

'I can see that, Trout,' answers the Corporal. 'But we must continue pushing forwards – and where is that Dexter? I thought—'

The Corporal halts mid-sentence as he hears the tapping of Dexter's claws coming briskly down the stairs. 'Dexter! Over here!' adds the Corporal 'Come quickly!'

Dexter quickly nods and rushes across towards the Corporal, holding very firmly onto the two large jars of dust he had acquired earlier from Mr Dylan's store.

'Oh my—' begins Dexter, staring in concern at the chaos all around him.'

'We need a distraction – and quick, Dex!' expresses the Corporal.

'Mind yourself there, Sir!' bellows Private Simmons, stepping onto a small wooden stool and launching himself through the air, before swinging hard at a white linen shirt, which suddenly flies towards the Corporal. The shirt instantly meets the end of Private Simmons' table leg and is knocked back across the room, hitting a wall and sliding to the floor. The Corporal turns to Private Simmons and nods, acknowledging his small, yet heroic act.

Another window smashes as various trousers and shirts push their way through the shards of broken glass, effortlessly sliding over the makeshift barricade of tables and chairs.

A few more shirts of a questionable material pound hard against the main door.

'Quick, Dexter…' begins the Corporal. 'Do your thing. We are struggling to hold them back – we need to advance to our camp.'

Dexter looks down at the two glass jars he has placed on the floor and hastily removes their lids.

'It might be a good idea to tell your men to hit the deck,' instructs Dexter. 'I've never attempted anything like this – and of such epic proportions. It could get rather unpleasant.'

The Corporal acknowledges with a gentle nod, before taking a cautious step back. He turns towards his men, who continue to hopelessly battle wave after wave of possessed laundry.

'Hit the deck, lads! Heavy artillery coming through!' yells the Corporal, his bellowing voice cutting through the chaotic sounds of shouts, cries and groans.

Dexter lifts his head to see the Corporal's men immediately lowering themselves to the floor of the tavern. They cover their heads with their arms.

Duncan, the tavern cook, and the other random villagers, duck behind the bar counter.

Dexter turns back towards his jars of dust and without hesitation, sticks his snout deep into one. He takes in a long sniff of dust; filling up his nostrils. He pauses and slowly backs away from the jars and rests himself up against the back wall of the tavern.

'Oh, very unpleasant,' mutters Dexter. 'Oh—'

◆◆◆

Mrs Stamps slowly crouches down behind a stone wall at the rear of Mr Dylan's store and hides herself from view. She pauses briefly before letting out a loud gasp. 'MY DARLING CHICKENS!' she shrieks. '*I've*—I've forgotten my poor babies. We have to go back!'

Mrs Stamps quickly turns around and grabs hold of Timothy's shirt with both hands as he falls to his knees, while catching his breath. He pushes the tines of Mrs Stamps' pitchfork deep into the damp grass below and clutches hold of it tightly to prevent himself from completely collapsing to the ground.

'Are you serious?' questions Timothy, taking in a deep breath. 'You really want to go back?'

'Yes, I'm deadly serious, Timothy!' replies Mrs Stamps. 'Those chickens are my world.'

Timothy sighs and lifts himself up slightly. He peers over the stone wall and glances across the green to the tavern entrance, where all chaos has broken out.

'How long do you need, Mrs Stamps? I mean, where are your chickens right now?' asks Timothy.

'At the rear of the post office – in a cage. I must go and release them—' There is a moment's pause as Mrs Stamps stares directly at Timothy. 'You are not going to believe this Timothy – but I'm now going to say something that I never thought I would say to you.'

'Oh, what's that?'

'I need your help, Timothy…'

Timothy raises his eyebrows at Mrs Stamps, slightly confused as he tries to determine whether he is in shock, or in delight at the fact that Mrs Stamps, of all people, is asking for his assistance.

'In that case, I will try my absolute best to assist you, Mrs Stamps,' announces Timothy, pushing himself against the pitchfork and lifting himself to his feet. He runs his hands through his hair and wipes the sweat from his brow with the sleeve of his shirt, before pulling the pitchfork out of the ground. He grasps it firmly.

'Oh, look out, Mrs Stamps!' instructs Timothy, placing one of his hands firmly onto Mrs Stamps' left shoulder and pushing her down, just as a large pair of elaborate cotton underpants leaps atop the wall and passes by.

'Come on, Mrs Stamps,' announces Timothy. 'Lead the way. We will go and rescue your chickens and then make our way back to the tavern – although I'm really not too sure what is going on in there.'

'What do you mean, Timothy?'

Timothy tries to focus in on the tavern entrance, where the sunlight seems to be reflecting off hundreds of tiny shiny objects, which are being forcefully ejected through the tavern's front windows. 'I'm not sure, Mrs Stamps – but from here…it looks like our tavern is erupting copper coins!'

'What do you mean…erupting copper coins?'

'Take a look for yourself.'

◆◆◆

'Keep your heads down, lads,' yells the Corporal. 'It looks like we are getting the better of them! Keep it going, Dexter…you're doing a grand job!'

'I don't think there is any problem in me doing that, right at this moment,' stutters Dexter.

AAAAAACHOO! AAAAAACHOO!

The Corporal smiles.

Dexter leans with his back up against the rear wall of the tavern and spreads his wings wide open. He digs the tips of his claws deep into the flaking masonry of the wall and struggled to maintain an upright position as copper coin after copper coin rapidly fire out of his nostrils.

AAAAAACHOO! AAAAAACHOO!

Dexter changes his position as hundreds of copper coins continue to launch at high velocity across the room, ricocheting off wood, metal and stone. He adjusts his position ever so slightly; attempting to alter the coins flight paths and engage their targets with maximum effect.

Splinters and chips fly off the makeshift barricade in front of him and fill the tavern with a cloudy blanket of fine wooden shards.

'Keep low, lads!' instructs the Corporal. 'They are backing off – keep it up, Dex!'

Duncan peers over the bar-counter and takes a huge gulp of honey mead from his tankard, before letting out a large cry of despair as he watches his beloved tavern being obliterated in front of his eyes. He lets out a bellowing roar, rises to his feet and throws his butcher's knife as hard as he can across the room. The blade shimmers in the dull light as it spins through the air, before coming into contact with a pair of leather trousers and slicing them in two.

The trousers groan in agony and both halves immediately fall to the floor. Duncan lets out a loud gasp as he observes each trouser leg still advancing towards him. In shear desperation, he throws his empty tankard directly at them, before ducking back down behind the bar-counter.

'You're slowing down, Dex!' yells the Corporal. 'Maybe another round of dust, huh?'

Dexter turns towards the Corporal and nods. He leans forward and carefully dips his snout back into the open jar of dust in front of him.

'Okay, lads…let's push them back outside!' yells the Corporal, signalling his men to move forward with a small hand gesture. 'Covering fire please, Dex!'

Dexter tries to remain calm and hold his random sneezes as the Corporal's men re-position themselves, ready to advance. Just as before, a multitude of copper coins fire out of Dexter's nostrils in great succession.

This time, each individual copper coin finds its target; bombarding a variety of trousers, shirts and other various pieces of clothing.

Each piece of attire moans and screams in pain as they are driven backwards by the wave of copper coins.

'Steady – steady now,' announces the Corporal, as a sudden humming noise begins to fill the room, causing everyone to look around in confusion.

'What's that noise, Sir?' queries Private Trout.

The Corporal turns towards Private Babe and listens for any intellectual or logical comment he may have. Private Babe stares back in confusion.

'I'm not sure, Trout,' answers the Corporal. 'But whatever it is…it is getting much—*WHOOOOAH!*'

Unexpectedly a brilliant flash of light illuminates the room, causing everyone to come to a sudden standstill.

THE AIR CRACKLES.

With a loud thud, three bodies drop to the floor and produce a small explosion of dust around them.

'Well, that certainly went a lot better than I expected it to,' announces Melvin, rising to his feet, but then ducking suddenly to avoid a whizzing sound that shoots past his left ear. 'What the—'

Melvin? Is that you, my handsome man?' queries the Corporal, squinting his eyes and trying to focus them through the dust filled room. 'It is you! Quick – move back here!'

'Oh, my Lord!' yelps the Reverend, pushing himself to his feet and aiding Samuel, who struggles to find his balance.

'Over here, gentlemen,' shouts Duncan, waving his arms in the air and directing them to the bar area.

'What on Earth is going on?' asks Melvin.

'Invasion,' answers Duncan, before chuckling. 'But

look! Look what they are doing to my tavern! But it's all good now...huh?'

'What do you mean – now?' answers Melvin.

'Well...you're back now – you can make everything better again, can't you? No?'

Melvin frowns and ducks down behind the bar-counter. He catches a quick glimpse of Dexter, who continues to fire vast amounts of copper coins from his nostrils. The coins ricochet off multiple surfaces, before scattering over the floor of the tavern.

'I'm afraid that's just not going to be possible at present, Duncan,' states Melvin.

'Not possible? Why—*hic*—ever not?' asks Duncan.

'I don't have the energy – I'm pooped from the last spell I cast. It takes a little while for me to regain my magical charge.'

'How long does that usually take?' enquires Samuel.

'Well, how long is a piece of string?' replies Melvin, placing his hands over his ears; attempting to shield them from the chaotic sounds going on around him.

Duncan raises an eyebrow at Melvin, before turning his attention to Samuel, who is frantically rummaging through his jacket pockets.

'Melvin?' asks Samuel.

'Huh? Yes?' replies Melvin.

'Can you please let me know the next time you use a teleportation spell? My hat is now probably floating around in some interstellar dimension.'

'Oh, that's a shame—' answers Melvin.

The Reverend lifts himself up and peers over the top of the bar-counter, just as the Corporal instructs all his men to advance forward.

'What are you going to do about this, Melvin?' asks the Reverend, holding on tightly to his crucifix.

'What am I going to do…? Surely you mean *we*?' replies Melvin, arguing that although most of this is his fault, is it still rather the problem of the whole village. He convinces himself that he did actually achieve what he set out to do, and that was to wash all of the villagers' dirty laundry, although afterwards, he didn't anticipate it all being very much alive.

'I think we may need to split up and start searching the village for Amelia,' suggests the Reverend. 'We need her help, especially if Melvin is unable to assist at present.'

'Yes, I agree,' adds Samuel. 'And no disrespect to you, Melvin – but we do actually need somebody who knows what they are doing – especially with laundry. Even if you did have enough magical charge, it may *not* be a good idea to cast another spell – just in case you make it worse than it is already.'

'Okay, but where shall we search first?' asks the Reverend. 'We are assuming that she is actually still in the village—'

'True,' interrupts Samuel. 'We must also search the surrounding areas.'

'Including the forest?' asks the Reverend.

'No need, people…' begins Melvin. 'I have a very good idea where she may be.'

The Reverend and Samuel huddle around Melvin.

'Where?' asks the Reverend.

Melvin raises his hands and points to the ceiling.

'Oh no! Really? She is with our Lord?' gasps the Reverend, placing his hand over his dropped jaw.

'What? Huh? No-no…I think she maybe upstairs,' responds Melvin, with raised eyebrows.

'Upstairs…?' queries Samuel. 'Would you care to explain, Melvin?'

CHAPTER XII

"Panic? I haven't got time to panic, Babe. Besides, how many times have you been chased around a water fountain by a pair of woollen pyjamas?"

Corporal Ringelstein

The sight of two people running frantically through an army of laundry that has magically and mistakenly been brought to life by a crazy eccentric wizard, is certainly something that many people would find rather odd and strange. However, the sight of two people running through laundry, followed by ten incredibly gormless chickens, is in itself, border lining on peculiar.

'This is the only way that they will follow me,' yelps Mrs Stamps, chucking handfuls of popped corn onto the grass in front of her chickens.

'I know that, Mrs Stamps,' replies Timothy. 'But we don't have the time for them to keep stopping and pecking at the ground – we must get a move on!'

Timothy looks up and quickly lifts Mrs Stamps' pitchfork around his head, before using all his strength to swing it at two pairs of trousers, which have crept towards him and Mrs Stamps. The pitchfork makes contact and knocks them both to the ground. The trousers moan in agony and slowly wriggle around in the damp grass. Timothy carefully steps over them.

'Come on, my little babies,' instructs Mrs Stamps, trying her best to usher her chickens onwards. She sighs as she watches them peck randomly at the grass.

Timothy stands firm; his shoulders held back. He begins to breathe heavily as he turns to a large mass of laundry that has now become extremely aware of his presence. He tightens his grip around the pitchfork handle and digs the heels of his boots deep into the wet ground beneath him.

'Mrs Stamps…I hate to tell you what to do – but we really must be going now,' whispers Timothy.

'I'm going as fast as I can, Timothy. Will you please be patient,' replies Mrs Stamps.

'That is something I don't have a lot of right now, Mrs Stamps – patience.'

Without any warning, a small group of bright white underpants descend from above and begin to attack Timothy; slapping themselves hard across his face, arms and any other exposed part of his anatomy. The stinging sound of wet cotton lashing on naked flesh, echoes through the air.

Timothy screams like a little girl, before rage takes over and he suddenly adopts some crazed attack mode; swinging the pitchfork around in the air, hoping that at least some of his uncontrolled swings will make contact with the underpants.

He continues to frantically slice through the air; the tines of the pitchfork eventually finding the freshly washed cotton-like material of the undergarments, ripping them to shreds and falling to the ground in front of him. He stares in disbelief as they continue to move around at his feet.

Mrs Stamps endures to aid her chickens across the village green, constantly looking around her as she takes careful steps backwards. The chickens slowly follow her, clucking erratically.

Timothy paces forwards, pauses briefly and checks for a suitable moment to make a rush for the tavern entrance; the tavern, which at this very instance has more laundry coming out of it, than going in. He ponders at why the laundry has changed direction.

'Oh, bothersome!' curses Mrs Stamps, stumbling over something on the ground at her feet, causing her to fall backwards onto her plump rear.

'Are you okay, Mrs Stamps?' asks Timothy.

'What on Earth is this…?' mumbles Mrs Stamps, reaching underneath her and picking up a magically bound book. 'Oh…it's Melvin's journal.'

'Melvin's journal?' questions Timothy, eyeing up two large white linen towels moving very cautiously towards him.

'Yes, Timothy,' replies Mrs Stamps. 'He must have dropped it earlier when he was casting the spell on the washing. We'd better return it to him – he may need it to solve this mess.'

'Where do you think he is? We did sort of run off and leave him in the middle of all this.'

'Well, he did tell us to leave him there, didn't he?'

'Yes, he did. But I don't think he actually—'

'I can assure you that Melvin is more than capable of looking after himself.'

Timothy approaches Mrs Stamps and assists her to her feet. For once in her life, she doesn't unleash her rage onto Timothy, but instead gives him a small nod, followed by a gentle smirk.

'LOOK OUT!' yells Timothy, grabbing Mrs Stamps by the arm and pulling her to the side as two linen towels pounce onto Timothy; knocking him back and pushing him to the ground. 'Get off me, you blasted—you…' continues Timothy, cutting himself off mid-sentence, struggling to come up with a suitable name for the possessed linen towels.

Timothy frantically spins around on the spot and tries his hardest to shake off the towels that grip tightly onto him. He curses at them loudly, waving his arms about through the damp grass, while desperately trying to hold onto the pitchfork. He attempts to push himself to his feet as one of the towels positions itself over his face, before wrapping tightly around his neck, causing Timothy to let out a gasp of air as the towel begins to tighten against his throat.

Mrs Stamps screams as another towel creeps up behind her and launches itself onto her head. It wraps itself tightly around her face and muffles her screams to a near silence. She drops down to her knees, while desperately using her hands to pull the towels away.

The towels continue to try and suffocate both Timothy and Mrs Stamps and during all of this, ten confused chickens continue to cluck uncontrollably.

Suddenly, a loud roaring shout resonates through the air and the sounds of footsteps pounding on damp grass are heard. They get faster and louder. Timothy tilts his head slightly; trying to take a look at what is heading their way.

Timothy finds it difficult to focus as the towel grips tighter around his neck. It causes his face to turn a slight bluish colour; struggling to breathe.

Without warning, the towel wrapped around Mrs Stamps' head howls in pain as it is ripped from her face and thrown to the grass. Mrs Stamps takes in a deep breath of air and rubs her eyes with both of her hands. She gazes in front of her to observe Officer Locks darting very quickly towards Timothy, with rage in his eyes. He reaches out, grabs the two towels that cling onto Timothy and with one swift movement he tears them both to pieces with his bare hands.

'Quick – get up!' yells Officer Locks, reaching out his hand towards Timothy.

'Officer Locks – is that you?' mumbles Timothy, taking Officer Locks' hand and rising to his feet.

'It is—' replies Officer Locks, picking up the pitchfork from the grass and handing it to Timothy.

Officer Locks turns towards Mrs Stamps and checks on her condition. He paces slowly towards her and stares at her, before his attention is re-directed to her chickens, which have gathered at her feet.

Mrs Stamps brushes herself down and straightens her dress, before reaching down to her chickens.

'Oh, my babies – did they hurt you?' mutters Mrs Stamps, grabbing another handful of popped corn from her pocket and throwing it to the ground.

Officer Locks turns back towards Timothy. He raises an eyebrow and looks for some explanation as to why Mrs Stamps is talking to a bunch of chickens.

Timothy shrugs his shoulders and lets out a smirk.

'We must move,' instructs Officer Locks.

'We are heading to our tavern,' responds Timothy.

'To our tavern we go, then,' replies Officer Locks. 'Quick – follow me and stay alert.'

Mrs Stamps stretches out her left hand and extends her index finger, using it to point at each and every one of her chickens; tallying them up. 'Okay – they are all here. Let's go!' she says.

'Now, don't forgot that diary of yours, Mrs Stamps,' responds Officer Locks, pointing to Melvin's journal laying on the grass.

'My what? Oh – yes—*ahem*—' replies Mrs Stamps.

'Okay…stay close to me and scream if you have to,' announces Officer Locks.

◆◆◆

The Corporal raises a clenched fist into the air to instruct his men to hold their positions. He shifts his body to face Dexter, who then acknowledges the Corporal with a gently nod.

Dexter attempts to hold his sneezes, but with the large amount of dust in his nostrils, it is proving quite difficult. He continues to fire off copper coins through the front window of the tavern, narrowly missing the Corporal's men.

Dexter takes a few careful paces backwards and leans himself up against the rear wall of the tavern. Hr lowers his head to the floor in a desperate attempt to minimise the amount of copper coins flying through the room. He shuffles his clawed feet and tries to avoid copper coins that continue to fly out of his nostrils. He lets out a painful cry as a few coins hit his scaly skin.

'What is it, Myles?' yells the Corporal.

Private Myles stares in relief as the laundry begins

to retreat from inside the tavern. Pieces of fabric groan and moan as they slither across the floor, over the barricade and make their way outside.

'They are retreating, Sir!' replies Private Myles.

'They are?' asks the Corporal.

'Yes, Sir! 'But wait…what the—'

Private Myles, in most situations he gets caught up in, likes to bend the truth; making them sound just a little more glamourous than they actually are. However, in this case, Private Myles says exactly what he sees, although it does sound rather peculiar.

'*It's*—it's that Mrs Stamps, Sir!' continues Private Myles. 'She is with Timothy and some other guy.'

'Some other guy?' queries the Corporal.

'Yes…and—well, they are being followed by a load of chickens, Sir.'

'A load of chickens? Seriously, Myles?' questions the Corporal. 'I sometimes consider whether that pea-sized brain of yours has finally—oh, you are right,' he adds, approaching Private Myles from behind and glancing out across the village green.

'They seem to be heading our way, Sir,' adds Private Myles.

'With the chickens?'

'It looks that way, Sir.'

The Corporal stares at Mrs Stamps leading her chickens very hastily towards them. He climbs up onto the make-shift barricade, scouts around and checks that the coast is clear.

'Okay, lads…let's get them all quickly and safely inside,' instructs the Corporal. 'We shall then make a push through the village and make way to our camp.'

'Sounds like a good plan,' replies Private Trout, joining his superior atop the barricade, before climbing down to the wooden decking outside the tavern. One by one, the remainder of the Corporal's men follow, each being very cautious of their surroundings.

'Where in blazes do you think you are all going?' hollers Melvin, from behind the bar.

The Corporal quickly turns around to face Melvin. 'It's okay, my sweet little Melvin. I know you'll miss me, but I will be back soon. The men and I are going to fetch our weapons from the camp at the river.'

Melvin cringes at the Corporal's response. He wishes that the Corporal hadn't breathed in as much of the Angel's Fern as he did, as his very loving comments are now getting very uncomfortable for everyone.

'Oh…and you are about to receive a few guests,' continues the Corporal.

'Guests?' queries Melvin, popping up from behind the counter and gazing across the tavern.

'That's right. Mrs Stamps and that Timothy fellow,' replies the Corporal.

'Oh geez…and they are coming this way?'

'That's right, they are – and with some other chap.'

'Some other chap?'

'That's what I said, Melvin – my sweet.'

The Corporal follows his men as they jump down off the barricade and onto the wooden decking; each of them holding their wooden table legs firmly in their hands and poised ready for battle.

'Mrs Stamps!' bellows the Corporal, waving his hand frantically through the air. 'Over here!'

'I don't think she can hear you, Sir,' says Private Babe. 'Those chickens of hers are making such an awful racket—'

'Sir?' interrupts Private Myles. 'We have a slight problem.'

Private Myles takes a small step forward. He points towards the centre of the village at a small area on the far side of the fountain, where multiple pieces of laundry are materialising into a large group. They form highly organised lines; placing themselves into packs, according to size, weight and colour.

The Corporal shifts his eyes to where Private Myles is pointing.

'Looks like they are forming ranks, Sir,' announces Private Myles. 'What are we going to do? They are right in our path back to the camp.'

The Corporal pauses, allowing his brain to conjure up some masterful and cunning plan that would get him and his soldiers to their camp without being spotted. In his head he visualises a tactful and well executed system of timed manoeuvres, which would allow him and his men to creep undetected, with utmost precision, past the army of possessed laundry that are lining up across the green. Of course, what the Corporal plans out in his head and what actually happens, are two completely different things.

'Okay, lads…' begins the Corporal. 'Private Trout and Private Myles – you go and assist Mrs Stamps with her chickens and bring them all back here safely. The rest of us shall make our way towards the camp.'

'Through that lot?' asks Private Myles, still pointing at the lines of laundry forming across the green.

'Yes, Myles,' replies the Corporal. 'We shall use our highly trained stealth abilities to sneak past.'

'Stealth, Sir?' questions Private Myles. 'If I may say so, Sir – and I don't want to come across as sounding rude…but, you are a rather large—'

'Silence, Myles!' interrupts the Corporal. 'That's the plan and we are going to stick with it. Now off you and

Trout go. We'll meet you back here shortly.'

Private Myles promptly salutes his superior and nods at Private Trout; indicating to him to move out towards Mrs Stamps.

'Right…now let's quickly move, lads!' instructs the Corporal. 'Follow my lead. Oh…and Dexter – best you hold here awhile until your sneezing subsides. We don't want any unnecessary sounds that will break our stealth. Keep your ears open though, Dex. I will yell if I require a distraction.'

◆◆◆

'A vampire, you say?' questions Samuel. 'What in the Lord's name would a vampire be doing here in our village, Melvin?'

'Well, come on – think about it,' replies Melvin.

Samuel turns to the Reverend and then slowly back towards Melvin; staring blankly at him. Melvin gazes back at Samuel and then quickly shifts his eyes across to the Reverend, awaiting a response from either of them.

'Seriously…?' adds Melvin, before a slight pause. 'Duncan…would you please be so kind as to describe the gentleman staying upstairs in room four?'

'Huh?' responds Duncan, taking a gulp of honey mead from his tankard.

'The gentleman staying in room four, Duncan – please describe him,' repeats Melvin.

Duncan shuffles towards Melvin. 'Well…he is a man – very tall – wears a pair of sunglasses – oh…and he has a pet rat.'

Melvin narrows his eyes at Duncan. 'Thank you for that amazing descriptive assessment, Duncan.'

'A pet rat?' gasps the Reverend. 'Now…that is very interesting you say that as Mrs Stamps mentioned that she saw a giant rat the other night. What's even more interesting – is the fact she said the rat spoke to her.'

'That she did!' responds Samuel.

'How many nights has the gentlemen in room four been staying here, Duncan?' asks Melvin.

Duncan lets out a loud belch. 'Oh, I would say a couple of nights, but I have hardly seen him at all – I occasionally bump into him at dust.'

'You see…' begins Melvin. 'A vampire!'

Samuel turns and leans up close to the Reverend. 'Do you think that he has actually lost the plot?' he whispers into the Reverend's ear.

The Reverend lets out a smirk. 'So…what are you getting at, Melvin?'

Melvin sighs. 'Don't you see – if I am right – and I pretty much know that I am – I believe that there is a vampire staying upstairs.'

'And?' questions the Reverend. 'There is nothing wrong with that. It is up to Duncan who he chooses to stay here. That is none of our business.'

'I believe that the vampire – who by pure chance I met on the stairs last night – is most likely holding our Laundry Fairy captive…in room four.'

'But why would he do that, Melvin?' asks Samuel.

'I haven't got the time to explain that now…' begins Melvin. 'Will you both escort me upstairs please? I believe that I would like to pay this vampire a little visit. Do you have a spare room key, Duncan?'

'Hang on a wee moment, *Mr Wizard Man*,' retorts Duncan. 'You just can't go around…letting yourself into people's rooms! They have to pay extra for that privilege.'

'Yes…Duncan is right,' states the Reverend. 'At some convenient point – why don't we just go and see if we can find Officer Locks – do it all properly?'

Melvin bites down on his lip in frustration, which he often does when he becomes impatient. He ponders at the Reverend's suggestion, before nodding his head in acceptance.

'Well, let's go and get him, then,' announces Melvin.

'No need, Melvin,' begins Samuel. 'Here he is right now – with Mrs Stamps, Timothy and—well, all of her chickens.'

'*MELVIN*!' shouts Mrs Stamps. 'Are you here?'

Melvin closes his eyes. He shakes his head from side to side and hopes that if he remained perfectly still, Mrs Stamps would not notice him.

'Ah, Melvin…it is you there,' adds Mrs Stamps. 'I'm so glad that you managed to get yourself to safety. I had complete faith in you – of course.'

'Darn it,' mutters Melvin, before instantly smiling as Mrs Stamps approaches him. 'Hello, Mrs Stamps.'

Timothy follows behind, while carefully avoiding the fragments of splintered wood and piles of copper coins that lay scattered about the floor.

'Ah, Timbers…it was extremely noble of you to run away like that, earlier,' roars Melvin. 'If it wasn't for the Reverend and Samuel dragging me into the church – then who knows what may have become of me.'

Timothy lowers his head in shame. 'Oh, my sincere apologies for that, Melvin. Please forgive me.'

Melvin gently nods and accepts Timothy's apology.

'Here, Melvin…I believe that this is yours…?' says Mrs Stamps, handing over Melvin's journal.

'My journal!' glees Melvin. 'I thought I'd lost it. I thank you from the deepest depths of my heart.'

'You do, Melvin?' replies Mrs Stamps, winking slyly.

A moment's pause is suddenly interrupted by a loud thud as Private Myles falls flat on his face onto the tavern floor. Private Trout lets out a roaring laugh and drops to his knees in hysterics; laughing uncontrollably at Private Myles, who had just misplaced his feet while climbing over the barricade.

Mrs Stamps turns towards Private Trout and blows him a kiss, before winking at him. She does this purposely in front of Melvin, who responds by raising an eyebrow.

'Where are the others?' asks Mrs Stamps.

'The others?' replies Private Trout.

'Yes...the large chubby one – your Corporal – and the rest of your squad?'

'The chubby one...' sniggers Private Myles, lifting himself to his feet and brushing himself down.

'Ah yes...' begins Private Trout. 'They are sneaking about the village – trying to make their way back to our camp to collect weapons...and anything else we can use to fight with.'

Mrs Stamps nods and turns towards Melvin.

Without warning, another loud thud hits the floor of the tavern, causing a small eruption of dust into the already cloudy and musty air.

'Ah...Officer Locks, I'm guessing?' asks Melvin.

'That would be correct,' replies Officer Locks. 'I'm guessing that you are the troubled individual who happened to crash right into our village fountain the other night, are you not?'

'Err...well—*I*—I can explain—' stutters Melvin.

'Never mind!' interrupts Officer Locks. 'At this very moment we have more important issues to worry about – have we not?'

Melvin smiles briefly and turns to Samuel. He tilts his head in the Officer's direction and prompts Samuel to ask Officer Locks for his assistance with a certain individual, in a certain room upstairs.

Samuel stares at Melvin in slight confusion, before realising what Melvin is suggesting.'

'Oh…right—err…Officer?' *I*—*I*—I mean *we*—we were wandering if we could possibly borrow you for a few moments? Melvin seems to believe he knows where our Laundry Fairy is.'

Officer Locks lifts his head suddenly. 'Really? How very interesting…do tell!'

'Well…' begins Samuel. 'Melvin believes that she is here in our tavern – upstairs – in room four.'

'Room four? I don't think I understand what you are saying,' replies Officer Locks.

'Yes, what are you mumbling on about, Samuel?' questions Mrs Stamps, taking a step forward.

Samuel pauses and lets out a sigh. 'I'm talking about a vampire…' begins Samuel. 'Melvin believes that a vampire is staying upstairs in room four – and that this vampire has captured our Laundry Fairy – and is hiding her in the room.'

Officer Locks growls. 'A vampire? How interesting – how very interesting. Well, if that is the case, I believe we should all go upstairs and knock on the door – see what this vampire character has to say for himself—'

'Edwin…' interrupts Duncan.

'Excuse me?' responds Officer Locks.

'The chap in room four…his name is Edwin.'

Everyone gently nods, before being interrupted by Dexter, who rushes across the tavern floor. 'I need water!' he screams. 'I think my snout is on fire!'

◆◆◆

Crawling very slowly on their hands and knees, the Corporal and his other men move silently behind a long stone wall, which lines the outer perimeter of the village church. The Corporal occasionally stops and peek over the top of the wall.

'I've already had my hands covered once in mud and dirt – with them stupid darn trees…' begins Private Simmons. 'And now I'm crawling through mud again – why did I sign up to this—'

'Be quiet, Simmons,' whispers the Corporal, looking back at him and the rest of his highly trained men, crouching behind the wall.

'How's the path ahead looking, Sir?' asks Private Babe. 'Any signs of the laundry?'

'I can't see much from here,' replies the Corporal. 'We need to move forward to take a look.'

The Corporal continues to creep forward, followed momentarily by Private Babe, who keeps a few steps between himself and his superior, on the unlucky event that the Corporal suddenly halts, causing Private Babe to push up against the Corporal's incredibly large rear.

Private Babe ponders to himself; wishing that the Corporal would buy himself some new trousers, or at least ones that would fit well around his waist area. The sight of a couple of plump bum cheeks sticking out of the top of his trousers, is beginning to give Private Babe some severe psychological issues.

'Okay…pass this message on, will you?' instructs the Corporal, turning towards Private Babe. 'We have to keep low and rush across to the fountain wall.'

Private Babe nods and turns to the next recruit in line and whispers to him exactly what the Corporal has just instructed. Private Babe is slow, clear and precise as he pronounces each and every word.

After a few moments, the message is passed along the full line of recruits, before being relayed to Private Simmons at the end. He pauses in confusion.

'We have to stay toned and rub ourselves up against the fountain wall?' mutters Private Simmons, before questioning the Corporal's intentions.

Suddenly, the line of men in front of Private Simmons advances forward. The men crawl carefully across the muddy ground beneath them, and one by one they each drop onto their stomachs and pull themselves across the green, towards the fountain.

Sitting upright, the Corporal and his men lean up against the wall of the fountain and keep their heads lowered. The men pause to catch their breath as the Corporal peeks over the top of the fountain.

'How's it looking, Sir?' asks Private Babe.

'Not too good – to be honest,' replies the Corporal. 'They now all seem to be gathering around the other side – I can't see any other way around.'

'What are we going to do, Sir?' adds Private Babe.

The Corporal pauses. 'Well…I believe we have two choices. We either engage them – or we try to sneak around them and hope that they don't spot us.'

Private Babe lifts himself up and takes a peek over the fountain wall, before promptly lowering himself back into position.

'I think I prefer the latter, if I had to choose, Sir,' answers Private Babe.

The Corporal nods in agreement.

'Okay…follow me,' instructs the Corporal. 'And for God's sake…keep quiet!'

The Corporal and his men continue to plough and

slide across the muddy grass, trying their best not to make any unnecessary sounds that will alert the mass of laundry, gathering nearby.

Suddenly, the Corporal halts and lets out a groan.

'What's up, Sir?' whispers Private Babe.

A slight grumbling sound is heard coming from the Corporal's belly.

'Sir...?' adds Private Babe.

'I really don't think I should have eaten two of those pickled eggs, earlier. You know? The ones that Duncan keeps behind the bar at the tavern.'

'What do you mean, Sir?'

'Well, they are giving me bad stomach pains and slight gaseous problems. I really feel like I need to let out a huge—well, you know...a large eruption of gas from a certain rear aperture.'

Private Babe remains silent; shocked by the choice of descriptive words his superior has chosen.

Without warning, and with no consideration for the close proximity of Private Babe, the Corporal lets out a very high-pitched squealing fart; a fart that ripples and resonates through the air, creating sonics that no human being should be capable of making.

The unpleasant sound of the Corporal's gaseous ejection, travels at speed across the village green. One by one, it attracts each and every piece of laundry that stands in unison, just several feet away.

'Oh—err...Corporal?' whispers Private Babe. 'We have a slight problem.'

'You think *we* have a problem?' says the Corporal. 'I think I've just pooped—'

'Look out, Sir!' yelps Private Babe.

◆◆◆

Melvin hesitates, before knocking firmly on the door to room four. He waits patiently alongside Officer Locks, the Reverend and Mrs Stamps, for any answer from within. Melvin slowly turns towards the Officer, who then gently nods at Melvin; indicating for to him to knock a second time on the door.

Melvin tightens his hand into a fist and thumps down several times on to the dry wooden face of the door. He pauses, before taking a small step backwards.

'Looks like there's no one in,' states the Reverend.

'Well…if what Melvin is saying is true…' begins Samuel. 'And there is a vampire on the other side of this door – then surely he *would be* inside? – staying out of the sunlight. I hear they don't like it; you see?'

Melvin nods and raises his fist to the door to knock for a third time.

Inside the room, Corbin awakes to the sound of Melvin's knocking and hurriedly scutters across the room. He stands perfectly still at the side of the door, with his back firmly against the wall and pauses briefly to steady his breathing.

Corbin shuffles himself down onto the dusty floor in an attempt to take a peek through the gap under the door, hoping to catch a glimpse of the type of footwear being worn by the person, or persons, on the other side. Being able to guess the type of person by their footwear alone, is a skill that Corbin has developed to perfection over the last few years and prides himself in being an expert at.

The gap under the door is too narrow for Corbin to see anything through. He lifts himself up and races back across the floor towards his Master, who lay atop the bed. Corbin ponders whether or not to wake his Master from his deep sleep.

There is another loud thump at the door, which stirs Corbin's Master from his sleep.

'Master?' whispers Corbin. 'There is someone at the door.'

Edwin lets out a small hiss and opens his eyes, before promptly elevating himself to a sitting position.

'Hello…is anyone in there…?' questions Officer Locks, from outside the room. 'This is Officer Locks. I demand you open this door at once!'

'What should I do, Master?' whispers Corbin, with a slight tone of panic in his voice.

Corbin's Master immediately swings his legs off the bed and places his feet firmly on the floor, before standing up. He instantly grabs his cloak and throws it into the corner of the room; covering the metal cage and hiding the Laundry Fairy from view.

The thick material of his cloak muffles the painful sounds still being made by the Laundry Fairy.

Corbin's Master then darts across to the window shutters and checks that they are firmly closed, before turning around and straightening his attire.

'I think there is someone in there…' announces Melvin, placing his ear hard up against the door. 'I can certainly hear someone rummaging around.'

Officer Locks takes a small step forward and reaches out to grab hold of the door handle. He gives it a careful twist and nudges the door gently with his knee. The door fails to open.

'Locked…I'm guessing?' asks Samuel.

Officer Locks turns to Samuel and nods, before turning back to face the door. 'I can hear you in there…' begins Officer Locks. 'I suggest you open this door right now, or I'll have no choice but to bust it open!'

'What do we do, Master?' murmurs Corbin.

'We answer the door, Corbin,' replies his Master.

'Will that not allow the light in, Master?

'I will stand back here, Corbin – by the wall. Just do your best to get rid of whoever is out there – and do it quickly! We haven't time for visitors.'

Corbin creeps back towards the door and reaches up on his tiptoes to turn the key in its lock. He turns to look over his shoulder at his Master, before turning the door handle and carefully pulling the door open. Corbin cautiously peeks around the ajar door and tilts his head up to Officer Locks and Melvin, who stand in front of Samuel, the Reverend and Mrs Stamps.

'Oh—err…hello there, little one…' begins Officer Locks, staring down at Corbin. 'I wasn't half expecting to be greeted by a—err…what means of creature are you—?

That's the giant rat I saw the other night!' interrupts Mrs Stamps, barging her way through Melvin and Officer Locks. 'Yes, that's him! I told you I saw a rat – I'm not going mad!'

'Debatable…' mutters Melvin.

Corbin shivers at the sight of Mrs Stamps and pushes the door slightly forwards; shielding himself from her.

'Calm down, Mrs Stamps,' instructs Officer Locks, glancing over his shoulder at her. 'Now then, *my*—my little—err, what do they call you…?' he continues, crouching down towards Corbin.

'My name is Corbin. I'm a mole-sprite,' announces Corbin, staring Officer Locks up and down.

'Very interesting…' responds Officer Locks. 'Well, Corbin – we are here to see Edwin, if you please?' turning towards Melvin, who nods gently back at him.

'Not here,' answers Corbin, before attempting to close the door in front of the Officer, who promptly wedges a foot between the door and its frame.

'Then I assume that you wouldn't mind if we just take a quick look around?' asks Officer Locks, pushing the door wide open and stepping into the room.

'Well, this is highly irregular,' announces Edwin, stepping out of the shadows, into the centre of room. 'I assume there is a good reason for this intrusion?'

'That's him!' shrieks Melvin, standing defensively behind Officer Locks and waving his pointed finger crazily over Officer Locks' shoulders. 'That's the vampire! What have you done with her?' he continues, huffing and puffing.

'Ah…it is you – the spellbinder…' begins Edwin. 'It is true what you say – I am a vampire – but I also have no idea what you are blathering on about.'

Mrs Stamps and the Reverend slowly enter the room, closely followed by Timothy, and also Samuel, who then closes the door gently behind him and turns the key in its lock.

Edwin stares hard at Officer Locks; his eyes narrow. 'You smell of fear, Officer,' states Edwin. 'Oh…and I'm sensing a slight tingling in your blood – maybe something to do with a celestial object? – just a guess.'

Officer Locks lets out a quiet growl at Edwin, which he cleverly hides from the others, by pretending to clear his throat. The Officer glances around the dull candle lit room, observing Corbin as he jumps up onto his Master's bed. He watches Corbin remove his yo-yo from his waistcoat pocket and begin playing with it.

'What have you done with her!' shouts Melvin. 'I know you've taken her – where is she?'

'Let's not jump to any conclusions, Melvin,' says the

Reverend, placing his hand on Melvin's shoulder.

Samuel shifts his eyes to look around the poorly lit room and tilts his head to look under the bed. He fails to notice Edwin's magical zynite cage, which sits in the shadows under his cloak, in the far corner of the room.

'Looks like there is nothing here,' states Samuel. 'Maybe you are mistaken, Melvin?'

'I know this *v—v*—vampire has taken her – *I*—I'm pretty sure—' stutters Melvin, before collapsing onto his knees.'

'Melvin? Are you okay…?' queries the Reverend, stepping forward and aiding Melvin to his feet. He pulls Melvin's arm over his shoulder.

'*S—s*—something is draining *m*—my power,' slurs Melvin.

'Okay…everyone stay where they are!' yells Officer Locks. 'There is something fishy going on here and I'm about to get to the bottom—'

'We haven't got the time for this!' interrupts Mrs Stamps, grabbing her wooden crucifix tightly in her hand and stomping across the floor towards Edwin. She reaches out and forcefully holds her crucifix in front of Edwin's face. 'Let the power of our Lord, compel thee!'

Edwin lets out a loud hiss and immediately backs up against the wall; cowering at the sight of Mrs Stamps' crucifix. He attempts to shield himself by wrapping his arms tightly around his head, before falling to the floor and cursing loudly.

Corbin, on noticing that his Master requires his assistance, grabs his yo-yo and jumps down from the bed. He hurryingly scutters across the floor towards Mrs Stamps.

'Not so fast!' bellows Officer Locks, reaching down

and picking Corbin up by the scruff of his neck. Officer Locks lifts Corbin from the floor and holds him out in front of him. Corbin smirks as he tries to wriggle himself free from the Officer's firm grip.

'Now…we can do this the easy way – or the hard way,' snarls Mrs Stamps. 'Tell us where our Laundry Fairy is – or things are going to get very messy. You wouldn't want to mess with a woman who is running out of clean outfits to wear!'

Edwin hisses, before turning himself into a bat, in a desperate attempt to elude Mrs Stamps' crucifix, only to fail instantly by crashing head first into the far wall and sliding down onto the floor in human form.

'Quick Reverend…help me!' shrieks Mrs Stamps. 'Use your crucifix on him – keep him to the floor!'

'I really don't think we should be doing that, Mrs Stamps,' responds the Reverend. 'Especially as we don't have any hard proof—'

'Just do it, Reverend!' yells Mrs Stamps.

The Reverend passes Melvin across to Samuel, who aids him in standing upright. Samuel ponders at what could possibly be making Melvin feel ill and drained of energy.

'Come here please, Officer…' begins Mrs Stamps. 'Help us lift the vampire into this chair. We can then tie him up in front of these shutters.'

'With what?' asks Officer Locks.

'Pardon me?' responds Mrs Stamps.

'With what would you like me to tie him to the chair with, Mrs Stamps? Oh, never mind, I shall just use this little chap's yo-yo,' replies the Officer, ripping it from the clawed hands of Corbin, who begins to whimper. 'Now then, little one – where to place you,' he adds, gazing at Corbin.

Officer Locks paces across the room and lowers Corbin down onto the end of a bed knob; hooking his waistcoat tightly over the top. He swings his little arms and legs through the air in an attempt to try and loosen himself, before sighing and realising he is not going anywhere fast.

Officer Locks and the Reverend take hold of Edwin's arms and legs and lift him off the floor and into the wooden chair.

'He feels very cold to the touch,' states Samuel.

'He's a vampire,' replies Mrs Stamps. 'What do you expect?'

Samuel holds Edwin's drooping body in place as the Reverend wraps the string from the yo-yo around him; finishing it off with a tight knot.

'Is that going to hold him?' questions the Reverend.

'That will have to do,' replies Mrs Stamps. 'Right …move him across here – in front of the shutter. When he eventually regains consciousness, I'm sure he'll answer all our questions if I threaten to open these shutters on him.'

Mrs Stamps carefully places her crucifix back into the top of her dress. 'Okay…how long does it take a vampire to awaken after knocking himself out?'

◆◆◆

The Corporal and his men stand poised, gripping their wooden table legs in their hands. They stare nervously at each other, before turning towards their superior, who grits his teeth in rage. He growls quietly at the oncoming mass of laundry and raises his table leg high into the air, before hurling it down into the palm of his sweaty hand.

'Well, lads…' begins the Corporal. 'It has been an absolute pleasure working alongside you all. I know that this is not what most of you were expecting when you signed up, but please do not be discouraged to venture into different professions – I will not hold it against you.'

'I'm here by your side until the end, Sir!' salutes Private Babe, quickly followed by cheers from the rest of the squad.

'So be it…' mutters the Corporal, charging forward towards the frontline of the laundry. 'Aggressive fire, Dex!' he shouts. Dexter then immediately dips his snout into the half full jar of dust and digs his claws deep into the damp soil below; finding a footing.

Within seconds, Dexter's nostrils flare up and go into overdrive and shower the village green in copper coins.

AAAAAACHOO! AAAAAACHOO!

A full blown force of hundreds of copper coins pelt the oncoming laundry; bombarding them from every possible angle.

The Corporal and his men charge hard at the laundry. They wave their tables legs frantically through the air, whilst dodging masses of copper coins that whizz past their ears; many pinging off the tips of their table legs and falling to the grass below.

The laundry starts to advance towards them. Many of them float through the air like ghostly apparitions, while others slowly slither and slide across the grass like snakes about to attack their prey. They begin to swirl around the Corporal and his men; surrounding them in a huge circle; blinding them from any sort of pathway out of the village.

Laundry flies off in all directions. It meets the

tipped ends of their table legs as the Corporal and his men hurl and thrash them through the air.

The Corporal and his men shout in rage as wave after wave of laundry starts to head towards them. The continued moans and groans from the laundry echoes around the village. Piece by piece the laundry falls to ground, only to seconds later, arise once again.

'I'm really not too sure how long we can hold them off, Sir!' shouts Private Babe.

'We must find a way through!' replies the Corporal. 'I thought maybe using Dex would of least caused *some sort* of distraction, but there are too many of them.'

'Do you think that maybe you could lead them away, Sir? asks Private Babe. 'The rest of the men and I could then try and make our way to the camp?'

'Me?' responds the Corporal, sounding surprised.

'Yes, Sir,' yelps Private Babe. 'You are the biggest and the strongest – you can at least give us a chance.'

The Corporal smashes his table leg into a pair of trousers; knocking them flying back into a group of woolly jumpers. The jumpers turn and suddenly pace towards the Corporal.

'Very well, then…' begins the Corporal. 'You lead the rest of the men to camp. Dex and I will create some sort of diversion – and Private…?'

'Yes, Sir?' replies Private Babe.

'Be careful!'

Private Babe salutes his superior and shouts across to the rest of the squad, who continue to fight a losing battle against the possessed laundry.

One by one the men nod and fight their way over towards Private Babe. They huddle around him, with their backs against each other.

'What's the Corporal doing?' asks Private Simmons,

adjusting his helmet to a more horizontal position.

'Err...I'm not sure,' replies Private Babe.

'He seems to have unintentionally collapsed to the floor,' adds Private Simmons. 'It looks as if he is rolling around on the ground like some huge beach whale.'

'Is he lighting a cigar?'

'What on Earth is he doing that for?'

'Beats me. He said he was about to distract them to allow us to proceed to camp. So be ready, will you?'

The Corporal remains still on the floor, obliviuos to the fact that a small group of finely stitched hats and scarves slide silently towards him.

Private Babe watches the Corporal, who then turns to face Private Babe.

'Matches!' yells the Corporal. 'I need matches!'

Private Babe immediately takes action and reaches inside his jacket pockets, frantically searching for his flare of matches. He grips them tightly in his hand, before throwing them across to the Corporal, who snatches them out of the air with minimal effort.

The Corporal sits up and calmly lights the end of his cigar. He tries to avoid asking Private Babe, why he now suddenly has matches in his pockets.

'Cover me, Dex,' instructs the Corporal, rising to his feet and taking a long drag on his cigar.

Dexter pivots himself towards the Corporal and showers the terrain to the front of him in copper coins. The coins steadily pound at the oncoming hats and scarves. It causes them to stop suddenly in their tracks and turn themselves away from the sting of the coins.

'What *is* he doing?' mutters Private Simmons.

Private Babe ponders at what the Corporal is trying to achieve. '*I*—I think...I think he is going to create some sort of smoke screen.'

‘A what?’ replies Private Simmons.

‘Quick now, chaps,’ begins Private Babe, pointing towards the river. ‘Be ready to make a sudden dash for the camp. The Corporal is going to give us cover.’

‘Okay, Dex…’ yells the Corporal. ‘I’m going to take another long drag of my cigar and then blow all the smoke in front of the laundry. That will hopefully blind them enough for you to create a pathway.’

Dexter, with no immediate control of the copper coins being ejected from his nostrils, nods quickly, which causes a few of the coins to plough into the grass beneath him.

The Corporal proceeds to suck hard on his cigar; the embers glowing bright orange as tobacco leaves burn at an accelerated rate. He raises his arm towards Dexter; indicating to him to be ready. The Corporal exhales; ejecting the smoke from his lungs, which causes a curtain of thick smoke in front of the laundry.

Now! shouts the Corporal. ‘Covering fire – give them a pathway through. Move, lads – move!’ adds the Corporal, before taking another huge draw on his cigar and blowing another smoke cloud out in front of him.

‘You heard the Corporal – move!’ instructs Private Babe, signalling to the men to push through the smoke filled air and streams of copper coins.

‘I can’t see a darn thing!’ moans Private Simmons.

‘Just keep moving forward,’ responds Private Babe. ‘We’ll make it through!’

With their table legs swinging through the void in front of the them, Private Babe leads his comrades through the thick smoke and towards the hill leading down to the river, occasionally fending off pieces of possessed laundry that have managed to elude the Corporal’s smoke screen.

'What's wrong?' asks Private Simmons to Private Babe, who comes to a rather sudden stop in the middle of the path. Private Babe turns around and stares on in horror at the smoke filled village centre. Private Babe's eyes widen.

'I can't leave them down there,' says Private Babe.

'We have our orders—' answers Private Simmons.

'Screw our orders – the Corporal is my friend – and the dragon doesn't deserve to be put into this mess. I'm going back for them! You take the rest of the men and gather what you can from the camp.'

Private Simmons nods and rushes to return to the rest of the men heading towards the camp. Private Babe turns and clutches hard at his table leg, before proceeding back into the village.

'Do you think that's enough smoke now?' splutters Dexter, trying to focus in on where his copper coins are disappearing to.

'I hope so, Dex,' replies the Corporal. 'As that was my last cigar.'

'You're kidding? Well…I do hope you have a plan, because I'm also out of dust.'

The Corporal squints as he tries to look through the smoke filled air. 'I don't see anything at all – where are you, Dexter?'

'Just by the fountain – where do you think they have all gone? They've like…just vanished.'

'Shush! – I'll come over to you.'

The Corporal follows the occassional sneezes of Dexter; sneezes that are gradually subsiding.

AAAAAACHOO!

'Well I think that's the last one,' annouces Dexter.

AAAAAACHOO!

No, one more,' he adds.

'I really can't see anything in this haze,' states the Corporal, reaching out in front of him with his arms.

'You're telling me!' responds Dexter.

As the dense smoke cloud slowly dissapates, the Corporal manages to locate the perimeter wall of the fountain. He cautiously crawls to the side of it, shuffles next to Dexter and places his back up against the cold and damp stonework.

The Corporal turns his shoulders to take a peek over the edge of the fountain wall; observing a few random pieces of laundry lingering on the other side.

'You are right, Dex,' states the Corporal. 'Most of them seem to have just disappeared – but where to?'

Dexter glances around at the village green and at all the shiny copper coins scattered across the grass. 'Oh my…did I do all that?' he mutters to himself.

'Um…Dex?' asks the Corporal.

'Yes?'

'What's that sound I can hear?'

Dexter twists his highly tuned ears up into the air. They twitch and flick as Dexter listens carefully to the sound.

'I think you mean two sounds,' annouces Dexter.

'Two?' questions the Corporal.

'Yes, two…' begins Dexter. 'Firstly, I hear a roaring and whistling sound; it sounds very much like—no it cant be? – It sounds like Melvin's bicycle.'

'You think?'

'I know that sound anywhere.'

'And the other sound?'

'Oh, that's just your faithful Private Babe, running and shouting, "I'll save you" – look!'

Private Babe races down the dusty pathway towards the centre of the village. He huffs and puffs as his stick-like legs propel him forwards. He clutches firmly at his wooden table leg in one hand and places his other onto the top of his helmet, preventing the battered metal headpiece from dislodging and sliding off his head.

He suddenly slows down to a gentle jog. He lowers his arm, which causes the tip of the table leg to drag through the wet blades of grass beneath him. He glances around at the centre of the village that only moments earlier had been a chaotic sight, filled with manic possessed laundry, fast flying copper coins and plentiful amounts of smoke. A look of complete and utter confusion creeps across his face.

'Over here, Private,' whispers the Corporal.

Private Babe turns towards the fountain and lowers his head slightly, catching a glimpse of his superior and Dexter as the tops of their heads poke over the rim of the fountain wall. He cautiously paces towards them, pondering to himself as to why the village green is now remarkably quiet and clear of any signs of laundry.

'What's happened?' enquires Private Babe. 'Where has all the laundry disappeared to?'

'Shush! A few pieces of laundry are still floating about!' murmurs the Corporal. 'Anyway...I thought I instructed you to stay with the men?'

'I came back, Sir,' answers Private Babe. 'I came back to save you.'

'You did?' replies the Corporal, honoured that his *number one* thinks so dearly of him, that he would risk *his* life to save his.'

'Yes, Sir – I couldn't leave knowing that you and Dexter were surrounded by that laundry – but you— err...you seem to have made them vanish...?'

'No...not vanished,' interrupts Dexter. 'But we believe that they have moved elsewhere.'

'Where?' responds Private Babe. 'They were all over the place a short while ago.'

'The Corporal and I believe that they may have headed over to the other side of the village – alerted by the sounds of what I imagine to be, Melvin's repaired bicycle.'

'What? The whole lot of them?' gasps Private Babe.

'I can't see them around here…can you?' responds Dexter.

Private Babe glances around the village. 'No…I suppose you are right there,' he says. 'Well, in that case, I think it would be a good idea to move back to the camp right now – and Dexter, would you please stop flapping your wings around? You keep clipping the surface of the water and sending cold splashes of it down the back of my neck.'

'Err…that's not me,' answers Dexter. 'My wings are securely tucked away behind me.'

Well, what on Earth is going on, then?' mumbles Private Babe, shifting his attention to the water. 'What in blazes is that…?' he adds, placing his hands onto the rim of the wall and pulling himself up to take a better look.

'Oh, my goodness—' responds Dexter, turning to face the fountain.

The Corporal rotates his head, joining Dexter and Private Babe as they stare in wonder at the water in the fountain, which ripples and swirls violently in front of them.

'What is this all about?' yelps Private Babe.

'Maybe it's some magical residual energy from the spell that Melvin created?' responds Dexter, leaning his snout down on top of the stonework.

'Magical what?' quizzes the Corporal.

'Magical residue, it's—oh, it doesn't matter,' retorts Dexter. 'However, it doesn't look good – I really think we should move.'

Without warning and to the complete surprise of the Corporal, Dexter and Private Babe, a pair of extremely large woollen pyjamas punches through the surface of the water. It slowly rises into the air and showers the Corporal in a misty spray. The pyjamas stand still as droplets of water stream down its strands of wool and fall back into the pool below.

The Corporal and the others remain perfectly still, staring up in horror at the over-sized pyjamas in front of them. They gasp simultaneously as the pyjamas lean down towards them, eyeing them up, one by one.

'That is one gigantic pair of pyjamas,' whispers Dexter. 'They're not yours by any chance, Corporal?'

'Not mine,' replies the Corporal. 'But I believe you are right in saying that we should at least try to—*WHOOOOAH!*—MOVE!' he shrieks, as the huge pair of woollen pyjamas jump out of the fountain and land on the grass in front of him with a loud thud.

'You're right there!' yelps Private Babe, trying to prevent his boots from slipping on the wet grass.

Suddenly, the pyjamas begin to lean backwards, before pausing briefly and letting out a deafening high-pitched squeal, which causes the Corporal, Dexter and Private Babe to immediately cover their ears to shield them from the loud resonant sonics pounding at their eardrums.

The squealing stops and the pyjamas lean forward, before letting out a bellowing roar.

'Quickly! Move!' instructs Private Babe. 'Let's run back to the camp.'

'You don't have to tell me that twice,' announces

Dexter, pushing himself to a vertical position and moving across to aid the Corporal to his feet; the Corporal, who at this very moment, is in a state of shock, caused by the unusual sight in front of him.

'Sir…we must move!' yells Private Babe,' tugging at the Corporal's bulky arm.

The woollen pyjamas take a giant step forward, followed by another.

The Corporal whimpers and lets out a loud girly scream, which causes Private Babe and Dexter to stare at him in concern; concern at how a large framed and masculine character, such as he, can produce a loud squeal of such magnitude and frequency.

Aided by Dexter and Private Babe, the Corporal rises to his feet. In his panic, he stumbles backwards and trips over the fountain wall.

SPLASH!

The Corporal collapses into the fountain's water pool. He gasps for air as the chilly water instantly takes his breath away.

'Move, Sir!' shouts Private Babe, trying desperately to attract the pyjamas attention from the other side of the fountain, by banging his wooden table leg hard against the fountain's stonework. 'It's coming for you!' he adds.

The Corporal claws furiously at the water, in an attempt to try and pull himself into a more upright position. Splashes of water fly out in all directions, before the Corporal manages to stretch out his bulky arms and wrap them around the highly decorative sculpture at the centre of the fountain.

The pyjamas continue to slowly creep towards the Corporal, not taking any notice of Private Babe, who tries to distract their attention, with no avail.

Dexter tries his best not to snigger at the sight of the Corporal climbing up and mounting the rear end of a crafted stone giraffe.

'Err...Corporal...?' begins Dexter. 'You'd better hurry up and get down – that loud squealing sound that the pyjamas have just made – wasn't random. I think it was a battle cry to alert the rest of the laundry - look!'

The Corporal and Private Babe redirect their attention to where Dexter is pointing, where in the distance, a mass of laundry is starting to march back towards the centre of the village.

THERE IS A SUDDEN CRUNCH OF STONE.

The back end of the sculpture breaks free under the Corporal's weight, sending it and the Corporal back into the waters below.

SPLASH!

Dexter sniggers as he watches the Corporal drag himself out of the fountain and tumble onto the grass.

'Behind you, Sir!' yells Private Babe, indicating that the pyjamas have moved around the outside of the fountain, quickly closing in on him.

The Corporal lets out another loud squeal; a squeal that this time sounds more like a drowning pig.

Dexter continues to gently snigger and chuckle at the Corporal's child-like antics, with no immediate care to assist him in anyway.

Without delay, the Corporal rises to his feet. He starts to pace around the outside of the fountain and tries to conjure up enough energy to force himself into a small run, which for the Corporal, is easier said than done. He struggles to catch his breath as his tree-trunk sized legs try to hold up and stabilise his bulky mass.

Behind him, the woollen pyjamas stomp down hard on the damp grass. They gradually move closer towards the Corporal, who maintains his pace by grabbing hold of the fountain wall and using it to pull himself along.

'What *is* he doing?' mutters Dexter, assessing any suitable way he could intervene and aid the Corporal.

Dexter cringes as he observes the Corporal slump to his knees and fall flat on his face. The Corporal rolls onto his back and stares in horror at the pair of pyjamas now standing over him.

There is a brief pause before the woollen pyjamas raises one of its legs high into the air and hovers it steadily over the exhausted Corporal.

'Oh, geez…' mumbles Dexter.

'Corporal, look out!' shouts Private Babe, as he hurls his wooden table leg towards the pyjamas, only to completely miss them. 'Move, Sir!'

In an absolute panic and in sheer desperation in trying to save himself, the Corporal fumbles to untie the laces on one of his boots, before removing the boot and clutching it firmly in his hand. Without hesitation and as hard as his strength allows, he launches his boot at the woollen pyjamas. The pair of pyjamas lets out a huge groan as the boot makes contact, causing the pyjamas to stumble backwards, before hopping on one leg and finally crashing to the floor.

'Quick, Sir…come to me,' commands Private Babe.

'*I*—I'm coming. *I*—I think *t*—that now would be a very *g*—good time to leave…' stutters the Corporal, his voice trailing off as shock begins to settle in.

Private Babe waves across to Dexter; instructing him to proceed to the camp. 'Yes, Sir…I think you are right. Let's move before that one gets to its feet and—oh my – and before the rest of them get here.'

Dexter scutters across and joins the Corporal and Private Babe, briefly looking over his shoulder at the mass of laundry, which is fast approaching the centre of the village. 'Think it's time to go,' he states, ushering the Corporal and Private Babe out of the village. 'Oh, Corporal?

'Hmmm?' responds the Corporal.

'What was the whole throwing the boot thing?' begins Dexter. 'Out of everything you could do – you throw your boot at it?'

'Oh nothing – nothing at all. It seemed like a good idea at the time,' answers the Corporal.

'I think that the Corporal just panicked a little, didn't you, Sir?' adds Private Babe.

'Panic? I haven't got time to panic, Babe! Besides, how many times have you been chased around a water fountain by a pair of woollen pyjamas?'

Private Babe turns to Dexter and raises an eyebrow.

'He's has got a point, Dex,' states Private Babe.

'Yes, maybe, but he's also got very smelly feet…' mutters Dexter.

CHAPTER XIII

"Arghhhh, look! A pair of Mrs. Stamps' frilly knickers have flown down the bell tower. We must cleanse the church of this demon. Fetch me a long pole, I'm going in!"

Reverend Clementine

Mrs Stamps stands with her feet spread apart and her hands placed firmly on her hips. She waits patiently in front of Edwin, who remains tied to the chair with his head hanging low.

'Just give him a poke or something, Mrs Stamps,' instructs Officer Locks. 'We simply haven't got all day to wait for him to wake up.'

Mrs Stamps takes a small step forward and leans down towards Edwin, giving him a gentle poke on his shoulder with the end of her finger. She immediately shuffles backwards and awaits a response from Edwin.

'A little harder than that, Mrs Stamps,' adds Officer Locks. 'He's a vampire – not a baby.'

Mrs Stamps repeats her action, only this time slightly harder than before. Edwin groans and opens his eyes.

Slightly dazed, Edwin lifts his head up towards Mrs Stamps, who places her hands back onto her hips and patiently waits for Edwin to wake up.

'Ah…you are awake, then?' asks Mrs Stamps. 'Right…let's get down to business – I haven't got all day to dilly-dally about.' Mrs Stamps leans forward. 'Right, this is how it's going to be, Edwin—oh you don't mind if I address you as Edwin?'

Edwin hisses and slowly tilts his head towards Corbin, who still dangles on the bedpost, under the watchful eye of Officer Locks.

'You may,' mumbles Edwin, shuffling around in the chair and trying to formulate a plan to save himself and his mole-like companion, only then to notice the good Reverend standing behind him, holding his silver crucifix firmly in his shaking hands.

'Right…well, you see this shutter here?' begins Mrs Stamps, stepping aside to reveal the wooden window shutters, of which Edwin is very much familiar with. 'If I feel that you are not answering my questions to a satisfactory level – my little hand may just slip on this here latch. It is certainly a bright and sunny day today.' Mrs Stamps pauses, before leaning down close to Edwin's face. 'You see where I'm going with this…?'

Edwin gasps in horror as he realises exactly what Mrs Stamps' intentions are.

'Don't worry, Master – I will save you,' murmurs Corbin, quietly trying to wriggle himself free from his waistcoat, only to suddenly freeze in place as Officer Locks takes a small step towards him, eyeing up Corbin's suspicious movements.

Edwin sighs and lowers his head.

At the back of the room, Samuel assists Melvin and lowers him onto the floor, leaning his back up against the wall. Samuel removes a cotton handkerchief from his jacket pocket and uses it to carefully wipe Melvin's sweaty brow.

Mrs Stamps casually picks up the wooden stool from underneath the window frame and places it down firmly in front of Edwin. She slightly lifts up her dress and lowers herself onto the stool.

'I will ask you a series of questions, Edwin,' states Mrs Stamps. 'If you value your life, then I suggest you answer them correctly.'

'Don't tell her anything, Master!' shrieks Corbin, before then being suddenly silenced by Officer Locks' hairy finger being pushed hard up against Corbin's dry and chapped lips.

Edwin sighs. 'Very well…you have my attention.'

'I guess the first question is – what have you done with our Laundry Fairy?' asks Mrs Stamps.

'I really have absolutely *no* idea what you are talking about,' responds Edwin, trying his best not to make eye contact with Mrs Stamps.

'I think you lie!' snaps Mrs Stamps. 'It seems rather strange, that for many a year we have had absolutely no issues with our Laundry Fairy, yet all of a sudden she disappears the moment you set foot in our village.' Mrs Stamps raises an eyebrow and awaits an answer.

'Purely coincidence…' answers Edwin.

'So, you are saying that you have absolutely no idea where she is?' continues Mrs Stamps.

'That is what I'm saying,' mutters Edwin, leaning towards Corbin and shaking his head very slowly from side to side.

'Hmmm, well as for your little pet here…' begins Mrs Stamps. 'Would you kindly tell me why he was rolling about in the mud in front of my post office the other evening? That *was* him that I saw – don't you dare say that it wasn't!'

'Why don't you ask him yourself,' replies Edwin. 'Actually, NO!' he then yelps. '*Ahem* – I mean no—'

'What do you mean…no?' interrupts Mrs Stamps, standing to her feet and shuffling towards Corbin. She reaches out and gives him a gentle pat on the head.

Although Corbin is incredibly loyal towards his Master and would do pretty much anything for him, Corbin is also very foolish, blunt and direct when faced with answering questions. His little brain cannot deal with multiple complex questions, or more to the point, questions that require a lot of thought in answering. This usually leads to Corbin blabbering out basic answers that either end up telling someone something they didn't want to know, or more worryingly, something they did, which more often than enough, ends up being the truth. After knowing Corbin for many years, this is something that Edwin is very aware of, and has got them both in some very sticky situations in the past.

'So then, little furry creature…begins,' Mrs Stamps. 'What were you doing outside my post office the other night? I know it was you.'

'You were just going for a stroll in the darkness, weren't you, Corbin?' interrupts Edwin.

'No, Master,' replies Corbin, nervously. 'I was with you the whole time – and you were just about—'

'No, Corbin! You went for a little walk – didn't you?' adds Edwin.

Mrs Stamps turns to Edwin and raises her finger up to her lips, indicating to him to be quiet. She points across to the window shutters, before slowly drawing an imaginary line with the tip of her finger from one side of her throat to the other.

Edwin immediately mutes himself.

'Err…No, Master. I was helping you…remember?' states Corbin.

Edwin sighs at Corbin's truthfulness and quickly turns to Mrs Stamps, who walks towards the window shutters. She stares at Edwin as she places her hand onto the shutter latch, before turning towards Corbin.

'And just what were you helping your Master with, Corbin?' asks Mrs Stamps.

'*I*—*I*—was helping *m*—*m*—my Master—err…I was helping *m*—my—' stutters Corbin.

'Spit it out, rat!' bellows Mrs Stamps.

'I'm a mole-sprite, lady – not a rat,' retorts Corbin, watching Mrs Stamps' hand creep up to the shutter handles, before hearing a defining click as the latch mechanism releases. The clicking sound echoes around the room. Edwin gasps and tries his hardest to rock the chair out of the way of the shutters, with little success.

'NO! Please wait!' shrieks Edwin.

'Something to say, Edwin?' asks Mrs Stamps.

Edwin inhales a deep breath of dry musty air, before exhaling it slowly.

'I'll take it from here, Corbin,' announces Edwin, turning slowly to his assistant.

Mrs Stamps lets go of the latch and checks to ensure the shutters are firmly locked into place. She returns to sitting upon the stool and waits for Edwin to speak.

'He was helping me *to*—to...he was helping me with,' mutters Edwin.

Mrs Stamps jumps to her feet and rushes towards the latch on the shutter.

NO! Please I beg you – wait!' yelps Edwin. 'I will tell you...please – please!' Edwin begins to whimper.

The Reverend slowly lifts his head and stares at Mrs Stamps. He moves to the side of Edwin and joins Mrs Stamps at the window shutters.

Samuel aids Melvin to his feet, guides him across the floor and sits him down gently on the end of the bed next to Corbin, who smirks back at Melvin.

'Tell me, then! Or I swear this hand of mine will slip,' responds Mrs Stamps, her eyes narrowing.

'Okay-okay...' begins Edwin. 'Corbin was helping me to capture your Laundry Fairy—'

Everyone gasps.

'Did you succeed?' asks the Reverend.

'What have you done with her?' yells Melvin, before letting out a spluttering cough.

'She is safe,' replies Edwin.

Melvin releases a sigh of relief, promptly followed by Mrs Stamps, who steps forwards and gives Edwin a firm pat on his shoulder.

'Now...that wasn't too hard...was it, Edwin?' asks Mrs Stamps.

Samuel holds tight onto Melvin, who mysteriously seems to be getting weaker by the minute.

'I have a question...' begins Samuel. 'Why have you decided to steal our Laundry Fairy? What exactly has she ever done to you?'

Edwin lowers his head in shame. 'I never meant to cause this much trouble,' he whimpers. 'I only wanted to borrow her a little.'

'Borrow her for what?' replies Samuel, pondering if a vampire needs his clothes washed, just like the rest of us do.

'To assist me in being able to walk in the sunlight,' replies Edwin, mumbling the last few words.

'But you're a vampire,' responds Samuel. 'Surely it is not normal for a vampire to be able to walk in the sunlight? Why would you think you'd be able to? That is clearly common knowledge…even for you?'

Edwin sighs. 'I'm not an evil person – you must believe that. But ever since I was a young boy, I always thought I was—well, a little different from all the other vampires. I simply had a certain curiosity to go out in the daytime – and so my obsession to find a way to be able to walk freely in the sunlight…began.'

'But why do you need our Laundry Fairy?' enquires Mrs Stamps, stepping towards Edwin.

'I've spent many years trying to find a way to walk in the sunlight…' begins Edwin. 'Most of them have failed, some have been dead ends and some have been just darn right ridiculous and dangerous. It is only just recently that I have come across some ancient text from my ancestors; text that describes a way in lifting this cursed vampire trait—'

'What a load of old cobblers!' interrupts Melvin.

'No…I'm afraid it is very much true,' replies Edwin. 'I have no reason to twist the truth. May I continue please?'

'Yes, please do!' replies Samuel, interested in what Edwin's motives truly are.

Edwin nods in acceptance. 'It was then that I spent a vast amount of my time and resources in trying to understand the texts. After deciphering them, I realised that there was only one more thing to do – and that was to track down and locate your Laundry Fairy.'

'Yes-yes! I get that!' interrupts Mrs Stamps. 'I don't understand why you needed to capture her. Do you realise the amount of problems that you have caused here in our village?'

Edwin nods. 'Well, I can understand how I may have started off a chain reaction of events, which has led the villagers in having a slight problem in keeping their washing up to a high level of cleanliness.'

'It's a lot more than that, Edwin!' roars Mrs Stamps. 'Anyway…as I was just saying…why do you need our Laundry Fairy?'

'She has to read the ancient texts of my ancestors,' explains Edwin. 'You see – she has to say the words – not me. Alongside using her unique magical powers – she should, according to my research…then be able to allow me to walk out in the sunlight.'

Samuel pulls himself closer to Edwin. 'Why don't you just simply ask her to help you?'

'She would not help my kind,' replies Edwin.

'What do you mean – your kind?' responds Samuel.

'Fairies and vampires have a very dark history together. Stories which I can't even begin to describe, where vampires hunted down fairies; killing them for their magical powers. I never intended to harm your Laundry Fairy. My association with my ancestors is something I cannot help, but believe me when I say – I'm ashamed of what they did. I thought that maybe if I just—'

'Just what?' interrupts Mrs Stamps.

'If I just threatened her a little by saying that I had captured her brothers and sisters – and kept her captive for a short while – then she would eventually give into my demands. To be honest, I think she would have eventually given in if you hadn't all shown up when you did. I was just about to get her to read out the text.'

A small emotional tear slowly appears in the corner of Edwin's eye and rolls down his cheek.

'Are you crying, Edwin?' asks Mrs Stamps. 'I didn't think vampires were capable of showing any sort of remorse or emotion.'

'Vampires don't cry…' begins Melvin. 'They eject a highly potent—*cough-cough*—oh never mind!'

Mrs Stamps turns to the Revered and then briefly towards Samuel. She lets out a long sigh.

'Where is our Laundry Fairy?' asks the Reverend.

'She is just over there,' answers Edwin, flicking his head back and indicating to the far corner of the room.

The Reverend turns, paces slowly towards the corner of the room and disappears into the shadows. He pauses a moment to let his eyes adjust, before reaching down to the floor to pick up Edwin's cloak.

'It's just a cloak, Edwin? I assume yours?' questions the Reverend, turning in confusion towards Edwin.

'Look underneath it…' mutters Edwin.

'I *am* looking under it,' responds the Reverend. There is absolutely nothing here at all – just the floor.'

'She is most certainly there…' begins Edwin. 'She was there just a few moments ago. Look for a cage.'

'No cage here, Edwin – look!' replies the Reverend.

Edwin rotates his head as far as he can and uses his ability to see into the darkness. He gasps.

'What's wrong?' enquires the Reverend, stepping out of the shadows towards Edwin.

'*Th*—that is not possible!' shrieks Edwin. 'She was right there under my cloak. I swear to you!'

'Excuse me everyone?' begins Samuel. 'But where is Officer Locks?'

◆◆◆

The Corporal picks up his sword from the sandy shore of the river and grasps it handle tightly in his left hand. He casually rotates the shiny steel blade from side to side, which seems to shimmer as the sunlight bounces off its surface.

The steel blade hums as the Corporal swings the sword out in front of him, violently cutting through the air, before pulling it back and carefully running the face of his thumb along its sharpened length.

He pauses for a moment, before lifting his head to glance around at his men, who are busy scavenging the camp in search of anything else that can be useful in defending off a mass of possessed laundry.

'Do you think that these swords are going to do the trick, Sir?' enquires Private Babe, pacing towards the Corporal. 'I mean…we gave them a good *seeing to* with the table legs, earlier. You saw what happened when Duncan cut one straight in half with his huge knife – they just don't seem to want to—well, want to die!'

'Yeah, Sir…' begins Private Simmons. 'We do seem to be fighting a losing battle here – and look at that Dexter – his snout is smoking. I really don't know how much longer we can keep this all up.'

'All very good questions and concerns,' answers the Corporal. 'If the truth be told – I really do not know.'

'We could just make a run for it, Sir?' announces Private Simmons, eyeing up his superior.

'Make a run for it? Make a *run* for it?' bellows the Corporal. 'We are men – not cowards! Only cowards run! Are you a coward, Simmons?'

'Err…no, Sir,' mumbles Private Simmons.

'Well then, we will all head back to the village and

do everything that we can to help defend it, and hope that my *Melvy* will find a way to sort all of this mess out, or better still, find the Laundry Fairy. Besides, you still want to get paid, don't you?'

'Yes, Sir!' salutes Private Simmons.

The Corporal slides his sword carefully back into its scabbard, which is held tightly around his bulky waist by a leather strap; a strap that barely stretches around his fat belly.

He reaches into a crate on the floor and pulls out another cigar, lifting it to his nose and running the length of it underneath his nostrils. He promptly places it into his mouth and awaits Private Babe to present him with a means of lighting it, realising quickly that *he* still had the matches in his pocket from earlier.

With the cigar lit, the Corporal takes a few long puffs of it, before exhaling three perfectly formed smoke rings into the air.

'Okay…**ATTENTION!** – Attention, lads! Line up – line up,' instructs the Corporal, before watching his men rustle up to form a straight line in front of him.

'Right…I'm not one for long drawn out speeches, so I'll keep this short and sweet…' begins the Corporal, pausing to take another long drag on his cigar. 'We are men…men of honour…men of statue. I look around at each and every one of you; you know what I see? I see fighters – not cowards! Fighters that will fight to the bitter end – fighters that will not give up! I will not lie to you, lads. We are about to embark on an epic battle – a battle that has near improbable odds of us winning – but we must hold the enemy back as long as we can – and give the people of this village a chance to survive. The eyes of our Lord are upon us! Our task will not be an easy one – we are up against an unlikely enemy. However, we are fully equipped and battle hardened. We will be savage – we will be fierce and give them hell. Make every second count, lads – the more time we can give Melvin – the better chance we have.'

The Corporal's men stand in silence, each of them expressing a look of shock and confusion. Their jaws hang fully open.

'Too much?' whispers the Corporal, leaning down towards Private Babe.

'Yes, just a tad, Sir,' replies Private Babe.

The Corporal turns red with embarrassment and lets out a slight smirk.

'Okay, lads!' begins the Corporal. 'Enough of this – now we march – we march into the village with our swords held high. Let us show them what we are all made of. Until the end, lads!'

'Err…Sir? I really think you are beginning to scare the men,' interrupts Private Babe.

'Nonsense,' mutters the Corporal. 'Now, Dexter? Where are you?'

'I'm over here!' yells Dexter.

'Why are you in the river?' bellows the Corporal.

'Excuse me…' begins Dexter. 'But if you've just fired off round after round of shiny copper coins from your nostrils at near super-sonic speed – wouldn't your snout be feeling as if it was on fire?'

◆◆◆

The Reverend rushes towards the door of room four, which has been mysteriously unlocked and left wide open. He sticks his head out into the long hallway and scouts along for any sign of Officer Locks, or more importantly, Amelia.

'How on God's Earth did we just miss that?' yelps the Reverend. 'He was just standing right next to us. It looks like he has managed to steal Amelia, sneak past us all, unlock the door and escape.'

'Why would he do that? I mean…what would he need Amelia for?' asks Samuel.

'I don't know, Samuel,' replies the Reverend 'What should we all do?'

'We must find her!' bellows Melvin, rising to his feet. 'Come…let's go! We haven't got time to waste!'

'Well, it sounds as if someone is certainly feeling a little better, huh, Melvin…?' says Samuel.

'Yes, for some bizarre reason, I suddenly felt rather drained and dizzy from the moment I walked into the room – as if there was something drawing and feeding on my already low magical powers.'

'Interesting,' answers Samuel. 'But yes, I agree with you. We have to find her – for all our sakes.'

'How do you propose that we do that?' enquires Mrs Stamps, from the other side of the room. 'We don't even know where she went.'

The Reverend pauses, before rushing down the wooden stairs, into the bar area and asking Duncan if he had recently seen anyone come down into the room. Duncan in his slight incoherent state, slurs a few words and shakes his head from side to side. The Reverend approaches Timothy, who is leaning up against the side of the bar counter.

'Timothy, we have a problem!' states the Reverend.

'Have you found her?' replies Timothy, pushing himself up into a more vertical position.

'Yes, we have found her, Timothy—'

'Oh, good-good!'

'But we have now lost her again—'

'What do you mean – you have lost her *again*…?' questions Timothy, pacing towards the Reverend.

'I haven't got the time to explain…' begins the Reverend. 'But did you by any chance see our Officer Locks come down the stairs?'

'I haven't seen anybody at all…why?'

'Quickly, come with me, Timothy,' shouts the Reverend. 'Myles and Trout – you both stay here. We may need your assistance shortly.'

Private Myles and Private Trout both nod in agreement, and watch as the Reverend and Timothy run back up the stairs and towards room four.

'Had any luck?' asks Mrs Stamps, as the Reverend pauses for breath in the hallway.

'No…no one has seen anything downstairs, but I really—oh bother it – look!' responds the Reverend, racing across to the end of the hallway. He comes to a sudden halt as his polished shoes crunch over broken shards of glass laying on the floor by a window; a window that has recently been shattered, leaving only a few pointed fragments of glass poking out of the framework.

'There he is!' he adds, turning his head back to room four and hoping that everyone heard.

'Who?' answers Timothy.

'Officer Locks…' begins the Reverend. 'He has stolen our Laundry Fairy!'

Timothy gasps. 'So, it wasn't the vampire, then?' queries Timothy, with a confused look upon his face.

'Well, it was the vampire at first – but now Officer Locks has stolen her.'

'I don't believe he would do such a thing – why would he?' remarks Timothy.

The Reverend pokes his head through the window

frame. He watches as Officer Locks runs at very high speed over the surrounding foothills and into the Darkened Enchanted Forest, holding on very tightly to the zynite cage containing Amelia. The cage swings violently from left to right as Officer Locks disappears into the dense trees.

'Looks like he has cut himself on the glass,' states the Reverend. 'Yes – look! There is blood all over the place. Some here…here…and lots over there. 'Looks like our Lord favours us this afternoon – we have a trail to follow.'

'You really can't be serious, Reverend?' questions Timothy. 'You want to venture into the Darkened Enchanted Forest? You'll never make it back out – that's just a darn ridiculous idea.'

The Reverend carefully pulls his head back through the window, tiptoes around the broken glass on the floor and paces towards Timothy. 'Well, what else do you suggest we do?'

'Maybe start by trying to find someone that knows the forest well?' replies Timothy. 'It's all well and good following a blood trail into the forest, but it's getting back out again that is going to be the hard bit. You hear stories of the paths disappearing around you; plants and trees mysteriously growing in places where the paths used to be. It's a complete maze in there!'

'Why don't we just ask Melvin…?' responds the Reverend. 'Didn't Mrs Stamps say a few days ago that he lived in the forest? I'm certain he will be more than happy to assist – he seems very keen to find Amelia.'

'True…let's ask him,' replies Timothy.

The Reverend and Timothy turn and race back down the hallway into room four.

'What's going on?' asks Samuel.

'We've found the Officer,' replies the Reverend. 'Well not found him, but located him - he has made a mad escape into the Darkened Enchanted Forest.'

'The forest?' blasts Melvin. 'Oh deary-me…that is not good – not good at all!'

'What do you mean…not good at all?' enquires the Reverend, stepping towards Melvin.

'We'll never be able to find him in there…' begins Melvin. 'The forest is full of mysteries and can be very dangerous at the best of times.'

'Are you saying you don't know your way around it?' asks Timothy. 'I thought that you lived there?'

'I do!' retorts Melvin. 'But it's not as simple as that. Things change in the forest and nothing is quite as it seems – I wouldn't even know where to begin looking. You can easily lose your mind in there.'

'We can start by following the trail of blood that the Officer has left behind…' begins the Reverend. 'He seems to have cut himself on some glass during his hasty escape. He was certainly running at a very high speed when I caught a glimpse of him a moment ago.'

'I keep thinking to myself, why though?' questions Mrs Stamps.

'A very good question indeed,' responds Samuel.

There is an eerie silence in the room as everyone ponders on Mrs Stamps' question, trying to answer and even make sense on why the village lawman would be interested in stealing their Laundry Fairy.'

'Her heart…' mutters Corbin, breaking the silence.

Mrs Stamps turns around and walks slowly towards Corbin, who bobs up and down on the end of the bedpost.

'Explain please?' commands Mrs Stamps.

'Let me,' interrupts Edwin, tilting his head in Mrs

Stamps' direction. 'Fairies have very unique hearts. They are made of a very special type of crystal called a hue, which they use to store all their magical powers in. They can be sold for a very high price to the right buyer, because of the fact that they are hard to come by – as a fairy is difficult to find, yet alone capture. I believe that is why the Officer has taken your Laundry Fairy. I've really just given your Officer a head start.'

'Oh my…that is dreadful. Will he kill her?' shrieks Melvin. 'Quick, we must find him before—'

'You won't catch him!' interrupts Edwin.

'Why ever not?' responds Melvin.

Edwin sighs. '*He's*—he's a…'

'He's a werewolf,' adds the Reverend.

'Precisely!' continues Edwin. 'He will be too fast for you – and certainly too strong.'

'But I'm a spellbinder,' announces Melvin. 'I can just cast a quickening spell—'

'Not in your state, Melvin!' interrupts Samuel. 'You may think you are okay, but to me you still look rather frail and weak.'

'Samuel is right, Melvin,' answers the Reverend. 'We must find another way…and quickly – as the judges are due to arrive shortly to assess us for the competition!'

'Well…it's not like that is going to go very well now, is it?' mumbles Timothy.

◆◆◆

'What are you staring at, Myles…?' questions Private Trout, as he casually rolls himself a small cigarette.

'A few moments ago, I swear I just saw the Corporal remove his boot and throw it at—well, at a very large pair of woollen pyjamas.'

Private Trout places his neatly rolled cigarette into his mouth and clamps it down gently between his dry and chapped lips. He reaches inside his jacket pocket, pulls out a flare of matches and uses one to light his cigarette. He huddles up besides Private Myles.

'I thought he was leading the rest of the squad to the camp…?' queries Private Trout. 'I'm sure the Corporal, with his expertise, has got all the men to the camp with no issues at all.'

'Hmmm, well I must be going crazy, then…' begins Private Myles. 'I swear he was just there – rolling around in the grass. However, what's more bizarre, is the fact that the village is suddenly now completely clear of laundry – look!'

'Going crazy?' I would never expect that from you Myles,' replies Private Trout, sarcastically. 'But you are right about the laundry. That's very unusual. We only turned our backs for a few moments. Where could they have all gone? And look at the state of the village green – it's all covered in shiny copper coins.'

'I'm not sure, but what's that sound?' asks Private Myles.

'I don't know,' responds Private Trout, glancing through the windows at the village fountain. 'Whatever it is – it's getting louder and certainly closer.'

At the back of the room, Duncan pours himself another tankard full of honey mead, before turning to face the random villagers. He continues to tell them about the time that he saw the biggest rat in the world and how he was going to make a large pie from him. He raises his tankard to his mouth and gulps down half its contents.

'Shush, Duncan!' whispers Private Trout. 'Listen!'

Duncan immediately silences himself and raises his

tankard into the air, signalling to Private Trout he has heard him. He lets out a few loud hiccups, which he promptly silences by covering his mouth with his hand.

Private Myles turns his ear towards the centre of the village, listens carefully and tries to deduce what the oncoming thudding and thumping sounds could be.

'Look!' yelps Private Myles, pointing across to the far side of the village green. 'There they are!'

'Quick…' begins Private Trout. 'Let's not stand here.' He places a hand onto Private Myles' shoulders and ushers himself back towards the bar counter and more importantly, out of sight of the approaching waves of laundry.

◆◆◆

Mrs Stamps places her right hand on her chin and rests her right elbow into the open palm of her left hand. She repeatedly taps her index finger onto the side of her cheek and stares down piercingly at Edwin.

'Surely there's another way?' asks Mrs Stamps.

'I'm not letting that swine anywhere near Amelia!' bellows Melvin, pointing his finger at Edwin. 'I don't trust him after what he's already put her through—'

Edwin frowns and accepts Melvin's statement, acknowledging him by gently nodding his head.

'Would you shut your cake-hole, Melvin!' interrupts Mrs Stamps, immediately muting Melvin. 'You've done quite enough damage for one day, don't you think…? Besides, what Edwin is saying does make *some* sense.'

'You surely can't be considering using—' begins Melvin, halting mid-sentence as Mrs Stamps widens her eyes at him.

'That spellbinder really doesn't like me, does he?'

murmurs Edwin, addressing Mrs Stamps as she leans down to face him.

'So, tell me, Edwin…' begins Mrs Stamps. 'Why would you offer your assistance? What possible reason would interest you? And like Melvin just said…why should we trust you?'

'For several reasons to be perfectly honest,' replies Edwin. 'Firstly, you are running out of valuable time; time that ticks away as we continue to speak. Secondly, the Reverend says that he has left a trail of blood?'

'That is correct,' responds the Reverend.

'I will surely be much quicker in locating the Officer and Amelia, as I will be able to follow the scent of the blood – being a vampire – and in bat form I shall be faster still. I'll be able to scout high above the trees.'

'And do you really believe that you will be able to find and save her?' asks Samuel.

'Yes…and what will you do when you have found her?' adds Melvin, narrowing his eyes at Edwin. 'Steal her back again, huh?'

Edwin turns to Melvin. 'Look – I know you don't like me very much at this particular moment – and that is quite understandable – but we are wasting valuable time; time which we really don't have. To save Amelia and get her back before the judges arrive is a near impossible task, but I can at least try to save her before Officer Locks does the unthinkable with her. But to answer your questions, that's simply a yes…and a no.'

'I do not trust that Edwin at all,' whispers Melvin, leaning casually towards Samuel's ear.

'I know you don't,' responds Samuel. 'And to be honest, it is a little unnerving to allow him to try – but we are running out of time…and options.'

Timothy stands at the back of the room and glances

across at Corbin, who listens very carefully to all the talking going on around him. Timothy gives Corbin a little wave, to which Corbin acknowledges with a cheeky smile.

'I don't like it one bit!' states Melvin.

'Are you absolutely sure that you will be able to save Amelia, Edwin?' enquires Mrs Stamps.

'I am fairly certain,' responds Edwin.

'How certain?' adds Melvin.

Edwin frowns. 'Well, Melvin…I can't promise you – but I will do my utmost best to try and rescue her – and bring her safely back to you.'

Mrs Stamps turns to Melvin, who shifts his eyes towards her. She shrugs her shoulders and upturns her hands, silently asking Melvin what extra harm it could cause by allowing Edwin to assist.

Melvin sighs, removes his hat and scratches the scalp of his head rigorously with his fingertips. He violently shakes his head from side to side, causing his glossy white hair to flare outwards, before carefully patting it down and placing his hat back atop his head.

'Very well…' mumbles Melvin. 'But I'm warning you, Edwin…the moment I smell something fishy going on, *I—I—*I will hunt you down and do some pretty horrible and naughty things to you. Are you hearing me, Edwin?'

'Steady on, Melvin…' begins Samuel. 'I think Edwin gets the point.'

Samuel paces towards Edwin, removes a small pocketknife from his jacket pocket and uses it to cut through the yo-yo string, releasing Edwin from the chair. Mrs Stamps take a precautionary step backwards towards the window shutters. She anticipates opening them if Edwin goes against his word.

'My cloak…if you please, Reverend?' announces Edwin, adjusting his attire and straightening his hair.

'Err…Master?' mutters Corbin, with a smug face. 'You seem to have forgotten one very small thing…In-fact you all have.'

Everyone pauses and stares around at each other in confusion.

'Oh, yes! Silly me,' retorts Edwin, picking his sunglasses up from the side table.

'No, Master…' begins Corbin. 'Unless you have completely forgotten – those sunglasses aren't going to be much help, unless you are going to be covering yourself in some sort of sunlight blocking cream.'

'Oh drat!' yelps Edwin. 'Of course – how foolish and silly of me…of us! In all that jabbering about, I completely forgot about the fact that I can't walk outside…I swear there is some very messed up irony in that somewhere.' Edwin chuckles at himself.

'Problem?' asks Samuel.

'A darn big one,' replies Edwin. 'It's called the sun. – or more precisely…the sunlight.'

'Well blast me down with a rubber duck!' titters Mrs Stamps. 'We certainly forgot about that one, didn't we people?'

'Seems like we are right back to square one, doesn't it?' responds Melvin. 'In that case, we must go and find her ourselves – and now!'

'Wait just a second,' interrupts Samuel. 'You're a spellbinder, Melvin. Can't you just create a little spell or something to temporarily allow Edwin—'

'Don't even think about it!' shrieks Mrs Stamps.' We already have enough problems at the moment. We don't need additional ones by *magic man* here making a monumental pig's ear of another spell. I'm sorry

Melvin, but with respect…you should at—'

'I can do that,' announces Melvin, pacing forward towards Edwin. 'It will probably drain all of the energy in me, but I have something up my sleeve that will allow you to walk in the sunlight, but—'

'Up your sleeve, Melvin?' enquires Mrs Stamps. 'I'm intrigued to find out if you *actually* have something up your sleeve, or if that was just a figure of speech.'

'Both,' answers Melvin. 'But this particular spell does have one minor flaw.'

'Oh, here we go,' mutters Mrs Stamps. 'There is always something with you, isn't there?'

'You can't live without me,' states Melvin, winking at Mrs Stamps.

Melvin takes his right hand and inserts it into his left sleeve opening. He sticks out his tongue and pulls some remarkable facial expressions as he rummages around deep inside his sleeve.

Everyone stares in amazement as Melvin's hand and arm mysteriously disappear up his sleeve.

'Ah, there we go!' exclaims Melvin, pulling out a small glass orb, no bigger than the size of a grape. 'This will help you, Edwin – but as I said it does have a teeny-weeny flaw.'

'What good is this going to be…?' questions Mrs Stamps, snatching the glass orb out of Melvin's hand, bringing it close to her face and scrutinising it in minute detail. 'What is it?' she adds.

'No time to explain…' begins Melvin, grabbing the orb back from the hands of Mrs Stamps. 'Right, Edwin…listen carefully. Oh, did I mention that this spell has one rather small flaw?'

Edwin nods. 'You have mentioned it has a flaw, but you never told me what it—'

'Good-good,' interrupts Melvin. 'Now, this is what is going to happen. I will begin by throwing this glass orb at you. As it flies through the air towards you, I shall mutter a few magical words – so please do not interrupt me while I'm saying them. It is very important that you—'

'Oh, would you just get on with it!' bellows Mrs Stamps, breaking Melvin mid-sentence.

Melvin narrows his eyes at Mrs Stamps, before throwing the glass orb at a completely unprepared Edwin. Melvin promptly mutters a few magical words.

THERE IS A BRILLIANT FLASH OF LIGHT.

'Well, would you look at that?' announces Samuel, gently rubbing his eye sockets, before focusing in on Edwin, who now stands inside some sort of clear protective bubble.

'How is this going to help?' enquires Edwin.

Melvin strolls forward towards Edwin and pokes at the protective bubble surrounding him with his finger. 'This bubble will, for a short time only, protect you from the sun's rays and should allow you to walk freely outside,' he states.

'A short time, Melvin?' responds Edwin, nervously.

Melvin smiles. 'Yes, that's right – a short time – we must hurry – chop-chop!'

'You might want to think about putting some sort of value to your term, "short" – and what do you mean should? I don't need to hear, "should" – I need to know it will!'

Edwin, being the man he is (well…vampire) – is very aware of the effect of what even the slightest ray of sunlight can do to his aged body, having in the past encountered some pretty close calls, after being briefly exposed to it. Standing nervously inside a protective bubble, which has just been magically cast by a weakened, panicked and hasty spellbinder, certainly sets alarm bells going in Edwin's mind. Based on Melvin's recent history with spells not going quite to plan, Edwin is a little hesitant to just simply open the window shutters and fly out across the village.

'Well, I really hate to say it…but I'm with Edwin, Melvin,' states Samuel. 'What do you mean…short?'

'I did say the spell has a small flaw, didn't I?' replies Melvin, letting out a small giggle.

'Yes, you did, Melvin…' continues Samuel. 'But I think it's important to tell us how short a time are we talking?'

'Err, well…' begins Melvin, struggling to start his sentence. 'Based on the amount of concentrated magical energy involved, the initial size of the orb, impact velocity, as well as the viscous composition of the bubble and the time of day – oh and also—'

'How long, Melvin?' blasts Samuel.

'Two hours, give or take—' responds Melvin.

'Well…that doesn't allow us very long at all, does it, Melvin?' questions Samuel.

'Not if we keep standing here and yapping on about it all,' bellows Mrs Stamps. 'Now, Edwin…hold out your hand in front of the shutters here – let's see if Melvin's bubble does what he says it does.'

Edwin paces across to the window shutters and nervously extends his arm out in front of them. The bubble stretches and reforms around him.

Mrs Stamps grabs hold of the latch holding the window shutter closed. She slowly begins to lift it off its hook. It instantly lets out a long creaking sound.

'Wait!' shrieks Edwin. 'Are you absolutely positive that this is going to work, Melvin?'

'Only one way to find out, Edwin,' gloats Melvin.

'And what if the bubble suddenly bursts or pops?' adds Edwin, in a worried tone.

'Well…then you are in a little bit of a pickle, Edwin,' answers Melvin. 'Simple as, I'm afraid.'

Edwin sighs and accepts that he will try to take his chances with Melvin's protective bubble. He turns to face Mrs Stamps, before giving her a gentle nod, indicating to her to open the shutters. He slowly closes his eyes and steadies his breathing.

As the shutters slowly open, a slither of sunlight bursts into the room, shining directly onto Edwin's arm. He opens one of his eyes to observe his arm still intact. He gasps at the spectacular sight in front of him; a feeling of realism and his first real moment of experiencing the sun's warmth on his pale skin.

Looking up at Mrs Stamps, Edwin pauses, before allowing Mrs Stamps to completely fill the room with sunlight.

'See…it works!' yelps Melvin, with a slight surprised tone in his voice. 'How do you feel, Edwin?'

'Relieved, for starters,' replies Edwin.

'Then there is no time to lose,' declares Mrs Stamps, pushing the two shutter doors firmly back to the wall; stretching their small iron hinges to their limits. She pushes the window to the side, which allows a warm breeze to enter the room. Edwin smiles with joy as the warmth of the sun hits his face; a joy that Edwin knows will not last forever. He takes a few steps towards the window, before turning towards Melvin.

'I'm going to rescue Amelia, Melvin,' announces Edwin. 'I promise you that. While there is strength in my body, time on my side and as long as this bubble holds, I will be back with her.' Edwin lowers his head towards Corbin. 'Try to behave yourself while I'm gone, Corbin – and if something happens to me—well, it's been a pleasure to have you as—as my friend.'

Corbin whimpers at his Master's kind words.

THERE IS A FLASH OF RED LIGHT.

Edwin instantly turns himself into a bat and darts out of the window into the morning sky. He pauses a moment before racing off towards the forest.

'Well, little one…' begins Mrs Stamps, staring at Corbin. 'You'd better come with us.' Mrs Stamps leans forward and reaches down to grip hold of Corbin's waistcoat, lifting him off the bedpost and lowering him to the floor.

'Where are we going?' asks Corbin, looking around at everyone in the room.

'Well, you are very welcome to stay here if you like,' replies Mrs Stamps. 'But I suggest we all go back downstairs and work out how we can solve this other issue. Oh…and Timothy – what time are you expecting these judges to arrive…? I really do hope you have thought about what you are going to say – or better still – what you are *not* going to say?'

'I'm sure I will conjure up something suitable to say,' responds Timothy, biting his bottom lip.

◆◆◆

Approaching the village of Baston from the south has always been a challenging task on foot, but to negotiate the rock covered hills while riding on the back of a donkey, is by all means, an undertaking on a whole different level.

The clattering of the donkey's hooves over jagged rocks, resonates through the air. The donkey struggles to support the weight of a rather plump woman sitting on its back as it steps down off a small embankment and onto the pebbled shores of the Cobalt River. The clattering of hooves turns into clinking as the donkey is guided across shale and pebbles, towards the edge of the water. It pauses for breath, before lowering its head, sticking out its tongue and slurping madly away at the refreshing crystal-clear waters.

Many people, who have the pleasure of owning a donkey, will usually name it something simple, such as "Donkey," or even refer to it as "boy" or "lass." However, this is not the case for this donkey, who has been given a very peculiar name by its owner. This donkey has been named, Dinkle.

Dinkle has been in the company of his owner for many years, although he sometimes wishes that he hadn't. Years of hauling his owner around on his back has taken its toll on his overworked legs, spine and—well, anything else that bares the weight of a rather large and plump woman, who at this moment is sitting on his back with her chubby legs dangling either side of his body.

Wrapped up in very colourful clothing and sporting a pair of oversized fancy spectacles, Felicity Fullers is certainly an eye-opener for any passer-by, or anyone standing in her presence. Sometimes it's not Felicity that people stare at in amazement, but Dinkle, as he struggles to plod along, with his legs shaking and taking the strain of the colossal weight above him.

'I think that's quite enough water for now, Dinkle,' mutters Felicity, pulling hard on the reins and raising Dinkle's head out of the river.

Felicity always talks very openly to Dinkle, knowing perfectly well that he cannot answer back, although she wishes that he sometimes would. She also likes to believe that Dinkle understands her every command, even if most of the time, he decides to do the opposite.

'We must be getting pretty close to the village of Baston now, Dinkle,' declares Felicity. 'Let's just pause for a moment and check this map and—oh yes, not too far from it at all – in fact…just over that hill Oh, look over there! There seems to be a group of gentlemen playing with their swords. They have tents – they must be camping. Come, Dinkle – off we go – *tut-tut*.'

Felicity pulls at the reins and directs Dinkle over the pebbled stones and up towards the Corporal and his men, who are just about to march back into the village. Dinkle pants loudly and lets out some strange coughing sounds. He tries to remain balanced and upright.

'Hello there, you fine gentleman!' yells Felicity, madly waving an arm through the air towards Private Simmons, who has to check twice at the unusual sight coming towards him.

'Err…Corporal, Sir?' asks Private Simmons, turning promptly to his superior.

'Yes, Simmons?' replies the Corporal.

'There seems to be a rather large lady trying to mount a donkey – coming this way. Well, it looks as if she is trying to mount it – no wait…I think she *has* mounted it – yes, apologies, Sir – she is riding it.'

'What *are* you blabbering on about, Simmons?' demands the Corporal.

The Corporal turns and faces to where Private Simmons is pointing. He squints his eyes and tries to focus in on what Private Simmons is desperately trying to describe.

'Well, I'll be damned,' mumbles the Corporal. 'You are right, Simmons.'

'What's going on, Sir…?' questions Private Babe, moving aside the Corporal.

'Fat lady on a donkey,' replies the Corporal. 'Now that is something you don't see every day, is it?'

'You're not wrong, Sir,' sniggers Private Simmons.

Private Babe takes a few steps forward. 'Oh, gosh! That must be the judges for the village competition. The Reverend did say that they are expected around this time.'

'Are you telling me that the donkey is a judge…?' queries Private Simmons. 'How very strange!'

Private Babe chuckles. 'No, Simmons…the rather large lady riding the donkey is the judge.'

'Ah, I see,' sneers Private Simmons. 'So, there's only one judge, then?'

'Looks like it,' replies Private Babe.

The Corporal, alongside Private Babe and Private Simmons, watch in concern as the donkey comes to a well-deserved halt in front of them; panting and struggling to catch its breath.

'Good day, gentlemen,' announces Felicity. 'I'm rather hoping that one of you delightful specimens could direct me to the village of Baston? In our haste we seemed to have wondered off the pathway.'

'Certainly…' responds the Corporal. 'If you take that path just over there, it will lead you over the hill and down into the centre of the village.'

'Oh, thank you – very kind…err—'

'Ringelstein, ma'am…Corporal Ringelstein,' replies the Corporal, before taking a slight bow.

'Oh, how absolute charming – a *real* military man,' responds Felicity. 'Well, I'm Felicity Fullers…it's an absolute pleasure to meet such a polite and respectful gentleman for a change.'

Private Simmons gently sniggers.

Felicity turns to face the rest of the Corporal's men who stand battle ready; their helmets securely fastened and swords in hands.

'What are you all doing?' questions Felicity.

'Well, it's a long story…' begins the Corporal. 'But if you come with us, we shall give you a personal escort back into the village.'

'How wonderful! I must say…I'm very impressed already.'

'Well, give it a few moments…' mumbles Private Simmons, under his breath. 'I'm fairly sure that you'll change your mind.'

◆◆◆

On the ground floor of the village tavern, Mrs Stamps, Melvin, Samuel, Timothy, the Reverend and Corbin stand behind the bar, alongside Duncan, Private Myles, Private Trout and the random villagers.

Everyone huddles together; one by one they each take a peek over the top of the bar counter. They stare nervously through the broken windows and towards the mass of laundry marching across the village green.

'It's that giant rat again!' slurs Duncan, stumbling to his feet in an attempt to grab his knife off the wall, only to be denied and pulled back down behind the bar counter by Samuel.

'Be quiet, Duncan…' begins Samuel, placing his hand firmly over Duncan's mouth. 'They'll hear you.'

Corbin turns to stare at Duncan, before smiling; safe in the knowledge that he has been saved, for a second time, from being turned into a pie by Duncan.

'Have you mulled over about what we can do with

all this laundry, Melvin?' asks the Reverend, crouching himself down next to Melvin.

'I'm afraid not, my holy friend…my magical energy is extremely low,' announces Melvin, stroking his beard softly. 'I believe it would be of great benefit to pray; pray that Edwin manages to find Amelia and bring her back to us safely. God only knows what will become of Officer Locks.'

'What do you mean …?' questions Samuel

'Well, vampires and werewolves don't mix very well, do they?' responds Melvin.

'I guess not,' mutters Samuel.

'We must also hope that Amelia *will* be able to help us with sorting out the possessed laundry. Maybe she'll be able to reverse it or do something remarkable—' adds Melvin.

'Like what?' interrupts Mrs Stamps.

'I don't know,' splutters Melvin. 'But I really am too low on power to do anything at the moment – I'm sorry I can't be of further help.'

Mrs Stamps crawls across the floor behind the bar, squeezing herself past the Reverend and Samuel. 'What about you two?' she asks, poking Private Trout on the shoulder and nudging her elbow into the ribs of Private Myles.

'Us?' responds Private Myles. 'What do you think we can do about it?'

'Yes…I really don't think that Myles and I can really do much about it, Mrs Stamps,' adds Private Trout. 'There is so many of them and—well, we can fight all we like, but they just don't want to stay down. These table legs are useless against them.'

Mrs Stamps sighs. 'Well there must be something that we can do? We can't just rely on Edwin coming back with Amelia. Even if he does, we can't be sure that she'll be able to aid us. We must take matters into our own hands!'

'What about if we set them all on fire?' questions Timothy, trying to project enough volume to reach Mrs Stamps, yet low enough not to attract attention from the laundry outside.

'Timothy, we have already had that conversation,' retorts Mrs Stamps. 'Although I believe that idea could possibly work – I don't think that seeing their clothes burning in some smouldering inferno, is going to go down too well with the locals. Besides, firstly…I'm near out of clean underwear and I haven't changed this dress since early this morning. Secondly…what would the judges think when entering the village and seeing a pile of burnt and charred fabric? You know, questions will be asked, Timothy!'

'Shush, Mrs Stamps!' commands Samuel. 'They are coming closer.'

Mrs Stamps shuffles forward and pulls herself up to take another peek over the top of the counter. A small army of laundry begins to form by the fountain.

'What are they doing?' questions the Reverend.

'What do they want? That would certainly be a better question to ask,' adds Samuel.

Everyone watches as wave after wave of laundry continue to appear from behind the village hall; each wave carefully making its way across to the fountain. Minute by minute the mass of laundry gets larger.

'Or, an even better question would be…where are they all going?' responds Timothy, watching as a few waves break away from the rest of the group and head through the village towards the river.

'It looks like they are going to intercept the Corporal

and the rest of the gang,' states Private Trout. 'I do hope they have managed to find something to fight them with.'

'Shall we go after them?' asks Private Myles.

'After who?' replies Private Trout.

'The Corporal and the rest of his men – surely you didn't think I meant that army of laundry?'

'I never know with you, Myles – and no, we'll be seen. We will just wait for the Corporal to arrive. I'm sure he will have a plan of attack.'

'So, we are just going to sit here?' asks the Reverend.

'Yes…for now,' responds Private Trout.

Samuel slowly releases his hands from Duncan's mouth and indicates to him to remain quiet, which for Duncan, in his incoherent and drunken state, is a task easier said than done. Duncan acknowledges Samuel's request with an uncontrolled nod.

Placing his hands atop the bar counter, Samuel raises himself up and takes a peek at the laundry still accumulating at the fountain. 'Why do you think those ones are just standing there?' he asks.

'I'm really not sure…' responds the Reverend. 'But I'm glad that most of the villagers have managed to escape the chaos and have locked themselves safely inside their homes and businesses.'

'Yes, that is a relief. I do hope my family are safe.'

'I'm sure they are – your wife is a strong woman.'

Samuel gently nods at the Reverend.

'Oh, my goodness!' shrieks Mrs Stamps. 'Look!'

Suddenly the laundry spreads out across the village; underpants, trousers and jumpers rising into the air and swirling around the fountain. Pyjamas, overcoats and shirts begin marching towards the village's various buildings. Socks, tights and undergarments dissipate outwards; sliding and slithering across the damp and sodden grass.

One by one, pieces of laundry begin to attack and then cling themselves to the surrounding buildings; each of them trying to find a way inside. The sounds of glass window panes shattering, and slated tiles smashing as they hit the ground, echo in the air.

'They are attacking all the buildings!' yelps Private Myles. 'But what are they looking for?'

'I'm not sure, Myles,' replies Private Trout. 'I really cannot understand what they are—'

'Perhaps they are after me?' interrupts Melvin.

'Why would they be looking for you?' enquires Mrs Stamps.

'Err…because—because *I—I*—I'm a—oh, I don't know. It was just a thought!' stutters Melvin.

Everyone continues to stare in horror as the laundry starts to engulf the buildings.

'We really need to do something!' declares Samuel. 'Has anyone got any ideas?'

'It's a pity that we don't have a huge iron – then we could iron them all,' says Corbin, before chuckling.

'Thank you little one…' begins Mrs Stamps. 'But I do believe we are looking for solutions—'

'Hold on one second…' interrupts Samuel. 'Our new friend may just be onto something.'

'I am?' glees Corbin, presenting Samuel with a smile.

'Yes-yes, I believe you are…' answers Samuel, before pausing to think. 'Melvin…I hear you have a steam-powered bicycle. Is that correct?'

'Yes, that is right – I do own such a contraption,' responds Melvin, positioning himself closer to Samuel. 'Err…why?'

Samuel leans up towards Melvin and places a hand

upon his shoulder. 'Steam, Melvin…steam.'

Melvin stares momentarily at Samuel's hand resting on his shoulder, before turning to face him with a complete look of confusion. Samuel waits patiently for Melvin's brain cells to catch up and relish him in Samuel's, or even Corbin's moment of genius.

'Aha! Steam…yes!' bellows Melvin. 'That could certainly work.'

'Steam?' questions Mrs Stamps.

'Yes, Mrs Stamps…steam,' responds Melvin.

'Is this another one of your crazy thoughts?' replies Mrs Stamps. 'I simply don't have the patience for you to mess up again. I'm dangling on the end of a very thin tether right now – and I'm about to—'

'Shush, Mrs Stamps!' interrupts Samuel. 'Corbin, our little— err, what are—'

'Mole-sprite…' says Corbin, sighing.

'Yes, our little mole-sprite…' begins Samuel. 'He may just have come up with an ingenious idea to use steam against the laundry.'

'Arghhh, look!' exclaims the Reverend. 'A pair of Mrs Stamps' frilly knickers have flown down the bell tower. We must cleanse the church of this demon. Fetch me a long pole, I'm going in!'

'You can't be serious, Reverend?' asks Timothy.

'Ah, yes…maybe you're right, Mrs Stamps doesn't do frilly knickers – or does she?'

CHAPTER XIV

"I used to think that I was indecisive. Now I'm not too sure..."

PRIVATE MYLES

Corporal Ringelstein marches his men across the foothills and down the dusty pathway that leads into the village of Baston. They are tailed sluggishly by Felicity riding on her donkey; Dinkle, who is very much on the verge of exhaustion; and Dexter, who dallies along behind, continuously fanning his snout with his claws, in an attempt to cool it down.

The Corporal and his squad of men wield their swords through the air; swinging them carelessly from left to right as they sing a multitude of comical battle songs. The Corporal occasionally gives his men a couple of his greatest inspirational and motivational quotes, which fail to impress.

'Do you know what…?' begins Felicity, shifting her attention towards Dexter. 'I can't recall ever meeting a dragon before—well, maybe a couple of little ones in the past, but certainly not one with your intellectual capacity. It's an absolute pleasure to meet you.'

Dexter nods his head and smiles back at Felicity. He chooses not to engage in any conversation, hoping that his temporary silence will soothe his snout and aching jaw bone.

'I'm a little curious, Corporal…' begins Felicity. 'I'm curious as to why you and your men are all marching into the village holding swords in your hands? Is it something ceremonial? I mean…you didn't have to go to such extremes in welcoming me into the village.'

The Corporal suddenly stops, causing his men behind him to come to a swift and unprepared halt. He unhurriedly turns to face Felicity, who sharply pulls back on Dinkle's reins, bringing him to a well- deserved stop, even if for the briefest of moments.

'Well…how do I put this?' responds the Corporal, scraping the blade of his sword carefully down the side of his stubbled face. He ponders for a few moments, trying to conjure up an answer that will satisfy Felicity, but at the same time, one that doesn't sound over the top, unlikely or ridiculous. He bites hard on his lower lip, before letting out a long drawn out sigh. 'Well Felicity, the village has been taken over by a small army of possessed laundry articles, that have magically been brought to life by a crazed and eccentric spellbinder wizard. The village's Laundry Fairy is also missing and the locals think that a vampire is to blame.'

Felicity lowers her head; allowing her perfectly formed brown eyes to stare over the top rim of her spectacles. She raises an eyebrow at the Corporal, and tries to deduce, to the best of her ability, whether the Corporal is being serious, or just simply joking with her. After a few seconds, she opts for the latter and lets out a loud chuckling laugh.

'Oh deary-me…you're so funny, Corporal,' roars Felicity, continuing to giggle, before pushing her spectacles back up the bridge of her nose.

'Well…I don't see what's so funny, Felicity? I was being deadly serious,' replies the Corporal, turning around and continuing to march towards the village. Felicity pauses in thought, before snapping at Dinkle's reins and instructing him to follow.

'I'm supposed to meet up with a gentleman called the Reverend Clementine – and also Mayor Timothy Oakes,' states Felicity. 'Do you know of them?'

Private Simmons turns towards Felicity and slows down his marching pace, allowing Dinkle to catch up with him. He continues to walk alongside them both.

'Yeah…we know them both,' responds Private Simmons. 'The Corporal and the Reverend are good friends. You'll probably find both the Reverend and Timothy inside the village tavern. They have most likely barricaded themselves behind the bar.'

'Oh gosh!' gasps Felicity. 'Men of their status – drinking at this time of the day?'

'I think *you'll* be needing a drink after you see the state of the village.'

Dexter lets out a little snigger from behind.

'What could you possibly mean by that?' questions Felicity.

'Well, take a good look for yourself!' replies Private

Simmons, pointing his finger towards the village.

Felicity's eyes widen in horror at the sight before her. In her shock, she pulls hard on Dinkle's reins, forcing him to a sudden, painful and abrupt halt. She glances across to the Corporal, who crouches down on the edge of the pathway. He scouts the immediate area and ponders over a plan of attack.

'Well, I wasn't expecting anything quite like this…' mutters Felicity. 'Are they dangerous?'

'I really haven't had chance to find that out yet,' answers Private Simmons. 'I clobbered a few of them with a wooden table leg…but that didn't seem to stop them. The trouble is – we have no idea what we are going to do with them.'

'What do you mean?' asks Felicity.

'You can bash them all you like – they just don't stay down,' responds Private Simmons. 'Every time we hit them and knock them to the floor – they just get back up again. We all came back to the camp to pick up our swords, hoping that they would be more effective against them.'

Felicity and Dinkle continue to watch from the hillside; looking down at the whirling mass of laundry flying through the air and around the buildings of the village. Trousers, aprons, blouses and sweatshirts skim over the rooftops and dart violently around the many protruding chimneys pots, which project into the sky.

Felicity refocuses her eyes to observe the village's smaller buildings being engulfed by a variety of fabrics; fabrics that spread themselves open and cling to the buildings' wooden frameworks and stone masonry.

Other smaller items of laundry force their way into the narrow cracks and crevices, just like a bee would prod at a flower in search of pollen.

The ground around the village fountain shines and flickers as the sunlight reflects off the many thousands of copper coins that lay scattered upon it. Felicity squints and tries to deduce through her thick lensed glasses, at why the ground also seems to be moving, gasping in shock as she observes an array of socks and woolly tights slithering like snakes, across the sodden grass. Felicity's jaw drops as she realises the severity of the village's problem and the amount of damage the laundry is causing.

'I'm pretty certain that I will not be needing this score sheet,' announces Felicity, removing it from her bag and tossing it over her shoulder. 'I can see perfectly well from here that I will not be able to tick a single one of those boxes.'

Dexter tilts his head and watches the score sheet float away down the hillside; carried gently by the soft morning breeze.

'ATTENTION, LADS! Attention now!' bellows the Corporal. 'We—'

'Excuse me?' interrupts Felicity. 'I may be a slightly larger lady, with a masculine build and questionable facial features, but please…please…I'm still very much a woman!'

'Oh—*cough-cough*—yes…apologies to you Felicity,' mumbles the Corporal. 'Force of habit, you see?'

There is an uncomfortable silence.

'Okay, lads and—err…lass. This is it! Let's charge in and give them all we have. Let's give Melvin plenty of time to—well, to come up with something.'

'Melvin…?' questions Felicity, a curious tone in her voice.

The Corporal turns towards Felicity. 'Yes…the spellbinder wizard who caused all this mess.'

Felicity's eyes suddenly widen. 'You don't by any chance mean Melvin Copernicus?'

'Yes, that's him!' answers Private Babe.

'How extraordinary…' glees Felicity. He certainly is—well, let's just say…a unique individual. I believe the last time I spoke to him was when I was writing a short piece for the local newsprint. Something about a remarkable tale of his parents dying to get into the afterlife, or—well, something along those lines.'

'Is that so…?' questions Private Babe.

'Oh, it would be an absolute marvel to see him again. Is he down there?'

'I believe so, yes…but no telling where,' responds Private Babe.

'Oh goody-goody,' replies Felicity, clapping her hands together. 'Maybe I could write a small piece on how he brought the village of Baston to its knees. People love that sort of story, you know!'

'Well, we are here to make sure that something like that does *not* happen,' retorts the Corporal. 'And for your safety I would advise you to stay out of the village – it could get very disordered down there.'

'Are you kidding me?' questions Felicity. 'I'm not missing any of this!'

'You can't be serious…?' coughs the Corporal. 'A battlefield is no place for a refined woman, such as yourself.'

'I assure you…' begins Felicity. 'I have had my fair share of battles in my time. Isn't that right, Dinkle?'

Dinkle chews on the long grass beneath him. His ears twitch slightly.

'Besides – I have this…' announces Felicity, pulling out a small hand-held device crafted of metal. She grasps it firmly in her hand.

'Oh, jolly-good show!' yelps Private Simmons, quickly breaking formation on noticing Felicity's toy. 'Is that what I think it is?' he adds, racing towards her.

◆◆◆

Edwin, in bat form, flies at speed over the Darkened Enchanted Forest, scouting for a suitable place to dive through the thick canopy of trees and into its mystical depths.

It is not uncommon to see a bat fly above the forest, but to see a *vampire* bat engulfed by a magical protective bubble, is extremely unlikely and improbable.

The forest is a mass of lush green vegetation, plants and flowers. Colossal trees rise up from the ground; huge trunks fill the void spaces as they intertwine with each other; projecting upwards into the sky. Branches and leaves shoot out at every angle, forming canopies, which cast gloomy shadows on the forest floor.

When the wind blows just right, multiple shimmers of sunlight penetrate through the vines; cutting the air like spiked daggers.

Seeing a small gap, Edwin quickly swoops down and bolts through the thick blanket of trees, entering the darkened depths beneath them. The sunlight instantly fades, which for Edwin is not a bad thing at all.

From the outside, the forest looks like any other. Edwin realises why, as he peers into its gloominess, it is known as the *Darkened* Enchanted Forest.

He darts quickly through the twisting branches and vines, before momentarily taking up rest on the wilted branch of a blackened oak tree. He peers through the low light and looks for any sign of Officer Locks, or any indication of where he is heading with Amelia.

His sensitive nose twitches whilst picking up the faint scent of fresh blood; a blood that Edwin instantly recognises as being that of a werewolf. He scouts the immediate area, trying to let his nose hone in on the scent, but more precisely, where it is coming from.

Being a vampire, Edwin refuses to acknowledge the meaning of the word fear, and wouldn't, or more accurately, *doesn't* get scared; a fact he is always constantly reminding Corbin of. However, hanging off a branch deep inside the Darkened Enchanted Forest, unsettles Edwin; hearing the sounds of the forest's many inhabitants echo through the trees.

The wind whistles gently. Fallen leaves rustle on the ground below and create an eerie and ghostly chorus, which sends a slight chilling shudder through Edwin's fragile body. His eyes stare into nothingness as he picks up voices; whispers and murmurs from the trees themselves.

Startled by the sounds of twisting and creaking wood from beneath him, Edwin swiftly flies down to the forest floor. The branch he rests upon suddenly bends and moves, as if the tree itself is alive.

The scent of blood hits Edwin's nose again, causing him to glide across to a pile of boulders, positioned very neatly underneath some un-earthed tree roots.

THERE IS A FLASH OF RED LIGHT.

Edwin instantly turns back into his human form. The protective bubble around him magically resizes around his body and adjusts itself to his altered form.

He steps forward towards the boulders, reaches out and slowly drags his fingernail through a thick red liquid, which streams off it and drips onto the ground below. He raises his finger to his mouth and runs his pointy nail gently over the tip of his tongue.

'Werewolf…' he mutters to himself, turning around and searching for any other signs of blood, or more importantly, a trail of blood to follow.

Edwin feels as if burning eyes are watching him. He cautiously strolls through the rich fauna, being very careful not to catch his bubble on anything that could cause it to rip, or worse…burst.

Although the forest is shielded from the majority of the sunlight overhead, slithers of light still find their way to the forest floor. They seem to dance and flicker as the trees sway gently back and forth. Edwin begins to realise, that if his bubble did burst, or he ran out of time, then he would certainly meet his fate. Even constantly using his lightning reflexes and speed, trying to dodge the speed of light is something even *he* is not capable of.

Edwin continues to pace through the overgrowth and looks around for any more signs of blood. He pauses as he finds another small droplet clinging to the edge of a bracken leaf, and further still, more random spots of blood on the long grass in front of him.

Edwin lifts his head and uses his night vision to try and penetrate the darkened depths of the forest.

'Must be this way,' he mumbles.

THERE IS A FLASH OF RED LIGHT.

Edwin transforms into his bat form and follows the trail of blood, which seems to be get more frequent. He keeps his eyes fully open and his ears tuned.

◆◆◆

Melvin pounds his fist hard against the bolted door of Eric's workshop, before spinning around and kicking at a few socks, which have followed him across the village green. The socks fly backwards, only to reform and once again, advance towards Melvin. He begins to panic at the sight of other oncoming laundry that he has attracted the attention of. His eyes widen at a group of linen shirts racing towards him. Melvin continues to pound harder on the workshop door.

'Eric? Are you in there?' shrieks Melvin, looking back over his shoulders. 'Open the door! It's me… Melvin.'

There is the faint sound of shuffling from behind the door and a couple of loud bangs, which are quickly followed by a long drawn out groan.

'Who is it?' moans Eric, his voice trailing off.

'I already ruddy told you that it's me, now will you please let me in!'

There is a pause…

'And who's me?' asks Eric, his voice now booming from the other side of the door.

'What the blazes do you mean…who's me? Who do you think you are?'

There is another pause…

'I know who I am,' responds Eric. 'I'm Eric.'

'Eric…it's me, Melvin. Now would you please stop dallying about and let me in….?'

Daring not to turn around and face the oncoming laundry that is creeping closer towards him, Melvin chooses to close his eyes and visualise himself at his happy place, which for Melvin, is somewhere hot, with a sandy beach and some of those colourful drinks with the little umbrellas in. This unique calming technique is something that Melvin often uses when he is feeling in a state of panic. However, this time, his attempt at a blissful, tranquil and soothing scenario of the mind is interrupted by a possessed sock nibbling at his ankle.

'Oh, what the sweet—' begins Melvin, instantly turning around and kicking the sock *so* hard that his sandal dislodges from his foot. It launches into the air and lands several feet away from the river's edge.

'Blast it! – Blast it! – Blast it!' exclaims Melvin, before gasping in horror at the group of white shirts approaching him.

'ERIC!' yelps Melvin. 'Let me in…it's your good pal, Melvin!'

There is another pause, before the sound of a key turning in its lock, breaks the silence. The clicking sound is followed by an assortment of clangs and scrapes as a complex system of cogs and gears begins to activate the doors unlocking mechanism.

'Hurry up, Eric!' continues Melvin. 'I'm about to be attacked out here and I don't think I have much energy left to create—Oh, screw it!'

THE AIR HUMS.

Melvin disappears in a flash of light, only to seconds later re-appear inside Eric's workshop. He briefly stands still, before rolling his eyes backwards and collapsing to the floor with a loud…

THUD!

'Melvin? Melvin is that you?' questions Eric, quickly rotating the key in the opposite direction; re-locking the door. He rushes across to Melvin and aids him to his feet, before lowering him gently down onto a wooden stool.

Melvin mumbles a few incoherent words.

'Get some of this down you, Melvin,' announces Eric, reaching into his pocket and pulling out his flask of brandy. He pops off the cap and lifts the flask up to Melvin's lips. 'That'll warm your cockles, huh?'

Melvin grabs the flask from Eric's hand, takes a gulp of its contents and hands the flask back to Eric.

'Anyway…what are you doing here, Melvin?' asks Eric. 'And how did you get past my security systems?'

Melvin shakes his head from side to side, whilst relishing and savouring the warm Dwarven brandy swirling around in his gullet.

'I've been banging on your front door for the last two minutes!' bellows Melvin. 'Didn't you hear me?'

'Steady on – was that you?' responds Eric, turning a slightly shade of crimson. 'I thought someone said Melton. I don't know a Melton. That's why I was a little bit hesitant in answering. Why didn't you just say it was you?'

'I did!' retorts Melvin. 'Several times!'

'Well I guess it's a good idea that you are in here and not out there. As the person out there, would surely be having a difficult time right now. But that person was you and you are—well, here.'

A bewildered expression falls over Melvin's face.

'Anyway, Melvin…you real shouldn't be wandering about outside – it's dangerous. Have you seen what's going on? Any idea how it has happened?'

'One question at a time please, Eric,' states Melvin, wiping the sweat from his brow with the sleeve of his robe.

'Ah, yes…silly me,' responds Eric. 'Guess I'm always looking for answers – Dwarven nature that!'

'Well to answer all of your questions, Eric…' begins Melvin. 'I *do* know what is going on outside – as I created it all.'

Eric gasps. 'You did? What in the Great Forges of the South, did you—'

'No time to explain,' interrupts Melvin. 'I really do

need my bicycle back. Is it finished? And if you must know – I teleported inside your workshop, which I really shouldn't have done – as I'm now feeling slightly light-headed and rather dizzy.'

'You can teleport? How very interesting. That is surely something I never thought about exploring. I must have a serious think about the physics of that – at some point. I assume that on a quantum level – a vast amount of energy is used to alter the mechanical state of particles through time and space – allowing them to physically transverse from one point to—'

'Eric! My bicycle!' blasts Melvin. 'I really don't have the time or the energy to explain the ins and outs of teleportation to you.'

'Oh, yes…apologies, Melvin,' replies Eric, pacing across to the side of his workshop. 'It certainly is finished, Melvin…but it was no easy task.'

Eric signals Melvin to join him by a large object, covered entirely by several large sheets of oil stained linen. He pauses, before removing the sheets one by one, to reveal Melvin's recently repaired steam-powered bicycle. 'There you go, Melvin…what do you think of that fine piece of craftsmanship?'

'That's brilliant, Eric!' replies Melvin, hurriedly. 'Now have you got any coal?'

Eric huffs and hangs his head low. 'Well…I thought that you would have sounded a little more excited, Melvin – considering the amount of time and effort I took into putting it all back together.'

'Oh…Oh, yes I am, Eric! I just don't have the time right now to thank you formally. Another time maybe?'

'Well, I guess so—'

'Good. Now, have you any coal please?'

'Already loaded.'

'Ah, good-good!'

'You'll also find that I have added a few features of my own design. I believe you will find them most fun – and I have optimised the furnace for maximum burning efficiency. It should give you a few more horsepower to those old cylinders.'

'I don't need any horses, just the bicycle.'

'Err…I mean—oh never mind.'

Eric walks around to the front of the bicycle. 'I have also added an ignition system by using a cleverly designed flint mechanism. When you flick this lever, a flint will strike against—'

'That's all very useful, Eric – but I haven't got the time to listen to all this at present. *I—I—*well, the village has much bigger issues – and I'm going to use my bicycle to sort this mess out. On top of that, Officer Locks has stolen the Laundry Fairy!'

'Officer Locks has stolen her?' gasps Eric.

'That's what I just said, Eric.'

'I don't believe it. Why would he do such a thing?'

'I *really* do not have the time to explain, Eric. But hopefully I'm going to use my bicycle to control the laundry. Now…have you got more coal?'

'Plenty over there in the corner.'

'Then grab it all! We are probably going to need it.'

'What are you planning to do, Melvin…? Run the laundry over with your bicycle?'

'Don't be so silly, Eric. I haven't got the patience for that!'

'Well what, then…?'

'Steam, Eric…lots and lots of steam.'

◆◆◆

Edwin continues to weave in and out of a variety of exotic trees; narrowly avoiding their twisting branches, which protrude out in all directions. The trail of werewolf blood becomes more visible; droplets and traces of thick red blood ooze off leaves, twigs and rocks, as Edwin ventures deeper into the forest.

Judging by the amount of blood, Edwin deduces that Officer Locks, in his haste, must have cut himself extremely badly on the glass shards, while escaping with Amelia.

Edwin slows down, noticing that the trees and bushes around him have started to become less dense. He darts up behind the trunk of a large oak tree, noticing a faint orange glow in the distance. His ears twitch; hearing the sounds of crackling leaves as they burn. His smell heightens; detecting the aroma of charred and burnt wood.

THERE IS A FLASH OF RED LIGHT.

Edwin transforms himself back into his human form and instantly turns to lean his back up against a tree trunk. He gently lowers and raises himself up against its bark, allowing the rough texture to scratch an itch he has developed; an itch that he couldn't quite reach while in bat form. He lets out a sigh of relief and grins in satisfaction.

Edwin turns his head, peers around the side of the tree trunk and into a large clearing. A roaring fire burns brightly in the centre of the clearing; bellowing out a fume of thick ash-like smoke while sparks and burning embers dance ferociously through the air, before quickly disappearing.

Feeling the warmth of the fire on his face, Edwin carefully sneaks out from behind the tree and tiptoes forward to take a closer look. He slowly kneels down behind tall bushels of thick grass and immediately gasps at the sight of his zynite cage resting atop a small rock. Edwin slowly elevates himself above the grass and gasps again as he catches a glimpse of Amelia laying on her side in the centre of the cage.

'This is too easy…' mutters Edwin, as he lowers himself back to the ground and pulls his black cloak tightly around him; shielding the bright light created by the fire, from reflecting off his shiny red waistcoat.

Edwin waits patiently and ponders at where Officer Locks could be; scouting the area for any signs of him. After a few moments, Edwin's thoughts turn to whether he could just simply run in, grab Amelia and make a mad dash back through the forest. Edwin then realises, that although a marvellous start to his plan; navigating through the forest on foot is certainly asking for trouble; and without Corbin, he would certainly struggle to carry the cage while in bat form.

Without any time to waste and checking that the area is clear, Edwin proceeds to advance towards Amelia. He decides that he will risk trying to obtain his magical cage containing her and make a desperate run back through the forest, long before Officer Locks realises that Amelia has gone.

Edwin takes a couple of careful steps forward and immediately halts on hearing the rustling of leaves, just off to the side of him. He quickly crouches and hides his shadowy figure amongst the long grass as he oberves Officer Locks pushing and ripping his way through the tall overgrowth towards Amelia.

Edwin's eyes continue to follow Officer Locks as he makes his way across to the cage; watching him give it a violent shake, which startles Amelia. Edwin lets out a long sigh as he observes Amelia struggling to lift herself into a sitting position. She rubs her eyes with the backs of her hands and begins to focus in on her surroundings, before displaying confusion at how she suddenly ended up in the middle of the Darkened Enchanted Forest.

Amelia continues to let her eyes adjust to the faded light and manages to pick up the lanky outline of Officer Locks as he removes a sharp knife from underneath his belt. The Officer glances at its shiny steel blade, before driving the pointed end deep into the top of a rotten tree stump, which stands nearby.

'Officer Locks?' murmurs Amelia, questioning to herself if it was truly him, and shocked at why the Officer, who after years of doing his washing, is now standing in front of her with a sharpened knife. She continues to ponder at where Edwin, her previous captor is, before letting out a smile; smiling at the fact that maybe Officer Locks has saved her.

Trembling and with little strength, Amelia finds the will to stand to her feet. She stumbles to the front of the cage and quickly clutches onto the thin metal bars in an attempt to keep herself upright.

'Excuse me, Officer?' mumbles Amelia, trying to project enough volume to make the Officer hear her, only to then splutter a few coughs, which finally catch his attention.

'Ah…she's awake,' mutters Officer Locks, before smiling and letting out a devilish chuckle. He strolls gently towards the cage, leans down and brings his face up close to Amelia. Amelia takes a small, cautious step backwards from the cage's metal bars.

'I'm guessing that you are wondering, what on Earth is going on?' continues Officer Locks, with a smug look upon his face. 'I also imagine that you would like to know how you got here and—err…oh yes, why I'm here and where that pathetic vampire called Edwin, has gone?' Am I right?'

Amelia gently nods in response to Officer Locks' questions. 'Have you not come to rescue me from that ghastly vampire?' she whimpers.

'Rescue you? *Rescue you*?' responds Officer Locks, standing upright, before slowly pacing back towards the tree stump and pulling out the knife with minimal effort. 'Oh, not at all, my dear. In fact, it is completely the opposite.'

'I don't understand,' sobs Amelia.

Edwin cautiously creeps forward, trying his best not to make any sudden sounds that could alert Officer Locks of his presence. He carefully pushes the long grass to the side and leans down; hiding himself from view. Edwin rotates his head to direct an ear towards Officer Locks, hoping to capture, in a little more detail, the conversation the Officer is having with Amelia.

'Well, I'm not going to beat about the bush – *pardon the pun* – but I'm here to take your heart,' explains Officer Locks.

Amelia gasps. 'Why would you do such a thing?' I have been doing your dirty laundry for years and this is how you re-pay me?'

'Oh, boo-hoo…' responds Officer Locks, raising his finger to his face and imitating wiping a tear from his left eye. 'Do you really think I care about all that…?' No! I've got bigger plans for you—well, your heart.'

Officer Locks reaches deep into his other trouser pocket and pulls out a small coarse stone, before slowly rubbing it along the side of the knife blade. The sound of stone grinding against metal, sends a shiver through Amelia's tiny, fragile body.

'You are going to kill me?' weeps Amelia.

'Yes, that is generally what happens when a Fairy's heart is removed, no?' replies Officer Locks.

'But…why?'

'Do you honestly think I'm going to stay around in that dump of a village forever? Being paid next to nothing to keep the village safe from harm and protect its inhabitants – whom, to be brutally honest, I really don't like that much – No! Your heart will fetch me a pretty price from the right buyer and then—then I'll be able to get far away from here.'

'But why wait until now…?' questions Amelia. 'I mean…you have had years to do this. Why all of a sudden have you decided—oh…oh-my…you needed Edwin, didn't you?'

'Clever girl,' responds Officer Locks, turning over the knife blade. 'Let's just say that I had a little tip-off that a vampire was staying in the village. Well, I say tip-off – but it was more like the incoherent and drunken blabbering of a certain tavern keeper – and when I was approached by the Reverend and some of the other locals – and told you had gone missing – I kind of put two and two together and—well, here we are.'

'Amelia starts to cry. '*But*—but I've done nothing to you…nothing,' she bawls. 'People are all the same; I try my best to help people out of the goodness of my own heart, but all they do in return is abuse my powers for their own childish schemes. Or worse still – take my heart.'

'Yes, that's pretty much the extent of it,' responds Officer Locks, with no trace of remorse or emotion in his voice.

Officer Locks quickly stuffs the coarse stone back into his trouser pocket, before scraping the edge of the knife blade slowly across the top of his left forearm. The blade effortlessly slices through the excessive hairs growing upon it.

'I guess it was just lucky that the stupid vampire caught you. If it wasn't for Mrs Stamps using her quick thinking and tying Edwin up in front of the window shutters – it would have certainly been much harder for me to sneak you out without anyone noticing. She made it extremely easy for me.'

'Someone will come and find me…' interrupts Amelia. 'Melvin the Spellbinder will come for me – I know he will.'

'That crazy old fool?' Somehow, I don't think he will. He is drained and weakened of energy from that stupid spell he cast earlier. Besides, he will not come to the Darkened Enchanted Forest. He would become completely lost in here and—'

'No, he would not!' shrieks Amelia, followed by a number of small coughs. 'He knows the forest well. He lives right in the centre of it – in a castle.'

Officer Locks lets out a roaring laugh. 'Melvin? Melvin Copernicus – knows the forest well? From what I've heard, he got lost in his own castle once.'

Amelia sighs.

'Well, I can't stand about all day…' begins Officer Locks. 'Besides, even if someone was looking for you, they would find it near impossible to find you here in the forest. They have also run out of time.' Officer Locks leans down to the latch on the cage. 'Now…I promise you this will be quick and painless. No one can save you now—'

'That is where you are *very* wrong!' gloats Edwin, stepping out of the overgrowth and revealing himself to Officer Locks.

'Oh, it is you…vampire,' responds Officer Locks, backing away from the cage and standing upright. 'Well, this is truly unexpected and rather inconvenient timing. I really wasn't anticipating on seeing you here. I thought that maybe you would have been tied up – *no pun intended* – for the majority of the day. How terribly troublesome.'

Edwin stares hard at Officer Locks. 'You are very much mistaken, then.'

'I guess I am, vampire. Now please tell me…purely out of curiosity – why is there a funny looking bubble around—Oh…yes, I have just answered my own question. You shouldn't be out in the daylight, should you? Hmmm…I'm guessing that bubble protects you from the deadly rays of the sun? One of Melvin's crazy spells, I would imagine? '

'Well, that is none of your concern, is it?' responds Edwin, taking a small step forward.

Officer Locks pauses and stares knowingly at Edwin. 'I'm taking a stab in the dark – again, *no pun intended* – but what would happen to you if that bubble suddenly burst?'

Edwin hisses and takes another step closer to Officer Locks.

'Hold it right there, vampire!' instructs Officer Locks. 'We wouldn't want anything to suddenly slip and puncture that protective bubble of yours, would we…? Oh…now there's a thought – a vampire that perished by sunlight – whatever would your mother think? She would be truly disappointed in you—oh wait! I believe that she suffered a similar fate, if I'm not mistaken?'

Edwin lets out a menacing hiss. 'Do not talk about my mother. She has no relevance here.'

Office Locks smirks.

'Oh, but she does…or do you not recognise your own kin, Edwin?' states the Officer.

'What do you mean, my own kin?' Edwin raises an eyebrow in confusion.

'Are you telling me that you don't recognise your own brother, Edwin?'

Edwin's eyes widen. *It—It—*It can't be…' he mutters. 'You were taken – we all thought that—that you had—'

'That I had been eaten by wolves…?' interrupts Officer Locks. 'Is that what you are asking?'

'Precisely,' answers Edwin, shocked at the sudden appearance of his younger brother.

'Well, to be perfectly honest…it was completely the opposite. I wasn't eaten by wolves, but I was certainly bitten by one of them – and raised as one of them.'

'But you are, or even *were* a vampire. How is it even possible to be bitten by a werewolf?'

'Well, let's just say that the werewolf that bit me was slightly poorly for a few days after tasting my blood. I have no idea why I was converted into a werewolf – although some might say, I'm sort of a half vampire… half werewolf.'

'You mean, you are a hybrid?'

'If that's what you call them…then yes!'

Edwin gulps. He had heard stories of hybrids, but never thought that they could actually exist.

'And after all this time, you never came back?' asks Edwin. 'Our family spent years looking for you, in the hope that you survived the attack.'

'Well, I'm here now, Brother.'

'Please do not call me that. I lost my brother years ago. You are something else…something different.'

Officer Locks gently taps the knife blade onto the palm of his left hand.

'Come on, Edwin…' begins Officer Locks. 'Let us share in the spoils of capturing this Laundry Fairy.'

'That is something I cannot allow you to do. I will not let you take her heart,' snarls Edwin.

Officer Locks continues tapping the blade of the knife onto his hand, gradually picking up pace and intensity. 'Such as shame – such a terrible shame,' he mumbles to himself.

Edwin stares at the Officer's knife, being cautious of its sharp edge, and the fact he is standing within striking distance of Officer Locks. He carefully takes a step backwards.

'What are you going to do, Edwin…?' asks Officer Locks. 'Are you going to attempt to stop me? Don't make me laugh – you are too soft and weak.'

'I may be soft and weak, but I'm still not going to let you take this fairy's heart.'

Edwin repositions himself into a defensive stance.

'I would very much like to see you try to stop me, Edwin,' growls Officer Locks. 'But you seem to have a very severe weakness in using that bubble of yours. A simple swing of my blade and I could slice that bubble right open – allowing the sunlight to fall upon your pale vampire skin.'

Edwin smiles. 'You seem to forget that I'm much faster than you and within the blink of an eye, I could rip that knife out of your very hand. Besides, you seem to have a couple of major flaws in your plan.'

Officer Locks ponders at what he could have possibly missed and why Edwin is so overly confident that he will defeat him. He shrugs his shoulders at Edwin, before prompting him for a reason.

'And what may that be?' quizzes Officer Locks.

Edwin steps forward and releases his arms from inside his cloak, which flies open and flaps gently in the breeze. 'You forgot that you are a werewolf and that you need moonlight and a full moon to shapeshift into your wolf form. I don't see any moon in the sky.'

'And the other flaw?'

'You seem to be depositing a lot of blood all over the ground. You clearly do not have any of your healing abilities while in human form, do you? You weaken by the second.'

Officer Locks smiles and slowly paces towards Edwin, being very cautious of any sudden movements. He reaches into his jacket pocket and pauses.

Edwin lets out a loud hiss and displays his white fangs at Officer Locks.

'You seem to severely underestimate my abilities and cunningness, Edwin…' begins Officer Locks. 'But I will give you your dues. You are right in stating that I do require the presence of moonlight, but…I do not require the moon at all.'

'What do you mean?' asks Edwin, concerned at Officer Locks' unusual confidence in his abilities.

'Just as I said, Edwin…I don't need the moon – one of the mysteries of being a hybrid, I imagine.'

'Well…how do you expect to transform yourself into wolf form without the moon for its moonlight?'

'I have this…'

Officer Locks pulls out a small vial from his jacket pocket and holds it out in front of him. The contents of the vial glow with an intense white light, which illuminates the immediate area.

Edwin gasps. 'Bottled moonlight,' he mutters.

'Correct, Brother…bottled moonlight. If I pour the

entire contents of this vial over myself – it will be more than enough to make me shapeshift.'

'Where did you get that from…?' enquires Amelia, shouting as hard as she can towards Officer Locks.

'I borrowed it,' replies Officer Locks.

'You stole that from the tribal fairies of Elladon Forest, didn't you?' continues Amelia. 'They are the only fairies that can bottle pure moonlight.'

''Hmmm, I haven't stolen it!' yelps Officer Locks. 'I have simply borrowed it for a time that I may need it…just like now.'

'You disgust me,' states Amelia, before sliding to the floor in agony.

Officer Locks turns back towards Edwin. 'So…do you still think you will be able to stop me, vampire?' he asks, placing his thumb casually underneath the vial's cork bung.

Edwin hisses.

Officer Locks growls.

◆◆◆

Just as the village of Baston thinks that it has seen the most peculiar and unbelievable possible sight, another one suddenly comes along and blows the previous one completely out of the water.

The sight of a small group of highly trained military men, running wildly down a hill, while wielding swords, is a sight that would go completely unquestioned, based on the village's current circumstances. But now a group of military men, running wildly down a hill, wielding swords, quickly being followed by a rather plump lady riding a donkey, whilst firing off explosive rounds of lead from a hand-held device, is now proving to be the forerunner of unusual and bizarre sights seen by the village of Baston.

'You're just putting huge holes in the laundry with that thing, Felicity!' yells Private Simmons, watching as Felicity continually reloads her pistol with small lead balls and fires them off at random pieces of possessed laundry. 'Those little balls really don't seem to be doing much damage to them at all!'

'And that sword of yours is doing a much better job, is it…?' retorts Felicity, as Dinkle canters past Private Simmons.

'Well, it is doing a much better job than simply putting a big hole in them, replies Private Simmons, swinging madly at an oncoming white linen shirt and shredding it into pieces. The shirt moans and groans as shreds of its white linen fabric fall onto the grass below; only to seconds later, group up and individually advance towards Private Simmons.

'Whatever you say – this is too much fun and it gives me a chance to play with my new toy,' continues Felicity, directing Dinkle to join Private Simmons, while observing the shredded fabric of the linen shirt, slithering across the grass. 'They really don't seem to be staying down, do they?'

'LOOK OUT!' yells Private Simmons, leaping to the side of Felicity and sticking his sword through the toughened leather lining of a pair of brown trousers. He crazily wields the sword through the air and cuts the leather trousers into several pieces.

'That was a close call!' yelps Private Simmons.

'Yes, indeed. I believe I owe you a thank you,' replies Felicity, loading her pistol with another lead ball, before discharging the round into the strips of leather at Dinkle's feet. 'Take that, you—you—'

'Trousers?' suggests Private Simmons.

'Yes, trousers!' responds Felicity. 'Take that…you trousers!'

The Corporal and Private Babe stand side by side, slicing and dicing their way through an assortment of underpants, shirts, jumpers, trousers and other items of laundry, which constantly attack them from every direction. Random shreds and slithers of leather, cotton and silk fly through the air around them as the sharpened blades of their swords effortlessly cut the laundry into pieces.

The Corporal pauses briefly to wipe the sweat from his brow, before swinging his sword with all his might and slicing a cotton dress completely in half.

'We're sort of fighting a losing battle here, Sir,' states Private Babe, adjusting his helmet and poising for another attack. 'I'm fairly sure that I have fought this pair of underpants three times now. I just keep slicing it into smaller pieces every time – and it still keeps coming back.'

'You are right!' responds the Corporal. 'But what do you suggest we do about it?'

Private Babe ponders for an answer to his superior's question, while continuing to fend off an onslaught of cotton shirts and woollen jumpers.

The Corporal and Private Babe push their way across the village green, using their swords to slice the oncoming waves of laundry to pieces. The Corporal curses loudly as he has to step back and take a second or third swing at the constantly moving fragments of fabric.

Pausing to catch his breath, the Corporal turns to face the rest of his men, who continue to fight against the odds. He watches as they stumble their way through piles of shredded fabric, which slither on the ground on top of a scattering of shiny copper coins. On noticing the coins, he immediately turns and scouts the area for Dexter.

'Ah, Dexter…there you are!' yells the Corporal. 'Come over here – I need some covering fire!'

Dexter races across to the Corporal, while dodging a few pairs of socks that weave across the grass.

'I told you – I'm now out of dust,' replies Dexter. 'Besides…it's really not going to do any good, is it? We'll be here forever trying to defeat this army of laundry. It is just stupid that we are doing this to defend the village. In essence, we are making it a lot worse by slicing them into pieces.'

The Corporal frowns at Dexter, 'You may have a point there. Anyway…make yourself useful and go and fetch Private Trout and Private Myles, would you? We need all the help we can get out here. Also, try and find Melvin while you're at it. He must have come up with some marvellous plan by now.'

Dexter gently nods, races through the rest of the Corporal's men and heads towards the tavern.

'Keep it up, lads!' shouts the Corporal. 'We are getting on top of them! Keep pushing!'

'Err…Sir?' interrupts Private Babe.

'Yes…what is it?' responds the Corporal.

'It might be the case that we are getting on top of them – but in several pieces. What I'm pointing out – and I believe I speak for everyone – is that the laundry isn't staying down. We can't keep this up—'

'We must!' bellows the Corporal. 'We must give Melvin the time he needs.'

'The time for what though, Sir?' enquires Private Babe. 'Do you even know where he is?'

'WATCH OUT!' shrieks the Corporal, pushing Private Babe onto the ground, before quickly taking a huge swing with his sword at a bulky woollen jumper and slicing it straight down the middle. It falls to the ground, groaning and moaning in pain. 'No…I have absolutely no idea where Melvin is,' he adds.

The Corporal raises his head and gasps at the sight of continuing waves of laundry still advancing across the village green. He looks around at the rest of the village; observing masses of laundry climb and scale the surrounding buildings; watching them closely as they thump down hard on windows and doors, rip tiles from the roofs, and try their best to find their way inside the homes and businesses of the locals.

'You know what, Private…?' begins the Corporal. 'You are absolutely correct. This is just not going anywhere. But surely there must be something that we can do?'

Private Babe pauses and tries to conjure up any logical solution to their immediate problem. He looks across the village for anything that would give him a spark of genius. He deduces that swords are not having any real effect on the possessed laundry, but nor is Felicity's hand-pistol, which will eventually run out of ammunition. He realises that setting the laundry on fire could be an option, although there would be a risk in setting the whole village ablaze, which wouldn't go down too well with the locals.

He ponders at whether drowning would work against them, but since they have already been swirled around in a watery vortex and the fact that they are laundry, he scraps that thought on the principle that laundry is probably used to being drowned in copious amounts of cold water.

'Err…Private?' says the Corporal, interrupting Private Babe's trail of thought.

'Huh?—*cough-cough*—Oh…err—yes, Sir?' responds Private Babe.

'Any ideas…?'

'Err…nope, Sir. But look at what we are doing with everyone's clothes. The locals are surely going to be furious at what we've done. I mean look at this mess!'

'I'm sure they'll be understanding of our actions – considering the circumstances. Besides, it's nothing that a good tailor or leatherworker can't handle.'

'Well, there are certainly enough remnants of leather and fabric to keep them in business for a very long time.'

The Corporal chuckles and swings his sword towards a crisp white cotton shirt.

◆◆◆

Edwin attempts to remove his hat and throw it onto the ground beneath him. He soon realises that the protective bubble around him only stretches and deforms so far around his body and doesn't allow any part of him, or his attire, to penetrate the bubble's thick membrane-like walls. He becomes conscious of the fact that he is stuck inside the bubble until either the spell wears away, it bursts, it is destroyed by his own doing, or by that of Officer Locks.

Edwin watches nervously as Officer Locks flicks out the cork bung from the vial with his thumb. The bung flies through the air, before disappearing into the thick layer of leaves in front of him. Edwin hisses at Officer Locks, who holds the vial high above his head and slowly begins to tip its contents over himself.

'Well, you leave me no choice, vampire,' states Officer Locks. 'I will entertain your courage and allow you to try and stop me. But I did tell you, Edwin – you are too soft and weak.'

In one swift movement, Officer Locks fully tilts the vial; allowing the pale light to seep out and drip over his skinny body. It flows out of the vial just like any fluid would. Edwin gasps in amazement, to the fact he was expecting the contents of the vial to simply shine some sort of beam onto Officer Locks, rather than to coat him in small, glowing droplets.

A brilliant pale blue light radiates from the liquid. It begins to run down Officer Locks' face, before spilling onto his shoulders and seeping down to his arms.

Edwin takes a small step back and awaits to see what becomes of Officer Locks.

There is a moment's pause…

'I'm not going to let you take her heart,' announces Edwin. 'I will die trying.'

There is no response from Officer Locks, who begins to tremble and shake. Edwin lets out another hiss as he observes Officer Locks' eyes turn from their normal bright blue colour, to a jet black; a black that makes even Edwin's hair colour seem like an extremely dark shade of grey.

The chilling sounds of breaking bones fill the air as Officer Locks' bone structure shifts, causing his arms and legs to grow and lengthen in an uncontrolled manner. Excessive blades of thick hairs start to protrude out of his skin, forming a blanket of rich dark brown fur over his body. The fabric of his clothes stretches and rips, before splitting open and falling to the ground. Claws as sharp as daggers begin to form and extend from his fingertips, which continue to grow longer by the second; fuelled by the mysterious effects of the bottled moonlight.

Officer Locks lets out a howling growl as his jaw dislodges and painfully shifts to form a long snout. Teeth begin to transform into razor-like fangs, which drip with saliva and gleam in the softened light.

Suddenly, the violent movements of Officer Locks, cease. Edwin stares in horror at the sight before him; a fully grown and developed werewolf, panting heavily. The Officer lets out a deafening howl, causing Edwin to cringe. Edwin then gasps as he notices Officer Locks' wound from earlier magically begin to heal itself; drawing the seeping blood back into his body; seamlessly closing the wound.

Edwin gulps and takes several steps back. Fear has never been an option for Edwin, but in this case, he is willing to make an exception.

Amelia begins to snigger uncontrollably. 'Looks like you've got yourself into a little spot of bother there, vampire?' she states.

Edwin quickly shifts his attention across to Amelia. 'Why are you laughing?' answers Edwin, with a *very* concerned look upon his face.

Amelia watches as Officer Locks takes a slow step towards Edwin, who stands poised and ready for any signs of attack.

'You deserve to be torn to pieces for taking me as your prisoner,' snarls Amelia. 'You could have avoided this by just letting me be, but no you—'

'No-no…you've got it wrong,' interrupts Edwin. 'I've come to save you from—*WHOOOOAH!*'

Edwin quickly darts to the side and stumbles flat on his face, avoiding a giant leap from Officer Locks, who smashes into the ground where Edwin had just stood.

THUD!

The ground shudders and disturbs the crisp dry leaves that lay upon it; causing the leaves to scatter into the air around Officer Locks' claw-like feet.

Officer Locks lets out several grunts, which Edwin assumes is Officer Locks' way of saying something very rude to him. The Officer stretches himself upright and makes a sudden charge towards Edwin.

Edwin's eyes widen in shock as he realises Officer Locks' heightened strength, speed and agility. He quickly reacts by leaping into the air, narrowly avoiding being knocked down by the Officer's head-on charge. Edwin gracefully lands back to the ground and quickly turns to face his foe, who comes to a grinding halt at the edge of the clearing.

Edwin turns to his side, noticing the fire still roaring and burning brightly. He quickly races across and pulls out a long branch from its fiery centre. He grips the unburnt end tightly in his hand, allowing the other end, still violently aflame, to steadily burn in front of him.

Edwin recalls that he had once read that werewolves are not at all fond of fire. Edwin has never had the opportunity to find out whether the information he read is true or not…but either way, he is about to find out now.

Edwin hisses loudly and reveals his shiny white fangs; they grow longer and sharper with every drop of rage that Edwin feels.

He pushes his cloak to the side with his free arm and waits for Officer Locks to make another advance. Almost instantly, the Officer races towards Edwin; pounding at the ground on all-fours and ripping through the leaves with his claws.

Edwin holds his position and waits for the ideal moment to launch the flaming log through the air. He bides his time, and just as the Officer pounces towards him, Edwin hurls the branch and knocks the Officer back to the ground in a cloud of burning embers and smoke.

Officer Locks lets out a pained squeal, before turning his head and growling at Edwin.

The Officer raises himself to his feet, and with inhuman like speed takes a huge swing at Edwin. He knocks him flying across the clearing; landing with a loud grunt next to Amelia. He lets out a series of spluttering coughs while pushing himself to his knees. He checks that his protective bubble is still intact, before letting out a sigh of relief.

'You were saying…?' asks Amelia.

'I said…' begins Edwin, placing his hand on his chest and taking in a few deep gulps of air. 'I said…*I—I*—I'm here to save you from Officer Locks.'

'And why would you do that?' responds Amelia, confused at the fact, that only a short while earlier, Edwin had held her prisoner himself. 'It is just an excuse for you to steal me back – so you can abuse my magic with your silly spell!'

'I must admit…that did cross my mind,' responds Edwin. 'But the truth of the matter is – that I have been sent by—*WHOOOOAH!*'

Suddenly a huge boulder crashes to the ground in front of Edwin. 'Playing that game now are we, Officer?' snarls Edwin, leaning forward and picking the boulder up from the ground. His protective bubble morphs itself around the boulder's rough surface and with all his might, Edwin launches it back at Officer Locks. In one swift movement, Officer Locks steps to the side and effortlessly dodges the boulder, much to the disappointment of Edwin.

'Sent by who?' continues Amelia, trying to regain Edwin's attention.

'The spellbinder sent me,' replies Edwin, cautiously eyeing up the Officer.

'You mean Melvin?'

'Yes-yes…Melvin sent me to rescue you.'

'I don't believe you. Why would he do that and not come himself?'

'Well, if the truth be told, he did…I can't explain right now – I'm a little preoccupied – and I do not have much time – my life literally depends on it.'

'Is that what the stupid bubble is about? One of Melvin's spells to keep you from turning crispy?'

Edwin pauses. 'Precisely…and I'm running out of time to rescue you and get you back safely.'

◆◆◆

Narrowly avoiding a small group of woollen socks, Dexter races across the side of the tavern and leans up against its exterior wall. He peers around the corner of the building and checks that the coast is clear. He rushes to the front of the tavern, takes a huge leap through the broken windows and lands with a small thud next to Timothy and Mrs Stamps.

'Ah, Dexter…you have returned, I see!' announces Timothy. 'You gave me a little bit of a fright just then. I also see the Corporal has returned and is hard at it – keeping the laundry at bay. Is he having much luck out there?'

'What do you think?' replies Dexter, eyeing up the tavern's occupants.

'Err…I'm guessing by your tone of voice – that would be a no…?' responds Timothy, taking another glance out of the window. 'Oh, piddle-sticks!'

Mrs Stamps turns towards Timothy. 'What's "Oh, piddle-sticks," Timothy?'

'I believe the judges – or should I say *judge* is here,' answers Timothy, pointing towards Felicity.

'You're right there,' replies Dexter. 'She really isn't too happy about the state of the village and has already thrown away her scoresheet. But she certainly seems to be having a good enough time firing off that pistol of hers.'

'She has a pistol…?' enquires Mrs Stamps? 'What a woman!'

'Yes, she certainly has,' responds Dexter.

'I was expecting more judges,' says Timothy.' Not just the one – unless that donkey she is riding can talk?'

'Do not be so darn stupid, Timothy!' interrupts Mrs Stamps. 'You have always got some stupid comment to make…haven't you? We simply don't have time to worry about the competition – that's now a dead end. We need to figure out how we can help Melvin!'

'Talking of Melvin – where is he?' asks Dexter, scouting the room for any sign of him.

'He snuck out a while ago to fetch his bicycle,' answers Samuel, from the other side of the room.

Dexter paces across the dusty floor of the tavern to join Samuel and the Reverend. He lets out a slight gasp as he notices Duncan, Private Myles, Private Trout and the other random villagers laying spread out on the floor behind the bar counter; each of them indulging in copious amounts of honey mead, having a slurred and incoherent conversation about how to achieve the best tasting pickled eggs.

'And what do you mean…gone to get his bicycle?' enquires Dexter. 'It's truly a fine time to worry about whether or not his bicycle has been fixed or not. What does he think he is playing at?'

'No-no…' interrupts Samuel. 'We all think that he will be able to use it against the laundry.'

Dexter pauses in confusion and stares back at Samuel. He waits for an explanation.

Samuel sighs at Dexter's ignorance to determine what they have in mind.

'Steam, Dexter…steam!' announces Samuel. 'We are hoping to use it against the laundry in some way - what way, we do not know yet.'

'Oh geez…really?' responds Dexter. 'It was his fascination with steam that got us into this mess in the first place…well, kind of. If Melvin hadn't of crashed into the fountain, then he wouldn't have destroyed his bicycle and forced us to stay here a few days while it is being repaired. He wouldn't have then had some crazy idea to meet the laundry fairy and—'

'Dexter? Stop blathering on, will you…?' instructs Samuel.

'I'm sorry…' begins Dexter. 'I do blather a lot when I get nervous – and I'm *very* nervous about this plan…in fact *any* plan that involves Melvin. Besides, how do you think that steam is going to help us against—oh…oh-my – that is brilliant! You know? – I think he could be on to something.'

'I hope so…' adds the Reverend. 'We have to try something. I continue to pray that Edwin rescues the Laundry Fairy from Officer Locks – and I hope that she can perhaps aid us in clearing up all this mess.'

This time, Dexter stares blankly at the Reverend. He tries to deduce, why not so long ago, his faithful friend

Melvin was not only trying to locate the Laundry Fairy, on his suspicions that she had been taken by a vampire, but also to now wondering why the vampire is now attempting to rescue her from Officer Locks, who was, in the first place, trying to rescue her from the vampire.

'Err…what on Earth happened while I was gone?' questions Dexter, shifting his eyes back and forth between the Reverend and Samuel.

'Well, basically – and without going into too much detail…' begins the Reverend. 'Vampire steals our Laundry Fairy – We then rescue our Laundry Fairy from vampire – Officer Locks then steals our Laundry Fairy – Vampire is now attempting to rescue Laundry Fairy from Officer Locks – Melvin has gone to retrieve his bicycle…and we are now just waiting to see what happens next. Pretty exciting – don't you think?'

'Oh, yes…truly riveting stuff!' responds Dexter. 'Anyway, I've been instructed by the Corporal to send Private Trout and Private Myles back over to him.'

The Reverend, Samuel and Timothy slowly turn in unison towards the two Privates, who now lay face down on the floor behind the bar counter, rambling and blabbering on about the perfect type of pickling vinegar.

'Um…Trout? Myles?' shouts the Reverend. 'The Corporal is asking of you.'

'Is*h* he now?' slurs Private Trout, attempting to raise himself onto his feet. 'We'll be over—*hic*—straight away, Reverend!' he adds, before, stumbling over and crashing back to the floor.

'I've got you, Trout…I've—*hic*—got you.' groans Private Myles, propping himself up against the bar counter and holding his hand out to Private Trout. 'We must do—*hic*—as the Reverend says—*hic*—and go back to the Corporal. He needs us…no?'

Private Trout mumbles a few slurred words, before extending his hand towards Private Myles. He pulls hard against Private Myles' arm, only to underestimate Private Myles' strength, resulting in him losing his balance and crashing back to the floor next to Duncan.

Samuel shakes his head in disapproval and runs the palm of his hand gently down his face. 'Well, I don't think that the Corporal is going to get much use out of those two,' he states.

'Here, let me have a go…' begins the Reverend. 'Err…Myles? Trout? You both still want to get paid, don't you?'

Private Myles sits up straight. He reaches back to aid Private Trout off the floor, who then slouches and leans up against him. 'Yes, Sir…we do – don't we, Trout?' replies Private Myles, quickly giving Private Trout a gentle shake.

'No, we don't!' slurs Private Trout, his head hanging low. 'Just leave me here.'

'We don't?' answers Private Myles.

'I mean yes, we don't want to…No, I mean no we do…?' stutters Private Trout.

'I used to think I was indecisive. Now I'm not too sure…' states Private Myles, scratching at the top of his head. 'That made no sense at all, Trout.'

The Reverend frowns. 'Well, I suggest you both get back to your Corporal – if you still want a gold coin placed in your hand at the end of all this.'

Private Trout and Private Myles help each other to their feet; struggling to find their natural balance. They cling onto one another as they both stumble out from behind the bar counter and advance across the tavern floor. Private Trout gives the Reverend a gently pat on the shoulder as he staggers past him.

'I really don't think those two are capable of doing anything right now, you know?' mutters Samuel, softly into the Reverend's ear.

The Reverend gently nods in agreement.

Dexter ponders about what he can do to help his friend Melvin. He contemplates about running across the green and towards Eric's workshop, but with the chaos going on outside, he decides to stay safe inside the tavern.

'Hello…' says Corbin, staring up at Dexter. 'Are you a real dragon?'

Dexter tilts his head to the floor to observe Corbin smiling up at him. He pauses briefly, before his eyes widen.

'Well blast me down! A living, breathing mole-sprite,' glees Dexter. 'And yes, I'm a real dragon.'

'Thank you!' yelps Corbin. 'Someone who actually knows what I am! Thank you-thank you!'

'Okay, steady on there, little buddy,' responds Dexter, wondering at what all the fuss is about.

'Corbin…' replies Corbin. 'My name is Corbin.'

Corbin gently tugs at Dexter's tail before staring in amazement at Dexter's claws, wings and other dragon-like features. Dexter flicks his tail in an attempt to deter Corbin.

'Is there a problem, Corbin?' asks Dexter.

Corbin pauses.

'Oh, no-no…please – I meant no disrespect. It's that I've only ever read about dragons and I have never had the chance to meet one in—'

'WHAT ON EARTH IS THAT?' bellows Mrs Stamps, pointing through the window and into the sky above the village.

Everyone who is currently standing, shifts their attention to where Mrs Stamps is pointing.

'*It's*—it's a large bird, isn't it?' responds Samuel.

'No…birds don't eject huge clouds of smoke from their rear, do they?' replies the Reverend.

'Maybe it's on fire…?' suggests Timothy, quickly realising his foolish statement as Mrs Stamps lets out a large sigh.

'See, Timothy? There you go again – another stupid comment!' blasts Mrs Stamps.

'That isn't a bird…' begins Dexter. 'That's Melvin on his bicycle – with Eric – and they are both—oh-my…they are flying!'

CHAPTER XV

"I am not crazy. I am special...no wait... maybe I am crazy - one second... I need to talk to myself about this—"

OLD JUDE

Officer Locks growls at Edwin; revealing his stained yellow teeth, which are drip trails of saliva onto the forest floor. Edwin stares in horror as he tries to formulate some sort of marvellous and ingenious plan, which will enable him to defeat Officer Locks, rescue Amelia and then get back to the village of Baston, all before the protective bubble surrounding him bursts or fades away.

Although Melvin had previously told Edwin that his bubble should last for about two hours, Edwin sensibly lacks the confidence in Melvin's calculations, feeling anxious to return to the village as quickly as possible, with the knowledge that his bubble could potentially fail at any moment.

Based purely on Melvin's recent misjudging and miscalculation of the spell he'd cast upon the local's dirty laundry, Edwin, with his high level of intellect, deduces that when Melvin said two hours, he probably and more realistically, only meant one.

'So…vampire. What you are telling me – is that you have absolutely no sort of plan at all…?' questions Amelia, trying desperately to squeeze her head through the thin metal bars of the cage.

'Please-please…it's Edwin - not *vampire*,' responds Edwin. 'And yes, that pretty much surmises the current situation.' Edwin raises his head, looks up at Officer Locks and keep a keen eye on him to anticipate his next move.

'Well…you are going to have to do something – and quick,' continues Amelia. 'I for one, do not intend to hang about here all day – and you certainly cannot afford to waste any more time, can you?'

A look of worry and concern falls across Edwin's pale face as he realises that while he stands about doing nothing, time ticks away from him. He audibly gasps at the severity of the situation.

Edwin takes another glance at Officer Locks, who begins to claw at the ground in preparation for a running charge. Edwin narrows his eyes and takes a small step forward, on the off-chance that he will be presented with a moment of divine clarity; one that will steer him towards a hasty solution in defeating the crazed Officer.

Amelia watches as Edwin creeps towards Officer

Locks He spreads his cloak out behind him, which flaps gently in the breeze. He clenches his fist and lets out a gentle hiss; knowing that any moment now, either he or the Officer, will make the first move.

Edwin sighs as he realises that his moment of divine clarity did not come and decides, in desperation, to take a racing charge towards Officer Locks, darting from left to right at near lightning speed.

Amelia closes her eyes and cringes as she hears the sound of Officer Locks take a huge swing at Edwin's body, which knocks flying to the ground in front of the cage. Edwin groans loudly and struggles to catch his breath.

'This is really not going too well is it, vampire...?' asks Amelia. 'Err...I mean, Edwin.'

Edwin rotates his head to face Amelia, spitting out fragments of damp leaves and mud, before raising an eyebrow at her.

'You know? I didn't have to come all the way out here to rescue you...' begins Edwin. 'In fact, I could just return to the village right now and tell them that I was too late – give them the bad news that you have perished at the hands of Officer Locks.'

Amelia hangs her head down low and begins to sob.

'But I will not...' adds Edwin.

'You won't?' whimpers Amelia. '*But*...but why?'

'My reasons are my own,' responds Edwin, pushing himself to his feet and brushing leaves off the front of his waistcoat. 'And you are right – this is really not going too well at all, is it? He is too strong for me to even do anything with – or I'm too weak. Either way, it's not good.'

'Have you anything in your pockets that you could use against him?' questions Amelia. 'Just a thought –

you know? Maybe you have some Wolfsbane or some silver bullets tucked away in—?'

'Oh sure!' interrupts Edwin, sarcastically. 'I carry those things around with me all the time – just in case.'

Edwin carefully watches Officer Locks from the corner of his eye. He decides to try his luck and begins rummaging around in his pockets for anything that may be of some use, only to pull out a couple of Corbin's candy wrappers and a handful of dried mud.

'LOOK OUT!' screeches Amelia, before suddenly halting her words and quickly wondering why she has even the slightest level of concern for Edwin's safety. After a few moments, Amelia realises that Edwin is maybe her only hope of surviving and escaping from Officer Locks.

Edwin immediately shifts to the left to avoid the extended hairy arm of Officer Locks, which quickly swings towards him. Edwin lets out a gasp as he catches sight of the Officer's long razor-like claws and how close he was to nearly getting shredded, or worse still, his bubble getting shredded.

Office Locks, upon realising he had again missed Edwin, lets out a loud screeching howl. He turns in frustration, and with the back of his hand knocks the cage containing Amelia off the top of the rock. The cage crashes to the ground, rolls over a few times and comes to a halt on its side.

Edwin hisses, before leaping up into the air and launching himself towards Officer Locks. He clenches his fists tightly, and with all the strength he can muster, punches Officer Locks cleanly on the end of his snout…

THWACK!

…knocking him to the ground. Edwin quickly darts forwards, punching and kicking a few more times at the Officer, before he has the chance to return to his feet.

THUMP! THWACK!

Edwin continues to unleash his fury upon Officer Locks, who starts to moan in agony.

Edwin stops and turns quickly towards the cage. 'Amelia? Are you okay?' queries Edwin, rushing over and dropping to his knees.

Amelia rubs her forehead with her hand and stands to her feet.

'Are you okay?' repeats Edwin, huffing and puffing in exhaustion.

'Just a bump – I'll be fine,' replies Amelia, looking on at Officer Locks, who lays on the ground several feet away. 'Quick, let's make a run for it!'

'Where do you suggest that we run to? I have no idea where we are. All I know is that the village must be back that way.' Edwin raises his arm and points his finger towards the lush overgrowth leading back into the blackened depths of the forest.

'Then we go that way – quick release me from the cage!' orders Amelia.

'Oh, no-no,' replies Edwin. 'I promised that I would come to rescue you and return you safely to the village. What assurances do I have – that you will simply not run away and leave me here?'

'What difference would it make?' retorts Amelia. 'You can fly out of here and return to the village at any time. Where else would I go?'

Edwin ponders at the fact, that indeed, what Amelia is saying, does make complete sense.

'Very well, then,' mutters Edwin.

'Besides…' continues Amelia. 'I need you to release my brothers and sisters – I'm not letting you out of my sight. I assume that your change of heart, or whatever you want to call it, hasn't forgotten about them?'

Edwin bites on his lower lip.

'Umm…well – about them…' begins Edwin. 'You see…I never really captured them. It was just a ploy to make you give in to my demands. I have never met them before in my life.'

Knowing that he had lied, Edwin lowers his head in shame and waits for Amelia's response.

'You mean that they are all safe?' questions Amelia.

'I imagine they are perfectly safe,' responds Edwin.

Amelia lets out a long sigh of relief.

'Quickly, then…' begins Amelia. 'Let me out of here before that beast gets up and realises what is going on. Oh…you will also need to carry me.'

'Absolutely not!' states Edwin. '*I*—I mean…no to carrying you. I am a slave to no one. I would find it extremely difficult to hold onto you with this protective bubble in place – I would not be able to get a firm grip on you. I can't even put you inside my pocket, as you would have to somehow step through the bubble. Besides…why don't you just fly?'

'I really don't think I have the energy to fly,' replies Amelia. 'That stupid cage of yours has drained most of my powers. I can barely stand. It will take some time to recover – time that we don't have.'

'How long?'

'Depends if the sun is shining or not.'

'You gain your powers from the sun?'

'Well, not technically – it's from the sunlight.'

Edwin chuckles. 'So, you need sunlight to charge

your powers and yet, it will kill me instantly if I step into it. What a unique couple we are.'

Amelia nods.

'So be it…' says Edwin, reaching down and flicking open the latch on the cage. 'I think you stand a better chance if I was in bat form. You might be able to wrap yourself around one of my ears.'

'Really? I have never ridden a bat before,' states Amelia, stumbling out of the cage. 'But hurry…the Officer seems to be getting back up from the ground!'

THERE IS A FLASH OF RED LIGHT.

◆◆◆

Just as the village of Baston thinks that it has seen it all, another peculiar sight presents itself, which makes all the other previous sights seem, relatively speaking, extremely normal. This time, the sight of a flying steam-powered bicycle being ridden by an old and skinny spellbinder wizard, wearing a pointy hat, with a fat Dwarve in pillion, is about to become the talk of the village. The fact that neither of the riders seem to have any idea how to fly the contraption, makes the situation even *more* comical.

'Pull that long lever there, Melvin!' squeals Eric, holding tightly onto Melvin's robe.

'Which lever?' yelps Melvin. 'They all look exactly the same!'

'The long one,' replies Eric. 'I would show you if I could, but right now, both my hands are rather busy – holding on for dear life!'

'They are all blinking long!' screams Melvin. 'Why didn't you colour code them or something?'

Melvin struggles to turn the newly rebuilt steam-powered bicycle. He grasps his hands tightly onto the bicycle's handlebars; pulling and pushing them from left to right, in a frantic attempt to change direction, while at the same time looking between his legs at the multitude of new levers and buttons that Eric has recently installed.

'Well, you'd better hurry up and do something soon, Melvin,' announces Eric. 'If not, we are going to crash right into the church tower – which I don't think would go down too well with the Reverend.'

'WHY-WHY-WHY is this ruddy thing not turning?' yells Melvin, frantically pushing and pulling at the bicycle's handlebars.

'Turning the front wheel in mid-air is not going to make it go anywhere, is it?' Eric sighs. 'That's for use on the ground. Pull on that long lever to activate the rudder!'

'Activate the what?'

'The rudder!'

'Don't you dare swear at me! I'm trying my best!'

Melvin continues to glance down at the multitude of levers between his legs, hesitating to pull even one of them, knowing that a wrong selection could cause much bigger issues. Melvin panics as he continues battling to control his bicycle, which gets closer and closer to the church tower.

'Listen, Melvin!' shouts Eric, against the wind. 'It's the long lever that has two large arrows on it. You can't miss it!' Pull it back. It will release the rudder brake. You can then use the lever as a joystick – to steer us.'

'A what?'

'A joystick.'

'How the blazes am I going to use the lever as a broomstick?' Are you insane?'

Eric sighs at Melvin's complete lack of engineering knowledge. 'Just pull it – and quickly!'

Melvin reaches down with his left hand, grips the top of the lever and pulls it firmly backwards. The lever slots into place with a small clunking noise.

'That's it, lad!' shouts Eric. 'Now steer us quick – or we are going to hit the—*WHOOOOAH!*'

Melvin pushes the lever fully to the left, causing the bicycle to suddenly turn and narrowly miss the church. Eric looks over his shoulder and lets out a sigh of relief as he calculates that if Melvin *hadn't* pulled the lever when he did, the bicycle would have had an undesired collision with the tower of the church.

'Okay…I think I've got the hang of what this lever does now,' states Melvin, pushing the lever gently in the opposite direction and bringing the bicycle to a horizontal.

'I'm glad…' mutters Eric.

'And will you please stop digging your fingernails into me! It's getting rather uncomfortable now.'

'I wouldn't have to dig my fingernails into you at all – if I could sit in the side car, would I?' retorts Eric. 'But no! You had to fill it will coal, didn't you? Abusing this highly crafted machine – with a complete and total lack of respect for my hard work and craftsmanship. That coal dust it going to take forever to clean from the upholstery.'

'We've got much bigger things to worry about than a speck of coal dust, Eric!' states Melvin.

'Oh, yes! What's the plan?'

'You are not going to like this one bit…' begins Melvin. 'But, in simple terms – I don't have a plan—'

'What! No plan?' yelps Eric. 'Well…in that case, we should put our heads together and try to formulate an epic plan of attack; one that we can execute with split-second timing and precision; a plan that is so complex in every detail – that it will make all other plans in the history of plan making seem like a stroll in the park. To truly make the plan work, we must understand the severity of the situation and its *pro et contra.* We must remain completely level headed and let nothing distract us – no matter how much we want to—'

'Oh look!' interrupts Melvin. 'I can just about see your workshop from up here.'

◆◆◆

'Lady, can you please stop your chickens from pecking at me?' squeals Corbin, whilst running and hiding behind Timothy's legs.

'They must be after something you have,' responds Mrs Stamps. 'They are not usually that friendly towards people they don't know – let alone a rat—*cough-cough*—I mean a—err…what exactly are you again?'

'I'm a mole-sprite, lady!' replies Corbin. 'They must be after my boiled sweets.'

Mrs Stamps smiles. 'Well, that will be why they're following you around, then.'

Corbin sniffs and frowns.

Samuel continues to look up in amazement at Melvin, who tries to control his steam-powered bicycle across the skies of Baston. He cringes at the anomalous and terrifying manoeuvres that Melvin is attempting, in order to prevent his bicycle from any sort of collision.

Timothy reaches down and picks Corbin up from the floor; rescuing him from the unceasing pecking of Mrs Stamps' chickens. Timothy raises Corbin up and places him onto his shoulder. Mrs Stamps' chickens continue to scout about the floor at Timothy's feet.

'I think that he is trying to signal us,' states Samuel, pointing up at Melvin. 'Look!'

'Do you think?' questions the Reverend.

'Well…it is either that, or his whole arm has gone into some sort of spasm,' responds Timothy, shuffling forward to prevent dislodging Corbin.

Dexter stares up at Melvin; watching him as he tries to control the bicycle with one hand, while frantically waving down at Dexter, with the other.

'You are right – I think he is trying to tell us all something,' announces Dexter. 'Or he might just simply be waving at us all.'

Dexter squints as he focuses in on Melvin, whose hand movements suggest that he wants Dexter to fly up towards him. Dexter looks at Eric, who continues to keep his eyes closed, while holding on very tightly around Melvin's skinny body.

'It does look like Melvin is indicating for you to go to him,' says Samuel. 'Do you think he wants you to fly up to him or something?'

Dexter's ears twitch as his super hearing picks up the faint sound of Melvin shouting and cursing at him from up above.

Dexter sighs at what he hears and turns to Samuel.

'What's he saying?' asks Samuel.

'You really don't want to know…' begins Dexter, muttering a few words under his breath, which Samuel doesn't quite catch. 'But it seems he does definitely want me to fly up to him.'

'I didn't know you could fly, Dexter,' says the Reverend, sounding surprised.

'Well, I am a dragon,' remarks Dexter. 'Why would you ever think that I couldn't?'

'Oh…err, no reason. I don't believe that I have seen you fly since you've arrived here in Baston,' replies the Reverend. 'It's just that you always seem to be walking everywhere.'

'Well, I can fly – I just choose not to most of the time,' responds Dexter, hopping up onto the wooden barricade and extending his wings.

With his eyes wide open, Corbin stares in wonder at Dexter; watching him flap his wings hard, which causes plentiful amounts of dust on the floor to rise up into the already musty-filled room.

Dexter lifts off and proceeds to fly high up into the sky to meet Melvin, who at this very moment is struggling to make sense of Eric's control mechanism for making the bicycle go up and down.

'No, Melvin!' roars Eric. 'Use the lever that's right next to the one you are holding. That will make the bicycle go up and down. It controls the side elevators, Melvin.'

'The what?' responds Melvin, gripping the lever tightly in his hands.

'Elevators!'

'I don't even know what they are, Eric.'

'They make the bicycle go up and down – and will you stop holding onto the handlebars. They aren't going to do anything are they? The bicycle is not going to drop out of the sky if you let go of them – well, unless we start to run out of steam pressure. You see…reducing the steam pressure produces less thrust, which creates less lift – so if we don't keep that steam pressure high – we will most certainly drop out of the sky.'

Melvin chooses to ignore Eric's comments, on the principle that Melvin has more important things on his mind; mainly being, rectifying the chaos of possessed laundry, which continues to cause havoc below them.

'Well, young Dexter seems to have the whole idea of flight pretty much sorted,' states Eric, as Dexter approaches the bicycle and perches himself on its handlebars.

'Ah finally, there you are, Dex,' announces Melvin, skilfully and carefully readjusting the two levers in his hands and steadying the bicycle, the best he can.

'You called me up, Melv?' asks Dexter, continuing to gently flap his wings to hold himself level. The bicycle continues to circle above the village.

'Yes-yes. I need you to deliver a simple message to the Corporal…' begins Melvin, scouting below and tilting his head in the Corporal's direction. 'I need you to deliver him some instructions.'

'What sort of instructions?' enquires Dexter. 'Are you telling me that you *actually* have a plan? I thought you don't do plans, Melv?'

'It's not a plan – I'm making stuff up as I go along,' replies Melvin. 'It's only a plan if I stick to what I planned in the first place – and I haven't planned anything – so it's not a plan. This is simply just a set of instructions that I would like the Corporal and his men to follow. If we are lucky, it might inspire me to come up with a proper plan.'

Eric sighs.

'A proper plan?' questions Dexter.

'Yes, that's right!' answers Melvin. 'A proper plan. I just don't know what it is yet.'

Dexter rolls his eyes.

Melvin looks down towards the village green, where the Corporal and his men are wildly causing almost as much havoc with their swords, as the possessed laundry is having with the village. He watches as wave after wave of laundry continues to appear from the wash-house, a plump lady riding a donkey fires off her pistol, and copper coins, which previously lay scattered across the grass, become slowly covered in a mass of freshly cut cotton, wool and leather.

'They are just going around and around in circles…' begins Melvin, before biting on his lower lip. 'The Corporal and his men are just making one big mess out of the laundry.'

'What do you suggest we do, Melvin?' asks Dexter.

Melvin pauses in thought.

'Err…Eric?' shouts Melvin. 'Can you hear me?'

'Barely, but yes I can hear you…' responds Eric.

'Exactly how much steam can this bicycle generate?'

Eric's right eye twitches as he precisely calculates the exact amount of steam the bicycle can produce, only to then give up and relish Melvin with an answer, or more precisely, one that Melvin will understand.

'Plenty, Melvin,' responds Eric. 'If the boiler is full and the furnace is burning hot – the steam will just keep flowing. I would imagine it can go a good while before the water tank needs topping up again.'

Melvin nods his head.

'Okay, Dex…' begins Melvin. 'I want you to go and instruct the Corporal to attempt to push the laundry towards the edge of the village – force them to the wash-house.'

'What are you going to do…wash them again?' retorts Dexter, letting out a chuckle.

'I'm guessing you are going to try and use the steam to control them?' questions Eric.

'That's what I'm thinking, Eric,' answers Melvin. 'I'm going to attempt to collect the laundry up in a big swirling vortex of steam—'

'And then what?' interrupts Dexter.

'Err…I'm not too sure,' responds Melvin. 'But I'll work something out. I'm really am hoping that Edwin will manage to save Amelia, and that she'll be able to do something on her return.'

'Have you thought about what you are going to do if he doesn't?' asks Eric.

'Don't talk like that!' snaps Melvin.

'I'm just saying,' responds Eric. 'But we must have a back-up plan…no?'

'He doesn't even have a main plan, Eric…let alone a back-up plan!' hollers Dexter.

Melvin pulls the lever in his left hand; turning the bicycle towards the wash-house.

'Steady on, Melvin!' blasts Eric. 'Small adjustments – small adjustments!'

'Okay-okay…' replies Melvin. 'This is the first time I've flown anything! Cut me some darn slack!' Anyway, Dex…please give the Corporal those instructions?'

Dexter nods. 'And what are you about to do…?'

'I'm going to drop a gear and disappear!' retorts Melvin, with a smug look upon his face.

Dexter stares at Melvin in confusion; thinking to himself how long it's going to take Melvin to work out that the bicycle doesn't have any gears. Dexter slowly shakes his head from side to side and tuts, before promptly releasing himself from the bicycle's handlebars. He watches as Melvin steers the bicycle towards the wash-house.

'Right…better get to it,' mutters Dexter, flying down to locate the Corporal.

◆◆◆

Edwin is usually very quick and agile when in bat form. However, the magical clear protective bubble that is surrounding him, is currently hindering his ability to fly smoothly through the Darkened Enchanted Forest.

Laying herself face-down on Edwin's back, Amelia desperately clings onto his bubble; digging her tiny hands and feet into its thick rubber-like material. She tries to remain completely flat against Edwin's body, minimising the risk of losing her grip and being dragged off by the turbulent air currents, which rush over them both.

'We must go faster, Edwin!' shrieks Amelia, looking over her shoulder; observing Officer Locks hot on their trail. 'I would also prefer it if you could try to go a little smoother. I'm really struggling to hold on here. I'm sorry if that sounds a little backwards.'

Edwin lets out a high-pitched squeal and swoops around the trunk of a large redwood tree. Tilting his head briefly, Edwin observes the Officer in full pursuit behind them, watching him as he gallops and leaps through the forest; crushing and tearing up plants and flowers with his razor-sharp claws.

Edwin quickly shoots up over the top of a pine tree in an attempt to try and elude Officer Locks.

The sound of leaves and grass being shredded to pieces gets louder as the Officer manages to close the gap on Edwin and Amelia; racing towards them at tremendous speed.

Edwin flies up into the trees, trying his best to gain a little height from the Officer. He narrowly misses tree branches that stick out and intertwine with other branches; darting over and under them at great speed. Amelia tightens her clench on Edwin's protective bubble.

The Officer races along the forest floor underneath Edwin and Amelia; gaining ground and closing the gap between them. Edwin darts left behind the trunk of an old oak tree, hoping to force Officer Locks through a cluster of trees, and slow him down; giving them a little extra time to find a way through and soar into the sky.

'He is gaining on us!' yelps Amelia, looking down at the forest below them. 'He is right underneath us!'

Amelia continues to watch in horror as the Officer ploughs through the lush, thick vegetation below them. Blades of long grass, leaves, twigs and flowers fly through the air; shredded to pieces by Officer Locks as he claws his way forward. He grows in rage at Edwin, who continues to focus on a way to escape the forest.

Amelia closes her eyes and tightens her grip on the bubble. Edwin tries to stay at height and out of the reach of Officer Locks, who Edwin now knows, can leap fairly high.

Although at this height and at a safe distance from Officer Locks, Edwin still has to negotiate the added danger of the thick tree branches that hinder a smooth flight. Edwin twists and tilts his body to avoid crashing head on into a cluster of oak branches, which grow out from the many densely packed tree trunks.

Amelia struggles to maintain her grip as Edwin shifts his body weight to try and squeeze his way through the small gaps in-between the branches.

'Edwin – Edwin please…you need to slow down a little bit!' yelps Amelia, nervously. '*I*—I'm struggling to hold on!' Amelia digs her heels into the bubble and tries to find herself a better footing.

Edwin lets out a squeal and a few clicking sounds, which instantly silence and confuse Amelia.

After a few moments, Amelia realises that Edwin

can undoubtedly not speak while in bat form. Instead he squeals out his replies; believing that Amelia will understand. She fails to deduce what he means when he produces the clicking sounds.

Despite the difficulty of flying at speed through the dense tree canopies, Edwin is doing rather well, thanks to his ability to map out a pathway using sonar. The ultrafast sonics penetrate deep into the forest and then echo back at Edwin, who adjusts his course to avoid any potential collisions.

'Please, Edwin…you *really* need to slow down!' shrieks Amelia.

Edwin squeals and continues to race through the forest.

'If you slow down, I may be able to talk to the forest,' adds Amelia. 'The forest may aid us in trying to escape Officer Locks, or maybe open a gap in the trees, so we can soar up into the shy.'

Edwin immediately slows down on understanding Amelia's request, and takes a moment to tilt his head towards the ground to look at Officer Locks, who persists in trying to recapture Amelia at all costs.

Amelia readjusts her grip and begins to mutter a few magical words under her breath. She glows a crimson colour as she repeats the words over and over.

'I'm really hoping that the forest will heed my call,' states Amelia, as she pursues to recite some old magical enchants and phrases; gradually increasing her volume out of desperation and panic.

Edwin continues to tilt his head to the ground below him, while not taking any notice of the obstacles that lay ahead of him and Amelia.

'LOOK OUT, EDWIN!' screams Amelia. 'You are about to—'

A small tree branch bends and snaps as Edwin clips it with the side of his body. He loses control and in his struggle to remain horizontal, tips Amelia off his back.

Amelia plummets to the forest floor.

Edwin hastily turns and squeals loudly as he watches Amelia fall through the branches. He quickly reacts and immediately darts down in an attempt to rescue her from a near certain death.

He flaps his wings as hard as he can and nose-dives towards Amelia, bringing his wings tight to his body; reducing the air resistance. He squawks as he fails to gain any distance between himself and Amelia, realising that catching her safely on his back is not an option. He decides his only choice is to transform back into human form, stretch out his arms and reach for her.

THERE IS A FLASH OF RED LIGHT.

Edwin transforms into human form, promptly extends his arm and opens his hand to grab hold of Amelia, who gazes back at him with fear in her eyes. Edwin wraps his pointed fingers around Amelia's fragile body.

THUD!

Edwin hits the floor, causing leaves that lay on the ground to fly up and scatter into the air above him. After a few moments they gently float back onto the ground around him.

Edwin lets out a groan, before rolling himself onto his side and opening his clenched fist. He lets out a sigh of relief on seeing Amelia unharmed and curled up in a ball in the centre of his hand. She wobbles gently back and forth on Edwin's bubble, which fails to morph itself tightly around the contours of his fingers.

'*You*—you saved me...' mumbles Amelia, carefully

sliding down the bubble's surface, onto the forest floor and stumbling over a few lush green leaves.

'It would appear that way—' states Edwin, sitting upright and brushing off a few leaves, which stick to his cloak and waistcoat.

'You could have just let me fall…' begins Amelia. 'Why did you—'

'I guess it was the right thing to do,' interrupts Edwin. 'Besides, I was not looking where I was going was I?'

'That is very true and—oh, Edwin…is that a smile you are showing?'

'Smile? Err…no not at all. It is simply a twitch on my cheek. I think I may have—'

'LOOK OUT, EDWIN! Behind you!' screams Amelia, pointing back at Officer Locks, who leaps through the air and crashes down onto the forest floor next to Edwin.

The Officer lets out a loud growl and swings his arms towards Edwin; knocking him face down to the ground. The Officer reaches down, clutches his hand around Edwin's neck and effortlessly pulls him off the ground; raising him into the air. Edwin's feet dangle just above Amelia.

Edwin wriggles; trying desperately to free himself from the clutches of Officer Locks, who is proving too strong for him.

The Officer lets out another loud growl, followed by a chilling howl. He briefly stares into Edwin's eyes, before tightening his hand around Edwin's neck. With all his might, he throws Edwin hard against the side of a nearby tree trunk.

Edwin lets out a cry of pain as his body hits the tree trunk. He slides down its rough bark and lands at the base of the tree; groaning in pain as he lays twisted on the ground.

'Edwin!' yells Amelia, immediately turning her attention towards Officer Locks, who gazes down upon her; his sharpened claws extending out in front of him. 'Edwin…help me please!'

Amelia stumbles and falls onto her back. She tries to push herself away from the Officer, only to struggle to move aside twigs and leaves that block her way. In her panicked state, Amelia tries to flap her wings in an attempt to fly away, but in her weakened condition, caused by the magical effects of Edwin's cage, her wings fail to provide any lift.

'Please…help me, *Ed*—Edwin,' whimpers Amelia.

Without warning, Officer Locks halts in his tracks. The sounds of bones crunching and flesh being torn, fills the air. The Officer, to Amelia's astonishment, starts to quickly transform back into his human form; weakened by the lack of moonlight, which has rubbed off his body while running through the lush fauna, moments earlier.

Realising his dilemma, Officer Locks growls and raises his paws into the air, before striking at Amelia. She screams as she observes the Officer's claws swipe down towards her. She closes her eyes and accepts that this may be her fate.

Suddenly, Edwin darts across the forest in front of Officer Locks. 'NOOOOOOOOO!' yells Edwin, spreading himself wide and shielding Amelia from the Officer's sharpened claws.

There is a tearing sound, before Edwin crashes to the forest floor.

The Officer growls in rage as he continues to be forced back into human form; fur shedding from his skin and dropping onto the ground below.

Bones crack and crunch as the Officer's skeletal structure adjusts itself to a more human-like form. Officer Locks drops to his knees in agony; his claws retracting back into the tips his fingers; his fanged teeth shortening and receding into his bleeding gums.

'Edwin? Are you okay…?' questions Amelia, in a worried and concerned tone.

With no immediate answer, Amelia starts to crawl her way towards Edwin, who lays shuddering on the ground; tightly clutching his stomach.

Edwin groans loudly.

Amelia forces her way through the leaves and broken twigs that lay on the forest floor; trying with her remaining limited strength, to get to Edwin.

'Not so fast!' bellows Officer Locks, raising himself to his feet and abruptly rotating his neck; snapping his jaw back into a less than werewolf-like position.

Amelia gasps and falls to her knees. 'No…please!' she yelps.

'I'm guessing that your time has finally come…' announces Officer Locks, as he takes a small step towards Amelia.

◆◆◆

'He wants us to what…?' bellows the Corporal.

'I know – I know…' replies Dexter. 'Please don't shoot the messenger. I'm only telling you what he told me – and that is to force the laundry towards the wash-house at the end of the village.'

'And what about all the laundry items that have attached themselves to all the village buildings…?' yells the Corporal, slicing his way through a multitude of coloured shirts and jumpers. 'What does he expect us to do with them? I can tell you now…you will not find me scaling up the walls of the post office to try and push the socks towards the wash-house.'

'Err…well I guess he would expect that they would just follow the other laundry as you push *them* back,' responds Dexter

'And what does he want us to do when we get them there?' questions the Corporal.

'I think he has a plan using that bicycle of his. Look!'

The Corporal looks up to the skies above him. His jaw drops as he follows Melvin and Eric flying towards the wash-house on Melvin's bicycle. Dexter watches the Corporal shake his head from side to side. He tries to deduce if the Corporal is simply disappointed in Melvin's attempt to solve the village's possessed laundry problem using a bicycle, or whether the Corporal is now on the same wavelength as him, and hoping that Melvin doesn't make the situation worse by doing something incredibly stupid.

'I dread to think what he is about to do,' states the Corporal. 'But he does look rather brave and heroic on that bicycle though – and very handsome – I must say.'

Dexter nods his head up and down whilst raising an eyebrow at the Corporal, wondering to himself how much longer the effects of the Angel's Fern can go on for. The comments that the Corporal is making at Melvin, simply do not go hand in hand with the Corporal's masculinity and size. Dexter cringes at the Corporal's sentimental and loving tone.

'Very well then, Dexter…' begins the Corporal. 'We'll try to force the laundry that way.'

Dexter flaps his wings rapidly and flies into the sky.

'Okay…listen up, lads and, err…lass?' yells the

Corporal. 'It looks like my *Melvy* is formulating some sort of plan and therefore wants us to force all the laundry towards the wash-house.'

Private Babe takes a huge swing at a large cotton shirt; slicing it into two pieces. He turns towards the Corporal. One by one the remainder of the Corporal's men re-direct their attention towards their superior.

'Sir?' questions Private Babe. 'He wants us to what?'

'He wants us to try and push the laundry back towards the wash-house,' replies the Corporal. 'He is going to try something.'

The Corporal points to the sky. He indicates to Private Babe, the faint outline of Melvin on his bicycle, as he, together with Eric, fly towards the wash-house.

'To push all this laundry back?' asks Private Babe, with a worried tone in his voice. 'How does he expect us to do that? It just keeps on coming and I have—'

'Just tell the others the plan, will you!' interrupts the Corporal. 'And where *is* Felicity?'

'Yes, Sir!' responds Private Babe, saluting at his superior. 'Oh, she is over there, Sir – blasting lots of holes into a couple of woollen jumpers.' The Corporal nods and watches Private Babe march away to rally up the rest of the squad.

'What do we have here…?' questions the Corporal, turning himself towards Private Trout and Private Myles. The Corporal's eyes narrow in anger.

Deliberately trying to annoy or make the Corporal mad, is not the typical etiquette of Private Trout, who prefers to use his natural charm and bluntness to do that for him. However, staggering towards his superior; slurring out phrases that make no sense, all whilst slapping the Corporal hard on the back with the palm of his hand, is now clearly testing all of the Corporal's patience. The added fact that Private Myles has fallen flat on his face, whilst mumbling a few incoherent sentences and then vomiting on the grass, is now *definitely* stretching the outer limits of the Corporal's anger management skills.

'What the devil are you two playing at?' blasts the Corporal, projecting enough volume to attract the rest of his squad's attention, who quickly turn towards him.

'Oh, this is going to be a laugh…' mutters Private Simmons, glancing across at the Corporal.

'Hello S*h*ir…' slurs Private Trout. 'Reporting for—*hic*—duty, S*h*ir!'

'Are you drunk, Private?' bellows the Corporal.

'N—*n*—not all, S*h*ir! I'm Abs*h*—*hic*—absolutely f*h*ine!' stutters Private Myles, crawling on his hands and knees towards the Corporal's feet.

'Let me at 'em!' splutters Private Trout. 'Gis a s*h*word, guv – I'll s*h*lice 'em—*hic*—up in—*hic*—no time! Please, S*h*ir – cherry on top—'

'Silence! You two had better sober up – and quick!' commands the Corporal, taking a step to the side and kicking at a random sock that has crawled across the grass towards him. 'As for swords…that is a no-no. In your state – you wouldn't know the top of it from the bottom.'

'Awwwwww—S*h*ir,' mumbles Private Myles, before collapsing to the floor.

The Corporal sighs and glances across to Private Simmons, who stares straight back at him.

'Is there a problem, Simmons?' yells the Corporal.

'Err…not at all—I mean…no, Sir!…I'm advancing forwards,' replies Private Simmons, aimlessly swinging his sword about in front of him, trying to make it look like he is fighting something. He waves at the Corporal.

The Corporal turns back to Private Trout, who with bloodshot eyes and sweat dripping from his forehead, grins back at the Corporal.

'I suggest you both take yourselves over to the water fountain and plunge your heads into the cold water – try to sober up,' instructs the Corporal. 'I simply will not have two of my men fighting under the influence of intoxicating liquids. We have a responsibility here. Besides, you could end up doing yourself some serious injury, or worse still – someone else!'

Private Trout raises an eyebrow in confusion and stumbles to his feet. 'Yes S*h*ir! Right away—*hic*—you gorgeous beast of a—'

'Now, Trout!' interrupts the Corporal, breathing heavily to control his rage.

Private Babe skips back to the Corporal. This is an act that the Corporal really despises. However, after checking the Battalion Hand Book several times in the past, the Corporal has failed to find any rule stating that a soldier should not perform such a manoeuvre whilst on duty. The Corporal takes in a deep breath and closes his eyes, before counting slowly to five in his head and exhaling.

'Everyone is aware of what we are planning to do, Sir!' announces Private Babe.

'Good. Now let's push them back as hard as we can,' answers the Corporal. 'Can you please also tell Felicity to cease discharging that pistol of hers in random directions? She seems to be doing a lot of—well…unnecessary damage.'

Private Babe nods and holds his sword high into the air. He suddenly lowers it to his side, in response to seeing a very strange old woman, pacing slowly towards him from the other side of the village.

'Err…Sir?' questions Private Babe.

'Yes…?' replies the Corporal, still trying to steady his breathing.

'There seems to be a very peculiar old lady heading towards us – holding what looks like a leg of ham.'

'That's just Mrs Stamps, no?'

'Err…no I don't think so, Sir. This one is wearing a large cowboy hat.'

The Corporal adjusts his position to gaze across at a wrinkly old woman taking very small steps towards them. She paces carefully; completely oblivious to the chaos that is happening all around the village. Her shabby appearance is heightened by the sporting of a black cowboy hat; a hat that is many sizes too big for her head, and looks completely out of place with the rest of her attire. She cradles a leg of ham in her left arm and carefully strokes it with the palm of her other hand.

'Excuse me?' says the old woman. 'Could you please tell me where I could find my bed?'

'Your bed?' replies Private Babe, looking at the old woman in confusion.

'Yes, my bed…' responds the old woman. 'My ham is rather tired and needs to rest—'

The Corporal shifts his eyes very slowly from the old woman towards Private Babe. He moves his lips; shaping them into a ring as if he is about to whistle.

'What's your name there?' asks the Corporal.

'Oh, well most people just call me Old Jude,' replies the old woman. 'But that's okay – that's my name.'

'I see…' replies the Corporal. 'And your ham is tired and needs to rest? – and you want to find your bed?'

'Yes, that's right,' says Old Jude. 'I took him for a long walk earlier and he is worn out.'

The Corporal tries his hardest not to laugh; relishing the conversation.

'So, Jude…' begins the Corporal. 'Does your ham have a name?'

Old Jude stares at the Corporal with a void look in her eyes. 'Don't be so silly. I would be crazy if I named a piece of meat, wouldn't I?'

'But you are not crazy, no?' asks the Corporal.

'Oh, come on, Sir,' replies Private Babe, shielding his voice from Old Jude. 'That is not a nice thing to say. She is just old and forgetful—'

'I am not crazy,' quickly interrupts Old Jude. 'I am special…no wait…maybe I am crazy – one second…I have to talk to myself about this—'

'Err…' begins the Corporal. 'Maybe you have to dismount your unicorn to do that?'

'Don't be so silly!' snaps Old Jude. 'My unicorn is at home – cooking my dinner—'

The Corporal raises an eyebrow. 'Well, that's me done here, Private. We really must get going, don't you think?'

The Corporal turns and promptly walks towards the rest of his men.

Private Babe nervously looks at Old Jude.

'I've never seen a horse talk before,' states Old Jude.

'Huh?' replies Private Babe.

'That horse that was just standing right next to you – he was talking—'

'Err…well—okay Jude…a pleasure to meet you,' interrupts Private Babe, taking a few cautious steps backward. 'Err…your bed is—is that way,' he adds, pointing in the direction of the village church, before jogging off to join his superior.

◆◆◆

Amelia begins to shake in fear as Officer Locks takes another small step towards her. She closes her eyes and starts to mutter the same magical enchants over and over again, hoping that if she keeps saying them, the forest will eventually hear her call and come to her aid.

She whimpers as she slowly whispers the words. Her voice slurs and breaks as she looks up to the Officer, who stares back down at her with a menacing rage in his eyes.

Again, Amelia attempts to flap her wings. She lets out a sigh of disappointment as they simply twitch; starved of sunlight and the mystical essence from it, that not only drives her wings, but also her magical powers and abilities; powers which at this precise moment are rendered useless by the lack of magical charge within her heart, and more importantly, by the lack of sunlight inside the forest.

'It seems like I may have caused a little problem with your vampire friend's bubble,' announces Officer Locks, letting out a chilling laugh. 'I'm guessing that it will only be a matter of time now before the sunlight begins to seep through the tear I have created in that pathetic bubble of his.'

Amelia turns and gasps at Edwin; watching as he tries desperately to close the tear in the bubble with his hands.

'Just look at you, vampire…' begins Officer Locks. 'Did you really believe that you would survive in that stupid little bubble of yours?'

'Hold on, Edwin!' yells Amelia. 'The sunlight is not that strong here. Keep holding the tear—'

'Silence!' bellows Officer Locks. 'That maybe true,

but I'm guessing that the bubble is not going to last much longer? So, it really doesn't matter either way, does it? I feel that as soon as that bubble disappears, the sunlight in here will be more than enough to—well, how should I put it? Slow roast you…?' The Officer chuckles loudly. 'You can't even get up, can you? You are in fear that the sunlight will simply weaken you more. Maybe I should just drag you near those rocks – the sun seems much brighter over there, does it not?'

Edwin hisses at the Officer and rolls onto his back. He grips the bubble tightly with his hands and squashes the material through his pointy fingers; minimising the amount of sunlight seeping through. He moans in pain; feeling the sunlight create a slight tingling on his pale skin, underneath his clothing. He lets out a sharp gasp in realising, that although in severe pain, it will be nothing compared to the pain he will experience if the bubble suddenly fades, or as Officer Locks stated, the sunlight in the forest intensifies.

For now, Edwin is safe in the forest, but time is running out for the bubble, and Edwin fears that without it, the sunlight in the forest will be more than enough to weaken and kill him.

Officer Locks gently pats his ripped trousers, which despite going through his dramatic transformation into a werewolf, remain on his body in reasonably good condition.

'Hmmm…' begins Officer Locks. 'During all that recent excitement – I seem to have misplaced my knife. Now, that is a shame. No matter…I will just have to take your heart at a later time. But for now, I will simply just have to squeeze the life out of you.'

Officer Locks takes a step towards Amelia, reaches out his arm and grabs Amelia in his hand.

Amelia lets out a high-pitched scream as the Officer's hairy fingers wrap themselves tightly around her fragile body; crushing her wings. She cries in pain as he tightens his grip.

'Any last words…?' announces Officer Locks.

Amelia coughs and splutters; struggling to catch her breath.

'What about you, vampire?' continues the Officer. 'Have you anything to say…?'

Edwin hisses and groans in pain.

'So be it, then…' mutters the Officer. 'I guess that this is your final—ARGGHHHHHH!'

Officer Locks lets out a loud roar as a large tree branch flies in from above and wraps itself around his waist. The branch twists around his body, which causes him to instantly release Amelia from his grip.

Amelia falls to the forest floor and lands softly atop a small red and white mushroom. She lets out a few more spluttering coughs, before pushing herself to her knees and turning to face Officer Locks.

Another branch suddenly appears from the side. It rushes across the forest and clings firmly onto the Officer's left leg. Moments later, a third branch appears from the opposite direction and wraps itself around his right leg. The twisting and creaking of wood is deafening as the branches stretch and change shape; winding tightly around the Officer's lanky body.

'What is this magic…?' snarls the Officer, pulling frantically at the branches with his hand, in an attempt to loosen them and free himself.

Amelia's jaw hangs open wide. She glances in amazement at the surrounding forest, which has mysteriously come alive around her.

A gentle whisper is heard in the air as the trees talk

to each other in some mystical ancient language. Amelia continues to watch the trees shift and move; stretching and reshaping themselves as more and more of their branches stretch out and wrap themselves around the Officer, until only his head remains visible.

'They have heard me…' mutters Amelia. 'Look Edwin! The forest has heard me.'

Edwin groans and smiles, before mumbling a few words that Amelia fails to interpret.

'Quick, Edwin…this is our time to make a run for it. We must go now!' announces Amelia, stumbling to her feet.

Amelia, with the little strength she has, makes her way across to Edwin. She pulls herself up onto his leg and moves up his body; climbing over his arm and coming to a halt at his pointy chin. She places a tiny hand on Edwin's cold lips.

'Edwin…*you*—you saved me,' says Amelia. 'And not once…but twice. *I*—I don't…I don't know what to say. I've never—I mean, I don't believe I have ever been so wrong about someone in my life. I never thought I would be saying thank you to a vampire – for saving my life. But I thank you, Edwin.'

'I aim to please…' mumbles Edwin. 'But you must run now, Amelia. Escape the forest – while you can. I'm afraid that my time in this world has nearly ended. I bid you to leave me here and run – run back to the village. I have fulfilled by promise—'

'No!' interrupts Amelia. 'There must be a way.'

'Don't be foolish. Run – run away!' replies Edwin.

Amelia turns her head back towards the Officer, who rises into the air; pulled up by the branches into the highest parts of the forest. The Officer continues to shout and curse as he tries to wriggle himself free.

'The forest is helping you, Amelia…' begins Edwin. 'They are giving you a chance to escape. You must get out of here!'

'No, Edwin. I will not leave you,' replies Amelia. 'You saved me and now I'm going to save you. Can you at least move?'

Edwin raises his head. 'I think so – but I dare not transform in bat form. I don't think the bubble will hold. I'm struggling to keep the tear closed as it is.'

'Well, Edwin – you can either lay there and see what happens, or at least try and let me help you. What have you got to lose?' I will hold onto your cloak while you rise to your feet. 'I'll then slide into your waistcoat pocket – if the bubble will stretch enough to allow me to climb inside.'

Edwin nods his head and proceeds to carefully roll himself onto his front. He lowers his forehead to the forest floor, and by using the little strength he has, pushes himself to his knees. He checks the tear in his bubble, before staggering to his feet.

'Now, Edwin…' begins Amelia. 'We must get out of here. We need to move quickly back towards Baston – or better still – try and find some sunlight.'

'Sunlight?' responds Edwin. 'That's not exactly what I need right now…is it?'

'Well, put it this way, Edwin. It will either be the end of you, or you may have a chance to survive – if I can charge up my heart.'

◆◆◆

Duncan pulls himself to his feet and staggers across to his large butcher's knife, which is hanging off the back wall, behind the bar. He reaches up and removes it off its hook, before stumbling towards Timothy, who quickly steps aside. Duncan then attempts to take a swing at one of Mrs Stamps' chickens, which has wandered off towards the other end of the tavern.

'What do you think you are doing, Duncan…?' bellows Mrs Stamps, leaping between her chicken and Duncan, who then suddenly falls to his knees and collapses on the floor. He mutters a few incoherent words; trying to structure a sentence.

'Were you just about to harm my poor little baby, Duncan?' yells Mrs Stamps, picking her chicken up from the floor and cradling it in her arms. 'I can tell you this right now…if you ever as even *look* at any of my chickens, I'll take your knife and I'll use it to cut off your—'

'Great balls of fire,' interrupts Samuel. 'What is Melvin doing? Look! He seems to be creating some sort of large smoke cloud – and right over the top of my wash-house. It is going to take ages to clean all that up. Why does he always seem to have no disrespect for other people's property?'

'And that's not smoke, Samuel – that's steam – hot steam, remember…?' responds the Reverend. 'Plus, it also looks as if the Corporal and his men are trying to push all the laundry in that direction.'

Mrs Stamps ushers her other chickens to the front of the tavern and away from Duncan, who has fallen asleep on the floor. She returns the chicken in her arms to the floor. It quickly joins her other chickens, wearing the same gormless look it had before Duncan took a swipe at it. Mrs Stamps points at each of her chickens and tallies them all up on her fingers and thumbs.

'Do you believe that maybe Melvin has some sort of plan…?' questions Mrs Stamps, stepping forward.

'Well, something is certainly occurring up there, Mrs Stamps,' replies the Reverend.

'Do you think we should try to assist in any way?' asks Timothy, reaching up to his shoulder and giving Corbin a little tickle. 'I feel a little useless here – doing nothing. I really do believe that I should try and meet the judge. She must be eager to start the judging process, don't you think?'

'Timothy!' howls Mrs Stamps. 'Don't be so stupid! Sometimes you are such a numpty. She is obviously having too much fun with that hand pistol thingy of hers. Besides, do you honestly think that with our current situation – we even have a chance at winning?'

'Err—well, I suppose not—' answers Timothy quietly, staring across at the mess in the village.

'Then shut up, Timothy!' responds Mrs Stamps. 'However, I do think that you are right in saying that we should do something to help.'

Samuel leans forward and focuses in on the Corporal. 'I agree. It looks to me as if the Corporal and his men are starting to fatigue, which is not being helped by Private Trout and Private Myles, who—well, who look as if they have absolutely no idea what they are doing. Drunken fools.'

'We'll need a lot more help…' begins Mrs Stamps. 'Maybe it would be an idea to get the villagers to assist?'

'What do you mean – villagers?' replies Timothy.

Mrs Stamps stares blankly at Timothy. She wonders how she can put the sentence any simpler.

'Seriously, Timothy?' snaps Mrs Stamps. 'You need me to explain what I mean by villagers?'

'Err…no,' answers Timothy. 'But it is just that—'

'That's actually a good idea, Mrs Stamps,' interrupts the Reverend. 'I think I can now see where Melvin is going with this whole steam idea of his. We need the villagers to help us direct the laundry towards the wash-house.'

'Do you believe that they'll help, Reverend?' asks Samuel. 'They must be pretty frightened. Look at them three behind us - they have hardly said a word since they have been here.'

The Reverend shifts his head towards the three villagers still hiding behind the bar counter. He nods his head at Samuel. 'Yes, you may have a point there, Samuel. But there is only one way to find out…'

'Excuse me…' begins Timothy. 'But you want me to go back out there amongst that chaos? What do you want me to do? Knock on everyone's door?'

'Well, that is the general idea, Timothy,' responds the Reverend.

'What about all the laundry that is surrounding the buildings?' asks Timothy. 'I'm really not—'

'What's the matter, Timothy? Are you chick—*cough*—I mean – are you scared…?' questions Samuel, with a smirk on his face.

'No-no,' replies Timothy. 'It's just—'

'Oh, shut up, Timothy!' blasts Mrs Stamps. 'Let's go and help save our village. Grab that pitchfork, will you?'

CHAPTER XVI

SQUAWK!

THE CROW

Edwin staggers through the Darkened Enchanted Forest. He clutches desperately onto the tear that has opened in his protective bubble; the tear caused earlier by Officer Locks' sharp claws. He grasps the bubble's material in his hands and tried his best to prevent even the smallest amount of sunlight from seeping through.

Edwin begins to panic. He realises that although the tear in the bubble is causing him discomfort and concern, it is a minor problem compared to the fact that at any moment, the bubble could fail completely.

Amelia stands in Edwin's waistcoat pocket and dangles her arms over the top of the neatly stitched trim that lines its top edge. She gazes down at Edwin's feet, which seem to be slowing down with every single step he takes.

'We must keep moving, Edwin,' says Amelia. 'Look! There is a gap in the trees up ahead and the sunlight is bursting through to the forest floor. Hurry, Edwin – take us over there!'

Edwin groans and takes a couple of steps forward, before collapsing to his knees. The sudden impact with the ground beneath him causes Amelia to clutch onto Edwin's waistcoat; preventing her from slipping out of his pocket.

'*I*—I don't think I can make it,' mumbles Edwin. 'You must go on without me—'

'What are you talking about, Edwin?' replies Amelia. 'We are nearly there – just head up past those rocks over there and beside them trees – head towards the sunlight.'

'That's really not a suitable thing to be saying to a vampire, is it?' Head to the sunlight – famous last words that, don't you think?'

'No, Edwin. If you take me to the sunlight – I can use the rays of light to charge my magical powers and then I—'

'But what will that achieve, Amelia…?' interrupts Edwin, whilst pushing himself to his feet. 'Let's face it – I'm done. There is no way I can get back to the village in time and there is certainly nowhere nearby to hide from the sunlight. This bubble will soon disappear and that will be—'

'No, Edwin – you cannot talk like that! If you take me to the sunlight – I will use my magical powers to make it…' Amelia pauses and lets out a long sigh. 'I will make it possible for you to walk in the sunlight – not just here and now – but forever.'

Edwin gasps. 'You mean you will—'

'Yes, Edwin – I will read out your ancestor's enchant and wash your clothes—well, cast a spell on them, at least. But I need to get to the sunlight. Without that, I don't think that either of us will be getting too far. So…get a move on!'

'But why would you do that—*cough-cough*—for me?' splutters Edwin, taking a step forward. 'You seemed so very certain that you would never help my kind – when I asked you before. Besides, you mentioned that by reading the spell…it could kill you?'

'Because, Edwin…I didn't know your true character before – and the last few moments have shown me a different side of you. You are not the typical vampire I would have expected. You are truly different.'

Edwin continues to take small steps forward, driven by the thought that if Amelia is true to her word, Edwin's worries about being frazzled by the sunlight could all be over. He relishes the thought of being able to walk out in the sunlight and experience what life is like during the day. He keeps putting one foot in front of the other.

'And you are right, Edwin…' begins Amelia. 'I did mention before – that if I read those dark enchants of yours – then it could all be too much for me – I, myself, could end up—well, I could perish; absorbed by the dark magic – It will overfill my heart and cause it to break. There is only so much magic it can hold. Besides, Edwin…we will die together if I fail, won't we? Well, perish is a better word…as you are already dead!'

'That is true – I am already dead. But why risk your own life – for mine? What have I done to deserve—'

'I could ask you exactly the same question, Edwin.'

'Okay…let me ask that another way. Am I worth risking your life for? I mean, you don't need me for anything – you can simply head back to Baston, and no one would care less about me,' states Edwin.

'You risked your life for me – and not once…but twice! Plus, I'm certain someone would care.'

'Who? Tell me who would miss me that much…?' replies Edwin, sadly.

'Your little assistant, for one – Corbin, isn't it?' replies Amelia immediately.

'Oh, yes…Corbin.' Edwin sighs.

Amelia watches Edwin cautiously approach an area of the forest that is illuminated by rays of sunlight; rays that are breaking through the thick tree canopies above; rays that shine a long slither of sunlight onto the forest floor.

Edwin stumbles forward. He groans in pain.

'I cannot let you risk your life – even for me…' mutters Edwin.

'That is my choice to make,' replies Amelia, firmly. 'I want to try and help you, Edwin. I really want to…'

'Even if it hurts you?'

'I'm prepared to take that risk. The question is…are you prepared to let me try? If you hadn't of come to my rescue – I would have surely perished at the hands of Officer Locks.' Amelia pauses. 'I will do my best to get your curse removed. It's ironic if you think about it. You've now got the chance to get exactly what you came for in the first place – just not in the way that you had planned.'

'That is certainly correct.'

Edwin comes to a halt at the edge of the rays of light and drops down on one knee.

'Hmmm…that should do nicely, Edwin,' states Amelia, climbing out of Edwin's pocket, sliding down his bubble and landing gracefully on the forest floor. She scutters through the leaves and broken twigs on the ground, and enters the beams of sunlight.

Edwin lifts his head. He watches Amelia begin to glow a greenish yellow as the sunrays shine over her body. Small shimmers of intense white light shoot out from her torso, while absorbing the sunlight's magical essence; charging her heart. She raises her hands high into the air; an aura forming around her.

The bright light causes Edwin to suddenly glance away and shield himself from the mixture of magical aura and sunlight. In the corner of his eye, he barely makes out the outline of Amelia as she is engulfed in sunlight. He turns to watch her unfold and flap her wings, which hum in the air, and just as quickly as the aura came, it disappears.

Edwin tilts his head back towards Amelia and watches her dart across the sky towards him; her wings in full motion.

'You – you are flying—*cough-cough*—I'm guessing it has worked?' asks Edwin.

'Yes…it has very much worked,' responds Amelia. 'But we don't have much time Edwin – that bubble is fading – look!'

Edwin lowers his head to observe his bubble slowly fading before his very eyes.

'This is bad,' announces Edwin. 'Very bad indeed.'

'Quick, Edwin…' begins Amelia. 'Where are the enchants that I need to read? Please don't tell me they are lengthy? We haven't the time to read out a novel.'

'They are in my pocket – my left waistcoat pocket – the inside one.' Edwin gasps. 'But it looks like we have a slight problem though, doesn't it?' he adds in a panicked tone.

'It does? What do you mean?'

'How are you going to reach through the bubble to retrieve the parchment?' I can't get to it – if I do, I'll let go of this tear and it will open up.'

Amelia ponders in thought. 'Do you trust me, Edwin?'

'Of course – I have no reason not to trust you. Why do you ask?'

'Well, Edwin…we don't have the time to mess about. It's going to hurt for a few seconds. But I want you to open the tear. I will then fly inside, grab your enchant and fly back out.'

Edwin frowns. 'How long will I have to let go for?'

'Not long…' responds Amelia. 'No pain-no gain. Are you ready?'

'As ready as I'll ever be.'

Edwin stares blankly at Amelia, who winks back at him. He softens his grip around the tear in his bubble, and lets out a few loud moans as the sunlight seeps through. There is a slight pause, and as fast as light itself, Amelia quickly darts through the tear, grabs the parchment containing the enchant from Edwin's pocket and returns outside, before Edwin even has time to realised what has happened.

'Right, hold on, Edwin,' instructs Amelia, watching him tighten his grip around the tear, and not taking any notice of the bubble itself, which begins to break down and fade.

'Hurry, Amelia,' pleads Edwin, with a look of sheer panic in his eyes.

Amelia quickly unfolds the parchment and scrolls her eyes over the ancient text. She goes over in her mind what the words mean and tries to figure out how to pronounce each and every word correctly, knowing that one false mispronunciation of even a single syllable, could cause Edwin to perish right in front of her. Amelia gulps as she realises that the enchant is very powerful and could end up sucking the very life force out of her, or worse still, fill her with so much darkened magic, her heart would simply explode.

'The bubble!' bellows Edwin, letting out a roaring scream as he feels the sunlight start to penetrate the bubble's wall. It seeps through his clothes and onto his aged pale skin. 'Oh, the pain. I don't know how much longer I can take all of this—'

'Be quiet, Edwin…' begins Amelia. 'I'm about to read out your enchant. I need to concentrate.'

There is a moment's pause. Amelia nervously and carefully reads out the enchantment on the parchment paper. From the first word spoken, she begins to glow with a pale orange aura; the aura changing colour as she reads out a new line, from orange to green and then green to red.

THE AIR HUMS AND CRACKLES.

Edwin shivers and shudders as he watches his protective bubble completely fade away. He falls to floor in agony, curls up into a ball and pulls his cloak around his trembling body. Trails of vapour rise from Edwin's clothes as the sunlight starts to breakdown and destroy Edwin's skin cells.

THERE IS BRILLIANT FLASH OF LIGHT.

Amelia falls to the ground.

There is silence in the air…

♦♦♦

Baston's Washhouse is a long and narrow building, constructed mainly of small rocks and stones, built over a large wooden framework of oak and pine. It sits on the outskirts of the village and it's the largest building for several miles, even giving some of the larger buildings in the nearby town of River's Bend, a *run for their money*. It is a truly majestic sight to stand before, but an even more majestic sight to look down upon from above; which is precisely what Melvin and Eric are doing as Melvin steers his steam-powered bicycle over tall stone chimneys, which protrude upwards into the sky from the buildings' slated roofs.

'Are you going to keep flying us around in circles Melvin?' yells Eric. 'Or are you actually going to do something? You are starting to make me feel rather nauseous.'

'I'm going to need to get this bicycle producing alot more steam than this, Eric,' replies Melvin, looking at all the bicycle's many additional dials and buttons. 'So, how do I do that?'

'Well, simple really…' begins Eric. 'You can make the bicycle go much faster and that will produce more steam. However, that all depends on whether or not you are able to control your bicycle at high speed, Melvin?'

'I can control anything!' retorts Melvin, with a crazed look on his face.

Melvin continues to grip tightly onto the joystick between his legs. He tries his absolute best to keep the bicycle steady; failing at it miserably as he crazily pulls and pushes the joystick in all directions. Clearly, the bicycle doesn't want to go where he wants it to go.

'Maybe...' begins Eric. 'But you must admit – you are really stuggling to control this bicycle, aren't you?'

'I'm perfectly in control, thank you, Eric,' responds Melvin. 'Anyway...how do I make the bicycle go faster, then?'

Eric sighs. 'You should of read the instructions Melvin! That would have been a good thing to do, no?'

'What instructions? I haven't got the time to read instructions, Eric! All I want to do is to get this bicycle to go faster and create more steam. Then, hopefully I will be able to do something with the possessed laundry – get it under control or something.'

'And then what...?'

'That is the bit I haven't worked out yet. I'm hoping that Edwin will rescue Amelia and return her to safety. She then may be able to do something—well, I hope she can.' There is a long pause as Melvin ponders on the thought of Edwin not returning with Amelia.

Melvin steers his bicyle towards the end of the wash-house. He looks down at the ground beneath him for an area large enough to accommodate the mass of possessed laundry. Melvin smiles as he realises that some sort of plan is starting to formulate in his head.

The Corporal and his men continue battling the laundry. They drive it towards the wash-house, in the hope that Melvin's idea of using the steam from his bicycle will attract the laundry to it, and give the Corporal and his men a much deserved relief from their constant fighting.

Melvin leans over the side of his bicycle and scouts the ground below. He searches for the ideal place to execute his plan; a plan for sorting out the mess he has caused. The bicycle continues to circle the skies above the wash-house.

'If you want more steam – you will have to fully open the furnace vent, Melvin,' instructs Eric. 'It will cause more air to flow into the furnace and make it burn hotter.'

'This vent here?' questions Melvin, tilting his head in the direction of the vent.

'Yes…that's the one, lad!' Eric reaches down and flicks a spring-loaded lever, which he had installed on the furnace door.

'What are you doing?'

'Now don't you be worrying about what I'm doing Melvin…just be ready with that joystick. Let's just say that the bicycle is going to get much faster – as soon as you open that vent.'

Melvin re-directs his attention to the centre of the village, where the Corpoal and his men are now struggling to hold their ground against the *non-stop* waves of laundry. Melvin also notices, to his surprise, that many villagers have started to appear, exiting their homes and businesses with a mass of bizarre objects, undoubtedly to be used as weapons.

'Is that Mrs Stamps and Timothy down there?' questions Eric.

'I believe it is,' replies Melvin. 'It looks like—I mean, I think she is trying to get the villagers to help to push the laundry our way.'

'Then we have not much time to lose, Melvin. Quickly…open that vent!'

Holding tightly onto the joystick between his legs with one hand, Melvin, with his other hand, reaches down and clutches tightly around the furnace vent. He rotates it fully open.

The bicycle howls and groans as air is drawn into the furnace. Eric stares through the grilled door of the furnace at the blazing fire within, before tilting his head around Melvin's body, and looking at the pressure gauge mounted near the handlebars.

'Hold onto that hat of yours, Melvin!' yells Eric. 'Any moment now…'

Eric continues watching the gauge. The needle that indicates the bicycle's steam pressure is forced all the way over to the right of the gauge's face, well past its maxmium readable pressure. It flickers back and forth, trying to a find a pressure value it wants to read; a pressure reading that the gauge is probably not even capable of showing.

'You know that small lever I flicked a moment ago, Melvin?' asks Eric.

'Yes,' responds Melvin, gripping tightly on the bicycle's joystick.

'Well, be ready – I'm about to flick it back!'

'Okay, I'm ready. Just tell me when you about to—*WHOOOOAH!*

With a slight ping, the lever disengages and the bicycle lets out a howling whistle. It hisses madly and gets louder as steam, under very high pressure, moves through the bicycle's valves and pipework, towards its pistons; pistons which Eric has clevily redesigned as a jet propulsion system, allowing the bicycle to fly at much faster speeds.

Eric quickly lowers his head and stares down at the exhausts. He watches in amazement as the steam exits them at a tremendous rate.

The bicycle jolts and shudders as it starts to gather speed. Mevlin gasps, tightens his grip around the bicycle's joystick and tries his best to keep it steady, as jets of steam push the bicycle faster and faster forward.

'Melvin!' shouts Eric. 'You are going to have to just

hold the joystick slightly to the left – maintain us on a circular course. Also, it is not going to be long before we are not going to be able to see anything – as we catch up the steam that has already been ejected.'

Melvin nods his head, sticks out his tongue and concentrates hard on holding the joystick in position.

'It looks like this needle is about to snap off, Eric!' yelps Melvin.

'Don't you worry about that, lad,' responds Eric, checking the huge trail of steam behind them. 'It will hold! Oh…and it's also going to get a little warm as we fly back into the steam, Melvin. Actually it's going to get a little more than warm – it's going to get *very* warm.'

Melvin continues to hold the bicycle joystick steady; allowing the bicycle to fly at high speed in a circular motion; creating a huge ring of steam, which floats mysteriously in the air. Just as the steam begins to dissapate, it is refreshed by the bicycle passing through it once again. This repeats for every circular revolution the bicycle makes.

'Keep it going, Melvin!' shouts Eric. 'You're doing a cracking job!'

Melvin tries to smile; however, the ever increasing turbulent air, triggered by the bicycle's high speed, forces Melvin's skin hard against his jaw bone, causing his attempt at a smile to end up a flapping mess of loose and wrinkly skin.

'You do realise, Melvin…?' begins Eric. 'That very shortly – we are not going to be able to see a darn thing through this steam. Do you still think that all this steam is going to attract the laundry? Even it is does, how on Earth are we going to know?'

Melvin pauses as he mentally digests all of Eric's

questions, only to then become frustrated at the fact he cannot give Eric an answer.

'I haven't got that far in my plan yet, Eric,' yells Melvin. 'I'm just sort of hoping that it will all work itself out. Besides…we can look down there – look!'

With his face still hugging Melvin's back, Eric rotates his head to the side and looks down through the centre of the steam ring; capturing a glimpse of the ground below him.

'If it does work and attracts the laundry – we will see it underneath us,' shouts Melvin.

'And then what?' repies Eric.

'Like I said, Eric. I have no idea – I haven't got that far yet!'

◆◆◆

Down below, in the centre of the village, the Corporal and his men continue to battle on against the possessed laundry. They try their best not to slice the oncoming laundry into multiple shreds with their swords, but instead, try to get the laundry to follow them towards the wash-house; a task that is proving to be easier said than done.

'We seem to be having difficulties in pushing them back, Sir,' annouces Private Babe. 'They just keep coming at us. If we continue on slicing up the people's laundry, we are going to be at the mercy of the villagers. They will not be too happy that we have destroyed all their clothes. We'll also cause ourselves much bigger problems – as we'll have much more laundry, or pieces of it, I should say…to re-direct.'

'Yes, Private…' replies the Corporal. 'I'm very aware of that fact.'

'Sir, look…' begins Private Babe. 'It looks as if Melvin has started to create some sort of steam ring in the sky above the wash-house. Maybe if we can get the laundry to notice it, they will turn and head over to it.'

'What do you suggest we do, Private? And will you please tell Trout and Myles to stop messing about in the fountain! It's not a swimming pool is it...? I'm seriously beginning to lose my patience with them two.'

'Play fair, Sir. You also swam a little bit in it earlier… didn't you?'

The Corporal frowns.

Private Babe glances around at the rest of the squad, trying their best to push the laundry back. His eyes suddenly lock onto Felicity riding Dinkle, who canters past him, followed by a line of woollen jumpers, some cotton shirts and a few socks.

'Look over there, Sir!' shouts Private Babe, pointing his finger at Felicity. 'Maybe they will all follow Felicity on her donkey? She seems to have attracted the attention of a few pieces of laundry. I'm guessing that if those pieces of laundry are following her – then there is no reason while other pieces will not.'

'Well, you could be on to something there, Private,' answers the Corporal.

Private Babe grins.

Felicity herself is having a whale of a time; firing off the last few rounds of ammunition from her pistol at pieces of laundry. The laundry pauses to look at the holes that she has put through them with her bullets. They all turn towards Felicty and proceed to join the long line of laundry that is following her, or more accurately, Dinkle, around the village.

'Felicity!' yells the Corporal, before motioning for her to head towards him.

Pulling hard on Dinkle's reins, Felicity directs him across the village green towards the Corporal.

'Yes, my lovely?' answers Felicity, as Dinkle canters past the front of the Corporal and around the far side of the village fountain, still followed by a continuously growing line of laundry. 'You'll have to shout a little louder – I can't hear what you are saying!'

The Corporal spins on the spot and follows Felicity with his eyes. He waits for her to steer Dinkle around the fountain and make another pass in front of him.

'I said…can you lead the laundry towards the wash-house!' instructs the Corporal, shouting a little louder at Felicity as she passes by. 'Lead all the laundry to the end of the village!'

Felicty turns her head and looks towards the wash-house at the end of the village. She then looks behind at the vast amount of laundry that is following her and Dinkle. Felicity gasps, turns back to the Corporal and raises a thumb into the air; indicating to him that she has understood his instructions. Snapping hard on Dinkle's reins, she leads the line of laundry towards the wash-house.

'That should hopefully help us, Private,' announces the Corporal.

'Yes, Sir, look!' yelps Private Babe. 'Other pieces of laundry seem to be following her.'

'It also looks like we have some additional help,' states the Corporal.

'Sir..?'

'Look over there…' begins the Corporal. 'That's Mrs Stamps. It looks as if she's rallying up the villagers to help direct the laundry towards Melvin.

Private Babe turns and watches Mrs Stamps, alongside Timothy and Corbin, lead a small group of villagers across the green and towards the washshouse. They use whatever means they can to try and remove laundry from the sides and roofs of buldings, hoping that they will also be attracted towards Melvin's steam cloud.

'Then, Sir, we shall take the fight to Melvin!' hollers Private Babe, waving his sword in the air.

'Yes! Oh…and did you manage to fetch Trout and Myles?' asks the Corporal.

'Yes, Sir!'

'What did they say?'

'I'm afraid that my innocent nature will not allow me to repeat such words, Sir. Besides, I don't think my vocabulary stretches far enough for me to pronouce some of them, let alone know what they actually mean.'

◆◆◆

Back in the skies above Baston, Melvin raises a hand in front of his face to shield himself from the hot vortex of steam that has been created by his steam-powered bicycle, which with every moment, gets faster.

'How are we for coal, Eric?' shouts Melvin.

'Plenty of coal, lad,' replies Eric. 'Don't you be worrying about that now.'

'How much longer do you think that we need to keep this up?'

Eric, holding on very tightly around Melvin's waist, shifts his head and looks down at the ground beneath them.

'I'm not too sure, lad,' answers Eric. 'I can't see anything at—oh wait!'

'What do you see?' yells Melvin, trying himself to take a peek down below, while controlling the bicycle.

'*It*—it seems to be a large lady riding a donkey.'

'A what…?'

'A large lady – riding a very tired looking donkey.'

'I'm sorry, Eric. I can't hear you very well. I thought you said that you see a large lady riding a donkey!'

'I did, lad! Look, she is being followed by a long line of laundry. Maybe your plan could work after all…? What do you expect will happen when they all get underneath us…? I'm hoping for something very exciting.'

Melvin pauses. 'I'm really not too sure.'

The bicycle continues to soar in circles around the skies over Baston; purring, hissing and producing excessive amounts of hot steam. Melvin holds on with all his might to the bicycle's joystick, which begins to shudder and wobble in his hands as the bicycle reaches its maximum speed.

Melvin shifts all his weight to the left and adjusts his centre of gravity to try and resist the large centrifugal forces acting upon him. Eric adjusts himself to follow Melvin.

'*WHOOOOAH!*—was that a pair of trousers I just saw fly past us?' yelps Eric, turning his head towards the rear of the bicycle.

'I belieive it was,' answers Melvin. 'Where did they suddenly appear from?'

Melvin squints his eyes and tries to look beyond the thick blanket of steam, which the bicycle continues to fly through. 'What is that?' he asks.

Suddenly a pair of leather trousers rushes past them both. They swirl around in the turbulent steam, before disappearing out of view.

'I think the laundry is being drawn into the steam, lad,' states Eric, looking down below to where the laundry, that had previously been following Felicity, is now being mysteriously attracted by the steam. Piece by piece, items of laundry leap up into the centre of the steam ring and are quickly dragged into its turbulent vortex; swirling around in one fast flowing circle.

'*WHOOOOAH!* I can't see!' yells Melvin, as a pair of white underpants hits Melvin hard in the face and clings to his facial contours. He shakes his head from side to side; eventually releasing the underpants, which fly off towards the rear of the bicycle.

'They are all being sucked up to us,' annouces Eric. 'And look, lad! – that Corporal bloke and his men – they are being followed by lots more laundry. We must keep going – suck all that lanudry up!'

'That's exactly what I'm trying to do, Eric!' screams Melvin. 'But I'm also trying to hold the bicycle steady.'

'What are you planning to do next?'

'As I said earlier…I haven't worked that bit out yet.

Eric sighs.

'Well…' begins Eric. 'We can't just keep circling around the skies of Baston, while a multitude of laundry spins around with us, can we? You do realise that this steam cloud can only last so long, lad? At some point, but not right at this moment, I will have to add more coal to the furnace. I can't do that while we fly – it's too dangerous!'

'I am aware of that. Give me a second. I'm thinking.'

'Well, think harder, lad!' shrieks Eric, noticing a couple of items from his own laundry basket, fly past him at tremendous speed.

From the ground, pieces of laundry continue to be sucked up into the vortex; following suit and joining all the other laundry that currently swirls around inside.

Eric re-directs his attention to the ground below,

where Mrs Stamps, Timothy and Corbin, together with some villagers, lead a mass of laundry from one side of the villlage towards the wash-house. They are followed momentarily by Samuel and the Reverend, who perform a similar action from the other side of the village; leading villagers and laundry towards Melvin's steam cloud.

'Seems like there is a lot of people down there, lad,' annouces Eric. 'In fact – it looks like most of the village has turned up.'

'Is there any sign of Edwin and Amelia?' questions Melvin, quickly reaching up and forcing his hat back down onto his head.

Eric slowly glances around and scouts through the familiar faces of the villagers. 'I can't see 'em,' he says.

Melvin sighs.

'I'm really hoping that Edwin does rescue her…' begins Melvin. 'I'm terribly worried about her safety. Thinking about it…I really do not have a clue what to do with all this laundry, now.'

'Why don't you cast another spell?' enquires Eric

'*NO!* I'm doing this without using magic. Besides, I wouldn't be able to think on how to begin to cast a spell on this mess – I would need my journal, which under the current circumstances would be difficult to retrieve. Even if you reached for it from my pocket, I would still need my hands to cast the spell. No…it's too risky – one of us could fall!'

'I thought you liked taking risks, lad?'

'I do, Eric. But when my life literally depends on whether I keep my hands on this joystick – the risk is too great…even for me.'

Eric nods. 'I must admit…we really didn't think this plan through…did we, lad?'

◆◆◆

A gentle breeze disturbs the leaves that surround the motionless bodies of Edwin and Amelia, who lay on the forest floor. Occasionally, a few leaves are picked up by the breeze and fly up into the air, before gently floating back down and landing atop Edwin's cloak.

There is an eerie silence, which is broken by the occasional sounds of rustling leaves as trees sway gently back and forth. A soft breeze murmurs through the forest.

Amelia lets out a spluttering cough, before picking herself up from the ground and turning towards Edwin. She immediately takes flight and darts across to him; stopping to hover in front of his head. She gazes down at Edwin's body and smiles, before giving him several pokes on his shoulder.

Edwin lets out a groan. He suddenly opens his eyes and shifts them from left to right; trying to work out whether or not he has ended up as a pile of dust, and is still in the land of the living, or if Amelia has actually succeeded in removing his cursive trait by allowing him to now walk in the daylight.

He reaches out his arms, spreads them forwards and pushes himself to his knees. His eyes widen as he feels the sun's warmth of his hands. He smiles; a smile of pure joy, realisation and merriment. Amelia chuckles at Edwin, who then tilts his head to meet her.

'It worked!' glees Edwin, turning over his pale toned hands to feel the sunlight on his palms.

'It has, Edwin…it really has,' replies Amelia, placing her hands on her hips.

Edwin stands to his feet and brushes himself down. His cloak hangs down off his shoulders and trails on the ground beneath him. Amelia flies up and sits upon Edwin's shoulder.

'*I*—I cannot thank you enough, Amelia…' begins Edwin. 'I feel like a new man—well, vampire, I can't even begin to describe the surreal feeling that I'm experiencing right now. It's as if I have been reborn. Are you sure that I'll be able to walk in full sunlight? I mean, I feel the sunlight on my skin and I'm very much still here – but will it last?'

'Only one way to find out, Edwin,' whispers Amelia, into his ear. 'Move yourself into the sunlight,' she instructs, pointing at the rays of light, which shine on the forest floor in front of them.

Edwin takes a step forwards and hesitates; reluctant to forcefully move himself into the light, on the principle that he knows, it will either be the last thing he ever does, or the start of a new lifestyle.

'It's okay Edwin – go for it,' says Amelia, softly.

Edwin nods and takes a few steps towards the beam of sunlight. He slowly and cautiously extends his arm and pushes his hand into the radiant waves of light. Edwin gasps in anticipation, waiting for the painful sting of the sunlight on his hand. With no surprise to Amelia, who continues to smile at Edwin, his skin doesn't react with the sunlight.

In one large movement, Edwin steps forward and enters the light. He pushes his cloak to the side, raises his head towards the roof of the forest and feels the sun's warm rays cast down upon his face. He smiles, before jumping up and down in excitement, which causes Amelia to take flight; hovering at his side. She claps her tiny hands together at a task well done, and one that has brought, not only her, but also Edwin great satisfaction.

'I can walk in the daylight!' yells Edwin. 'Look at me, Amelia! Look!'

Amelia lets out a giggle. 'All in a day's work, Edwin.'

'Oh, drat! I almost forgot!' exclaims Edwin. 'I'm afraid your work may not be quite done for the day, Amelia. The villagers may need your help.'

'What do you mean – need my help?' replies Amelia.

'You mean…you don't know about the mess that the spellbinder has caused?'

'How would I know, Edwin? I've been locked in the cage of yours. I haven't seen the outside of that tavern room until the Officer ran out into the forest with me. I'm also guessing that you mean Melvin?'

'Yes, that's him. Quickly – we must get back to the village. I believe Melvin is trying to solve a huge problem; one that he has caused with the villagers' dirty laundry. I sense it's not going to be as easy as he thinks – he may need your assistance.'

'Oh, my-my…what has he done? He hasn't tried to attempt to wash all the dirty laundry with his bare hands, has he?'

'No…not quite.'

'Phew! He is a man…no man can do that! Oh, he must have forgotten to separate the colours from the whites – and the colours have run, haven't they? Well, that's no problem – getting whites gleaming clean is my speciality.'

Edwin sighs. 'It's a little more worrying than that.'

'What could possibly be more worrying than all the colours running?' responds Amelia.

Edwin pauses and tries to construct an answer that will not only put the situation into perspective for Amelia, but also one that is realistic, to the point and will not make Amelia have a nervous breakdown.

'Err…well, how well do you know Melvin?' asks Edwin, raising his eyebrows at Amelia.

'Not very well. I only met him the other night,' replies Amelia. 'Seems like a nice enough fella though.'

'Have you heard that he can sometimes cast magical spells and get them very—and I mean *very*…wrong?'

'No, I can't say that I have heard that – I would have remembered if I did.'

Edwin chuckles. 'Well you are certainly not going to forget this one, Amelia. I promise you that!'

'Oh, what has he managed to do?'

'Come, I will show you. We must head back to the village right away – again…time is valuable.'

Amelia nods.

THERE IS A FLASH OF RED LIGHT.

Edwin transforms into bat form.

'Lead the way, Edwin,' instructs Amelia, as they both dart up through the trees and into the sky away from the forest.

◆◆◆

Mrs Stamps leads the Reverend, Samuel, Timothy and Corbin, over the top of the make-shift barricade at the front of the tavern. With their backs against the exterior wall, they each sneak along the front of the building.

They are all followed quickly by the three random villagers, who are either relieved that they have the chance to escape the constant ramblings of Duncan, or they genuinely want to try and aid Melvin in helping to save the village.

'I believe it would be a very good idea if we all split up,' suggests Mrs Stamps. 'There is no point in us all knocking on the same door, is there?'

'A good idea,' replies the Reverend. 'But I've been thinking. How can we be sure that the villagers are going to answer their doors? They will just think that it is the laundry banging up against them.'

'Maybe if we use some secret door knock, then they would know that it is one of us and not the laundry,' proposes Timothy, pushing the tines of Mrs Stamps' pitchfork into the damp grass and leaning up against its handle.

Mrs Stamps peers past the Reverend and stares at Timothy. He stares back at her briefly, before realising that he has perhaps said something that has displeased Mrs Stamps, and lowers his head in shame.

'Do you know what, Timothy?' begins Mrs Stamps. 'I really have had quite enough of your idiotic thoughts and comments for one day. How exactly do you think that your secret door knock is going to work if the villagers don't have a clue what the secret door knock is?'

'Yes, Timothy,' responds the Reverend, turning towards him. 'It's as if you would have to knock on their door as normal – get them to answer – and then tell them the secret door knock. They could then close the door and you knock again, only that time – using the secret door knock – so they will then know – that it is you, who is knocking. Does that make sense?'

Timothy pauses in confusion at the Reverend's comment and shifts his attention towards Mrs Stamps; waiting for her to relieve the Reverend of his comment. It doesn't come, but instead Mrs Stamps lets out a long sigh.

'What's the plan, Timothy?' asks Samuel, creeping up behind Timothy.

'I'm not too sure at the moment,' replies Timothy. 'Mrs Stamps is suggesting that we split up and go knocking on everyone's doors – to rally up as many villagers as we can. But we need to be persistent – as the villagers may just think it's the laundry banging on their doors.

'Yes, that would definitely be what I would think if there was banging on my door, right now,' responds Samuel.

The three random villagers join Samuel at the back of the line. Samuel immediately turns to greet them and acknowledges them with a gentle nod of his head. He motions for them to remain quiet by pressing his pointed index finger tightly against his lips and making a long shushing sound.

'It looks as if the Corporal and his men are starting to push the laundry back—well, in the right direction,' states the Reverend. 'I hope the steam that Melvin is going to create will attract the laundry towards it. We can then, along with the help of the other villagers, try to force all the remaining pieces of laundry that lay scattered about – across to him.'

Mrs Stamps nods.

'Okay, then…' begins Mrs Stamps, 'Let's split up. Timothy you come with me and we'll go down the west side of the village. Reverend…you and Samuel take the east side – and you villagers take up everything in-between…okay?' The random villagers nod and proceed to make their way across the village.

'Right, let's go!' announces Mrs Stamps. 'We will all meet where Melvin will be, okay?'

'Sounds good to me,' answers the Reverend, straightening his attire and stepping back to allow Timothy to pull the pitchfork from the ground.

Mrs Stamps leads Timothy towards the far side of the village. They both cautiously avoid attracting any attention to their presence; hiding from the laundry. They knock on the front doors of each of the village buildings they arrive at, and in the event that the villagers *actually* answer their doors, Mrs Stamps instructs them all to assist in aiding Melvin. She does this with pure eloquence; tainted with a tone that can only come out of her less than elegant mouth.

Many of the villagers accept Mrs Stamps' request as it wouldn't be the wisest of choices to refuse. They grab a variety of objects to use as weapons, while exiting their homes and businesses; one man in-particular picking up a fishing rod, which to Timothy's amazement is not a bad choice at all, as it could be used to pick off laundry from hard to reach places.

The Reverend and Samuel perform similar actions on the other side of village.

'No point on knocking on that door, huh?' states the Reverend, pointing at the church. 'As I am right here…'

Samuel chuckles. 'I'm just thinking, how are you actually going to get back into the church when all this is over?'

'What do you mean?' asks the Reverend.

'Well, you locked and bolted the doors from the inside…remember? Melvin then teleported us out.'

'Oh, drat!'

◆◆◆

Edwin leads Amelia across the tree tops of the Darkened Enchanted Forest. They head back to Baston, where on the skyline at the end of the village, a huge mass of steam and laundry swirls violently around in circles above the wash-house.

'Oh my—' begins Amelia, muttering to herself. 'What in goodness-gracious?'

Amelia tries her hardest to catch up with Edwin. You would think that it would be no trouble for her to keep pace; however, Edwin, being a vampire, is very quick and nimble in his bat form, and darts at lightning speed towards the centre of the village.

Edwin lets out a loud squawk and darts down underneath the steam vortex, before perching himself on the roof of the wash-house.

THERE IS A FLASH OF RED LIGHT.

Seconds later, Edwin, who is now in human form, is joined by Amelia. She hovers beside him with a look of shock and confusion upon her face.

'What's going on, Edwin?' asks Amelia, staring up at the mass of steam and laundry. 'Is that laundry alive? I swear I just saw a pair of trousers and a cotton shirt, wriggling about up there.'

'It very much looks that way,' answers Edwin.

'And is that Melvin up there? On some sort of bicycle…?' adds Amelia

Edwin tilts his head, squints his eyes and tries to focus through the thick dense steam. 'Yes, I believe it is,' he replies.

'I really don't know what to say…' begins Amelia. 'What has caused all this mess?'

'I think you'll find that was Melvin .'

Amelia gasps as she watches shreds of fabrics between sucked up into the steam vortex; fabrics that once were jumpers, shirts, trousers and all other forms of clothing.

'What has happened to all the clothes?' whimpers

Amelia. 'Oh, this is such a mess, Edwin. I don't know what to do.'

'I'm not sure…but I'm guessing it has something to do with that group of soldiers over there,' replies Edwin. 'They all seem to be wielding swords around. Logic suggests – that is not a simple coincidence!'

Amelia nods.

Edwin looks up at the sky above Melvin and notices dark clouds creeping over the village. 'Looks as if it is about to rain,' he annouces, before pausing. 'I think everyone is hoping that you will be able to cast some sort of reversing spell. Is that something you can do?'

'Well, I suppose I can try, but all that flying has considerably drained my power. Also, to solve a laundry problem of this magnitude…I will need to be fully charged. I really wasn't expecting this from Melvin. I thought that maybe it would be something simple. I never thought I would ever see laundry that is—well, alive – let alone laundry that is being tossed around in a large spinning steam cloud!'

'Why don't you just take a few moments to recharge – then we can try to come up with something?'

Amelia stares up at the sky. She watches as a large grey cloud crosses in front of the sun, blocks out its light and casts a darkened shadow across the village.

'Ah, well that idea is now out of the question,' adds Edwin.

'Yes, looks like its going to stay clouded over for a while. I can't charge up in this…it would take ages!'

'Quick, lets fly down and see what the others say,' suggests Edwin, noticing and then pointing at the recognisable posture of Mrs Stamps. He smiles as he catches a glimpse of his assistant Corbin, perched very comfortably on Timothy's shoulders.

Edwin jumps down from the roof and lands with a thud onto the grass below. He adjusts his hat and straightens his attire, before strolling casually towards Mrs Stamps. Amelia follows.

'Edwin! You are back!' yells Mrs Stamps, turning to face him. 'But, did you—oh—*cough*—hello there…it's you…isn't it?' she adds, upon noticing Amelia. 'It is! You are our little Laundry Fairy. By the way – I'm Mrs Stamps.'

'I know exactly who you are, Mrs Stamps,' answers Amelia. 'I've been doing your laundry for as long as I can remember.

'How is it that I can see you?' questions Mrs Stamps.

'I've just simply slowed myself down for all to see me,' replies Amelia.

'I see…' begins Mrs Stamps. 'Do you think it is a good idea that everyone can now see you? Oh my-my, Edwin…I've just noticed that you are walking in the daylight! How did that—'

'Too many questions, Mrs Stamps!' interrupts Edwin. 'I believe we have more important matters at hand – don't you think?'

Mrs Stamps nods, paces over to Timothy and taps him on his back. 'Timothy, look! She is here…'

'Who?' answers Timothy, carefully turning towards Mrs Stamps. 'Oh, my goodness' he adds, noticing Amelia floating in the air next to Edwin.

'Master!' yelps Corbin, excitedly, before jumping off Timothy's shoulder and onto the ground; landing with a small thump. He scutters across the grass and wraps his arms tightly around his Master's left leg.

'Ah, Corbin—*cough-cough*—how are you?' responds Edwin. '*It's*—it's good to see you again.'

'Master…you can walk in the daylight!' yelps

Corbin, who fails to notice Amelia floating above him. 'You have managed to get that troublesome fairy to change—'

'Troublesome?' interrupts Amelia, causing Corbin to tilt his head towards her.

Corbin gulps. 'Err…hello again, little fairy.'

Amelia frowns at Corbin.

'Enough of this!' exclaims Edwin. 'There is plenty of time for questions and answers later – but right now we need to be thinking about how we can aid Melvin, do we not? He seems to be losing control of his bicycle, up there.'

◆◆◆

'I'm struggling to keep this bicycle under control!' shrieks Melvin, tightening his grip around the bicycle's joystick, which shudders in his hands.

'You're telling me!' replies Eric, desperately clinging onto Melvin's robe. 'But keep it going, lad! I believe I just spotted our Laundry Fairy with that vampire character you mentioned.'

'Amelia? She is down there?'

Eric tilts his head and looks down through the centre of the swirling steam ring, which to most people would seem a fairly simple task. However, doing it on a bicycle that is travelling at excessive speeds through a vortex of hot steam, is easier said than done. Also, trying to accomplish it while a mass of possessed laundry swirls and flies past at lightning speed; making the task just a little more difficult.

'I think so, lad,' responds Eric. 'Unless there is some other fairy that you know of – who hangs around with a vampire?

Taking a look for himself at the ground below is not an option for Melvin. He puts all his concentration and effort into making sure he doesn't lose control of his bicycle, while at the same time, shielding himself from various items of possessed clothing that continuously speed towards him.

'Then what is she waiting for?' yelps Melvin. 'She must be able to sort this laundry problem out quickly and effortlessly – cast some sort of spell. We can't keep this up forever!'

'Aye…I agree, lad!' answers Eric. 'But we've come this far. We can't turn back now.'

Melvin grits his teeth and continues to maintain his bicycle on its circular path, which is now, to Melvin and Eric's relief, reaching its maximum flying speed.

'We need to find out what is going on down there,' states Melvin.

'And *how* exactly do you suggest that we do that?' replies Eric.

'I'm really not too sure, Eric. I've got a lot more to think about right now…than that.'

'So, what you are saying – is that we just keep going around in circles and wait for something to happen?'

'Sounds like a good plan, Eric. Which is good – as we needed a plan…no?'

Melvin attempts to smirk at Eric, however the turbulent currents pounding at his face, prevent him from doing so.

Possessed laundry continues to be forcefully sucked up into the centre of the steam vortex. An eerie hum is heard as the laundry groans, moans and resonates through the dense steam.

'We need to find Dexter!' yells Melvin. 'For some bizarre reason – he always seems to disappear when I need him the most. We could then ask him to fly down and try to get a message to Amelia.

Eric laughs; a laugh that is muffled by the increasing noises around him.

'What?' begins Eric. 'You seriously believe that he will be able to fly up here? Somehow I don't think so.'

'Pardon me…' responds Melvin. 'But you have no idea what that little dragon can do – when he puts his mind to it!'

'Err…it's funny that you talk about Dexter.'

'Why…?'

'Because I've just seen him fly underneath us – followed very closely by a large and angry bird. It looked very much like a crow…if I'm not mistaken.'

◆◆◆

The Reverend Clementine ducks his head to avoid Dexter, who suddenly swoops down low in an attempt to shake off a very large and angry crow. Dexter tries his best to out run the crow that continues to peck and claw at his tail.

The Reverend's unprepared and sudden ducking motion attracts the attention of Samuel and a few other villagers, who lift their heads and watch Dexter fly crazily around them.

'It looks as if that blasted crow from our village hall is back again,' states Samuel.

'You shouldn't be talking about Mrs Stamps like that, Samuel,' sniggers the Reverend, turning towards Dexter, who is still trying his best to elude the crow. Samuel chuckles.

'Master, look!' yelps Corbin. 'That dragon, Dexter, is struggling with a giant bird. Can you not help him?'

'I'm sure the dragon can fend for himself against a crow, Corbin,' replies Edwin. 'Besides, I think we have more important matters to deal with – and that being…what are we going to do about all this laundry? Isn't that right, Amelia?'

'Yes…I'm sure a dragon is more than capable of dealing with a simple crow,' responds Amelia. 'I'm trying to think about how to deal with the more *important* matters at hand.'

Corbin sighs and continues to follow Dexter with his eyes; cringing as he watches the crow constantly peck at Dexter's tail. He reaches into his pocket, in search of his yo-yo, only to be disappointed upon realising that Officer Locks had taken it earlier.

Corbin searches the ground at his feet and eyes up a small pebble, which he picks up and holds gently in the palm of his paw.

Corbin can be extremely clever when it comes to problem solving and can usually produce a solution very quickly when he puts his mind to it. This is certainly the case as he removes the shoe lace from his left shoe. He holds the shoe lace in his hand and wraps the end of it around the pebble; making a slingshot.

Edwin continues to discuss options with Ameila, while unaware of Corbin's antics.

Corbin starts to swing the sling shot around his head; spinning it faster and faster. If he builds up enough centrifugal force on the stone, then he hopes, that when released, it will come into contact with the crazed crow. He sticks out his tongue and closes his right eye; accurately.lining up his target.

Dexter flies frantically across the skies overhead. Corbin waits patiently for Dexter to come into range and the ideal moment to launch the pebble.

As Dexter swoops down over the heads of the villagers, who look on in amazement, Corbin releases the pebble from the sling. It flies through the air at great speed, before hitting the crow on the forehead, causing the crow to lose its concentration and crash into the grass below.

SQUAWK!

A few loud cheers are heard from the villagers as they gather around to see the dazed, but still very much alive crow, quivering on the grass.

Dexter stops, turns and hovers mid air. He swings his head from side to side, seeking what had caused the crow to just suddenly fall out of the sky and crash underneath him. He gently flaps his wings to steady himself, before noticing Corbin staring up at him with a shoelace wrapped around his claw. Dexter swoops down and lands softly besides Corbin.

'Err…' begins Dexter. 'Was it by any chance… *you*…that knocked that crow out of the sky?'

Cornin smiles and lowers his head in shyness.

'Oh. well—err…I guess *I*—I should thank you,' responds Dexter, reaching out his claw and giving Corbin a gentle nudge on his shoulder, which nearly knocks him off his feet. 'What did you do to the crow?'

'I just fired a small pebble at him,' answers Corbin.

'And you managed to hit him from here – using only your shoelace?'

'Yes—'

'Very impressive!'

'I wish I could fly,' states Corbin, watching as Dexter leaps up and hovers gently in front of him.

Dexter smiles back at Corbin's comment, before looking at the steam vortex above him. 'What *is* he doing up there?' he shrieks, raising an eyebrow at Melvin's bizarre movements.

'Oi! Mole-sprite!' yells Mrs Stamps. 'Would you please tie—*cough*—err, I mean…would you please replace your shoelace? You are making the place look very untidy.'

Corbin frowns. 'Lady…how many times do I have to tell you? My name is Corbin – and untidy? Have you looked around lately…?'

CHAPTER XVII

"HEE-HAW! HEE-HAW!"

DINKLE THE DONKEY

A single raindrop falls onto Amelia's fluttering wings; knocking her off balance. It is immediately followed by several more raindrops as the heavens open up and unleash a downpour over the village of Baston.

Edwin opens his cloak and gestures for Amelia to take shelter underneath it. He smiles, as he knows that this is the right thing to do, considering everything that Amelia had done for him recently.

'It looks as if it is going to rain quite hard,' states Edwin. 'I don't think that we'll be seeing the sun for a while – which is a shame…as I was getting rather used to feeling those rays on my skin. I also have a proper use for my sunglasses now.'

Amelia gently nods and stares at the mass of laundry, which swirls overhead. She sighs at Melvin's honourable, but darn right stupid idea to solve the laundry problem.

'What's the hold up, then…?' blasts Mrs Stamps, leaning down in front of Edwin and towards Amelia.

'Hold up?' questions Amelia, poking her head out from Edwin's cloak.

'Yes, the hold up…' begins Mrs Stamps. 'Are you not about to cast some marvellous spell that will solve all of this mess? I thought that you would have at least done something by now? With all due respect, you are the Laundry Fairy – and this is laundry…no?'

'It's not that easy, Mrs Stamps,' answers Amelia. 'Besides, I usually deal with laundry that—well, is not so much alive!'

'You must be able to do something?' continues Mrs Stamps. 'What about you, Edwin?'

'I fail to see what I can do,' says Edwin. 'I suppose we will just have to wait for the sun to come out.'

'The sun?' responds Mrs Stamps, pulling her blouse over the top of her head; shielding herself from the heavy rain.

'Yes…Amelia can use it to recharge her powers – and then hopefully she'll have enough magic in her to try and solve all of this.'

'I don't have the time for that!' bellows Mrs Stamps 'I need an outfit for—'

Suddenly, the sounds of the Corporal and his men arriving, cuts off Mrs Stamps, mid-sentence. She turns to observe the Corporal shouting and wielding his sword around in the air at a group of white linen shirts; pushing them all underneath the centre of the steam vortex, which continues to swirl overhead.

Mrs Stamps gasps as she observes a plump lady riding on the back of an extremely exhausted donkey. 'Oh my goodness,' she mutters, taking a step forward. 'Now that's something that you don't see everyday.'

As the Corporal and his men advance closer to the vortex, each and every piece of possessed laundry is dragged up into its whirling currents; currents that are caused by the circulating steam; steam that continues to swirl faster and faster; fuelled by Melvin and Eric on a flying steam-powered bicycle.

'Would you look at that, Sir?' yells Private Babe, pointing at the vortex with the tip of his sword.

The Corporal lowers his sword and tilts his head towards the sky; watching the last white linen shirt disappear into the thick, dense steam. He shifts his attention to his side, checks on the rest of his men and then sighs loudly as he realises that he and his men can now take a well deserved rest.

'Ah, Corporal…' begins the Reverend, striding across to meet him.'Was that the last of the laundry?'

The Corporal wipes the sweat from his brow with the cuff of his sleeve and stares hard at the Reverend. The Reverend waits patiently for an answer.

'Well, Reverend…we've gathered up all we can,' answers the Corporal. 'I can only say that we've done our best to round up all the laundry – although I fear there maybe a few pieces that still linger about the place. The men and I are extremely tired and fatigued. I'm just so glad that was the last of them. This rain is something that we could of done without – we were slipping and sliding everywhere!'

'I'm sorry, my good friend,' replies the Reverend. 'But I'm afraid there is not much I can do about the weather.'

'I would of thought you would have had a little word with your boss about that?' states the Corporal.

'My boss?'

'Yes…' interrupts Private Babe, pointing a finger into the sky. 'The man upstairs.'

'Melvin?' queries the Reverend, slightly confused. 'Why would I ask Melvin about why it is raining?'

'I meant our Lord, Reverend,' responds Private Babe, running the palm of his hand down his face and wiping off all the rain droplets that have acummulated there.

The Reverned nods. 'Oh, yes…of course. I was just testing you!'

'Yes, I thought you were, Reverend,' replies Private Babe, raising an eyebrow.

Private Babe's attention is suddenly shifted to Private Simmons, who rushes towards him; huffing and puffing loudly. Private Simmons halts in front of Private Babe, before approaching the Corporal.

'Sir!' yelps Private Simmons, pausing a moment to catch his breath. 'Sir?'

'Yes, Simmons?' replies the Corporal., stepping forward and holding Private Simmons upright; preventing him from falling to the ground.

'Sir, we have a very big problem!' continues Private Simmons.

'Go on…' instructs the Corporal, placing his sword carefully back into its scabbard. 'Anytime now would be good, Simmons. I haven't got all day!'

'Well, Sir…' begins Private Simmons. 'A number of the lads and I were trying to round up a few pieces of laundry that had clung to a couple of the buildings. I'm afraid I think we may have left some; some that we couldn't quite reach or get to. I also—'

'I wouldn't worry too much about them, Private,' interrupts the Corporal, while tilting his head up to the steam cloud. 'I imagine that my *Melvy* is almost ready to do something marvellous to all this laundry.'

'That's not all, Sir!' continues Private Simmons. 'We all saw – what looked like a huge pair of woollen pyjamas rising to it's feet near the village fountain. They were huge, Sir! Huge!'

Private Babe gasps. 'It sounds like those pyjamas from earlier. We need to get them to follow us here.'

The Corporal sighs.

'No rest for the wicked, Corporal,' states the Reverend, before politely smirking.

'You're certainly right there, Reverend!' answers the Corporal, pulling his sword out of its scabbard in one swift movement. 'Oh…and by the way…' begins the Corporal. 'The judge for the competition is over there. She is looking for you!'

'Which one is she?' asks the Reverend.

'The one riding the donkey,' answers the Corporal, pointing across towards Felicity, who sits on top of Dinkle. 'Plus, do you actually know what my *Melvy* is planning to do with all this laundry, Reverend? Oh…is that your fairy over there with—with a vampire?'

The Reverend turns. 'Ah yes, that's Edwin and our Laundry Fairy.'

'Is he dangerous?' enquires the Corporal, gazing at Edwin.

'No…he isn't. He saved our Laundry Fairy.'

'I see….so all is well now, then?' She can make this all better?'

The Reverend nods. The Corporal promptly turns, rallies up his men, and much to their dismay, leads them back to the centre of the village. The Reverend shifts his attention to Dinkle, who with a painstaking trot, carries Felicity towards him. Felicty pulls on Dinkle's reins and draws him to a gently stop in front of the Reverend. Dinkles leans down and chews on the grass at the Reverend's feet.

'I'm guessing from your attire, the crucifix around your neck and your angelic facial features, that you are the Reverend Clementine…? asks Felicity, glancing around at the chaos surrounding her, whilst waiting for the Reverend's response.

'Oh—*ahem*—yes, that's me,' answers the Reverend. 'I assume that you are one of the judges – here to judge the village for the competition?'

'I am the only judge. The others, they—err, let's not talk about what happened to them. My name is Felicity…Felicity Fullers. A real pleasure to meet you Reverend.'

'Please, call me Der—*cough-cough*—Reverend is fine.'

'I was also instructed to meet the mayor of the village…Timothy Oakes, I believe. Is he available?'

'Yes, he is just over there. So…err—Felicity…how are you finding our village…?' I hope that it's to your satisfaction?' The Reverend twiddles his thumbs and stares directly at Felicity, knowing perfectly well that he is not going to like her answer. He watches as Felicty removes her glasses, wipes them on her blouse and returns them onto the bridge of her nose.

'Well, my very good Reverend…' begins Felicity. 'In a nutshell…no! My impressions of the village did start off remarkably well, but to then be greeted by laundry that is very much alive, a couple of drunken soldiers laying on the grass next to the fountain, a huge whirling cloud of hot steam in the sky, which I can only assume has been caused by Melvlin Copernicus, and the fact I have just noticed a Laundry Fairy standing near a Vampire that can day walk, is really making me think about how serious you are in wanting to win the *Village of the Year Award.* Oh, is that a near dead crow on the grass over there?'

The Reverend gulps. 'So, that is a no?'

'At the moment, I'm very much indecisive,' replies Felicity. 'I am having quite alot of fun though. Now…I would very much like to meet Timothy Oakes, but I guess that can wait a little while.'

'Yes, I think it would be a good idea to wait a little – considering the situation.'

'Do you know what is going to happen?'

'Our Laundry Fairy is trying to think of how she can solve the dilemma with our laundry. The problem at the moment – is that she is low on magical power, or something like that. She can only charge up her powers by using sunlight – and since the sun is behind the clouds at present – it is proving difficult for her.

Felicirty raises an eyebrow. 'Oh, how very—very interesting,' she mutters. 'Seems like we *are* in a little bit of a dilemma, doesn't it?'

'It is very much that way, I'm afraid.'

'I imagine something will have to give soon. I really can't see Melvin staying up there all day. Besides, I have just seen a lightning bolt in the skies above the mountains – looks as if it's heading this way. He really doesn't want to get caught up in that…does he?'

'No, he doesn't. However, knowing Melvin, he would probably enjoy that excitement. He is a little crazy, you know?'

◆◆◆

Mr Dylan stands at the front window of his store. He stares with concern at a pair of bright red underpants that have attached themselves to the glass window pane.

He rarely ventures outside his store and for the last few hours, Mr Dylan has barricaded himself behind his counter top. However, the utter silence from the village green, that not only an hour ago had been filled with the sounds of a group of highly trained military men shouting, together with the moans of possessed laundry, has Mr Dylan intrigued to what has happened.

He turns his head looks through the window to the end of the village and gasps upon noticing the huge cloud of steam whirling above the wash-house. He stares in amazement; his eyes glistening at the sight before him. His stare is interrupted by movement from the other side of the village fountain. Letting out another gasp, Mr Dylan immedaitely steps back from the door as he watches a large pair of woollen pyjamas pound at the ground, before making their way towards the end of the village.

Not one to be eluded from the ongoings of the village and despite his nervousness and anxiety, Mr Dylan decides to open his front door, being careful not to make any loud sounds from the door bell hanging overhead. The bells makes a small jingle as he pulls the door open. He pops his head outside and glances at the underpants that remain on the glass window pane.

Mr Dylan closes the door behind him and quietly locks it with a small key. He cautiously makes his way towards the wash-house at the end of the village. He keeps himself close to the walls and the edges of the buildings, minimising the chance of attracting attention to himself. He pauses briefly to watch the large pair of woollen pyjamas pass behind the village hall and out of sight

◆◆◆

'As I was saying…' begins Mrs Stamps, turning herself around to face Amelia. 'I do not want to come across as being rude or ungrateful, but can I suggest that something be done quickly. I've run out of clean clothes to wear, and if this rain continues, my new hat is going to be completely ruined.'

Amelia sighs. 'I really don't know what you would like me to do, Mrs Stamps. I do not have the magical energy to cast any type of spell that has the capacity to sort all of this mess out.'

'And you need the sun to charge up do you? If you were fully charged you would be able to cast a spell and get my frilly dress washed and ready for this evening?'

'Yes, Mrs Stamps…I believe I could.' Amelia bites down hard on the end of her tongue, which stops her from releasing a variety of unladylike words at Mrs Stamps' demands.

'Then we must get the sun to appear,' annouces Mrs Stamps.

'Get the sun to appear? I think you mean to get the rainclouds to disappear,' retorts Edwin. 'The sun is already there – just hidden.'

'Don't you get smart with me, Edwin!' blasts Mrs Stamps.

Edwin raises his eyebrows in response to Mrs Stamps' tone of voice.

'Calm down, Mrs Stamps,' says Timothy, on hearing

Mrs Stamps' rant at Amelia and Edwin. 'I would imagine that Amelia is doing everything that she can. Remember…none of this is her doing, is it?'

'Timothy does have a point, Mrs Stamps,' adds Samuel.

Mrs Stamps turns to face Samuel and stares at him briefly, before shifting her eyes towards Edwin. She hangs her head low and accepts defeat. 'I guess you are right,' she mutters, before letting out a long sigh.

Everyone glances at the steam cloud above them, occasionally capturing sight of Melvin and Eric as the bicycle speeds around in circles through the steam.

'He must be thinking *what on Earth they are all doing down there?*,' says Samuel. 'He really can't keep flying around in circles can he? If he is going to do something himself – he would have done it by now, wouldn't he?'

'I believe that your assumption maybe true and accurate,' responds Edwin, adjusting the rim of his top hat and allowing rain water to drip onto the grass below. 'Oh, Amelia – just a question, if you please?'

'Yes, Edwin?' replies Amelia.

'How confident are you – that if you *were* fully charged you would be able to solve all of this mess that Melvin has created? It is possible that you can reverse his spell?'

There is a moment's pause as everyone looks across at Amelia; their eyes placed firmly upon her.

'Ummm, well…I guess if I was fully charged up, then—yes, I believe that I would be able to solve it all. I probably would not be able to do anything with all the laundry that has been torn to pieces, but I believe I can get all the other articles washed and back to their correct owners.'

'Then we just need to find some sunlight,' responds

Edwin, going into deep thought.

'Have you formulated a plan, Edwin?' asks Samuel

'Hmmm? Err…nope! What about you?'

'No…nothing at all.'

'It looks as if we are a little bit stumped, doesn't it?' adds Timothy.

'*H—h*—hello everybody…' begins Mr Dylan, who suddenly appears from nowhere. '*W—w*—what is everyone *d*—doing here?'

'Oh my-my, Mr Dylan!' yelps Samuel. 'Please do not sneak up on me like that – you nearly gave me a heart attack! But…hello to you also. It is actually nice to see you out and about in the village.'

'*I—I—I* was *w—w*—wondering *w*—what the blazes is *g—g*—going on?' replies Mr Dylan, looking in concern at the choas all around him.

'Where have you been all this time, Mr Dylan? On the moon?' quizzes Mrs Stamps. 'I guess you decided to shut yourself in that little store of yours, didn't you?'

'Yes…*t—t*—that is *pr—pr*—pretty much the extent of it, *M*—Mrs *S*—Stamps.'

'Well, Mr Dylan…' begins Samuel. 'We are trying to find a way to stop of all this madness with the laundry. Amelia, our Laundry Fairy, needs to charge up her powers and she needs the sunlight to do that. We have to try and—'

'Oh, be quiet Samuel,' interrupts Mrs Stamps. 'We don't have time for all these explanations to everyone that comes along. We need sunlight and we need it now!'

'*S*—sunlight?' enquires Mr Dylan. '*W*—why do you *n—n*—need sunlight—Oh good God! Is *th*—that a *v*—vampire?' he mutters, noticing Edwin standing nearby.

Samuel nods at Mr Dylan.

'Yes, Mr Dylan – sunlight,' answers Mrs stamps. 'As you can see, we are a little low on it at the moment.'

'*W*—*w*—what do *y*—you need that *f*—*f*—for?' asks Mr Dylan.'Oh my Lordy-Lord…is *th*—that our *L*—*L*—Laundry Fairy?'

Mrs Stamps sighs. 'Didn't Samuel just say why, Mr Dylan? I swear you are going deaf on us!'

Samuel nods his head again at Mr Dylan, surprised at Mr Dylan's cool and relaxed approach on seeing, not only a day-walking vampire in front of him, but also the village's Laundry Fairy. Anyone would think he had seen both of them before.

Mr Dylan stares at Edwin. Their eyes meet and Mr Dylan quickly re-directs his attention to Amelia.

'Hello, Mr Dylan…' says Amelia. 'To answer your question, and as Samuel has already said, I need the sunlight to charge up my magical powers. Without them I cannot cast any spells. I need to be fully charged to cast any spell capable of reversing this mess and I—

'I *h*—have *s*—*s*—sunlight!' interupts Mr Dylan.

'What do you mean – you have sunight?' asks Mrs Stamps. 'Sunlight is not something you just have, is it? Next you'll be saying that you have got some bottled up in your store –stored on some dusty shelf – in some dusty corner.'

'*T*—*t*—that's right, *M*—*M*—Mrs Stamps, *I*—I do,' responds Mr Dylan.

Timothy steps forward. 'Now, Mr Dylan…let's not get confused. We need proper sunlight and not some gimmick.'

'No-no…*I*—I have some *b*—*b*—bottled sunlight at *m*—my store,' retorts Mr Dylan. '*I*—If I rememeber it is *fr*—from the *f*—*f*—fire fairies of *El*—*El*—Elladon Forest.'

'You are telling us that you have rays of sunshine bottled up in your store?' enquires Amelia.

'Yes *t*—*t*—that's *r*—*r*—right,' responds Mr Dylan.

'That's wonderful news, Mr Dylan! I think I'm crying tears of joy right now,' adds Amelia.

'*I*—*I*—I have *t*—that also,' replies My Dylan, smiling softly.

'You have what?' questions Mrs Stamps.

'*T*—tears of *j*—*j*—joy,' answers Mr Dylan.

'You have got to be kidding me!' exclaims Mrs Stamps. 'You've got tears of joy bottled up?'

'*Y*—yes. *I*—I caught them *w*—when she was *cr*—*cr*—crying,' replies Mr Dylan.

Everone turns to each other in complete confusion and wonders if Mr Dylan is simply pulling their legs, or whether in fact he had bottled up the tears from some woman named Joy.'

'Never mind that…' begins Amelia. 'Would you mind terribly if we sort of borrowed a bottle of sunlight, Mr Dylan? Well, when I say borrowed – I actually mean…have.'

'Do you want me to go back and get it?' asks Mr Dyaln.

'No need for that…' begins Edwin. 'I have already taken the liberty of getting it for you.'

'What could you possibly mean – already got it?' enquires Timothy.

Edwin smirks. 'Well, during those moments that you were all talking about tears of joy, I, at lightning speed, dashed back to Mr Dylan's store, found the rays of sunshine and brought the jar back here.'

'H—h—how d—did you get inside the s—s—store,' asks Mr Dylan, knowing very well that he had locked his front door.

'Ah…well – yes…' begins Edwin. 'I sort of had to break in through a window. I'm terribly sorry about that. I will cover the costs of any repairs.'

'I—I thought *th—th*—that *y*—you have *t—t*—to ask *per—per*—permision *t—t*—to enter *a*—a premises, *Ed*—Edwin?' questions Mr Dylan.

'Only if it is a private residence,' answers Edwin. 'If it is a business, I can generally get away with it. I had to be invited into the tavern on arrival in the village, as Duncan lives there – as well as others – even if only temporarily…if you get my meaning.'

Mr Dylan nods.

'You must have done that very quickly, Edwin,' states Mrs Stamps. 'I hardly noticed that you had gone.

'Neither did I,' adds Amelia, with a confused look on her face, and wondering how he had returned so quickly, and yet not a single droplet of rain had fallen onto her tiny body.

'Let's not worry about the technicalities of how I can travel quickly,' exclaims Edwin.

'We have no time to lose, Edwin,' says Amelia. 'Quickly, empty the bottle of sunlight over me.'

'It would be much better if you hover over the bottle,' suggests Mr Dylan. 'The sunlight doesn't pour very easily – it likes to just shine out.'

Amelia nods, before flying out from underneath Edwin's cloak and into the rain.

She turns to face Edwin, who holds the bottle of sunlight tightly in his right hand. Edwin clutches around the screw on lid and slowly rotates it, loosening it. He lowers himself down and holds the bottle underneath Amelia, who hovers in the air in front of him. She tries her best to dodge the large raindrops that fall all around her.

Edwin glances at Amelia, who nods back at him; signalling to him that she is ready. With a quick flick of his wrist, Edwin unscrews and removes the bottle's lid.

Brilliant rays of yellowish light shine out of the top of the bottle and engulf Amelia in a blur of light and sparkles. There is a faint ringing sound; sounding like a thousand tiny angelic bells all ringing at the same time.

Edwin watches in amazement as Amelia absorbs the sunlight and charges her magical heart with its essence. The light radiates through her tiny body as she rotates slowly in the air; allowing her to absorb as much of the sunlight as possible.

Mrs Stamps gasps as she watches a small rainbow appear over Amelia; a result of the sunlight refracting through the many rain droplets that continue to fall to the ground around them all.

'Looks like the bottle is near empty,' states Mr Dylan, staring at the depleting bottle of sunlight.

'Is that going to be enough to charge up your heart Amelia?' questions Mrs Stamps, as Edwin drops the empty bottle, which lands softly on the damp grass.

'How do you feel, Amelia?' asks Edwin.

'I feel wonderful!' replies Amelia, flapping her wings excessively, before flying at speed around Edwin's head and landing on his shoulder.

'I believe I have enough energy to try and sort all the laundry out,' announces Amelia, lifting her head and staring up into the whirling steam cloud.

'Well, you'd better hurry…' begins Mrs Stamps. 'I have just lost sight of Melvin and Eric amongst that dense steam – and that lightning cloud seems to be getting a lot closer.'

Everyone turns and raises their heads. They stare at the dark rain clouds that begin to creep over the end of the village, before shifting their attention to the steam vortex overhead; a vortex full of swirling laundry.

'What are you going to do, Amelia?' asks Timothy, wiping the rain water off his face.

'I'm not too sure how, but I'm going to try and reverse Melvin's spell,' answers Amelia, removing her wand from underneath her belt. 'I'm going to need a little space to work here, Timothy. Could you get the villagers to move back please? I'm not sure what is going to happen when I attempt to reverse the spell.'

'Allow me—' says Edwin, brushing his cloak aside.

'Wait – please, Edwin!' interrupts the Reverend. 'It's probably not the best idea to barge into the crowds of villagers and demand they move.'

'Why ever not?' questions Edwin.

'Well, you're a vampire, aren't you? People are going to get a little scared and confused on seeing a vampire walking about in the village, especially during the daytime. Probably better to just let me and Timothy instruct them to move – don't you think?'

'Hmmm, yes I guess that is true and certainly a more logical approach,' responds Edwin, wrapping his cloak back around himself.

The Reverend and Timothy head towards the crowds of villagers; shouting and instructing them to move back from the steam cloud. To their surprise, the villagers listen to them, and they move like a herd of wildebeest towards the far wall of the wash-house.

Edwin looks down to the ground at his feet, feeling the fabric of his trouser leg being tugged hard by Corbin, who stares up at his Master, in hope of finding some shelter from the rain. Edwin smiles, picks up Corbin and cradles him in his arm, under his cloak.

Amelia flutters her wings and moves underneath the

raging storm cloud. She lifts her head and watches in concern at the ever-swirling mass of laundry articles overhead. She grits her teeth and holds her wand out in front of her.

There is a violent flash of light, (lighting to be precise!) that startles Amelia. She immediately retracts her wand as she observes Dexter crashing to the ground in front of her.

'ARGHHHHH!' screeches Dexter, as he rolls around in the damp grass, while attempting to extinguish a small fire that has started at the end of his tail; blowing down on it hard.

'Oh my, Dexter!' yelps Amelia. 'Are you okay? I'm guessing that you have just been hit by a bolt of—'

'Lightning,' interrupts Dexter, raising his tail to his mouth and sucking on it. 'I think I'll stay on the ground for a while,' he adds.

'Probably a good idea,' responds Amelia, returning her attention to the steam cloud above and pointing her wand towards it.

'We must hurry!' announces the Reverend.

Amelia starts to mutter some magical words under her breath and aims her wand into the centre of the steam vortex. The tip of her wand glows and radiates a soft orange light, before Amelia herself, begins to glow with an intense aura of light. Her wings flap back and forth; a perfect synchronised motion, full of harmonic rings and hums. She continues to speak enchants and magical words; words that to anyone else would be difficult to pronounce, let alone, understand.

The crowd of villagers stare up in amazement; mesmerised by the colourful aura of light projecting from Amelia.

Timothy and the Reverend stand aside one another

and clutch gently onto each other's attire.

Mrs Stamps, Samuel and Mr Dylan huddle together; shielding themselves from the intense rain that pours down hard around them.

Edwin stands still and embraces the rain. He moves not a single muscle as he stares at Amelia. Corbin pokes his head through a gap in his Master's cloak and glances up at the steam cloud.

THE AIR HUMS AND CRACKLES.

Suddenly, a piercing high-pitched tone is heard from the tip of Amelia's wand, causing everyone around to cover their ears with their hands; apart from Edwin, who continues to remain perfectly still.

BOOM!

A loud sonic boom resonates across the village, causing ripples of turbulent air, which then quickly dissipate around Amelia. Her wand glows brighter as she continues to speak her magic words; repeating them over and over again. Her voice projects power and intensity as she channels the magical energy from within her heart, through her body and towards the tip of her wand.

The rain changes direction upon meeting Amelia; momentarily pouring horizontally, before continuing to the ground in a way that you would expect rain to.

Amelia lifts her head and focuses her efforts on keeping her wand steady at the end of her trembling hand. She extends her arm out as far as it will go.

Without any warning, there is a huge explosion of orange light, and a continuous ray of magical energy shoots out from the end of Amelia's wand, and up into the centre of the steam vortex; a ray that is so intense it causes everyone to shield their eyes, including Edwin, who promptly pushes his sunglasses back up the bridge of his nose.

Edwin tilts his head towards Amelia, to observe the end of her wand pulse and emit a powerful ray of magical energy. With his eyes wide open, Edwin watches the rays of light penetrate the steam above them. Small explosions of light are seen deep within the dense cloud, followed by several crackling sounds.

The high-pitched tone continues to pierce the rain and steam; producing sonics that are out of the range for human hearing.

With a huge flash of light and a deafening boom, Amelia's wand stops emitting energy. The glow from her wand's tip fades as Amelia drops it to the ground, before she herself, plummets to the damp grass below; drained of all magical power and energy.

Edwin immediately rushes to her aid, stretching out his right arm and catching her safely in his open hand. He cups his other hand around her and shields her from the rain.

There is an eerie silence in the air. It is broken only by the continuous patter of rain on damp grass, the occasional rolling of thunder and the distant roaring of Melvin's steam powered bicycle.

◆◆◆

'What is happening, Eric?' yells Melvin. 'It seems as if all the laundry is starting to disappear!'

'I don't know, lad,' replies Eric. 'But you are right – the laundry is disappearing and some of it is not even moving – it seems as if it's not alive anymore.'

Melvin lowers his head. He watches as item after item of laundry vanishes before his very eyes or becomes suddenly lifeless. He gasps at articles that continue to spin through the rotating vortex of steam.

'Slow us down, Melvin!' shouts Eric. 'We may be able to get a better idea of what's going on. I'm hoping Amelia has managed to cast a spell to sort all of this mess out.'

'I truly hope so,' answers Melvin, turning a couple of dials and slowing down the bicycle. Much to his relief, the thick dense steam ejecting at high pressure from the rear of the bicycle, begins to dissipate; clearing a view around them.

Laundry that had been very much alive just a few moments earlier, starts to gracefully fall to the ground. It sways back and forth as the turbulent current starts to slow down. Pieces of laundry continue to vanish in flashes of light.

'Look, Melvin!' yelps Eric. 'I think she has done it!'

'She has?'

'Yes, I believe so. She is down there, cheering with everyone. The laundry doesn't seem—well, so much alive anymore. I think she has solved it.'

'But where is it all disappearing to?'

'I'm not sure, lad. But I'm guessing it is all being returned to their owners.'

Melvin smiles. 'What about the other bits?'

'The other bits?' quizzes Eric.

'Yes, the shredded bits? Pieces of laundry that the Corporal and his men have sliced into pieces.'

'It looks as if they are all falling to the ground.'

Melvin and Eric continue to watch as pieces of laundry fall to the ground below; some of which barely touches the damp grass, before quickly disappearing.

'Maybe we should land and see what is happening?' suggests Eric.

'Yes…good idea,' responds Melvin, shifting the joystick to the right and guiding the bicycle out of the steam; cautiously avoiding pieces of laundry.

Eric squints his eyes.

◆◆◆

The crowd of villagers cheer as they watch the laundry miraculously returning to its normal state (well the majority of it.) They stare at each other in confusion and wonder to themselves, where each piece of laundry is disappearing to. A few of the villagers moan and cry as they watch pieces of shredded fabric fall to the grass; pieces that had previously been parts of their shirts, trousers and various other items of clothing.

'You've done it!' announces Edwin. 'You've really done it!'

'That she has,' adds Mrs Stamps. 'Very well done – but the laundry seems to be disappearing in a flash of light. Where is it all going to?'

Amelia smiles. 'Please don't worry about that, Mrs Stamps. I think you'll find that when you go back to your washing basket, all your laundry should be back to normal.'

'All of it?' interrupts Timothy

Amelia lowers her head. 'I'm afraid not all of it Timothy. I can only do so much…you know?'

Timothy gasps. 'You mean there is nothing at all you can do with all these shredded pieces?'

Amelia turns and watches strips of shredded linen, cotton and silk fall from the sky. 'I'm sorry…but no.'

'Then, what shall I tell the villagers about their clothes?' asks Timothy.

'Come, Timothy…' begins the Reverend. 'I think

that now would be a good time to address the village and explain what has happened?'

'Do I really have to?' responds Timothy.

'Well, you can either do it right now – addressing everyone in one big hit,' replies the Reverend. 'Or later, when they'll be lining up outside your office – you'll be busy for weeks.'

Timothy sighs and nods his head.

Suddenly, the roaring and howling sounds of a steam-powered bicycle landing on the grass, grabs everyone's immediate attention.

'Amelia!' screams Melvin, dismounting the bicycle and knocking Eric to the floor.

'Watch it, lad!' bellows Eric, picking himself up and wiping himself down.

Melvin rushes across to Amelia, who is still being cupped in Edwin's hand. 'Edwin, you—saved her?'

Edwin nods. 'I did.'

Melvin, lost for words, takes a small bow towards Edwin. 'Then I thank you, sincerely – I really do. I must admit I had my doubts about you, Edwin. But I guess that no harm is done. Oh! I have just realised that you can walk in the daylight. Did she—'

'Melvin…is that you?' says Amelia, standing to her feet, in the palm of Edwin's hand, before fluttering her wings gently. She hovers across to Melvin, smiles and then gives him a gentle kiss on his forehead. Melvin instantly turns a bright shade of crimson.

'Dexter, ole chum!' yelps Melvin, reacting to Dexter's smoking tail. 'Are you okay?'

'Do you really want me to answer that question, Melv?' screeches Dexter.

Everyone laughs.

HEE-HAW! HEE-HAW!

'Seems like your donkey is happy, Felicity,' states the Reverend, patting Dinkle gently on the head.

'Yes, he does, doesn't he?' replies Felicity. 'So what happens now, Reverend? Oh, and this fine gentleman must be Timothy, yes?'

Timothy approaches Felicity, drops down to his knees and begins to cry at her feet.

'Oh, come on Timothy…it is not that bad, is it?' questions the Reverend, while Felicity looks on in concern.

'What are you talking about, Reverend? It is bad. I've just seen a pair of my favourite trousers ripped to shreds – no doubt hacked to pieces by the Corporal and his men. I'll never find another pair like them.'

'Talking of the Corporal and his men…where are they all?' asks Samuel.

CHAPTER XVIII

"Remember friends...without stupidity, there is no intellect - and without ugliness, there is no beauty."

FELICITY FULLERS

Timothy and Felicity sit side by side on top of the fountain wall. Felicity pushes her glasses up the bridge of her nose and gazes across the village. She shifts her attention to the ground in front of her and stares in amazement at thousands of shiny copper coins, an assortment of shredded fabric and Private Trout and Private Myles, who have both passed out on the grass in front of her.

She watches as many of the villagers try to make sense of what they are going to do to get their beloved village back to its former condition; many of them already picking up pieces of broken tiles, bricks and woodwork that has fallen or broken off from their homes and businesses.

'Does the village have some sort of bank, Timothy?' asks Felicity, staring across at Eric, who starts to fill his pockets with handfuls of copper coins.

'No, ma'am,' replies Timothy. 'Why do you ask?'

'All these copper coins, Timothy. There must be quite a lot of money scattered about the village? Maybe you could gather it all up and use the money to help the village get back to how it was? Just a thought.'

'It would certainly have to be an extremely large bank to accommodate all of it. Besides, I'm sure Eric, our blacksmith, will make very good use of it all. He is always complaining about the ever-increasing price of copper. But we must remember…all of this copper isn't technically ours – it all belongs to Dexter.'

Felicity pauses in thought. 'What would he need all this copper for, though?'

Timothy chuckles. 'True – very true,' he replies.

'Anyway, Timothy…' begins Felicity. 'I've called you over here – as I imagine you are dying to find out about my decision to whether or not to award you with the *Village of the Year Award*?'

Timothy turns towards Felicity and twiddles his thumbs in anticipation. 'Yes…very much. How did we do?' he says, knowing very well that unless Felicity has some very weird way of judging, the village has not won the award and he will not be receiving a chest of gold coins.

Felicity looks over the top of her glasses and gives Timothy a bemused look. She tilts her head towards the far side of the village green and nods at Timothy;

indicating to him to take a good look at the damage and untidiness around him.

Timothy sighs. 'We didn't score well, then…?'

'You didn't score at all, my good man.' Felicity laughs loudly. 'But, I did have a lot of fun – I must admit. There is always next year if you are still up for it? I feel as if this village is going to get pretty darn interesting over the next few months.'

'What do you mean?'

Felicity stands to her feet. 'Well, look…' begins Felicity, pointing across the village green. 'You have a vampire that walks in the daylight and a mystical fairy that does your dirty laundry for you – both walking about – plain as day! People love that sort of thing. All it takes is one little review in the local newspaper and people will flood into your village.'

'How would we get a good review?'

Felicity winks at Timothy. 'You leave that to me. I'm a resourceful woman – I have my ways.'

Timothy smiles.

'Ah…there you are, Timothy,' voices the Reverend, stepping over the motionless body of Private Myles. 'And we meet again, Felicity,' he adds, offering a hand out to Felicity.

Timothy shakes his head inconspicuously at the Reverend and hangs his head low; indicating to him that his mission to succeed in winning the *Village of the Year Award*, has been unsuccessful.

'Oh…that is such a terrible shame,' mutters the Reverend, turning to Felicity, who smiles back at him.

'I hope that you understand, Reverend?' responds Felicity. 'There was no way I could tick any of the boxes on my scoresheet.'

The Reverend nods. 'But I have spent a great deal

of time and effort ensuring the village is ready – surely we deserve a—'

Suddenly the sound of the villagers screaming, cuts the Reverend off mid-sentence.

'What's going on over there?' questions Timothy, lifting himself to his feet and looking across to the outer limits of the village.

'Melvin!' yells the Reverend, shouting across to him. 'Please tell me that you haven't performed another one of your spells and it's gone wrong again? We've only just sorted all the laundry out.'

Standing outside the entrance to the tavern, Melvin turns towards Timothy and holds his hand up to his ear; cupping it to indicate to Timothy that he can't hear a word he is saying.

The commotion at the other end of the village, immediately grabs Melvin's attention, and he watches in confusion as masses of villagers begin to scarper in all directions; screaming and rushing back into the surrounding buildings.

Mrs Stamps steps up beside Melvin and places her hands firmly on her hips. She joins Melvin in trying to observe what is causing all the screaming and shouting at the end of the village.

'What *is* that?' questions Mrs Stamps, raising her hand to her forehead and shielding her eyes from the sun. 'Whatever it is – is it travelling very speedily.'

Melvin squints his eyes and tries to focus in on what Mrs Stamps is seeing.

'I'm really not sure what to make of it, Mrs Stamps,' replies Melvin. 'Something bad – as it seems to be causing the villagers to run away from it. They are screaming and shouting. Look at them all!'

'Do you think that maybe you've forgotten some

random pieces of laundry, Melvin?' asks Mrs Stamps. 'Maybe a few pairs of underpants from earlier – have managed to elude you …?'

In a bright flash of blurred light, Amelia suddenly appears and lands very gracefully on Melvin's left shoulder. She sits herself down and wraps her arms around her bent knees. Her wings gently flap behind her.

'I don't think that it's laundry, Mrs Stamps,' answers Amelia. 'I'm pretty sure that I have accounted for each and every piece of laundry, including all the ones that have been ripped to shreds by the Corporal and his men. All the villagers' laundry is neatly washed and with its correct owner. But I'm afraid there is a limit to my repairing skills.'

'It could simply be Edwin taking a little walk through the village…' begins Mrs Stamps. 'Now that he can walk in the daylight – maybe he is just meeting the locals and they are having—well, they are a little shocked and scared at the sight of him?'

Melvin nods his head up and down.

'No…no that is certainly not the case,' responds Edwin, stepping out from inside the tavern, alongside Corbin, Dexter and Samuel. 'I'm right here. But I guess I could go have a look and see what's going on.'

'Yes, good idea—' replies Mrs Stamps. 'You've got exceptionally good hearing, did you know?'

'Here, Melvin…hold this,' instructs Edwin, placing one of Duncan's pickled eggs into the palm of Melvin's hand. Melvin stares down at the greenish coloured egg and cringes at the pungent aroma it gives off. 'That I have, Mrs Stamps…' adds Edwin.

THERE IS A FLASH OF RED LIGHT.

Edwin instantly transforms into bat form, soars into

the sky and heads towards the end of the village. He looks beneath him at a crowd of villagers that run off in every direction. He tilts his head and lets out a loud squawk, upon observing Officer Locks rampaging through the village, holding a large tree branch in his hands and swinging it angrily at everything and anything that gets in his way. Edwin quickly changes direction and heads back to the tavern entrance.

THERE IS ANOTHER FLASH OF RED LIGHT.

'It's the Officer – he is back!' announces Edwin, slightly panicked and shifting his eyes towards Amelia.

Melvin gasps.

'But—but how did he escape?' questions Amelia, knowing that Edwin is probably asking himself exactly the same question. 'Is he a werewolf? Or is he in—'

'Human form,' interrupts Edwin. 'But he looks very enraged. He is hitting everything he sees with a large tree branch. I'm not sure how he escaped. That's not important right now, is it?'

'Is he still after you, Amelia?' asks Mrs Stamps.

'Yes, I believe he must be,' replies Amelia, taking flight from Melvin's shoulders.

'Well, he is certainly persistent,' adds Mrs Stamps, gripping her hands tightly around the handle of her pitchfork. 'What shall we do?'

Timothy, the Reverend and Samuel, join the rest of the group, and they gaze across towards the area where the others are looking.

'Oh, my goodness…' begins the Reverend. 'Is that Officer Locks back again? I must say…he does look slightly—well, how do I put it politely…? Annoyed?'

'The Officer?' questions Felicity, turning to the Reverend. 'Who, or what, is the Officer?'

'He is a very nasty man who broke my yo-yo,'

whimpers Corbin. 'But he is also a horrible and smelly werewolf.'

'A werewolf…?' yelps Felicity, in a shocked and panicked tone.

Amelia turns towards Felicity. 'Yes, a werewolf – the same one that tried to kill me earlier – and if it wasn't for Edwin, he probably would have succeeded.'

Felicity places a hand over her open jaw.

'We must get the law to arrest this crazy madman!' announces Melvin. 'Lock him up in the jail and throw away the key – and then lock him up again, just to make sure!'

'Err…Melvin…' begins Dexter, taking a couple of steps towards him. 'I think you'll find that he is the law…remember? You great numpty!'

'Oh…oh, yes,' mumbles Melvin, turning a slight shade of crimson in embarrassment.

'As Mrs Stamps said…what shall we do?' questions the Reverend. 'He is getting closer and closer. Maybe we can ask the Corporal and his men to help in dealing with him? Where are they anyways?'

'They all went back to their camp by the river,' answers Dexter. 'Something about – many of them complaining of psychological issues after battling a colossal pair of woollen pyjamas.'

'Well, that is just great, isn't it?' states Timothy, before letting out a loud sigh.

Edwin takes a few steps forward and pushes his cloak aside. 'Don't worry people – I will deal with this demon. It's time to put an end to him for once and—'

'I will not have blood spilt in this village, Edwin!' interrupts the Reverend. 'Besides, if you are planning to do what I think you are, it is not going to look too good for you is it? You are trying to adapt into the village – and the villagers will see you as a cold-hearted killer – if your first act while being able to walk in the sunlight…is to kill!'

Edwin pauses. 'Yes, that is very much true. Oh, Amelia…is there anything that you can do with your powers?'

'I'm afraid I can't, Edwin,' answers Amelia. 'My spells are not really suitable for dealing with enraged werewolves. I don't think they will be much use at all. Unless you want his clothes washed—'

'What about you, Melvin?' continues Edwin. 'Surely there must be a spell in your arsenal that can deal with the Officer in a more—*cough-cough*—humane way?'

'NO!' screeches Dexter.' You seriously think it's a good idea to cast another spell, Melvin? Look what happened with the last spell you cast!'

Melvin turns towards Dexter. 'Actually, Dex – and I believe Edwin will agree with me. My last spell turned out exactly the way I planned it to – did it not, Edwin?'

'I must admit that statement it true,' replies Edwin.

'Well, the spell before that, then!' snaps Dexter, in a frustrated tone. 'That one didn't go too—'

'Enough of this!' interrupts Mrs Stamps. 'He is heading this way. Quick do something!'

'I could just go over and talk to him man to man,' suggests Timothy, taking a small step forward.

'Do you seriously believe that an enraged werewolf is going to listen to you, Timothy?' retorts Mrs Stamps, letting out a couple of tuts. 'Don't be so stupid!'

'I don't think that you will have much of a choice, shortly,' says the Reverend. 'Quick, Melvin…you must be able to do something?'

Melvin scratches his head. 'Err, I'm not sure how much magical energy I have left. I'm still rather—'

'Anything, Melvin!' interrupts Dexter, watching the raging Officer get closer. 'Anything at all will do right now, Melvin! I give you my full permission to cast any spell and I'll take full responsibility if you get it completely wrong.'

'Okay-okay…give me a few moments,' responds Melvin, reaching into his robe pocket and removing his journal; opening it with a wave of his hand, and with the muttering of some magical enchants.

'Hurry, Melvin!' yelps Amelia. 'He is getting closer!'

'Don't rush me…' mumbles Melvin. 'Patience is a virtue, you know?'

Mrs Stamps increases her grip around the handle of her pitchfork.

Edwin takes a step forward and flares out his cloak. He stands defensively in front of his newly made friends, and will do his best to protect them from the Officer, who with every second, is getting closer and closer towards them.

Melvin nervously flicks through the pages of his journal. 'Nope…err, no not that one…hmmm, err… nope…absolutely not! Hmmm maybe-maybe…' he mutters to himself.

'Have you found anything useful?' asks Dexter, trying to look over Melvin's arm at the pages of his journal, while keeping a watchful eye on Officer Locks.

'Err…well unless he has a sudden craving for some tomato chutney, there is really not—oh wait!' Melvin lets out a chuckle. 'Oh my-my, yes…this could work. You're going to love this spell!'

'Get on with it, Melvin!' blasts Mrs Stamps.

'What have you found, Melv?' asks Dexter.

'Be patient, Dexter,' replies Melvin, before going over some magical words in his mind.

'ARGHHHHH!' Where is she, vampire…?' howls Officer Locks, leaping into the air and landing in front of Edwin. 'Where is the Laundry Fairy?'

'Now, that is none of your concern, is it?' responds Edwin.

'You stole her from me!' roars Officer Locks.

'Err…no, I think *technically* you'll find that I rescued her, after—well…yes I suppose I stole her in the first place, but that—'

'ENOUGH!' yells Officer Locks. 'I will take her back from you – take her heart.'

'I'm afraid I can't let you do that,' snarls Edwin.

'Oh…is that so…?' begins Officer Locks. 'And you are going to stop me are you?'

'Well, maybe not me, but I know a man that can—' replies Edwin.

There is a moment's pause…

Dexter leans slowly towards Melvin. 'Err…Melv?' whispers Dexter. 'Now would be a very good time to cast your spell. I think that was your cue. You've just made Edwin look a little stupid. He practically set you up to cast your spell!'

'Oh, hang on one moment, Dex,' mutters Melvin. 'I'm struggling to read my own handwriting here—'

The Officer tilts his head; looking to the side of Edwin. He gasps as he notices Amelia hovering next to Mrs Stamps. 'Oh, there you are, little one,' he states, taking a small side-step around Edwin.

Edwin hisses. 'I will not let you take her!'

The Officer continues to stare at the familiar faces gathered up behind Edwin. 'Look at you all! You are all pathetic! Do you honestly think that you have the combined strength to stop me? You are all weak – and you would have to be as hard as a rock to defeat me.'

The Officer threateningly cracks his knuckles.

'It's funny that you say that, Officer…' begins Melvin, looking up from his journal and pointing a trembling finger towards the Officer.

'Enough of this petty and pointless talk!' shouts Officer Locks, clenching his fists together and readying himself to leap into the air.

THERE IS AN INTENSE FLASH OF LIGHT

A crackling bolt, of what can only be described as lightning, shoots out from Melvin's fingertip and hits Officer Locks; instantly freezing him in place. Mrs Stamps gasps in horror at the ghastly pose that Melvin has captured the Officer in.

Melvin and the others watch as the Officer's skin begins to change colour; turning from a pale pink to a darkened grey. Every part of his body stiffens and creaks as it comes to a sudden stop. His skin hardens and coarsens; opening up small pores on its surface, and shedding small dust particles, which drop to the grass below. The sound of stone crunching echoes in the air as Melvin's finger ceases to cast out the magical lightning bolt.

Everyone gasps at the sight before them.

'Oh, my Lord…' begins the Reverend. 'What sort of spell was that, Melvin?'

'*I*—*I*—I don't know what went wrong there,' stutters Melvin. 'I really didn't mean to do that!'

'What do you mean?' asks Mrs Stamps. 'You've just turned the Officer into stone – surely that is what you were meant to do?'

Melvin smiles and stares back down at the pages of journal. He turns over the page to check if he has misread something, or if there is an extra part of the spell he hadn't noticed.

'Err…not really…' begins Melvin. 'That was meant to be a **shrinking spell**. I must have perhaps written the wrong spell down on this page in my youth. I imagine I have mixed up the **shrinking spell**, with the ***rock and a hard place spell*** – that would make complete sense.'

Edwin steps slowly towards the stone version of Officer Locks. He pauses briefly before flicking his pointy finger onto the Officer's hardened forehead; causing a few small fragments of stone to fall to the floor.

Dexter looks on in amazement. 'Well that's certainly impressive, Melvin,' he states. 'I'm truly impressed with that one.'

'Aim to please!' answers Melvin, with a smug look on his face.

The Reverend cups his hands behind his back and strolls slowly around the frozen body of Officer Locks. 'Yes…very impressive, Melvin,' he announces.

Amelia flies across to Edwin. 'There is some irony in the fact that the Officer has turned to dust—well rock, rather than you,' she states.

Edwin smiles.

'What on Earth are we going to do with this monstrosity, then?' questions Mrs Stamps.

'You know…you could replace the statue in the fountain – the one the Corporal broke earlier?' suggests Dexter, letting out a small chuckle.

'Don't be so idiotic, Dex!' snaps Melvin. 'Why would the good people of the—'

'Actually, wait…' interrupts Felicity, stepping aside Melvin. 'I actually think that is a wonderful idea and it would not look out of place in the fountain. It will be a reminder to the village of all the heroic events that took place today.'

'Exactly what I meant to say…' expresses Melvin, with a slight grin on his face.

'Remember friends…without stupidity, there is no intellect – and without ugliness, there is no beauty,' announces Felicity.

'Are you calling me stupid and ugly…?' queries Dexter, flaring his nostrils.

'Oh, not at all little dragon,' whispers Felicity, into Dexter's ear. 'But maybe he is, huh?' she adds, tilting her head towards Melvin.

CHAPTER XIX

"I'm very disappointed that I didn't get to claim the Village of the Year Award, but at least I've found this new venture... now, was that sweet or salted you asked for?"

Timothy Oakes

Not less than a week ago, the village of Baston lay peacefully on the eastern banks of the Cobalt River. Today, although still on the banks of the river, it is far from being a tranquil and peaceful haven.

Word of recent events have travelled afar; tales of a mystical place where dirty laundry is instantly washed by a magical fairy; a vampire can greet you in the middle of the daytime and the village mayor does some *pretty* amazing things with kernels of corn.

With the increased amount of people expected to

flood into the village in the near future, Duncan the Tavern Keeper is planning to build an extension to the tavern; allowing many more characters to stay at his establishment. The village itself is also in need of a new Officer of the Law and is currently taking applications from all realms of life.

Many of the locals have recently signed a petition, barring any hairy-like humans from applying for the position, hoping to not have a repeat of a certain recent incident involving a werewolf.

At present, it is looking most likely that the new Officer of the Law could be a mermaid, although certain highly intellectual villagers have voted that the practicality could be hindered by a certain lack of interconnecting water around the village. There is also a concern that turning the village water fountain into a jail, is an engineering task that is *simply* out of the question.

◆◆◆

Duncan digs deep inside his pocket for another iron nail and places it between his lips; biting down on it gently. He picks up a mallet from the floor and whilst holding a new piece of freshly cut glass into position with his other hand, he drives the iron nail into the wooden frame with several strikes of the mallet.

He takes a step back to admire his craftsmanship, before reaching back into his pocket to remove a handful of nails. One by one he frantically hammers them into the framework; tightly clamping the glass pane into place.

Loud knocks, taps and bangs echo around the main room of the tavern, as the Corporal and his men put their combined carpentry skills to the test; attempting to repair the wooden tables, chairs, windows, doors and anything else they'd broken a few days earlier, whilst attempting to protect the village from an invasion of possessed laundry.

'Seems like we are always putting things back together,' moans the Corporal. 'I really can't wait until I get back to River's Bend and can have a nice hot soak in my bath tub.'

Private Babe, holding a table leg and half a broken chair, turns towards his superior 'This is the least we can do, Sir.'

'Huh?' replies the Corporal.

'We did sort of wreck the place in the panic, Sir,' adds Private Babe, inspecting the damaged table leg.

'Hmmm…I suppose you are right!' retorts the Corporal, turning an up-turned table to its correct orientation and bashing a new table leg into a slotted hole with his huge bare fist.

'Besides…' begins Private Babe. 'The Reverend will be allocating our payment shortly. Just think of all the pleasures you can have with that shiny gold coin.'

'For starters – buying myself some new clothes! Look at me…I have completely soiled my clothes over the last few days.'

Private Babe scrolls over the Corporal's attire and tries not to smirk or grin as he observes his superior bending his body into some very uncomfortable and disturbing positions; showing Private Babe the extent of his troubles.

'OUCH! Ruddy hammer!' yelps Duncan, dropping the hammer to the floor and immediately placing his thumb inside his mouth; sucking on it hard. 'I think I need a mead,' he howls, pacing towards the bar.

'I believe that you also need a bandage,' chuckles the Corporal, tucking his shirt inside his trousers.

'Anyone for drinks?' declares Duncan.

Loud shouts and cheers fill the room, and the Corporal's men huddle around Duncan, at the front of the bar

'Sir? Hello, Sir?' says Myles to the Corporal.

'Yes, Myles?' replies the Corporal.

'Err…how much longer are we going to be doing all these repairs? It's just that—'

'As long as it takes, Myles!' bellows the Corporal. 'If you hadn't decided to launch several pieces of furniture out of the main window – then we could have been out of here a lot earlier…couldn't we?'

'Oh, right…yes—my fault, Sir,' whimpers Myles. 'It's just that I was about to get attacked by an incredibly huge leather apron…and I sort of panicked a little. I didn't know what else to do, Sir.'

'Well, it's all done and dusted now, but due to your little panicked episode – we have been asked to stay and pick up the pieces.'

Myles lowers his head and turns slowly back towards Private Trout.

'Seems like he is in a foul mood with me, Trout,' states Private Myles, scratching the side of his neck.

'Ah…just ignore him,' responds Private Trout. 'He is just missing his *Melvy*.'

Private Myles and Private Trout snigger, and then promptly stop themselves as the Corporal gives them both a menacing stare.

Duncan proceeds to pour out several large tankards of honey mead. He lifts his head up to Private Babe.

'Oh, go on then, Duncan…one for the road, huh?' announces Private Babe, with a slight gulp.

'You know what?' begins Duncan. 'What on Earth do you serve a vampire to drink? It's been bugging me all morning.'

'I assume you are talking about Edwin?' asks Private Babe.

'I am, yes. He doesn't drink anything of the stronger variety…I already know that.'

'Well then, Duncan…I imagine that has pretty much limited his options, hasn't it?'

'Sorry to interrupt…' begins Private Myles. 'But you could just give him some water – that's a good enough drink—no wait! No—no, that's not going to work – forget that!'

'Why?' questions Duncan. 'Something wrong with my water?'

'Oh, not at all. It's very refreshing,' replies Private Myles. 'But I've seen that the Reverend also regularly drinks in our tavern. We don't want him inadvertently and mistakenly blessing the water, do we?'

'No—no…not at all!' yelps Duncan. 'That could get very nasty.'

Myles nods gently at Duncan.

'Right, troops…I think it's time for a little sing-song,' announces the Corporal, raising his tankard up high. 'Grab yourselves a brew, chaps – and let's sing the afternoon away.'

With tankards in hands, the Corporal, his men and Duncan, burst into a lively chorus of song and dance, whilst filling their stomachs with warm honey mead.

Before long, the heightened sounds of tankards clashing and feet stomping on the wooden floor, begin to fill the room. As the symphony of untuned singing voices reaches a climax, it is interrupted by a couple of very loud screams and lots of cursive shouting from outside, which brings everyone inside the tavern to a sudden and still-like halt.

'Ah, now don't worry everyone...' begins Duncan. 'That's probably just Melvin. Sounds like he is still struggling to control that ridiculous contraption of his!'

'MELVIN!' squeals the Corporal, dropping his tankard to the floor and clapping his hands together excitedly.

◆◆◆

Melvin's steam-powered bicycle whistles and hisses, before letting out a small squeak, and coming to an abrupt stop outside the front of the tavern. Melvin frantically rotates a few dials and pulls on a couple of levers, which reduces the bicycle's noise to a gentle purring sound. A small trail of vented steam steadily ejects from the exhausts and into the air.

'Apologies all...sorry about that!' shouts Melvin, turning to face a small array of villagers, which have had to suddenly dive out of his way, for risk of getting knocked over by Melvin's *less than perfect* driving skills.

'Melvin, you really need to take a little more care,' expresses Amelia, sitting on Melvin's shoulder and revealing her presence.

'Oh, Amelia...it's you,' replies Melvin, shifting his head to face her. 'Where did you pop up from?'

'I get everywhere these days, Melvin. I thought a man of your intelligence, would have worked that out by now?'

Melvin blushes and then forcefully kicks at a piece of bent metal with his foot. It springs out and locks into place; holding the bicycle upright. Melvin then disembarks the bicycle in the most elegant manner he knows of; raising his robe to his knees and swinging his left leg over the bicycle's framework.

'I really should spend a little more time trying to understand how this bicycle operates,' states Melvin. 'Eric has added all these extra levers and gadgets, and I have absolutely no idea what they all do. They truly puzzle me.'

'You must remember, Melvin. It's not just a simple bicycle, anymore,' states Amelia.

'What do you mean…a simple bicycle? I have you know that this bicycle is a mass of complex individual engineered systems that work in complete unison with each other—'

'I mean…it can now fly. You'll have to get used to that as well.'

Melvin giggles. 'I can hardly get used to controlling it on the ground – let alone in the air. I might leave it a little while before I venture into that again.'

'Probably best,' answers Amelia, taking flight in front of Melvin.

'I'm actually glad that I don't have to keep winding up my watch every time I want to try and find you,' says Melvin, adjusting his hat.

'Well it's so much easier to simply slow myself down…relax a little,' responds Amelia. 'Oh, and I don't do that for just anyone…you know?'

Melvin briefly smiles, before a saddened expression creeps over his face.

'What's wrong?' asks Amelia, fluttering her wings a little faster to move closer to Melvin.

'Err…well—no it doesn't matter,' stutters Melvin.

Melvin lowers his head gently, using the rim of his spellbinder's hat to mask his face from Amelia. He whimpers gently; hiding the fact from her by sneakily pretending there is something in his eye; poking it repeatedly with the tip of his finger.

'Are you crying, Melvin?' asks Amelia.

'Nope, not at all. Spellbinders don't cry. They eject watery concoctions of toxins and endorphins that are triggered by emotional responses—'

'Melv…?'

'Oh, okay—okay. I may have shed the tiniest of tears, but that's because I'm going to miss you terribly.'

'I'll miss you too, Melvin. I really will,' expresses Amelia, leaning forwards and giving Melvin a gentle kiss on his forehead. 'Besides…I can always come to visit. You're not that far away…are you?'

'Well, for a little one such as yourself – it may be a little bit of a distance,' replies Melvin. 'In fact, I may even have to draw you a map of how to find the castle.'

'A map? Why would I need a map, Melvin? Surely the castle is big enough to see?'

'No, it's not. I've cloaked the castle to be invisible to the outside world – it saves any unnecessary or unwanted visitors. There is however, a path that leads straight to my front door, but it can only be seen in the moonlight – and by invitation by myself.'

'A path?' questions Amelia.

'A *secret* path,' adds Melvin.

'Well, it's certainly not so secret anymore, is it?'

'Oh, I guess not,' responds an embarrassed Melvin. 'But, still let me explain how to find it—*ahem*—Okay…after you enter the forest…'

'Melvin?'

'Take an immediate left past a large blue—'

'Melvin! It's okay. I will just ask for directions,' interrupts Amelia.

'What do you mean – ask for directions?' enquires

Melvin, scratching his head in confusion.

'I do know a lot of creatures in that forest, Melvin.'

'Oh, I see…well, I guess that is that sorted, then. Anyway…as I was saying – you would be more than welcome at the castle. Don't wait too long until you visit…I make a cracking chilli!'

'MELVIN! OH, MEL—VIN!' bellows a voice from across the village.

'Looks like another one of your admirers has just turned up,' says Amelia. 'She's a fiery one!'

Melvin turns to see Mrs Stamps pacing towards him from across the green.

'Oh, darn it!' curses Melvin. 'Mrs Stamps again.'

Melvin scouts across the village green; looking for any signs of his pal and best friend Dexter.

'Dexter! Dexter!' shouts Melvin.

'Melvin!' repeats Mrs Stamps. 'Don't you dare go without giving me a little snuggle time.'

Melvin hastily gets back onto his bicycle, furiously turns the dials, pulls the levers and brings the bicycle up to full power. The bicycle howls and groans as Melvin desperately continues to locate Dexter.

'MELVIN!' roars a voice from inside the tavern.

'Damn…not him as well?' mutters Melvin, with a hand poised nervously over the bicycle's brake lever.

He turns to Amelia and smiles shyly.

'I must shoot, Amelia,' explains Melvin. 'As you can see, I'm a little overwhelmed with admirers…some a little larger than others.'

Amelia laughs and smiles back at Melvin.

'See you very soon, Melvin…and take care,' replies Amelia, clearing herself from the bicycle as Melvin releases the brake lever. The bicycle shoots across the village green at tremendous speed.

'DEXTER! Now would be a very good time to jump up onto the bicycle,' shouts Melvin. 'DEXTER! Where are you…?'

◆◆◆

The Reverend Clementine leans casually up against the white picket gate at the church entrance. He raises his eyes up to the church bell as it tolls twice, and smiles at the bell gleaming in the sunlight. He draws in a huge breath of fresh morning air and exhales it slowly.

'I'm so very thrilled that you have decided to stay a while and assist in helping with church activities, Edwin,' says the Reverend.

Edwin stands tall and proud on the other side of the gate, with his eyes closed and his head raised; feeling the warmth of the morning sun on his pale skin. He lowers his sunglasses to the end of his nose, slowly opens his eyes and stares briefly at the Reverend.

'You seem to be enjoying the sunshine, Edwin?' adds the Reverend, with a slight smile.

'That I am,' replies Edwin. 'It's surely a surreal feeling – and no doubt it will take me a little time to get used to the fact that I can walk out in it. I feel so alive…well, you know what I mean, Reverend.'

'I most certainly do,' chuckles the Reverend.

'And it is not a problem at all in staying a little while. It's the least I can do to show my gratitude to the village – especially for all the problems that I've caused.'

'Don't be so silly, Edwin. I fear that without your assistance in defeating Officer Locks and saving our Laundry Fairy…our village would have gone into complete disarray.'

Edwin gently bows his head. 'A pleasure to aid you.

I achieved what I came for, although the whole outcome was not the way I expected it to be. Staying here to help the village seems the right thing to do.'

'Good-good…' begins the Reverend. 'I'm glad you feel that way. Now, Edwin…there are certainly a few things that you will need to remember; a set of rules as such. For example, you must be completely aware that, although it is now possible for you to walk in the sunlight, you are very much still a vampire…and still very much have vampire weaknesses.'

Edwin clutches the bottom of his waistcoat with both hands and gives it a sharp tug; straightening his attire.

'That is true, Reverend,' replies Edwin, pushing his sunglasses back up the bridge of his nose.

'So firstly…' begins the Reverend. 'You must remember that you cannot step *at all* through this gate and onto the church grounds. As much as I would love to try and convince our Lord to make the church an un-holy sanctuary, I'm afraid I don't believe he would honour my request. So, we'll just have to deal with that inconvenience.'

Edwin smiles and gently nods his head up and down in acceptance.

'Secondly…I would normally expect a member of the church to wear a pendant…just like this,' adds the Reverend, holding up his silver crucifix. 'But that's not going to work for you either, is it?'

'That would be correct,' states Edwin, smirking at the comedy of the situation.

'Yes-yes…I would suspect that even a wooden crucifix would not work either?

'That would also be correct.'

'That's completely understandable…no problem at

all. Well, I think that's about it…unless you can think of anything else?'

Edwin raises his hand and gently cups his chin with his pointy fingers. He ponders to himself whether or not the Reverend has failed to mention anything else that could cause him great harm.

'No, I believe you've covered about everything Reverend,' replies Edwin. 'I really can't think of—'

'Garlic!' yelps the Reverend. 'What about garlic? Not that I have any laying around the church.'

'No…that's just a silly myth, Reverend,' replies Edwin, raising an eyebrow.

'Oh, I see. Well, that's about it, then…I don't believe there is—no wait!' voices the Reverend, leaning over the gate and staring down at Edwin's boots.

'What are you looking for?' asks Edwin, shuffling his feet around; wondering if he had stepped in something bad.

The Reverend lifts his head and addresses Edwin. 'I recommend you keep your bootlaces tied securely.'

'And why is that?' questions Edwin, with a curious look upon his face.

'Well, I don't want you tripping over and impaling yourself on anything? You know—all that stake through the heart business?'

Edwin grins and shakes his head; acknowledging the Reverend's concern.

'That would be most unfortunate,' mutters Edwin.

The Reverend reaches inside his tunic, pulls out a pile of papers from his inner pocket and holds them gently in his hands. He glances over the pages text.

'What are those?' asks Edwin, eyeing up the papers.

'Your first job,' responds the Reverend. 'Would you be kind enough to distribute all of these flyers around the village? I would truly appreciate it. You'll have to excuse the locals if they seem a little disturbed by your presence. I'm sure they'll get used to you eventually.'

Edwin takes the flyers from the Reverend, lowers his glasses and reads the scribbled text on the first piece of paper. The Reverend smiles.

'Morning service?' questions Edwin, shifting his eyes towards the Reverend.

'That's right, Edwin…' begins the Reverend. 'Every morning at nine.'

◆◆◆

'It certainly looks like your Master is getting stuck in with the whole *helping the church thing*, Corbin,' states Dexter, carefully dipping his snout into the cool and refreshing waters of the fountain, in an attempt to soothe his nostrils, which of late, have experienced plenty of explosive action.

Corbin sits quietly on the newly built fountain wall. He dangles his little feet over the edge and swings them gently back and forth, while looking across the green at his Master. A small tear runs down his cheek.

'Hmmm?' replies Corbin, sniffling softly and wiping the tear with the back of his hand.

'What's wrong?' asks Dexter. 'Surely you must be pleased that your Master is making himself useful?'

'I am…but—'

'But what?' interrupts Dexter, trying to push Corbin for an answer.

'Well, you see…I have served my Master for many years – and now it seems like he is doing everything for himself.'

Dexter shifts his attention towards Edwin, who is

busy handing out pieces of paper to the villagers. They seem to take them very promptly from Edwin; possibly in fear of being attacked by him if they refused.

'I just thought that he would have got me to hand out those flyers…you know?' sobs Corbin. I just feel like he doesn't need me anymore.'

'I'm sure that is not the case, Corbin,' states Dexter. 'He perhaps just wants to experience life in the sunlight – do normal things for a change – meet the locals.'

'I guess,' whimpers Corbin.

Dexter shifts up alongside Corbin and gives him a gentle nudge with his wing.

'Anyhow, it gives you a chance to do some of the things that *you* want to do…no?' suggests Dexter.

'I suppose so…' mutters Corbin.

'So, tell me…what have you always wanted to do or try? There must be a dream that you have?'

'Me…? Err—well, after seeing Eric flying on that bicycle – I was thinking that I would like to see what it's like to fly…well, to experience it at least. Just the thrill of flying through the air.'

Dexter smiles. 'Ah, I remember now…you did say you wished you could fly. Well, I'm a much too small at the moment and you are certainly a little too big, but one day I'll be much larger and perhaps I can take you for a ride?'

Corbin turns to Dexter in excitement. 'Really?' he shouts, with a huge smile on his face.

'I can't see why not,' responds Dexter. 'However, in the meantime…I have got a *little* something for you.'

'What do you mean?'

'I've got a little present for you, Corbin.'

'You have?'

'I certainly have…just a little something to say thank

you. I asked Eric to make something in exchange for a handful of copper coins, plus first claim to all the coins scattered across the village.'

Dexter reaches down to pick up a small wooden box from the ground beside him. He hands it over to Corbin, who then carefully reaches inside and pulls out a pair of crafted goggles. Rotating them in his tiny hands, Corbin inspects the thick glass lenses; held tightly in place by a thin copper frame. He slowly runs the tips of his fingers along two leather straps attached either side.

'I thought they'd be of great assistance to you when you go flying,' states Dexter, grinning.

Corbin pulls the goggles around his head and fastens the leather straps securely. He turns to face Dexter. 'How do I look?' he says.

'Perfect!' answers Dexter.

'And what are these?' questions Corbin, reaching deeper into the box and pulling out some folded pieces of copper plate attached to a large pin. Several strands of thin corded leather dangle below it.

'Well, until you get the chance to soar through the air, I thought this would get you ready.'

'What does it do?' queries Corbin, with a confused look on his face.

Dexter extends one of his claws and flicks the copper blades. They spin fast around the pin, slicing the air with a soft humming sound.

'Eric calls it a propeller. It creates lift or something technical like that. He is making something on a much larger scale that uses one of them…only much bigger!'

'Oh, I see…' glees Corbin.

'So, this little piece can go here on top of your hat – like so…and then we can thread these cords through there and ta-dah! A propeller on your head!'

Corbin chuckles as Dexter spins his new propeller around. It makes a buzzing and humming sound.

'Better not catch the wind in the wrong direction, Corbin,' says Dexter. 'Or you'll take flight…or worse still – people will think a mass of giant bees are coming their way.'

Corbin lets out a small and cute giggle.

'Anyway, Corbin…' continues Dexter, jumping down onto the ground. 'Looks like I'm being hailed. I must dash! Until we meet again – and probably sooner than you think…I'm running out of cheese.'

Corbin waves goodbye to Dexter.

◆◆◆

Eric quickly removes his soot-coated leather gloves and forcefully tucks them into his apron. He vigorously rubs his hands together.

He smiles and waves at Melvin and Dexter, as they disappear from view in a long trail of hot steam, which lingers gently on the landscape, before dissipating into the air.

'Pretty impressive what you've done with that bicycle, Eric,' says Timothy, nodding his head in the direction of the bicycle, as the last few trails of steam disappear.

'Aye…you're right there, lad,' replies Eric, wiping his forehead. 'Seems to be running a lot better with a good boiler full of coal.'

'Looks like it.'

'Pretty nice chap, that Melvin…and his pet dragon, Chester—err no wait…what's his name again?'

'Think you mean Dexter? Yes, I really don't know

what we would have done without them to be honest.'

'Ah, yes…that's it…Dexter. I would have loved for him to stay a little longer. Those copper coins would surely come in very handy in the near future. Copper is so expensive these days – don't you think?'

Timothy nods to agree; knowing he has absolutely no knowledge about the economy of the local mining industry.

'Anyway…try this,' instructs Eric, pulling from his pocket a small copper pipe with a hole drilled in the end. He hands it across to Timothy, who raises it into the air and turns it slowly with his fingers. The copper shines as it reflects the sunlight.

'Perfect!' concludes Timothy. 'I think that will do the job just nicely, thank you,' he adds, placing a small silver coin into the palm of Eric's hand.

'Not a problem at all, lad. I'm just happy that I—' responds Eric, pausing mid-sentence.

Eric glances around the village and smiles at the villagers getting back to their normal routine, and noticing that the recent overhaul to the village has not been a complete waste of time. In fact, it had never looked better. Occasionally, some of the locals still find a random sock hanging on tree branches or a pair of frilly knickers stuck on roof rafters, but in all…nothing that can't be retrieved.

'So, what are your plans for the day, Timothy?' asks Eric, completely forgetting his previous sentence.

'I've been thinking…' begins Eric. 'About all that stuff that Melvin mentioned about bending time. I thought perhaps I would see if I can craft some kind of special goggles…that could make it easier for us to see the Laundry Fairy.'

'Oh, right…and how would that work?'

Eric chuckles. 'I have absolutely no idea, lad. But it will be fun and games trying to work it all out.'

Timothy smiles and kneels down onto the grass next to a small array of copper pipes mounted inside a metal framework. He takes the copper pipe he had received from Eric and holds it steadily in front of him.

'Yeah…that's right, put it there…right there, lad,' instructs Eric, pointing at a large bent piece of pipe.

'I don't see why you need to bother with the goggles to be honest, Eric,' states Timothy. 'Amelia is just over there. All she has to do is to slow herself down if she wants to socialise.'

'Aye, lad…you're right. But maybe she has some friends? Perhaps I could use the goggles to see them?'

'That just sounds a little bit freaky, Eric,' chuckles Timothy. 'I think weird would be a better word.'

'Aye, it does…Dwarven nature that!'

'What is?'

'Being a little freaky. Talking of freaky…that Felicity woman is a right little catch, don't you think? What do you think my chances are with her?'

Timothy turns and looks across the green towards Felicity. 'Well she is rather tall, Eric – maybe a little too tall? Do you not think that could be an issue?'

Eric grins. 'That's not a problem. Where there's a will…there's a way! Besides, I thought I could perhaps butter her up a little bit…you know? Because there's always next year's competition…you see where I'm going with this, lad?'

Timothy sighs and pauses. 'I'm really disappointed that I didn't get to claim the *Village of the Year Award*, but at least I've found this new venture…now was that sweet or salted you asked for?'

'Salted please,' replies Eric.

Pop! Pop! – Pop!

'Okay then…' begins Timothy. 'Let's see if we can get this machine up to speed!'

THE END

Until our next adventure . . .

"Stories of imagination tend to upset
those without one."

– Terry Pratchett –

DISCLAIMER

This book is a work of fiction: names, characters, businesses, places, events and incidents are either the products of the author's imagination or used in a fictitious manner. Any resemblance to actual persons, living or dead, or actual events is purely coincidental.

In saying that…
I was once taught by an English teacher who talked too much and was a bit of a dragon…honestly!

SPECIAL THANKS

Thank you to all those who have guided me through the darkest of times. For your kindness, devotion and endless support. Your heartfelt selflessness will never be forgotten.

To my Mum, who is always there, pushing me to do, and for the rest of the family, who still love and care for me, even if I didn't. For understanding the demons that I faced and for believing in me…even when I started to doubt myself.

To Lorraine, for stating, "I'm never going to grow up – that's boring." I treasure how you have inspired me. Your undivided support and attention through the writing of this book is something I will never forget.

.

AUTHOR'S NOTE

THIS BOOK IS A WORK OF FICTION. However, many of the characters within this book are based on real-life people that I'm extremely close to, or have had the company of – if only for the briefest of moments. Their mannerisms, physical appearances, attire, how they talk and even the words they speak, have been used to great effect in developing each and every one of the key characters within this book.

I chose not to directly base a particular character on the characteristics of one real-life figure alone, but instead morph together some of the most fascinating, marvellous and elaborate features of many different real-life people; creating some *pretty* unique characters.

For example, Corporal Ringelstein may be based on the physical features of a key male figure in my life, but his mannerisms and actions are taken from a close close family member; people that have such presence and attitude; people who's pure real-life character is exactly what I was looking for when developing the Corporal. It was such fun in already having a real-life back-bone as a starting point to create, not just the Corporal, but also all the other characters in this book. People's speech, quotes and actions, down to the smallest details, have been used greatly, and without blending them in some magical way, I would have truly struggled to bring any of the characters to life.

Now, for the one character everyone is asking about – Edwin. Well, you see, Edwin has been one of the most difficult characters to write, if not the most difficult character to develop. Edwin has two sides to his personality that have such a bold appearance in this book. There is his more intelligent, serious and sinister side, and then there is his funny, witty and smooth side. It has been a challenge to show both sides of his personality at the appropraite times in this story. I took the intelligent/serious side from an old work boss of mine – the only difference is – I exaggerated it a little bit. Then there is his funny and comical side; this I took from a cousin of mine, who even in real-life still leaves me baffled and red from laughing. Thankfully, Edwin doesn't get his wittiness from me, as it normally would take me at least six hours to come up with any witty response to a comment, and it would usually come while I'm laying in bed; about to fall alseep. Instead, his wittiness is inspired by a young family member

Very early on in the creation of this story, I decided that I wasn't going to write pages upon pages of descriptive writing and describe each character down to every last detail, but chose to literally let the dialogue do all the talking. My aim was to take the reader on their own imaginative journey; letting them create and visualise in their own mind, their own version of the characters. I wanted to allow them to get a sense of the character's personality through their speech, their responses to comments made by other characters and their reactions to certain situations.

Many of the phrases, words and sayings used by the characters have also been said by real-life people. I chuckle when I think about the characters in this book saying exactly the same things that they have. The words "numpty" and "diddling" will never be the same again. To date, they are still a vital part of my everyday vocabulary.

This story is special to me because it was written for someone special. There are many easter-eggs that have been placed in this story. These are comments made by certain characters, or phrases and certain words used by them, that to the reader may seem strange and random. However, they are reference to certain parts of my life: happy moments; happy memories, which when I think about, make me smile and laugh.

How have I grown as I writer? Hmmm, now that is extremely difficult to say. I mean, I absolutely love writing and telling stories, and next to reading, it's one of my greatest passions, therefore my perception of writing hasn't dramatically changed. I have learnt one thing from writing this book – how to separate and space dialogue more effectively, so it's much easier for the reader to read and understand. There are many characters in some of the scenes and I aspired to make it clear to the reader, who was speaking and when. If the dialogue was too mashed together in a paragraph, it then became very difficult to comprehend. I'm also still having fun with my commas, but it's apart of learning how to write better and something I believe I will get much better at, as time goes by. I want to spend more time telling stories – as that's what I'm good at.

This book isn't just a fairy tale. It's a tale about

finding myself through the darkest of times and taking comfort in the people closest to me, even if some of them are just pages in this book. This story is about how the smallest things can make a big difference and realising that sometimes what you've been looking for, has been there all along. This book represents some of the tears that I couldn't cry and some of the terrors behind my smiling eyes. This book exists, because one morning as the sun came up, I looked out of the window and told myself that I had to swallow up all the fear and garbage around me, and once I had it inside me, I had to then transform it into something magical – because a little bit of magic – changes everything.

J.R.Buckley

Printed in Great Britain
by Amazon

59104892R00329